"SUSPENSE, DRAMA, AND ACTION
AS HOT AS A FIGHTER JET'S AFTERBURNER."
—*Publishers Weekly*

"[A] RIVETING, IRREVERENT
PORTRAIT OF TODAY'S NAVY."
—Stephen Coonts

"ENTERTAINMENT
OF A VERY HIGH ORDER."
—*The Philadelphia Inquirer*

"AN HONEST LOOK AT
THE LIVES OF NAVAL AVIATORS."
—Monty Ashliman, Former Topgun Instructor

continued . . .

"For your bookshelf to rest alongside *The Caine Mutiny, The Bridges at Toko Ri*, and *Run Silent, Run Deep*."
  —*The Hook*, official journal of the Tailhook Association

"Controversial because of its forthrightness about today's military."   —MilitaryLifestyle.com

"This is a fine tale of today's post–Cold War military, where pilots patrol no-fly zones, watch their exploits on CNN, and then send e-mails to buddies complaining about careerist superior officers. If you want to know what life is like in the U.S. Navy today, this would be a good place to start."
  —Thomas E. Ricks, author of *Making the Corps* and
   A Soldier's Duty

"*Punk's War* has it all: the action of the best techno-thrillers, the emotional drama of Coonts, the realism of Keegan, and the craftsmanship of a true professional."
  —John F. Lehman Jr., Secretary of the Navy, 1981–87,
   and author of *Command of the Seas*

"All military aviators will relate to the characters and the situations that Ward Carroll very clearly presents. . . . Beyond its compelling action this brutally accurate account of carrier aviation provides an answer to why some of us elected to stay in the service in the face of more comfortable and lucrative career options."
  —Vice Admiral Tony Less, USN (Ret.) Commander,
   Naval Air Force, U.S. Atlantic Fleet, 1991–94, and
   former Blue Angels commanding officer

"Ward Carroll brings you into the fold of a fighter squadron for an honest look at the lives of naval aviators. The thoughts and emotions captured through the characters in this novel are too accurate for *Punk's War* to be considered fiction."
  —Monty Ashliman, former Topgun instructor and
   F-14 Radar Intercept Officer of the Year

"Tom Clancy meets Joseph Heller in this riveting, irreverent portrait of the fighter pilots of today's Navy. At last somebody got it right. I couldn't put it down." —Stephen Coonts

PUNK'S WING

WARD CARROLL

A SIGNET BOOK

SIGNET
Published by New American Library, a division of
Penguin Group (USA) Inc., 375 Hudson Street,
New York, New York 10014, U.S.A.
Penguin Books Ltd, 80 Strand,
London WC2R 0RL, England
Penguin Books Australia Ltd, 250 Camberwell Road,
Camberwell, Victoria 3124, Australia
Penguin Books Canada Ltd, 10 Alcorn Avenue,
Toronto, Ontario, Canada M4V 3B2
Penguin Books (N.Z.) Ltd, Cnr Rosedale and Airborne Roads,
Albany, Auckland 1310, New Zealand

Penguin Books Ltd, Registered Offices:
80 Strand, London WC2R 0RL, England

First published by Signet, an imprint of New American Library,
a division of Penguin Group (USA) Inc.

First Printing, May 2003
10 9 8 7 6 5 4 3 2 1

*For Matt, the
first among us to go*

ACKNOWLEDGMENTS

For me, writing gets no easier with repeated attempts, and because of that I'm indebted to the following people:

- Giles Roblyer for his dedication and love of the craft, and for assuming the role of literary alter ego.
- Dan Slater and all at Penguin Group (USA).
- Stephen Coonts.
- Ethan Ellenberg and Michael Psaltis.
- Lieutenant Commander "Nose" Dickerson, USNR, for his LSO inputs.
- Commander "Sprout" Proano, USN, for his naval aviation expertise and war stories.
- My parents, Ned and Nancy Carroll, for their open minds and big hearts.
- My boys, Hunton and Reid, for their innocence and understanding.
- My wife, Carrie, for protecting my sanctuary and for her love.

CHAPTER ONE

Lipstick might help, he thought.

As Lieutenant (junior grade) Evelyn Greenwood described the workings of the F-14's fuel pumps while seated in one of the eight tight-fitting desk/chairs about the cramped briefing room, Punk wondered about how she might look with a little makeup. Greenwood was a handsome woman, strikingly tall, and, although a flight suit tended to mask such things, appeared to have a decent figure. She sported the sort of hairdo many of the females in the Navy seemed to favor: a low-maintenance coif that gave a half-assed nod to the burden of femininity while simultaneously broadcasting disdain toward it. From behind the briefing podium in the stark white room—the kind that mental health experts would find conducive to accelerating the slide into insanity—he considered that if she just let her brown locks grow beyond her collar and painted on a well-cut cocktail dress . . .

Punk snapped back into the role of flight instructor. Greenwood was just another pilot, one who happened to be climbing behind the controls of an F-14 Tomcat for the very first time today. And he would be in her back seat because instructor pilots rode there for the initial flights instead of instructor radar intercept officers—RIOs, as they were known. In theory, instructor pilots, more versed in the layout and "gotchas" of the front cockpit, would be better than those who normally sat in the rear cockpit at untangling the webs student pilots might weave during their first real attempts to get the aging leviathan of a fighter jet into and out of the air.

Tomcat pilots flying with Tomcat pilots was just one of the many unique elements of instructor duty at Fighter Squadron Ninety. The Death Boxers were the F-14 training squadron, or RAG, an acronym from the archaic Replacement Air Group. The squadron was officially labeled the Fleet Replacement Squadron, but FRS—*furse?*—didn't dance off the tongue like "rag" did, so the old term obdurately remained in the aviators' lexicon despite its absence from any official documents.

The RAG's primary mission was turning newly winged pilots and RIOs into fleet-ready Tomcat crews, and Punk and his fellow instructors were given roughly nine months to get each RAG class ready to fight as carrier-based aviators. The working days were generally long, but Punk was grateful for a shore-based flying job. When he'd called about orders more than a year and a half before, his detailer—one of the flesh peddlers at the Bureau of Naval Personnel in Millington, Tennessee—had hinted at some god-awful staff billets, the sort of positions no self-respecting fighter pilot of his rank would be caught dead in.

The student, or more correctly, the *replacement* pilot (hearkening back to the days of heavy combat losses), finished her description of the fuel system. Punk reviewed the last few items in the briefing guide.

"I'll meet you in maintenance control in fifteen minutes," he said.

Greenwood nodded and gathered her kneeboard cards. He watched her exit and made a mental note that the brief had gone smoothly, better than many of the first flights—FAM-1s—he'd conducted over the last ten months.

Punk returned the briefing guide to the small shelf on the wall next to the white board. He grabbed an eraser from the trammel and was cleaning the board in broad strokes when he heard a commotion in the passageway.

Stepping into the hall, he was blinded by a white light. He shielded his eyes and saw that a cameraman and a reporter had cornered Greenwood. The replacement pilot stood with her back against one of the white cinderblock walls that ran the length of the long building's second deck. Large hand-painted reproductions of fighter squadron insignias dotted the walls, and the female replacement was currently leaning against that of Fighter Squadron One-Zero-Four, the *Arrowslingers*, the carrier-based squadron Punk had served in before joining the RAG.

Two officers flanked her, and as Punk drew near he was just able to catch the end of Greenwood's response: "I'm looking forward to my first flight in the Tomcat. I don't view myself as a female pilot, just a naval aviator." She excused herself through the small crowd and continued on toward the parachute riggers shop to don her flight gear.

Punk approached one of the uniformed members of the gathering, a short lieutenant commander sporting a surface warfare officer pin above the left pocket of his khakis—a fish-out-of-water tipper that caused Punk to assume the man was a public affairs officer, PAO, one of the Navy's media handlers. "Mind if I ask what's going on?" Punk asked.

"Just your basic TV drill," the lieutenant commander said, forced to crane his neck back to look the pilot in the eyes. The man's head looked a size or two too big for his body, and he had a thick swirl of black hair across his forehead that reminded Punk of a cartoon rooster. "If that's all right with you, Lieutenant . . ." The PAO's eyes danced around Punk's head, certainly measuring hair length and military bearing in return, and then he fished around the pilot's flight suit for a nametag. ". . . Punk? What's your real name? I can't stand using those cute little nicknames you flyboys give each other."

"Rick. Rick Reichert, and actually, it's not all right," Punk said. "She's a replacement, and I'd prefer that she be allowed to focus on her flight."

"Oh, yes, Rick," the lieutenant commander mocked, "I forgot how intense your flying business is. Regular ninja warrior stuff, isn't it? I should've noticed from the look in her eye that she was in *the zone* already."

Punk was in no mood nor did he have the time to deal with a chip on another officer's shoulder. Punk had never been able to suffer a guy, regardless of rank, who was both an obstruction *and* an asshole. "Does our skipper know you're here?"

"Who's your skipper?"

"Captain Williamson."

"*Captain* Williamson? I'm here as a representative of *Admiral* Knowles, the commander of the Atlantic Fleet. Perhaps you've heard of him." The public affairs officer pointed toward a thin, matronly woman now talking to the reporters. "You see that woman there? That's *Senator* Eleanor Meyers, chairperson of the Senate Armed Services Committee."

"Okay . . ."

"She's taken a personal interest in female fighter pilots, and it's my job to make sure she has access to them." The PAO looked over both shoulders with darting eyes and then grabbed Punk by the elbow and ducked into the nearest briefing room with him. He closed the door behind them and gave his face an exasperated rub.

Punk knew his type; they seemed to migrate to the military business. Even now, he looked at Punk like a referee looks at a player just before throwing a penalty flag. He broadcasted the tacit expectation of one who very much cared about the difference in shape and color of their collar devices, and Punk, like any good junior aviator, couldn't help but half-dare him to make an issue out of it.

Just as Punk was sure the man was going to launch into a one-way ream session, the PAO's posture and expression softened. "Look, we all stress out any time Senator Meyers is around, and it seems like she's been around a lot lately," the PAO said.

"Oh?" Punk said, mollified by the sudden change in tone. "Why the interest in female fighter pilots? That was last decade's issue, wasn't it?"

"You'd think that, wouldn't you?" The PAO rubbed his face again and let out a weary exhale. "One of the senator's staffers presented her with some data showing the career progression of female naval aviators since 1991. Most of those who didn't get thrown out during flight school lost their wings during their first sea tours. The few who made it past that point all quit during their first shore duties. The senator was looking at her watch thinking we were about ready to select our first female fighter squadron commanding officer, and she finds out we don't even have any female aviators around to promote to lieutenant commander. She's convinced the Navy—especially in aviation—is slow-rolling gender integration, like the South tried to slow-roll civil rights.''

Punk rolled his eyes. "Excuse me. I've got to go do my part in aiding the cause.''

"This is no joke," the PAO said to the pilot's back. "Careers can be ended here. And that's not just me talking. Do you have any doubt how high this concern goes?''

"None whatsoever, I'm afraid.''

Punk walked back into the passageway, and as he neared the news crew, he heard a reporter ask the senator, "Are you saying the Navy still doesn't want women in combat roles?''

"All I'm saying," the senator said in a piercing nasal whine that Punk found instantly grating, "is that there is evidence that our initial efforts at integration have not taken hold." She turned to the preppy-looking, late twentysomething guy with perfect, thick black hair who was at her elbow. "Ferguson, give me that stat sheet we were looking at before." He rifled through the bundle of folders he was cradling in his arms and quickly produced the document. She scanned the sheet and then held it out like a lawyer displaying an exhibit to the jury. "These numbers don't lie. I'm heading a move to get to the bottom of the situation and to reinstitute the fixes, if required.''

The lines of her face were razor sharp, like a video game character, and her collar-length gray hair looked like molded steel wool. She gestured down the passageway, her arm nearly hitting Punk in the face as he passed. "I consider Lieutenant Greenwood to be a pioneer just as the women who first entered this building over a decade ago were pioneers. Today we are witnessing the beginning of the second wave of gender integration, and I'm going to make sure this one makes it over the dam.''

Punk moved out of earshot and decided he needed to make the skipper aware of the situation. He walked past the locker room door and entered the executive spaces—the only carpeted and paneled rooms in the hangar—and was immediately embraced by the scent of perfume. "Is he in?" he asked the yeoman second class sitting behind a large wooden desk in the outer office, a desk larger and in better shape than any others in the building except the skipper's.

"No, sir," the pretty blonde replied. Her smile reminded him that attractive enlisted women had a way of showing up in executive secretarial/receptionist roles. He wondered if Senator Meyers had noticed. "Captain Williamson is over at Fighter Wing at a commanding officer's meeting with the commodore. Can I leave him a message for you?"

"No, thanks," Punk said, stepping past her toward the CO's office. "I'll just leave him a note." He scribbled, *Did you know Senator Meyers is here? Very respectfully, Punk,* on the notepad on the skipper's blotter. Then he rushed to get dressed for his flight with the latest aviation pioneer.

The F-14's variable geometry wings were a marvel of twentieth-century aerospace technology. Swept fully forward, they gave the Tomcat impressive turning characteristics. Swept fully aft, the fighter became a high-speed interceptor. But from a new fighter pilot's perspective the wing sweep mechanism was designed to make a replacement, or "conehead" in instructor parlance, look like a dumb ass. It was a cantankerous system that required the operator to be both forceful and dexterous.

Punk looked through the Plexiglas above him and considered the clouds whisking across the airfield in the mid-May sky, feeling the airplane buck repeatedly as Lieutenant (junior grade) Greenwood attempted to bring the wings forward as part of the poststart checks. He quickly glanced to either side of them to make sure they were clear of the adjacent jets on the line and then watched the right wing jerk back and forth a few times.

"Easy with it," he said over the intercom. "The trick is to smoothly move the handle forward."

"I can't find the detent," Greenwood said, referring to the groove the handle fit into that allowed the wings to be controlled either by the flight computer or by the pilot via a button on the inboard throttle. Her exasperation was evident in her voice and in the movement of her head. "I'm fishing for it, but it's not there."

"Hit the master reset button," Punk said. "That moves the detent fully forward."

Greenwood depressed the button and the handle jumped into place. She sighed across the oxygen mask dangling from her helmet.

"Don't sweat it," Punk said. "The wings are a bitch." He winced. *Bitch? Couldn't you have come up with another word?* "You'll get the hang of it after a while," he said, attempting a recovery.

With the wings fully forward, Greenwood continued with the checks, dropping the flaps and cycling the spoilers on the wings in concert with the ground crewman's signals. "I'm having trouble seeing our plane captain," she said. "He's surrounded by cameramen."

Punk craned his head around and saw the news teams on either side of the enlisted man in front of the jet. Just behind the sailor, directing the cameramen while looking very much out of place, her cranial and goggles contrasting with skirt and heels, was Senator Meyers. She was accompanied by her well-groomed assistant who was trying in vain to keep his tie under control in the stiff spring breeze.

Jesus Christ, this is only a FAM-1, Punk thought. *Why all the attention?*

Greenwood managed to get the wings back to their fully aft position without too much trouble, and after the ground crew performed their final walk around the jet, she eased the Tomcat out of its parking place. Once clear of the jets to either side, she returned the enlisted crewman's final salute and steered left and out of the ramp area. The cameramen followed the F-14 as far as they could, running to keep pace at one point, each with one hand on his camera, and one on his ill-fitting hearing protection, until they sensed they were beyond their bounds. Before losing them, Punk wrestled with whether or not to render a thumbs-up or something equally cheery but decided to feign concentration on the checklist tacked to his kneeboard.

"Sorry about that," Greenwood said.

"What are you sorry about?" Punk said. "It's not your fault."

"I guess not. I'm really as surprised as you about the interest."

After passing through one of the throats between oblong islands of roughly mowed grass, they were headed down the taxiway. At that point, Punk initiated the take-off checklist: "Brakes . . ."

Greenwood took her cue without missing a beat: "Check okay. Accumulator pressure up."

"Fuel total. I'm showing sixteen thousand pounds on the totalizer back here."

"Okay. Normal feed, auto transfer, dump off, transfer checked. I show sixteen-two on the totalizer, two thousand pounds in each wing, five point eight aft and left, six point two forward and right. The feed tanks are full, and bingo is set at four thousand pounds."

"Canopy is closed, locks are engaged, light's out, stripes are aligned, handle is in the close position."

"Closed, locks engaged, light out, seal inflated, handle in close position."

"My seat is armed top and bottom, and the command ejection handle is aft."

"I'm armed top and bottom, and my status window shows you have the handle aft."

"Stability augmentation switches . . ."

"All on."

Punk twisted around and looked under each armpit at the six panels of circuit breakers along the back half of the rear cockpit, surrounding him like keys around a cathedral organist. "All my breakers are in back here," he said while he scanned the rows again to be sure.

"Okay, let me see . . ." Greenwood replied as she directed her attention to the rows of a dozen or so circuit breakers lined vertically along the bulkheads outside of each of her lower legs to see if any of them were popped out. After several seconds with no response Punk looked around the left side of Greenwood's ejection seat and saw her head down and moving from side to side. He wondered what was taking so long and then glanced beyond her, through the canopy, and saw the Tomcat was drifting to the left, nearly off of the taxiway.

"Watch where you're going!" Punk shouted over the intercom.

Greenwood jerked her head up and let out a shriek. She booted the right rudder pedal to get the jet back to the centerline, but pushed it too far. The F-14 swerved hard to the right, and before she could recorrect back to the left, the right wheel rolled off the asphalt and sank to the stub of the mainmount in the wet spring mud that bordered the taxiway.

"Shut the engines down!" Punk said as he leaned against

the jet's newly acquired right tilt. "Shut 'em down before we suck something down an intake!"

Greenwood pulled both throttles fully aft and within seconds it was dubiously quiet. "Safe your ejection seat," Punk called across to her, intercom now lost with the rest of the electrical power. "I'm opening the canopy."

The canopy opened with a whoosh of compressed nitrogen. Punk gathered his kneeboard, unstrapped, and made his way across the top of the F-14 to the left horizontal stabilizer from which he made the four-foot leap to the ground. He walked under the wing to the left side of the nose and unlatched the ladder and the pilot's step so that Greenwood could dismount the conventional way. She sat motionless, head down, still strapped into the seat.

Punk moved under the jet to see how far buried it was. A base operations pickup pulled up. The vehicle came to a halt with a screech, and the driver bailed out as if he feared the Tomcat was going to explode.

"What the hell happened?" the man asked as he briskly strode around the rear of the jet. The lieutenant considered the man's bald head and potbelly and realized he was one of those airfield employees who popped out of the cracks in the tarmac when something bad happened—those whom most aviators hadn't met and didn't want to meet.

"Nose gear steering failure, I think," Punk said cryptically, peering down toward the brake lines to see if they were still intact. The bald guy was followed by four more guys in an ominous-looking, lime green crash crew truck that bore down on the stricken Tomcat like a pit bull rushing a soup bone. Punk spotted one of them perched over the nozzle above the truck's cab, and he rushed out with his arms extended over his head to preempt an overzealous attempt to quell a nonexistent fire with foam that would turn the metal parts of the jet into corroded mush.

A few more yellow trucks pulled up, flashers blinking in earnest, and Punk wondered about all the fuss for one F-14 stuck in the mud. They didn't need a fleet of trucks idling around with the drivers passing judgment; they just needed a tow tractor.

After what seemed like several hours of standing against the unhindered breeze across the runways and making small talk with the airfield workers while waiting for the

squadron's maintenance crew, one of the chiefs pulled up
in a four-door pickup. The enlisted man saw Punk's expression and didn't ask any questions. Punk motioned for
Greenwood to get in the back seat and then slid in beside
the chief.

The pickup reeked of hydraulic fluid and wet rags. The
occupants remained silent for the short trip back to the flight
line until they got close enough to see that the camera crews
had reformed along the hangar bay doors, waiting for the
return of Lieutenant (j.g.) Greenwood from her historic
first flight. "Don't stop, chief," Punk said. "Drop us off
around the other side."

Punk avoided eye contact with the news people and the
public affairs officer as they passed, hoping they wouldn't
be noticed, but just as he was sure they'd slipped by he
heard one of them shout, "There she is!" Punk twisted
around and saw that they were being chased like the
Beatles in their early days.

"I'll drop you at the skipper's entrance," the chief said.
"That stairwell gives you the quickest route to the ready
room." He sped around two corners and came to a quick
stop next to the awning that marked the commanding officer's ceremonial entrance. The aviators bailed out and ran
inside, and the maintainer drove back to the taxiway to
check on the crew rescuing the Tomcat.

A small crowd of replacements and instructors had gathered in the ready room with the word of the mishap. As Punk
knew they would, a few were congregated at the main dry
erase board at the front of the room, working on a list of
new call signs for Greenwood. He caught "Baja," "Off-road,"
and "Bog" among the other offerings on the still-growing list
before rerouting the slump-shouldered lieutenant (junior
grade) to one of the briefing rooms, sparing her the indig-
nity of the moment.

Punk shut the briefing room door behind them, pulled a
chair around, and directed her to take a seat across from
him.

He started to speak. "I'm not sure what—"

"I don't want any special treatment," she said. "There's
no excuse for the stupid thing I just did."

"I'm not offering any special treatment," Punk said.

"Whether you want to admit it or not, I think the media coverage was a distraction."

She considered his words and then shook her head. "I've earned my wings. I should be able to taxi an F-14 safely to the duty runway."

The door flung open, and the public affairs officer rushed in. "What the hell do you think you're doing?" he asked Punk. "I've got two networks and one senator down there waiting to hear about Miss Greenwood's first flight. This may seem like a big bother to you, but the admiral—"

"Did you notice we were in an airplane when we left the flight line and in a truck when we got back?" Punk asked. "I know you're not an aviator, but even you should be able to figure out that something happened to our jet." Punk ushered the PAO out of the room, showing just enough respect to keep him from further losing his temper. "Now if you'll excuse us, we have to debrief."

CHAPTER TWO

"Ironically, when you came by to talk to me, I was over talking to Fighter Wing about Senator Meyers and her interest in Greenwood," Captain "Eagle" Williamson said. "I know the PAO was a pain in the ass, but he was right. The senator has been banging on the Chief of Naval Operations, and the CNO instructed Admiral Knowles to deal with our production of female fighter pilots." He leaned back in his leather chair with his hands clasped behind his head and propped his flight boots on his big wooden desk. Eagle's marbled physique showed that the years had been good to him since his days as a lacrosse standout at the Naval Academy. His call sign alluded to his prominent Roman nose that had obviously been broken a time or two. Punk had enjoyed serving under him for the past year. As skippers went, Eagle was low maintenance and didn't seem overly impressed with himself. He also had proved to be a tough pilot to beat in a dogfight.

Eagle winced against the afternoon sunlight streaming through the row of windows that lined the upper quarter of one wall and scooted his chair a few feet to his left to return to the shadows. "I'm not sure the timing is right for her to get a 'down' on her first flight."

"Well, skipper," Punk said, seated in one of the two armless leather chairs in front of the desk, "I think she'd be more pissed off about not getting a 'down' after what she did. She doesn't strike me as the type who's looking to use her gender to her advantage."

"That's nice, comma, but unfortunately what happens to her at the RAG isn't up to her." Eagle had a habit of audibly punctuating his sentences—an affectation that would've worn on the junior officers in the ready room had they been serving in the crucible of a carrier at sea instead of a training squadron ashore. The skipper also tended to overuse the term "great American" when referring to people he either liked or was impressed with. "At the same time, I'm not about to start compromising standards in the name of some political agenda."

Eagle ran a hand over his thin black hair combed straight back, and picked up one of the three phones on his desk. "Ops officer? Skipper. Could you come down to my office for a sec? And bring Lieutenant (junior grade) Greenwood's training jacket with you." The captain looked back to Punk as he hung up. "Like it or not, you've become part of this committee."

"Which committee is that?"

"The quote-unquote 'nip this little problem in the bud' committee. I'm not going to have this issue dominate the few months I have left as commanding officer of this outfit. Life's too short, and there are too few flights in the Tomcat left."

The operations officer appeared in the doorway. "Spud," the skipper said. "Come on in."

Punk still wasn't used to seeing the lanky and balding lieutenant commander without his signature "birth control" glasses, the Navy-issue specs that looked like a cross between those once worn by Buddy Holly and Truman Capote. Spud had undergone corrective eye surgery over at Portsmouth Naval Hospital a few weeks before and his vision had been corrected from 20/100 to 20/20 in each eye. He took the seat next to Punk and smiled toward the pilot he'd been crewed with during their last tour.

"What are you grinning about?" Punk asked.

"Peripheral vision," Spud said, eyes focused straight ahead. "I can still see you even when I look over this way."

"You're a marvel of modern science."

Punk and Spud had flown more than one hundred and forty sorties together, including the one over southern Iraq where they'd managed to keep the bad guys off of a squadronmate who'd had the misfortune of riding with their com-

manding officer when he was shot down by a surface-to-
air missile. Spud and Punk had each been awarded the
Distinguished Flying Cross for their actions. Spud was further honored with selection for command of a fighter
squadron, a true long shot for a prior enlisted officer known
for bucking the system and nearly a decade older than most
of his peers. He'd been ordered to the RAG to await "slat-
ing," the follow-on command assignment to a carrier-
based squadron.

"Don't tell me, skipper," Spud said, one hand on top of
his bald head as he feigned clairvoyance. "Punk wants the
ground school syllabus modified. Instructors are now to put
out the fact that the Tomcat should be taxied on prepared
surfaces only."

"Don't start, jerk-off . . . sir," Punk muttered back.

The skipper got up and shut the door to his office. "All
right, gentlemen, certainly we're all on the same sheet of
music with the idea that taxiing airplanes into the mud with
a high-profile female pilot at the controls is not a good
thing." He looked to Punk as he paced the length of the
wall by the door. "Aren't we?"

"Yes, sir," Punk replied.

"So what happened with the FAM flight?"

"Skipper, the PAO was more than just a pain in the ass,"
Punk said. "Those camera crews were a distraction."

"Maybe you didn't hear me," Eagle said. "Admiral Knowles
is going to bury the Chief of Naval Operations in human
interest stories about the *success* of the second wave of
female integration, and we're caught in the middle. What
pisses me off as much as anything else is I didn't see this
coming. Female fighter pilots? Didn't we already go
through this?" He stopped pacing and leaned against the
wall, hand on his forehead. "They're never going to hit you
where you're expecting it. My entire professional life has
been about being ready for the next fight. First it was the
Russians, then the Iranians, then the Libyans, then the
Iraqis, then the Serbians, and now the Iraqis again. It turns
out all I really needed to be concerned about was one female officer. And I hate to say it, comma, but we haven't
learned a thing since that female pilot flew a Tomcat into
the water behind the *Lincoln* years ago. The burden for
success here is squarely on the shoulders of Miss Green-

wood." He looked up from the floor and grew a quizzical expression. "She is a Miss, isn't she?"

"As opposed to what?" Punk asked.

"If she was married I'm sure we'd know about it by now," Spud said as he paged through her jacket. He stopped on one of the forms and ran his finger along it. "Here it is: She's single."

"Boyfriend?" the skipper asked as he moved across the room and plopped into his chair again.

Spud and Punk looked at each other and shrugged. "Why?" Spud asked.

The skipper leaned forward. "I want to know everything I possibly can about her. We're against the ropes here, boys. There's only one right answer as far as the chain of command is concerned: She needs to make it through the RAG successfully and get out to the fleet, and so far I'm not convinced she's capable of holding up her end of the bargain. How were her grades in flight school?"

"Above average mostly," Spud replied. "It looks like she struggled through the intermediate phase, but she managed to pull herself together in advanced. She got Tomcats thanks to the quality spread."

The skipper rolled his eyes. "*Quality spread* . . . right. Where did she got to college?"

"Naval Academy."

"WUBA, huh?" the skipper thought aloud with a glance toward the door. In the early days of female integration at the Academy, WUBA had stood for "working uniform blue alpha," but the acronym was also used to tag the initial cohorts of female midshipmen as, among other things, "women with unusually big asses." It quickly became a taboo reference; in fact, the name of the uniform was changed to "working blues" so that the brigade of midshipmen might stop saying "WUBA" altogether. "Well, if she got through Annapolis she must be able to handle some bullshit."

"I don't think her attitude is going to be a problem, skipper," Punk said.

"That's what scares me," Spud said. "I'd rather have a bad attitude and flying talent than the other way around. Attitude is easier to fix."

"No matter," the captain said. "Give her a 'down' but

keep it quiet. I don't want Senator Meyers on our case already."

"Why are we so concerned about Senator Meyers?" Punk asked. "Why would we accommodate one legislator's agenda over everything else around here?"

"Spoken like a man who's never had a tour at the Pentagon," the commanding officer said. "In practice one legislator is all it takes, especially when it's a legislator with the power that Senator Meyers has. And right now the Navy needs her to like us. Let me go big picture on you. We're in a crucial part of the procurement cycle, and we need Congress to make some serious moves toward replacing what we've got sitting on our flight line. I love the Tomcat like my mother, but most of those beasts out there are older than you, Punk." He reached across his desk and grabbed a newspaper. "By the way, did you see the article in the business section of today's paper about Raynotec Defense Industries? They're taking it in the shorts. We may be making our own parts soon."

"So how far do we lower the bar to keep the senator happy, sir?" Punk asked.

"I thought the last thing I said was give her the down . . . but keep it quiet. We're not going to lower any bars, but we're damn sure going to keep the senator happy." Eagle turned to Spud. "Have the FAM phase leader sit down with Miss Greenwood for a chalk talk and then get her scheduled to fly again right away." He pointed to Punk. "And not with him . . . no offense."

"Roger," Spud said. "Punk, you owe me the paperwork for today's adventure."

"You'll have it minutes after we finish here."

"You're both great Americans," the skipper said.

Spud nodded graciously and said, "You want me to call an all-instructors meeting to put word out on this?"

"No," the skipper said. "If she got wind that a special meeting was held on her behalf it wouldn't exactly help her state of mind. Get the word out informally." He leaned back in his chair and studied the ceiling for a few moments before lurching forward and hunching over the desk. "What is the rest of her class like? What are they, Class Two?"

"That's affirmative, skipper," Spud replied. "It's hard to

tell. They've finished ground school and are just starting to fly. So far it's mostly been we-talk-they-listen sort of stuff."

"Let me take a look at the roster." Spud handed the sheet across the desk and Eagle studied it for a few seconds. "Robert Bellingham? Is he any relation to King Bellingham?"

"His son," Spud said.

"You've heard of King Bellingham, Punk?" Eagle asked.

"The only Vietnam-era Navy ace?" Punk said. "Yes, believe it or not; I read his book when I was at the Academy."

"I guess what they told us at the last leadership conference about you youngsters being addicted to TV and video games isn't all true," the captain replied. "Spud, take a note and get me the admiral on the line. He'll want to hear about this way before anything about Miss Greenwood. What's the Bellingham kid like?"

"He's a wiseass," Punk said.

Spud paternally patted Punk's shoulder and added, "The jury's still out, skipper. As I said, these guys are relatively new in the program. This class of coneheads has a long way to go before we bless them as deployable."

"Speaking of that," Eagle said as he tossed the class roster back to Spud, "what call sign did the instructors finally settle on for Greenwood?"

"It was a close one," Spud said, "but I think 'Muddy' was the winner."

Lieutenant Cal "Crud" Workman was a slightly shorter, darker haired version of Punk. Handsome and athletic looking, Crud earned his call sign on his first cruise after spending two weeks in sick bay with a flulike disease that had baffled the carrier's flight surgeons. He now entered the operations office carrying a stack of officer records and stood with his back against one of the stark white plaster walls, staring at Punk with a sly smile until the other lieutenant was forced to react.

"Okay," Punk said from behind one of the three plain metal desks in the room. "I give up. What's up?"

"We've been elected," Crud said.

"To what?"

"To be the class advisors for Class Two. You've got the pilots; I've got the RIOs."

Punk and Crud had met several years ago at the outset of their own replacement days. Like most new fighter pilots, Lieutenant (j.g.) Rick Reichert hadn't been sure what to make of the radar intercept officers in his RAG class. He'd never flown with anyone else in the jet except flight instructors, each one a veteran pilot. But after several grueling simulator sessions with Ensign Cal Workman in the hot seat behind him, despite all the negative backseater stereotypes he'd caught in passing during his days in flight school in Meridian, Mississippi, Punk warmed to the idea of RIOs in general, and to Crud in particular.

The two of them pooled their resources during those months and rented a small house on the beach five miles due east of the air station. The place wound up being the venue of choice for replacement parties and a crash pad for husbands in the collective doghouse. Even some of the instructors sought refuge there from time to time. Now they had both returned to the RAG as instructors, fleet veterans with three-year sea tours and a thousand Tomcat flight hours under each of their belts.

"You mean this class is into FAM flights and they don't have class advisors yet?"

"They did: Rimshot and Hurl. But, as you know, Rimshot's now on terminal leave getting ready to become an airline pilot and Hurl's back at sea as a catapult officer."

"How did those two get picked in the first place?"

Crud shrugged. "Classic Navy-style administrative oversight, I guess. I'm not sure how much thought goes into picking class advisors, except in our case." He set the stack of records on a desk, handed Punk a copy of the Class Two roster, and plopped down on the battered couch that lined one wall, careful to position himself around the gooey pieces of duct tape applied years ago to keep the stuffing in place. "Spud recommended us. He fears Class Two's going to need special attention."

"Thank you, Spud."

Crud considered his copy of the lineup. "The first order of business is call signs." Although RAG call signs normally didn't last very far into a fleet tour—if the replacements made it through RAG at all—they had their utility during training: teaching replacements how to address each other over the radios fighter style and introducing them to the culture of fighter aviation. "Let's start with the RIOs."

"Shouldn't we have a few beers before we do this?"

"Probably, but let's give it a whirl straight. First guy: Ensign Travis Dover."

"Ben," Punk said immediately.

Crud raised his eyebrows. "Remember we have a female pilot in this class, a high-visibility one at that."

"So? You haven't got a hair on your ass if you don't agree to 'Ben.' "

"Actually, I don't have a hair on my ass. Workman is an English name and we gentlemen of northern European decent aren't hirsute like you Slavs."

"Reichert is German, not Slavic."

"Then how do you explain all the hair on your ass?"

"My mother was from Greek stock."

"Does she have a hairy ass?"

"I won't dignify that with an answer, and, for the record, my ass isn't *that* hairy. So are we taking a stand here, or not?"

"All right. Ben Dover it is. Next: Next is Ensign Fred Giles."

"Smiles."

"Smiles Giles? That's a bit too cute, don't you think?"

"It's the new Navy. There's no such thing as too cute."

"If you say so. That brings us to Ensign Saul Kaplan."

"Kosher."

"Kosher Kaplan," Crud said. "Okay, I guess. I'm a sucker for good alliteration."

"Although he did play baseball in college. We could go with Kofax Kaplan."

"That little guy played baseball? What position?"

"Shortstop, I think."

"What school?"

"Umm . . . Lehigh?"

"Kofax Kaplan . . . Kofax Kaplan. No, there's too much going on with that one. As a rule, replacement call signs shouldn't require an explanation, not to mention the minor detail that Sandy Kofax was a pitcher, not a shortstop. We'll stick with Kosher."

"All right. Next victim."

"Ensign Kendall Smith."

"Smitty."

"That's original. Smitty Smith."

"Yeah," Punk said. "He's another jock. He told me he played fullback at Grambling."

"Fullback? Well, he's big enough. Maybe we should go with a football theme."

"That would require an explanation."

"You're right. Smitty it is." Crud moved to one of the dry erase boards that dominated three of the four walls in the place. "We'd better write these down as we go along." He wrote, "Official Class Two Call Signs—Do Not Erase" across the top of the board and under that he listed the call signs they'd come up with so far.

"Let's not lose our momentum here," Punk prodded.

"Sorry. Ensign Perry Thomas."

"T-dog."

"T-dog?"

"Yeah. Every group of aviators needs a something *dog*, you know, like Moon *dog* or Joe *dog* or Bob *dog*."

"All right. T-dog." Crud refaced the board. "Now is that spelled *dee oh gee* or *dee ay dubble-yew gee*?"

"Just stick with *dee oh gee*. We don't want to get too rural with it."

"That's probably best. The last RIO is Lieutenant (j.g.) Brian Williams."

"Why is he a rank senior to the rest of the RIOs?"

Crud rifled through the stack of records until he found "Williams." "Here we go: He's a year senior to them," Crud explained. "It looks like he originally wanted to be a submariner, but he flunked out of nuke school. His class standing at the Naval Academy was in the single digits, so they must've given him the option of attending flight school as a naval flight officer."

"A smart boy, huh? I knew there was something that bothered me about him. He's got that smug know-it-all thing going on."

"And if there's any people we don't want flying fighters, it's smart people."

"That's right," Punk agreed. "We didn't spend all these years lowering the bar for nothing. So what about the call sign for Mr. Williams?"

"This former submarine link opens up a lot of options," Crud said. "Nuke, Bubble, Dolphin, Sinker—"

"That's it," Punk proclaimed. "Sinker Williams. It's going to require an explanation, though."

"True," Crud agreed, "but it's a Navy-themed explanation, so that's okay."

"There are so many rules here."

"But keeping track of them isn't a problem when you make them up as you go along."

"Momentum . . ."

"On to the pilots. Lieutenant (j.g.) Robert Bellingham." Pilots were normally senior to RIOs as replacements because the drivers' flight school, up to the point they were awarded their wings, was nearly a year longer than the backseaters'.

"I've already thought about this one," Punk said. "Remember that show *The Addams Family*?"

Crud's face lit up. "*Pugsly*. Bellingham looks just like him."

"Bingo."

"Oh, he's going to love that one." Under the "Pilots" column Crud wrote "Bellingham—Pugsly," and then he returned his attention to the roster in his hand. "Lieutenant (j.g.) Aurelio Clover."

"What sort of name is Aurelio?"

"Hispanic, or Italian, maybe. So that gives us Taco, Beaner, Siesta, Guido, Pasta . . ."

"All taken by instructors."

"He's kind of tall . . ."

"Not tall enough for Stretch."

"How tall does a Stretch have to be?"

Punk thought for a moment. "At least six-four. Let's work with the last name: Clover."

"Four-leaf?"

"Sounds too Indian."

"Leprechaun?"

"Too many syllables." Punk fitted his hands over his mouth like an oxygen mask and spoke as if he were talking on the radio: "Lep-re-chaun, break right—oh, too bad, the SAM got him."

"How about Lucky?"

"Genius. Next is Lieutenant Hank Ford."

"Full lieutenant?"

"Yeah." Crud paged through his record. "Looks like he went to grad school for a couple of years right after he got commissioned out of the Academy."

"Another smart guy? I'm going to have to crack open my copy of *Word Power*. Is Hank his real name or is it Henry?"

"Ah . . . Henry."

"Henry Ford? That gives us a definite theme. Detroit? No. Model-T? No, too many syllables again. Hmmm . . . Auto?"

"Auto it is."

"That brings us to Greenwood."

"Muddy."

"Copy," Crud said as he wrote on the board. "*Muh-dee.* You have to love a conehead who helps us like that. Oh, by the way, Spud said he wants us to keep close tabs on her."

"I know. I was on the ground floor of that one, remember?"

"He actually used the term 'CIA-style.' "

"What the hell does that mean? Phone taps? Hidden cameras?"

"I love it when you talk dirty." Crud ran his finger down the roster. "Lieutenant (j.g.) Michael Rhodes."

"Dusty."

"Naturally. *Duss-tee*, like every other Rhodes in the fleet. And our final contestant, Lieutenant (j.g.) Richard Norman."

"Greg."

"No, it's Richard."

"No, Greg as a call sign, as in Greg Norman."

"That definitely would demand an explanation."

"Greg Norman is a very famous golfer."

" *'Very famous golfer'?* There's only one very famous golfer these days and his last name ain't Norman. Plus call signs that are simply other people's names are confusing on the radio."

"What about 'Ben' Dover?"

"Irresistible sexual overtones, especially homoerotic ones, eclipse the fact that Ben is just a person's name."

"You have a bright future as an expert in tax law," Punk said. "How about Stormin'?"

"Let's take a look." Crud scanned the list of instructor

names along the opposite wall. "This has got to be the only squadron in the Navy without a Stormin' Norman already."

"If we don't have a Smitty and a Dusty already you shouldn't be surprised that there's no Stormin'."

Crud scrawled on the board again. "Stormin' . . . Norman."

The two instructors reviewed the list with silent satisfaction until Crud said, "Well, I'm outta here. Suzanne expects me for dinner. This is the first night this week I haven't had to fly." He tipped an imaginary hat and exited the office but reappeared in the doorway a moment later. "Oh, are we on for tomorrow night? All systems are go: We got a baby sitter, weather's looking good, neither of us is scheduled to fly . . ."

"I guess we're on—if you don't mind me coming along as the third wheel."

Crud sat down on the couch again. "Third wheel? What happened to the Rick Reichert of old, the man I used to know when we were RAG students together? That guy would've never been caught without a date."

"I'm not caught without a date," Punk said. "I'm just not sure what's going on with the person I'm supposedly dating right now."

Crud winced. "Anita? Trouble in paradise?"

"Right . . . paradise."

"Call her and make nice."

"I'm not sure I want to make nice. There's no telling where that might lead."

"C'mon, it's one of the first concerts of the season, and the weather is supposed to be perfect. Suzanne is going to be very disappointed if you don't come out with us. I don't have to remind you that she'd be married to you if I hadn't asked her first."

One morning three summers ago Suzanne had arrived on the doorstep of their beach house acting as an intermediary between her brother, Ritzo, a RAG instructor pilot, and her sister-in-law, a long-suffering fighter pilot's wife. Rick answered the bell dressed only in gym shorts.

"Oh," Suzanne said, as if she'd expected someone else to answer the door, somebody with a shirt on, perhaps. "Is Kip here?"

"Who?" Rick asked, head pounding. The day was already too bright. It had been another one of those nights. But the haze wasn't too thick for him to note that she was well put together. He reminded himself that he was already spoken for.

She stepped back and double-checked the rusted numbers on the side of the cedar house. "Twenty-seven. This is the number my sister-in-law gave me. Kip . . . oh, you guys call him Ritzo."

"*Kip?* Yeah, he's here." Punk crossed his arms over his chest, suddenly uncomfortable with his half-nudity. It had taken guts for her to come over to a well-known snake ranch early in the morning on a weekend, and the last thing she probably needed was him leering at her.

"Can I talk to him?" Suzanne asked.

Punk realized he'd been staring at her anyway. "Sure, sure. Come on in." He cleared a path through the empty beer cans, leading her to the choicest piece of beanbag furniture, and rushed off to rouse her brother from his drunken slumber. On the way, he did Cal the favor of shaking him awake and telling him that he needed to get his shit together and go meet Ritzo's sister.

That summer the roommates and their girlfriends had been a single unit. Cal and Suzanne were married the following spring just before the class left the RAG and went off to their various squadrons to start working for a living defending freedom around the globe. It taunted Rick that the relationship with his girlfriend, Jordan, had ended during his second deployment and that Cal and Suzanne had always seemed so happy.

Jordan. Just the sound of her name still affected him deeper than he was willing to admit. They'd been on the brink of engagement before his last deployment and by the time he returned she had disappeared from the face of the earth. He'd never been afforded a full explanation from her, just a letter she'd mailed in the final month of cruise that said things like the time had come for her to start thinking about herself. He'd always thought that they were destined to be together, but in the last year he'd been made to understand that life was seldom so poetic. Punk had worked hard to get over her but deep down it still felt unfinished, and he couldn't suppress the notion that there was more to come between them.

Now the last thing Punk wanted to do was bask in the glow of Crud and Suzanne's wedded bliss while he tagged along with a reliable standby, one of the boomerang girls, a circle of players so named because of their tendency to return to the officers' club from which they'd been figuratively thrown the Friday night prior. Although the availability and willingness of the boomerang girls was the stuff of military cultural legend, to travel in their circles after too long at NAS Oceana was to admit stunted emotional growth as a naval officer or, as in Punk's case, bad luck in matters of the heart. Boomerang girls were a dalliance, a check in the block, for RAG students and the occasional aviator in town on a cross-country, not RAG instructors. But Anita had done better than most at distancing herself from that persona.

"Anyway," Crud said, breaking Punk out of his daydream, "we would *both* be very disappointed if you couldn't make it. You know how I dislike rock concerts. I need you there."

Punk stretched and said, "I'll think about it."

Punk stood in the line of people waiting to get into the amphitheater, Anita on one arm and a blanket under the other, watching the men who happened by attempt not to stare at his date's chest. He tried to preempt the attention by locking forceful eyes with those of potential voyeurs as they approached, but they always managed to miss him on their way to her.

He glanced furtively at her profile and wondered whether the blank scan she cast across the crowd was a sign of ignorance or aloofness. She stood akimbo, right arm threaded through his left, long red hair cascading over an unbuttoned cardigan sweater and a painted-on T-shirt that featured the logo of a seafood restaurant with the slogan "Suck the Head, Eat the Tail" in prominent letters stretched to their limits. Her black skirt was cut above mid thigh and revealed nearly the full length of her tanned and shapely legs.

Hers was a beauty and style that didn't so much deserve

as demand attention. She wore a bit too much makeup and was tanned a shade too dark. Her face was pretty but with a hard edge to it when she spoke or laughed. She had sexy eyes—bedroom eyes—but in them Punk occasionally caught glimpses of sadness. Overall she was trying for wholesome, Punk thought, but it was a work very much in progress.

They'd dated off and on for more than a year now. She made Punk meals, cleaned his condo, showed up unannounced wearing nothing but a raincoat, and hoped his reaction to her efforts would grow from episodic enthusiasm into love. For his part Punk enjoyed her company, but it annoyed him that wherever they went for dinner the bartenders all knew her by name. But he didn't ask questions he didn't want answered. She was there when he called and, in the wake of Jordan's disappearance, that was enough for now.

"I'm glad you called, Rick," she said, stroking his forearm.

She was using his real name. Trainable, he thought. The first few times they'd gone out she'd steadfastly stuck with the boomerangesque tendency of using his call sign in spite of the hints he'd dropped. Just as it was awkward when squadronmates used his real name, it was awkward when civilians, especially girlfriends, used call signs.

"Thanks for coming," he replied before giving her a peck on the lips. "I wasn't sure whether you were a fan or not."

"Who doesn't like these guys?" Anita said dryly.

"I don't," Crud said from behind them. He also didn't like crowds, but he respected that the band was his wife's favorite and had waited in line for three hours months ago on a rainy winter day for these tickets—lawn seats, but tickets just the same.

"Suzanne," Punk called over his shoulder, "talk to your boy. I suppose he'll be complaining next that the weather is too nice."

"Don't worry about him," Suzanne replied. "He'll be fine once we claim our piece of the lawn."

The way Suzanne smiled at her husband reminded Punk of the way things had been with Jordan. But thoughts of Jordan brought on the dull ache he'd tried to suppress for months now, so he returned his attention to Anita and dotingly worked her hair behind her ear. She nervously jerked with his first touch, but then relaxed, pleasantly surprised by the overt display of affection.

After surrendering their tickets to an attendant and pushing through one of the turnstiles, they were in the amphitheater's main courtyard. On their way to the beer line, they passed several booths occupied by charity organizations and other nonprofit groups, including one called "People Against Aircraft Noise."

Punk approached the table that lined the front of the booth, picked up a pamphlet from one of the handful of stacks and began thumbing through it. Inside the book were diagrams of the crash zones around NAS Oceana and the field's departure and arrival patterns. On the next page was a chart that listed decibels at various power settings and altitudes. Punk quickly flipped through the rest and then took another look at the cover, a montage of a menacing-looking F/A-18 Hornet, shown head on, flying over a crying baby.

"What is this all about?" Punk asked the girl standing behind the desk. She looked like most of the coeds he'd seen from St. Johns, the philosophy college in Annapolis— straight hair, round glasses, and baggy clothes—except she was older, early forties by his estimation.

"PAAN is a citizens' initiative to stop a pandemic that threatens all of us: personal health risks and property damage from prolonged exposure to excessive noise."

"It sounds terrible," Punk said. "Cal, come over here."

Crud wandered over, slightly irritated that he'd been rerouted from his quest for beer. "What?"

Punk handed him one of the pamphlets and gestured toward the woman who repeated, "PAAN is a citizens' initiative to stop a pandemic that threatens all of us: personal health risks and property damage from prolonged exposure to excessive noise."

Punk and Crud exchanged looks of concern. "What causes this excessive noise?" Punk asked.

"You're not from here, are you?" the woman said.

"We're new to the area," Crud said.

She nodded her understanding and pointed skyward. "Military jets. You'll learn to hate them soon enough. They terrorize the city morning, noon, and night." She opened a pamphlet to the crash zone chart. "Where do you guys live?"

Punk leaned in and ran his finger over the page. "Let's see . . . um, right here. In this red-shaded area."

"Oh, my," she said.

"Is that bad?" Crud asked. "Our Realtor told us we were in a prime location, close to shopping and good schools."

"We intend to adopt," Punk added.

The woman turned around and hailed a portly man who was stacking boxes in the back of the booth. "Leo, we've got some Zone Oners here."

The man wiped his brow and waddled over. "Zone One, eh?" he said ominously. "That's the heart of the envelope."

"Heart of which envelope?" Punk asked.

"The crash envelope," the man said, growing fatter as he got closer to them. He placed a stubby finger against the chart. "This red area is where the fighter jets fly when they're taking off and landing."

"How often do they crash?" Crud asked.

"Yeah, how often?" Punk echoed. "I heard those fighter pilots were pretty good."

"Not as good as they think," the man said and emitted a snort. "Wait here." He lumbered to a briefcase near the boxes he was stacking, grabbed a folder, and then returned to the table. "These are statistics compiled by the Naval Safety Center that PAAN obtained through the Freedom of Information Act. Take a look."

Punk opened the folder and reviewed the top sheet inside. "Only two mishaps for every one hundred thousand flight hours flown? Maybe I'm wrong, but that sounds low to me."

"Yeah," Crud added. "And they do some really dangerous training, too. I saw it on a cable TV special a few months ago."

Punk ran his finger down the summary of mishaps. "It looks like the last time an airplane crashed in Virginia Beach was the late eighties."

The man stole the folder back from Punk. "The potential for a crash is always there, fellas. Not to mention the noise and the exhaust. You wait. Your quality of life will suffer. Your ceiling will crack and your cars will be covered with jet fuel. Your property value will drop like a rock. We even have medical evidence that, over time, the noise causes the human heart wall to thicken. Take one of our cards. You'll be calling PAAN soon enough, trust me."

"No wonder we got such a good deal, Cal," Punk said. "Our Realtor sold us a bill of goods."

"You're right, Rick," Crud replied. "Leo, when was the air station built?"

"I'm not sure. World War Two, maybe?"

"And how old is our house, Rick?"

"Five years old."

"It just doesn't make sense," Crud mused. "Why would they build houses where airplanes had been flying for years?"

"I'm a believer, Leo," Punk said. "What can we do to help stop this menace?"

"Well, we're having a rally next—"

Suzanne and Anita pushed up behind them. "Come on, you guys," Suzanne said. "The show's about to start. If you want a beer you'd better get it now."

Anita approached the table and started flipping through one of the pamphlets. The fat man studied her with great interest and very little discretion. "Have you ever been to Key West?" he asked while staring unashamedly at her breasts.

She looked up from the pamphlet to his eyes and then traced his gaze past the opening in her sweater down to her T-shirt. "No," she said. "This was a gift."

"Do you live in Crash Zone One, too?" the man asked, reluctantly shifting his greasy leer to her eyes.

"Where is Crash Zone One?" Anita asked back.

"Right here," he said, pointing to the diagram in the booklet.

She got her bearings around the tip of his finger and said, "Then I don't live in Crash Zone One." She cast a sideways glance at Punk. "And neither does he. He lives over here on the beach." She patted Punk's back maternally. "It's kind of scary that a fighter pilot can't find where he lives on a city map, don't you think?"

"Fighter pilot?" the man said. He narrowed his eyes at Punk. "You fly jets out of the air station?"

Punk calmly closed the pamphlet and replaced it on one of the stacks. "Does this mean I can't come to the rally?"

*   *   *

Beers in hand, the two couples claimed the first reasonably
spacious piece of lawn they came across, fearing there
might be no more available. Punk spread the blanket as
the house lights went down over the covered portion of the
amphitheater and the warm-up band took the stage. He
gave the act the benefit of the doubt for half a song, decided they were forgettable, and began people watching.

The slope of the hill positioned them above the walkway
that separated the seats from the grass. The crowd continued to pour in, cued by the music to hurry through the
lines and take their places in the audience. Punk noted
there were as many moms as daughters and collars as
crew necks.

The ambient light continued to fade with the setting sun,
casting an orange hue over those on the grass, a seemingly
more gregarious bunch than those in front of them confined
to padded chairs anchored into the concrete floor. Beach
balls took to the sky joined by mammoth bubbles created
by two longhaired lasses in short shorts and bikini tops who
fanned the air with head-sized hoops. A small dog smug-
gled in by its owner chased down a Frisbee, much to either
the chagrin or delight of those along its path, while a lone
freak strolled by decrying the fact that he couldn't score
any acid in spite of the fact that it was required to properly
hear the notes.

A boisterous group to his left diverted Punk's attention.
A burly black guy hoisted a tall woman on his shoulders
while others formed a chain and danced around them in a
circle. The woman was lowered, and in turn she put one of
the smaller men on her shoulders while the black man
joined the tail end of the procession. Punk wondered if
they could sustain the exuberance for the entire show, and
then he realized who they were: the coneheads from
Class Two.

The warm-up band finished, and while waiting for the
headliners, Punk convinced Crud to put on his advisor's
hat and join him in saying hello to the replacements. The
two threaded through the islands of blankets and bed-
spreads between them and the younger officers.

"Hey, the manager asked me to tell you to settle down
over here," Punk hailed as he approached.

"Damn," Lucky Clover said, "we can't get away from you guys."

"This is part of the RAG syllabus," Crud said. "We're here to ensure you're learning how to have good, clean fun."

"We're not interested in clean fun," Kosher Kaplan said.

"That's right," Smitty Smith agreed. "Although this white boy music ain't my thing, I'm showing my classmates here how to get down to it." He did a couple of fluid dance moves that little Kosher unsuccessfully tried to imitate.

"Did you two take advantage of the senior citizens' discount?" Ben Dover asked as he joined the semicircle of replacements forming around the two lieutenants.

"Yeah," Sinker Williams added. "Are you sure you're in the right place? I'm pretty sure that the Virginia Beach Symphony is playing at the civic center across town."

"I'd say something witty about your performance in the RAG so far," Punk countered, "but the skipper told me I'm supposed to be nice to you guys."

"Well, since you're being nice to us," Smitty said, "we'll be nice to you." He turned to Muddy Greenwood. "Give them a taste from your magic goat bladder, or whatever it is."

"You want some?" Muddy asked, holding up the teardrop-shaped bag with a plastic tip at the small end. It appeared to be covered with a dirty animal hide.

"What's in it?" Punk asked.

"Ah-ah," Lucky said with a waggle of his finger. "It's not polite to ask."

"I'll take some," Crud said as he reached out to take the bag from Muddy. She drew back.

"And it's also not polite to touch the container," Lucky said, protectively stepping in front of his female classmate. He was the only one in the group, including Smitty, taller than she, and only had her by an inch. "This is your first goat's bladder, isn't it?"

"No," Crud replied. "I've used one on a ski trip before."

"Were you the bag master?"

"The bag master?"

"Did you touch the bag?"

"Yes."

"Did others touch the bag?"

"Of course."

"What do you mean, 'of course'? Only the bag master is allowed to touch the bag. What kind of ski trip were you on, anyway?" Lucky teetered a bit, having partaken of the bag a few times already this evening.

"Just open your mouth," Muddy said as she pushed past Lucky. She sprayed a stream against the back of Crud's throat, and he forced the contents down until he could take no more. Much to the replacements' delight, she kept spraying for a few seconds after he closed his mouth, dousing his chin and neck.

Muddy turned to Punk with the bag poised in front of her like a pistol. "Now your turn."

Punk looked over to Crud, who was trying to suppress a cough while wiping tears from his eyes, and asked, "What was it?"

Crud shook his head and waved his hands, apparently unable to speak.

"No questions," Lucky instructed in his best POW camp provost voice. "Just drink."

The semicircle closed on him and he saw from the eager looks on the replacements' faces there would be no backing out. He closed his eyes and tilted his head back slightly and waited for Muddy to render his dose.

The female pilot took aim and bore down on the belly of the bag. The stream hit Punk's tongue, and he instinctively shut his mouth but reopened it quickly as her sinister laugh suggested she wasn't about to stop spraying.

Punk forced the liquid down with audible gulps, trying not to taste it and unsure of how his body might react. His resolve grew as a cheer welled up from the circle of replacements around him, the same reaction a rodeo cowboy might get after staying on a bronco beyond the bell. He was showing the youngsters the stuff fleet veterans were made of. After a half dozen more swallows the flow from the bag slowed to a trickle. Relieved and emboldened, Punk opened his eyes and leveled his head.

But as he met their high fives, Punk was hit by a burning in his gut. At the same time his brain registered the sickly sweet licorice flavor of the liqueur. As the wave overwhelmed him, he managed to turn most of the way around before a violent convulsion caused the liqueur, along with the better part of a steak dinner, to surge back out of his innards. He tried to cover his mouth, but the reaction lagged the first half of the stream, which found the feet of a well-groomed man in his thirties seated on a blanket cross-legged.

Accompanied by hoots and groans from the replacements and Crud, the civilian contemplated his shoes with disgust before standing up and squaring off with Punk. But before he could push too far inside of the fighter pilot's personal space, he was surrounded by several of the young officers, most effectively Smitty, who convinced the man with a look that, regardless of his impression, starting a fight over being on the receiving end of an inadvertent vomiting was a bad idea.

Smitty and Muddy tried to smooth the man's ruffled feathers, but to no avail. The man muttered his ire and dislike for the military as he wiped his loafers on the grass and then balled up his wool blanket and moved away with his female companion in tow. The replacements focused their attention back to Punk, who stood with fouled hand, red face, and sheepish grin.

"You did so well with our call signs," Smiles Giles said as Punk struggled to keep his dignity while doing his best to clean up with a single napkin. "Allow us to return the favor." The replacement scanned the faces of his classmates with a wry grin and then looked back to the instructor. "You're not Punk. You're *Puke*."

Punk started to say something about how established fleet call signs couldn't be changed, but stopped, knowing from experience that sometimes it was just best to take the hit earned. Plus, it wasn't true. Many times aviators eclipsed their own low-water marks of infamy and were awarded new call signs as a result. Boomers became Boogers; Potsies became Pissers; Skis became Skidmarks.

Instead of making an issue out of the notion of a new appellation, Punk rinsed his hand and face with the dregs from discarded bottles of water that were scattered at their feet. Muddy offered a stick of gum. "My date thanks you," Punk said. A stirring from the stage told that the show was about to restart, so Punk and Crud gave a courteous nod to the still-guffawing replacements, and hurried back toward the girls.

"I wouldn't worry about the new call sign," Crud said, stepping over a cooler. "It'll never stick. There's already a Puke flying Tomcats."

Halfway back to their blanket they ran into Pugsly, who was loaded down with cups of beer. "What the fuck happened to you?" he asked as he sized up Punk, whose golf shirt was soaked down the front from the dousing he'd given himself.

"He had a little run-in with Muddy's bag," Crud said.

"Muddy, huh?" Pugsly said with a sardonic chuckle. "I think the call signs you guys came up with suck." He pushed between the two lieutenants and continued on.

The sky turned dark, and during slow parts of the show, which seemed numerous, Punk gazed above the heads behind them to the red flashing lights that passed to the west of the amphitheater, jets just out of earshot by virtue of the volume of the PA. The fact it was Friday night meant nothing to the squadrons about to go on deployment. In many ways the weeks before the long separation from family and loved ones were worse than the separation itself. Punk thought of the purgatory of precruise, of being neither here nor there. On paper, cruises were six months long, but the emotional toll made them seem so much longer. Just before his last deployment the final "romantic" dinners with Jordan had been exercises in pushing food around plates and forced conversations, if any words were exchanged at all.

He looked again to the lights dotting the sky. He'd been where they were: on final approach to the airfield, peering along the canopy rail out to the bright glow of the amphitheater, yearning for that innocent world between scans of instruments in the cockpit, knowing full well that more than half the year to come would be spent wrestling with the challenges of deployment.

Later the band retook the stage for their encore, and all around the grass hillside women were being hoisted up on men's shoulders. Punk leaned over to Anita and said, "Want to get up?"

"I don't think that's a good idea," she replied.

"C'mon," Punk insisted. "Don't be a drag."

"No," she said, "I'd rather not."

"You're not getting it," Punk said playfully. "I'm putting

you on my shoulders." With that he snaked his head behind her and between her legs and quickly hoisted her up. As he stood erect, a soft grating of hair and folds of flesh against the nape of his neck evinced why she'd hesitated to get on his shoulders. He considered putting her back down, but didn't; it was only rock 'n' roll and he liked it. He felt himself getting aroused and was buoyed by thoughts of what the postconcert portion of the evening might offer. Anita stopped her protest and raised one hand into the air in synch with the beat while she tugged her skirt down with the other to keep the crack of her ass from showing.

Punk flexed his knees in time with the music and looked over to see if Crud had taken his cue and put Suzanne on his shoulders. The couple was standing in deep embrace, making out like hormone-saturated high schoolers. Punk watched as they kissed and Crud's hand slid down and cupped his wife's butt, envious that they'd seemingly captured both stability and passion. Punk was sure that what Crud had was what he ultimately wanted, but, with Anita's warmth against him, he was just as certain it could wait one more night.

CHAPTER THREE

The brief was quickly going south. In the time it took for one of the three replacements to stumble over the fourth step of the spin procedures he was supposed to know by heart, the mood in the cramped space went from professionally congenial to us versus them.

"So what is it, Pugsly?" Flex asked from an adjacent desk while he fiddled with the pair of beach volleyball shades that he constantly wore around his neck like a St. Christopher's medal. As he was going to be the replacement's RIO for the upcoming flight, Flex had a stake in ensuring his guy knew his shit. "You're in the strike phase now, not FAM. You've got almost forty hours in the Tomcat; stop acting like you've never flown before."

Flex had just rolled into the instructor role from a deployed fleet squadron after a three-year sea tour, so the salt on him from the wave tops of the Pacific and Indian Oceans was thick and fresh. He exuded every cliché of the West Coast Navy: flowing peroxide-blond hair, year-round tan, and an "I'm only here to fly" attitude. He was the military version of the target audience of men's lifestyle magazines—the kind of guy featured sporting a tank top and knee-length cargo shorts with a kayak slung across his broad shoulders in advertisements.

"We're spinning," Flex continued with a swirl of his calloused right hand. "What are you going to do about it?" Pugsly nervously tugged at the main zipper of his flight suit as his prominent jowls reddened to still-deeper shades and his mouth jerked without forming the answer. His instructor RIO continued to apply the pressure: "Fourteen thousand feet . . . thirteen thousand feet . . . I'm reaching for the ejection handle . . . we're about to waste fifty million dollars' worth of jet . . ."

"Somebody help him out," Punk said from behind the podium.

"If no recovery . . ." Smitty started, hesitant to bilge his peer, but eager to make a good impression on Punk, his instructor pilot for the event.

"Oh, yeah," Pugsly said, mental lapse apparently complete. "If no recovery, stick in the direction of the turn needle."

"Start again," Flex commanded.

Pugsly sighed and worked to regain his composure like a harried contestant at a spelling bee. While staring an angry hole into the wall under the dry erase board at the front of the room, he dove into the spiel again, maniacally throwing the steps out in a single breath: "Stick forward neutral lateral lock your harness both throttles idle rudder opposite turn needle/yaw if no recovery stick in the direction of the turn needle/yaw—"

Punk waved for him to stop. "Pick it up, Lucky."

Lucky was unfazed by Punk's check to see if he was paying attention and didn't miss a beat as he continued with the same flurried cadence of his classmate: "If recovery indicated neutralize controls and pull out at seventeen units angle of attack if flat spin verified by flat attitude lack of pitch and roll rate increasing eyeball-out G canopy jettison RIO command eject." He signaled completion with a drum roll on the surface of his desk.

Punk decompressed a tad, as relieved as the students that things hadn't grown any uglier. A "ready room down" was not pleasant for either the instructor or the replacement. The instructor assumed the burden of proving to the operations officer that the replacement's performance in the brief was so gross that it eclipsed his opportunity to prove himself in the air, and justified wrecking the flight schedule for the day and the training plan for even longer. The replacement who received the preflight down wore a label of incompetence from that point that was hard to shake. Like a professional golfer who squanders a two-shot tournament lead by triple bogeying the final hole, the fighter pilot suffers with any blow to his confidence. Many times, he ends up walking through the door that those no longer wearing wings pass.

"All right, let's quickly review what we've talked about here." Punk looked down at his watch. "We need to walk in about ten minutes. We'll press from here, hit the head or whatever, and then swing through maintenance control and check the gripes. Get out to our jets and do a good preflight, including a thorough check of the racks, inert bombs, and gun. Look under the boarding ladder at the belt and make sure you have bullets. Hop in. Go through the start-up procedures and wait in spot until I'm ready to go. I'll taxi first, followed by Lucky, and then Pugsly.

"The ordies will arm the bomb racks and guns in the hold short. Take the duty runway. Ten-second interval take-off rolls. Safe but expeditious joinups. Check each other clean and dry. Press down to the target at Dare County. Work the bombing pattern first." Punk moved to the dry erase board and pointed to one of the diagrams he'd freehanded earlier. "Run-in heading one-zero-zero. Hit the numbers and work hard to get a good solution. RIOs will record the hits for the debrief. Once we're all out of inerts we'll work the strafe pattern. We'll rendezvous overhead the target at five thousand feet and then drop down to fifteen hundred feet and do the spacer pass for the strafe pattern. Wings back at sixty-eight degrees, targeting four hundred and fifty knots. I pitch off. Five potatoes later, Lucky. Then Pugsly.

"Establish your strafing pattern, run-in heading one-seven-zero. Again, hit the numbers. Do the first two runs dry. After that, you're cleared hot until you get rid of all your bullets. At the roll in, aggressively maneuver to get the picture right through the sight. When you get the in-range cue in the HUD, squeeze the trigger once deliberately. Hold it until the firing stops and then get the nose above the horizon. Don't try to see the tracers all the way to impact. That's a good way to fly into the ground.

"Once we're complete with the strafing runs, we'll rendezvous overhead the target again at five thousand feet. Check each other clean and dry. At that point, we'll head back to the field." Punk returned to the podium and looked up at the small "weathervision" monitor mounted in a front corner of the briefing room. "Weather looks good for the rest of the afternoon, although it's July, and you always have to worry about thunderstorms at the end of the day. We'll plan on coming into the VFR pattern with the wings back for three-second interval breaks. Remember, you never know who's watching you around the field so make it look good. Crisp rolls, level turns. Wings sweeping forward at two hundred and eighty knots. Wheels down at two-fifty; flaps at two hundred. Full landing checklist on the downwind leg of the landing pattern. I'll full stop first pass. You guys get touch-and-gos until you run out of gas. Carrier qualifications are coming faster than you realize, and you need all the landing practice you can get."

Punk threw his hands up. "Any questions?" The aviators seated before him remained still. "Okay, let's do it."

As the small crowd dispersed, Pugsly approached Punk and sneered, "You know I know my procedures. I choked. It's no big deal."

Punk was in the instructors' locker room working the long zipper of his G suit up the length of his right leg when he asked his counterparts, "What do you guys think of Pugsly?"

Flex stretched his arms behind him and expanded his upper torso until it appeared as if his flight suit might shred and said, "Not much. I *do* think you really made him sweat over that spin procedure, though."

"Flex," Punk said, "you know what's interesting about you? Most guys show up here from the fleet ready to be buddies with the replacements, and then they turn into assholes after a few months of watching them make the same mistake over and over. You're way ahead of that timeline."

"I'm fair," Flex said. "And what does this guy have now, forty hours in the Tomcat? He just learned how to run an intercept on a bogey, but he's got the attitude of a Desert Storm vet with a MiG kill or two."

"Well, you know where he gets that, don't you?" Crud said from the far corner of the locker room. "His dad."

"Who's his dad?" Flex asked.

"Does the name King Bellingham mean anything to you?"

"No."

"King Bellingham?" Crud continued. "As in the only

Vietnam-era Navy ace King Bellingham? Didn't you ever read *King of Eagles*?"

"Was it made into a movie?" Flex asked.

"No," Crud said. "I think the American entertainment machine decided to torture the American public that time by forcing them to read the book." He concentrated on mating the hooks to the rings at the base of his survival vest, straining to look over the bulky flight gear around his middle, like a fat guy trying to find his belt buckle. "*King of Eagles* is King Bellingham's autobiography."

"How is it that you've never read *King of Eagles,* Flex?" Punk asked. "That's like a fighter pilot saying he's never seen *Top Gun.*"

"*Top Gun* changed my life," Crud said dryly.

"Mine too," Flex agreed without matching Crud's sarcastic tenor. "I know it sounds corny, but I won't lie about it: That movie is the main reason I went to flight school. Anyway, I don't give a shit what the cone's dad did, even if he was an ace. I got to deal with the cone, not his dad." The muscular RIO slung his harness over his shoulder. "Hell, my dad owns the most successful Mercedes dealership in southern California, but you don't see me going around making a big deal about it." He picked up his helmet and started out of the locker room, but then paused with his back against the door. "Don't worry, boys. Ops scheduled Pugsly with the right man. After this flight he'll be mellowed; I guarantee it."

The noise of Flex slamming through the locker-room door on his way out died off, and Crud gathered his gear and made his way across the line of lockers that separated him from where Punk stood taking inventory of the contents of his navigation bag.

They ambled out of the locker room jingling like cowboys as fittings and fasteners and snaps clinked against each other and the cinderblock walls. They entered the stairwell and their metallic tinkling grew louder as it echoed off the cement steps and down the well. Crud paused at a bulletin board next to the landing and studied a homemade flyer that advertised a catamaran for sale. "Summer's underway," he said. "I should get one of those."

"Remember that one we had at the beach?" Punk asked.

"How could I forget? The first time Suzanne and I porked was on that thing, a mile out after the wind died on us."

"That's more detail than I need, thank you."

"I'm sure that's not the first time I told you about that."

"I must have mentally blocked it out of my conscious-ness," Punk said. "I can handle the thought of Suzanne naked, but I refuse to picture you that way."

"Me naked is certainly not a new concept to you, Punk. We've done our fair share of hot tubbing together."

"Let it go, Crud."

The lieutenants pushed through the swinging door and into the hangar bay and were greeted by the cacophony that was the cavernous space's everpresent soundtrack. Life had its constants: death, taxes, and broken F-14 Tomcats. Walking down the nonskid path that ran along the front doors of the maintenance shops dotting the hangar's ground floor, the aviators found it sobering, after an hour or so in the preflight brief discussing the acts of derring-do they were going to perform as invulnerable cheaters of gravity, to see the sleek machines for what they were: a joining of pieces provided by lowest bidders like Raynotec Defense Industries, held together by rivets, screws, fasten-ers, wire, tape, and the grace of God.

Punk passed the first F-14 and flinched at the sound of a rubber mallet repeatedly pounding on a panel just above his head. He caught sight of a technician perched on top of the jet, arching his back and then striking the fighter behind the canopy with the two-handed determination of John Henry driving a railroad spike. There was anger in the work, much different from the calm, analytical evoca-tions of the high-tech aerospace surgeons seen in Navy cat-alogs and on TV commercials. Punk rationalized that from time to time even surgeons had to resort to good old-fashioned force.

The two instructors were the last aviators from the three-jet event to arrive at maintenance control. Punk and Crud entered the busy space and wedged themselves next to their respective students against the chest-high counter that ran nearly the length of the room.

"How are we looking, Smitty?" Punk asked his RIO as the ensign studied the aircraft discrepancy book for the jet

they were about to man up. Before each flight, aviators
reviewed the books. The binders full of loose-leaf computer
printouts documented problems discovered by aircrew during each of the airplane's last ten flights, as a way of antici-
pating how their machines might act up. The printouts were
placed to the left or the right on the inside of the binder,
depending on whether the maintainers had been able to fix
the gripe—problem—or not.

"Pretty good," the big replacement replied with a confident nod as he quickly flipped through the balance of the
binder's pages and then pushed it across the counter to
Punk. "The radar transmitter failed on the last hop, so they
stuck a new one in for us. Otherwise I didn't see anything
to be concerned about."

Punk let out a hum that signaled to Smitty that the next
test, in a series of many that would take place throughout
the flight, was about to occur. The lieutenant opened the
binder and began to page through the printouts with a pace
that, to the untrained eye, barely afforded the pilot time to
absorb the text. Punk made it halfway through the sheets
and then stopped abruptly on one of them before looking
up and flagging the attention of one of the maintenance
chiefs working behind the counter.

"Has this jet had a drop check?" Punk asked the khaki-
attired chief as he approached.

The chief knitted his thick black brow, twisted the binder
180 degrees on the counter, and quickly read the gripe
aloud. "When gear handle was lowered, left main landing
gear took fifteen seconds to go from barber poled to down
and locked." He momentarily relaxed his expression and
then again contorted his face in confusion while he tapped
on the page as if loosening additional bits of information.
After a few seconds passed without enlightenment, the
chief lifted his head from the page, excused himself, and
went in search of more clues.

Punk watched across two rows of metal desks on the
business side of the counter as the chief conferred with one
of the more junior maintenance clerks dressed in dungarees. While Punk waited for resolution, he pushed the
binder back toward his backseat charge and directed his
attention to the printout in question. "I'm assuming you
missed this one," he said to Smitty.

The RIO studied the page with the most stoic visage he could muster considering the circumstance. He slowly turned to the adjacent printouts, retracing the steps taken during the first run-through and testing whether the pages had a tendency to stick together.

"I appreciate the fact a Tomcat needs a working radar in order to be fully mission capable," Punk continued, "but I would also suggest that, regardless of how well it worked, the success of the flight would be questioned once we landed without all three of the landing gears down."

Smitty nodded contritely and waited for the knife to be twisted some more, but Punk turned his attention to the discussion between the maintainers across the room. Punk knew from the bemused and frustrated expression that the replacement longed to be the guy who caught the mistakes and stood in judgment. Instructors waxed nostalgic about their carefree days as coneheads—self-centered times without collateral duties and political snafus—but from where the coneheads stood, the instructors were guilty of selective memory. Punk remembered the perception well. However keen the feeling was, Smitty and the rest of Class Two still had a long way to go.

Punk noticed the other aviators filing out toward the flight line. "What's the story, chief?" he hailed across the fifteen feet that separated them.

His question drew the attention of a third party: the maintenance master chief, Master Chief Aviation Technician (Air Warfare) Bobby Callaghan, who was seated at his large wooden desk in the far left corner of maintenance control, a perch from which he could keep track of all the goings-on in his domain. He contorted his ruddy face, shook his head, which was freckled and sparsely covered with thin strands of red hair, and slowly pushed back from his desk to investigate the situation.

The chief involved in the discussion caught the master chief's approach out of the corner of his eye and became mute. The sight of a man as tall and muscular as Master Chief Callaghan barreling down on a group was likely to shut down the conversations in the room, the same way it had in South Boston dives before a single punch was thrown. The master chief silently relieved his subordinates of the aircraft discrepancy book and studied the gripe in question for a few seconds before calmly closing the book and shaking his head again. He said something to the others that Punk couldn't make out and then moved to the main counter, fishing under the ledge for another discrepancy book and placing it before Punk.

"You're in aircraft one-eleven, sir," the master chief said in his New England brogue.

Punk attempted to be gracious and unaffected while the master chief stood attendant before him and the other chiefs in the room pretended to be busy with other matters. The lieutenant knew there would be activity behind the woodshed following his exit, and he wanted to perform as much damage control as possible. However correct his query to the chief might have been, the maintainers' perception of the situation would determine the reality. Life could be rough for an aviator viewed as a troublemaker by the chief corps, especially a guy who in recent memory had been involved with an incident that made work for maintenance: for instance, an instructor who allowed his student to plant a jet in the mud next to the taxiway. Those sorts of flyers found themselves going down in the chocks more often than their lower-profile squadronmates.

Punk flipped cheerily through the discrepancy book, even faster than his normally brisk pace, and then closed the book with a lighthearted slam. "Looks like this dog will hunt, master chief," he said loudly enough for all to hear.

"It's a good jet, sir," the master chief replied as he rose to his full height. At six-foot-one, Punk had always thought of himself as tall, but he felt short in the company of the master chief who had nearly four inches on him. "Have a great flight."

The pilot paused for a second and feigned a study of the cover of the book and then leaned over toward the master chief and addressed him in hushed tones. "You guys deal with a lot in here, master chief. In the grand scheme of things, it really wasn't that important."

The master chief's eyes defied the ranks between them as he spoke. "Maintenance control is supposed to control maintenance. Besides, sir, I said, 'Have a great flight,' and once I say, 'Have a great flight,' our business is over until you bring my jet back safe and sound."

The pilot smiled and nodded and moved for the door. He took a few steps with his bulky replacement RIO in close trail but stopped to speak across the counter: "You up for a run around noon?"

"Have a great flight, *sir*."

"One, that hit was nine o'clock, one hundred meters," the spotter said over the radio in his guttural North Carolina waterman's twang, an accent that sounded like Cockney crossed with Swedish, as Punk climbed away from the target after delivering another Mark-76 inert bomb.

"One copies," Punk replied, disgust barely hidden in his radio voice. "Master arm safe."

He'd made five runs so far, leading the two replacements around the bombing pattern and planned on doing one more. At that point all of his Blue Death, the mock-lethal tag for the two-foot-long pale blue training bombs, would be expended, and from what he'd been able to glean over the radio his wingmen were in the same boat.

Punk looked over his left shoulder and verified that the white puff of smoke blooming where the last Blue Death impacted the ground was collocated with the spotter's call. He cursed something into his mask about how his heads-up display (HUD) must've been miscalibrated because he'd lined the symbology up perfectly before mashing the bomb button with his right thumb, and there was no way that the bomb should've missed the bull's-eye, although he had yet to come any closer than forty meters to it.

Punk reached twenty-five thousand feet while scribing a level arc toward the roll-in point and watched Lucky pull off target. Another smoke cloud appeared on the dirt, this one closer to the center of the five concentric rings.

"Two, three o'clock, twenty meters," the spotter reported.

"Two copies. Master arm safe."

"Man," Smitty said to Punk over the intercom, "Lucky's doing pretty good, isn't he?"

"Three's in hot," Pugsly said on the target frequency before Punk could respond to Smitty's observation. Punk shifted his focus to the roll-in point and he picked up Pugsly and Flex hurtling toward the planet. A few seconds later they had bottomed out and were climbing back up behind Lucky, who had Crud in his backseat as the instructor RIO.

"Three, six o'clock, five hundred meters."

Punk waited a few seconds for Pugsly's reply, and when it didn't come he said, "Three, understand your master arm is in the safe position?"

"Three's safe," Pugsly said resignedly. The period had not gone well for him in terms of putting Blue Death anywhere near the bull's-eye. For the past ten minutes he'd been spraying bombs all over Dare County, North Carolina—long, short, left, and right of the aim point. There hadn't been any consistency in his misses, and Flex was at a loss about how to advise him on his technique. But an instructor had to say *something*, so he reverted to bombing boilerplate: "Make sure you've got the pipper on the target before you pickle the bomb off."

Punk held the target off his left wing until he got over the access road that marked the roll-in point. He mentally reviewed the dispersion pattern of his previous five hits and mused at how bombing was like golfing: On some days it just wasn't there. His mind went to a place where he was standing over the ball with driver in hand, knees slightly flexed, body bent at the hips, club back, arc on plane, full shoulder turn—and then doubt creeps in, and he has no control over where the ball's going to go. A golfer had to accept that in spite of all the practice and lessons and high-tech equipment, some days were like that.

Punk came off the links and banked hard left, dragged his nose level for ninety degrees, and rolled nearly inverted until Smitty and he were aimed forty-five degrees below the horizon. Once happy with the dive angle, Punk leveled the Tomcat's wings. "Master arm's coming on," Punk said to his RIO before keying the radio: "One's in hot, last run."

"Roger one," the spotter said. "Cleared hot."

Smitty called off altitudes and airspeeds as Punk concentrated through the shapes projected against the glass before him. With the replacement's call of "ten thousand feet, four hundred knots," the pipper, a cross with a dot in the middle of it that marked where the bomb should hit at any given moment, came alive and began to track vertically up the

HUD. Punk anticipated the pipper's crossing of the bull's-eye and depressed the bomb button at what seemed the perfect moment. He fought the crush of G as he raised the nose back above the horizon and waited seemingly forever for the spotter's ruling.

"Bull's-eye." And some days a golfer could win the U.S. fucking Open.

Punk fought the desire to crow over the radio as he studied the white puff dead smack in the middle of the target and instead transmitted, "One's safe and out of bombs. Climbing to five thousand feet for rendezvous before entering the strafe pattern."

Punk noted from the lower altitude how the glint of the sun off the puddles scattered about the target looked a lot like the muzzle flashes that had greeted him that day over southern Iraq. He often contemplated how close the bullet that smashed through the rear portion of the canopy had come to hitting Spud. Hell, one foot to the right and it would have caught Punk right between the eyes. A few feet lower and it might have cut through hydraulic lines, and they would have joined their skipper and his RIO on the ground.

"Bull's-eye," the spotter called as Lucky pulled off target after his final run.

"Roger," Lucky sang. "Two's safe, one in sight."

Punk keyed his radio, tuned to the squadron common frequency. "Lucky, haven't you ever heard about letting the boss win?"

"Sure," Lucky chucked back. "But I joined the Navy so I wouldn't have to play those games."

"Really? Wait until you see your grade sheet."

Lucky had *it*. Class Two was just shy of halfway through the RAG syllabus, but it was already obvious to the instructor corps who among the replacements had that intangible quality that separated good fighter pilots from face-in-the-crowd fighter pilots. It was more than just stick-and-rudder stuff; it was the ability to stay confidently ahead of the situation, to deftly ply the gray areas of naval aviation. They could say what they wanted about the decline of American youth; the culture was still capable of producing folks like Lucky, pilots who had *it*.

"Three's in hot," Pugsly called.

"Cleared hot, three."

As Lucky smoothly attached himself to his flight lead's left wing, Punk watched Pugsly dive through his last run, halfway hoping that he'd score well this time. Even an irritating SOB like Pugsly needed an injection of confidence now and again.

But as the third Tomcat pulled off target, Punk saw a puff growing well beyond the outermost ring. The target frequency was silent, and Punk figured the hit was so far off that it was beyond the limits of where the spotter normally scoured the area through his binoculars.

"Three, did you drop?" the spotter asked.

"We think so," Flex said.

"Yeah, you did," Punk confirmed. "Long and left. Do you have us in sight?"

"Three has one and two in sight," Pugsly said.

"All right. Expedite the joinup and let's get set up to strafe."

Punk flashed a fist at Lucky, and the replacement complied with the signal by crossing under the lead Tomcat and reestablishing himself on the right wing. Punk focused his attention down the left canopy rail toward Pugsly whose F-14 was pointed at the other two as he tried to effect a quick joinup from below. At first, the replacement's attempt at rendezvousing looked good, but Punk watched with growing concern as Pugsly aimed his jet at them too long.

"Slow your closure," Punk commanded. "Align the fuselages."

Pugsly started to comply, but it was too late to salvage this attempt at an expeditious joinup. "Under run, under run," Punk said sharply. Pugsly bunted his nose just a bit and sailed his Tomcat swiftly under the other two. Once on the other side he threw his right wing up and halted his growing separation from the rest of the flight, and then more cautiously joined on Lucky's right wing.

"What was that, Pugsly?" Punk asked on squadron common.

"I was trying something new," Pugsly said. "Don't worry. I'm ready to strafe."

Punk shook his head, scribbled a quick note on his kneeboard card, and decided to wait for the debrief to chew the replacement out. "Range control, Boxer flight is transitioning to the strafe pattern. We're setting up for our spacer pass."

"Roger. Center banner in use today."

"Copy. We'll be shooting at the center banner." Punk started a slow desent while swinging the three jets along a wide arc toward the southerly run-in heading for the spacer pass. They'd been bombing toward the east, but the day was clear and the mid-July sun burned high overhead, so there weren't any atmospherics to worry about.

Once the flight was headed one-seven-zero, Punk steadied up and leveled off at fifteen hundred feet. Just over a mile away from the observation tower, Punk motioned toward his wingmen, as if slowly fanning his ear, then rolled his head forward, and when he brought it sharply back he flipped the switch on the inboard throttle, the one that commanded the wings to sweep.

"One's off, spacer pass," Punk said on the frequency.

He put his jet into a climbing left turn until he reached five thousand feet and was headed opposite the run-in course. He situated the Tomcat for the first strafing run, quickly reviewing the air-to-ground gunnery checklist on his kneeboard.

Punk's first indication that something had gone horribly wrong was Smitty repeatedly screaming, "Oh, no!" The pilot looked into his mirrors to figure out the RIO's problem and saw the replacement was focused out the left side of the jet.

Several lines of fire snaked out from a main plume of black smoke, marking the path of some of the larger pieces of jet headed for earth. The forward half of one of the Tomcats had hit the trees and then exploded across the swamp like a napalm hit in a Vietnam War documentary.

Smitty's frantic disbelief was drowned out by the sickening caw of emergency beacons over the distress frequency. Punk scoured the sky for parachutes. He spotted two of them and feared there were no more. Then he thought of Crud and a wave of dread washed over him. He wanted answers, but he took a long draw of the oxygen flowing through his mask, checked his emotions, and started his new role as on-scene commander.

Punk told his replacement backseater to calm down and

began to orbit the crash site at one thousand feet. He keyed the radio to talk to the spotter: "Range control, this is Boxer flight lead. Request you have the base launch the rescue helicopter."

"I already done that," the spotter replied, shock evident in his voice. There were a loud series of clicks and static over the frequency that sounded to Punk like the spotter had dropped the handset.

"Range control," Punk said. "Range control, radio check." There was no response. "Range control, how do you read Boxer lead?" Silence.

Punk circled above the target complex for a time, watching the sickly towers of black smoke rise into the sky and waiting for answers. None were forthcoming.

"Punk, are you up?" a voice asked over the radio after nearly fifteen minutes.

"Crud, is that you?" Punk said as he rolled his Tomcat to the left and looked down on the closest of the two crash sites.

"Negative. It's Flex. I'm up here in the spotting tower."

"Do you have anybody with you?"

"Just the spotter."

"Where's Pugsly?"

"I don't know. I think he got out of the airplane, but I didn't see where he came down."

"Where's Crud?"

"I don't know that either. I doubt it's good, Punk. It's *not* good."

Punk was hit by the mental image of Crud and Suzanne kissing at the concert weeks ago, and he refused to believe that Crud might be dead.

"Are you okay, Flex?" Punk finally thought to ask.

"Yeah, I'm fine," Flex said. "My fucking sunglasses broke. I'll bet the warranty covers jet crashes . . . *not*."

"What the hell happened?" Punk asked.

"We hit them right before they pulled off for the spacer pass . . . I don't know why, but we rolled into them . . . hit them with our left wing."

"Any chance they got out?" Punk asked as he looked down on one of the spires of smoke rising out of the swamp. He knew what Flex's answer would be.

"No," Flex said.

"Range control, Guardian six-ten is checking in," the pilot of the aging H-3 Sea King rescue helicopter said over the frequency. "We're over the northern part of the area at cherubs five. Crash locations in sight."

"Roger, Guardian," the spotter said. "Say intentions."

"We're going to scout the sites first and then let our swimmers out to tend to any survivors." The rescue swimmers were trained primarily for at-sea pickups, but their skills as field medics lent themselves to emergencies like these. Punk watched the helicopter pass underneath him just above the swamp's vegetation and then noted his fuel level. He cross-checked his fuel flow gauge and figured he could loiter above the scene for another quarter-hour or so. Though there was little left for him to do in his role as on-scene commander, he couldn't bring himself to leave.

"Guardian's got a parachute in sight," the helicopter pilot transmitted. "Looks like a survivor is stuck in a tree here. He appears to be alive; I can see his arms waving. I'm lowering a swimmer down to him at this time."

As he dropped the Tomcat down to a lower altitude and picked up a tight circle over the helicopter, Punk muttered a prayer. He watched as the swimmer left the helicopter and descended to the swamp. Once satisfied with his footing, the swimmer detached from the wire and moved to the base of the tree while the Sea King resumed the search for other downed aviators.

The emergency beacons attached to the ejection seats were still saturating the primary emergency frequency, so Punk assumed that the swimmer was using a survival radio tuned to the secondary emergency frequency to talk to the helicopter pilot.

"Smitty, keep your radio on the target frequency," Punk said to his replacement. "I'm switching mine."

The fighter pilot dialed in just as the swimmer relayed "—name is Pugsly. He appears to be unhurt. He's too far off the ground to release himself, but I'll be able to reach him."

"We copy," the helicopter pilot replied before keying his other radio dialed to the target frequency. "Targets, the first swimmer is with a survivor who has identified himself as 'Pugsly.' We've also dropped the other swimmer over the other site."

"Roger," the spotter said as he caught sight of a cloud of dust coming down the access road. "Looks like the Dare County paramedics are here, if you happen to need them."

"Copy," the helicopter pilot said before talking to both swimmers on the emergency frequency. "Gents, we need to expedite the discovery and pickup of the remaining survivors. We have an ambulance on station by the spotting tower."

"Oh, God," a new, more distressed voice passed, a voice Punk reasoned must belong to the other swimmer. "Boss, we ain't going to need an ambulance for these boys."

"Say again," the helicopter pilot said. "What do you have there?"

"I've got both of them nearby. They landed pretty close together, I guess. Not much left of them, really."

"Knock it off, Simmons!" the helicopter pilot said. "Use standard terminology, goddam it!"

Fighting a wave of nausea, Punk switched his radio off with trembling fingers and started the long flight back to the base.

CHAPTER FOUR

On most Friday afternoons during the summer the ceremonial hangar at Naval Air Station Oceana was filled with a well-appointed crowd of naval officers, their spouses, and prominent civilians celebrating a change of command or a retirement. This Friday afternoon held no such promise. Now the building had assumed its secondary role: The place was home to the shattered remains of two F-14 Tomcats that had collided over a North Carolina swamp.

The scene as Punk entered the hangar was macabre, and he felt like a cop contemplating a couple of ambushed associates on the city morgue's forensics slabs. The two jets, or thousands of scraps that were once joined to form the jets, lay across the white painted cement floor, gigantic jigsaw puzzles with pieces that didn't fit cleanly together anywhere. The cheerful semaphore pennants that hung in rows from the rafters seemed out of place, and the massive wall-sized American flag on the far wall behind the folded dais had picked up the darker half of its split personality and now bespoke sacrifice instead of achievement. He reflected on the awards ceremony, nearly a year ago now, when he'd stood on that stage and received the Distinguished Flying Cross from the Chief of Naval Operations. The event seemed like it had just happened yesterday; at the same time, it now felt like a few lifetimes had since passed.

He walked the length of waist-high yellow tape used to mark crime scenes and took in the wreckage of the first jet, starting with what used to be the radome and radar antenna followed by the smashed control surfaces, black boxes, and twisted actuators with the same horror one might have had to suppress stumbling over roadkill. The appearance of the mechanical innards testified to the violence that had exposed them to the light of day. The mess was painstakingly arranged, the pieces ranging in size from as small as a quarter to as large as the left vertical stabilizer, which rose fifteen feet above the floor and appeared basically untouched. The squadron logo—a flying skeleton wearing boxing gloves—that once proudly adorned the tail now seemed to mock the fact that flying fighter jets was ultimately an undertaking subject to both the laws of nature and human error. After pausing to study the twisted and mud-encrusted exhaust nozzles, he moved to the second line across the hangar floor.

A few of the mishap investigators, the same men who'd helped dig the remains out of the crash site, gathered over what had once been the second Tomcat's left engine afterburner section and scribbled notes onto the screens of their handheld computers. He wanted to talk to them, but their body language advised against it. These were more of the guys aviators never wanted to see, even more so than the airfield emergency personnel who'd descended on Muddy Greenwood and him weeks ago, because the investigators' presence indicated that the shit had somehow *really* hit the fan, that airplanes had been destroyed or people had died.

And when the investigators did show up it was with a cool and detached precision that implied that they had no real emotional ties to the business. They had gone through this sort of drill many times. If the Naval Safety Center's statistics were to be believed, in spite of the assertions of People Against Aircraft Noise, naval aviation had become safer since the day Ely made the first arrested landing with his biplane aboard the USS *Langley*. But airplanes still hit the ground, or, in this case, each other, and when they did somebody had to clean up the mess.

Punk walked with heavy steps down the second line of smashed airplane parts, starting at the tail and working his way forward. He hadn't been sure which jet was which until he got to the cockpit section of the second one down. There he saw a recovered ejection seat with its headrest twisted around one hundred eighty degrees, the fuselage cut in two about where the aviator's ribcage would have been. *Crud's jet* . . .

Punk shook his head and thought of the replacement pilot with the call sign "Lucky." The name seemed to carry the irony of a black comedy.

"They never felt a thing," a voice said from behind him. He turned to find a thin, gray-haired man in shirtsleeves, wearing a thin, limp loosened necktie. Corky McBride was the chief field representative for the base's largest military contractor, Raynotec Defense Industries. RDI was one of the few companies to survive the end of the Cold War, and its staying power had allowed it to gobble up the smaller firms that had dotted the landscape of the Reagan era. Nearly a dozen companies had originally come together to manufacture the F-14, but RDI now had its stamp on everything from the altimeters to the latch that held the tailhook up. In fact, the only components that RDI didn't manufacture were the ejection seats, the engines, and the tires. "Good to see you, Punk." Corky smiled and deepened the cracks across his tanned and weathered face. He extended his arm in a manner that seemed too buoyant for the setting.

"Hello, Corky," Punk said.

"This whole thing is too bad, huh?"

"Yeah," Punk said just shy of mockingly. "Too bad . . ."

"You were leading that flight, weren't you?"

"Yep."

"Did you see anything?"

"Nope," Punk replied with a shake of his head.

There were a few minutes of silence between them. Owing to the mood the scene created, too much chitchat would have been unprofessional, and Corky never wanted to come off as unprofessional. "Did you know Crud very well?" he asked after an appropriately reverent period of time.

"Yeah, I did," Punk replied. "We were RAG students together—roommates, actually—before we went off to different fleet squadrons for our first tours."

"I didn't really know him myself," Corky explained. "I mean, I saw him around and everything, but I didn't really know him. Was he married?"

"Yeah."

"Kids?"

"One . . . a two-year-old boy."

"And the conehead?" Corky asked. Punk knew he was trying to come off as tough and unemotional in the face of death and naval aviation, but to Punk he just sounded rude. Corky constantly wrestled with the fact that he'd never actually been in a squadron himself. If he was guilty of anything in his quest for professional acceptance, it was that he often tried too hard to be an insider.

"Don't know," Punk shrugged as he looked at his watch. "I'd better get going."

"Oh, yeah," Corky said while shooting a glance at his own watch. "I'm headed that way too." He sanded his hands against each other. "Hey, Punk, before you go, let me ask you the same thing I've been asking a lot of other people the last few days: What do you think caused the jets to collide?" Punk shrugged, and Corky pressed him further. "Pilot error or mechanical failure?"

Punk shrugged again as he ran his thumbs along the front of his white uniform's beltline in an attempt to smooth the wrinkles where his shirt tucked into his pants. "I guess that's for the board to figure out." He pointed to the investigators. "Along with those guys over there . . . and you. You're the engineer, Corky. Why don't you tell me what happened?"

"Well, I think I know the answer," Corky said. "In the end, I'm sure we'll prove the same thing we always prove during this process."

"What's that?"

"That there are no new mishaps—just new people reinventing the same old mishaps."

Punk raised his eyebrows in an expression that politely accommodated the field rep's clichéd wisdom and walked back toward the hangar entrance.

"I'll see you over there," Corky called after him, as if they were headed for the nineteenth hole instead of a memorial service for two men whose lives had ended much too soon.

Punk sat next to Anita in the third row of the chapel and nervously flipped through the pages of the memorial service program as he waited for the families of the deceased to arrive. He stopped at Crud's biography and skimmed the write-up: Born and raised in Moorestown, New Jersey,

Eagle Scout, all-state high school wrestler, cum laude grad-
uate of Villanova University, Top Scope in his F-14 RAG
class, two-time nominee for Fighter RIO of the Year. The
last line summed up the tragedy: "Lieutenant Workman is
survived by his parents, Mr. and Mrs. Calvert Workman, Sr.,
his wife, the former Suzanne Denardo, and a son, Jason."

Punk studied the photo of Crud in the upper left corner
of the page, a head shot with shoulder boards, ribbons, and
wings of gold on prominent display. As always, his black
hair was neatly combed, punctuated by a ruler-straight part.

"Anal," Punk would say.

"Meticulous," Crud would reply.

Punk's thoughts turned ethereal as the volume of the
chapel's organ grew. He looked deeper into the portrait
and wondered if there was something in Crud's expression,
beneath the confident smile and warm brown eyes, that
predicted his untimely demise. Where was he now? Was he
up there on a balcony of clouds comparing notes with all
the other naval aviators who'd died when they were his
age?

Punk shifted his attention to the massive cross behind
the altar, its golden surface highlighted by the flicker of
candles reflecting off of it, until immediate families began
filing into the rows of pews just in front of him. A sobbing
young female who was aided by a more elderly woman led
the procession. Punk turned to Lucky's bio and ran his
finger to the bottom of it. He *was* married. *What are coneheads doing getting married?* Punk wondered. *Why would
you drag somebody else into this way of life at such a
crazy stage?*

Crud's family followed, and Punk got a glimpse of Suzanne through the protective wall of brothers and brothers-
in-law that surrounded her. Although her eyes were hidden
behind sunglasses, she appeared composed. Punk knew that
Crud had discussed a widow's conduct with her long ago,
and her loyalty to her husband even now made the scene
that much sadder.

Punk had been the best man at their wedding and wanted
that to continue to define his relationship with them. He
had been part of the team that first went to the house but
had steadfastly insisted that he not be the one to break
the news.

A day later she'd gathered herself enough to call and insist that everything was okay and asked Punk if he'd speak at the memorial service along with Flea Parker, the commanding officer from Crud's first fleet squadron. Punk had readily accepted, but now his nerves threatened to get the better of him as he reviewed the bullets he'd scrawled on a few sheets of paper during the last forty-eight hours.

The chaplain opened the service and began to wax spiritual about young lives prematurely lost and the search for answers that seemingly did not exist, and then countered with sentiments about the beauty of faith and God's master plan. Punk had been raised a good Episcopalian and, in spite of lazy attendance habits, retained a concept of a higher power, but the chaplain's statements made him want to utter "bullshit." He looked up from the program and felt a surge of adrenaline wash away his anxiety as he focused on the man's well-rehearsed smile of enlightenment. This ceremony wasn't going to be just another check in the block, a feel-good event designed for those who didn't even know Crud.

After the testimonials on Lucky's behalf, reflections offered by his brother the stockbroker and his grief-stricken father who fell to his knees on his way back to the pew, it was Punk's turn to speak. His courage had faded now, and as he approached the pulpit, he hoped his emotions would remain in check.

"I met—" Punk's voice cracked, and he turned away from the microphone, cleared his throat, and tried to start again. "I met Cal Workman the day I showed up at the RAG for training." He wiped a bead of perspiration off of his forehead. "Now Commander Parker will certainly tell you about Cal the officer and gentleman; I must admit I never saw any of that." The audience laughed, and Punk relaxed a little.

"Now you have to understand that pilots fresh out of flight school have little to no idea what a radar intercept officer is for. The only other people we'd ever had in the jet with us were flight instructors who were generally interested in making our lives more difficult. So, I walked into the student lounge to find my new mailbox and get the lay of the land, and there was this guy sitting there dressed in a flight jacket with the collar turned up, mug of coffee in one hand and an issue of—I'll never forget this—*Fortune* magazine in the other. He had his feet propped up on the table and this stupid look on his face, the classic Cal look."

Punk attempted to imitate the expression. He raised his eyebrows, pursed his lips, and nodded slightly as if in possession of great wisdom. Many in the audience recognized the look and chuckled again.

"He kept staring at me as I moved around the room, so finally I asked him what his problem was. 'You've got your ribbons in the wrong order,' he said. 'Your Defense Service Medal should come before your Expert Pistol Shot.' " Punk shook his head. "I'd been in the lounge all of five seconds.

"I remember another time Cal and I were enduring a particularly grueling flight simulator session. The instructor had me against the ropes: I had one engine on fire, a hydraulic failure, and the weather went from clear to a thunderstorm in the space of a few seconds. Cal was in the backseat walking me through the various checklists and trying to keep me calm. Just before we both sensed the instructor was about to issue the coup de grace and throw on one more emergency, Cal said, 'This simulator has ceased to simulate real life.'

"Now this guy couldn't believe what he was hearing, and he spent the next ten minutes yelling at Cal for having the gall as a replacement to judge what would or wouldn't happen in real life. The next thing you know, the crew for the simulator period after ours showed up with their instructor, and we had to move on. Our instructor didn't know what to do with us, so he just gave us an incomplete on the event. We repeated the simulator the next day with a different, kinder instructor and aced it.

"Cal taught me much more than what a great radar intercept officer could do in the F-14. He was a walking recruiting poster. Even his flight suits were freshly pressed." The crowd laughed again. "I'm not kidding." He smiled at the memory. He could get through this without breaking down.

"I used to kid him about his knowledge of naval history, but Cal was grounded. He had a feeling for context. Cal also loved to read and, although he was very guarded about letting the bubbas in the ready room know about it, was a big fan of poetry. Whenever things got tough during our RAG training, Cal would recite a William Butler Yeats poem." Punk straightened the sheet before him and began reading:

> Nor law, nor duty bade me fight, nor public men, nor cheering crowds, a lonely impulse of delight drove to this tumult in the clouds.

"I didn't understand that poem then. Sometimes Cal would repeat it just to annoy me. But as I thought about it over my years of flying fighters, it increasingly struck me as one of the most honest statements ever made about what we do. Cal's understanding of that was about half a decade ahead of mine.

"And I'm convinced that much of what I do right as an officer is a direct result of the lessons Cal taught me. It still hasn't hit me that he's gone because if it had I'm sure I wouldn't be able to stand up here and talk to you about him. I take some comfort in the fact that Cal died doing his job. And while I must admit I don't fully appreciate the chaplain's explanation for why he died, I do ask the aviators in the room to look at yourselves and check your approach to our business, an occupation that's inherently dangerous." Punk paused again and scanned the gathering. "Whatever happened over Dare County a few days ago wasn't due to a mistake made by Lieutenant Cal Workman."

He wiped another drop of sweat away before it passed across the bridge of his nose. "This is about the point where Cal would be telling me to shut up, so I will. Let me just finish by saying Cal Workman had a lot left to do in this life. He would've been a great squadron commanding officer; he could've been the Chief of Naval Operations, for that matter. And as a father . . ." Punk looked to the front pew and saw young Jason, innocently waving a program like a toy, ignorant of the crash's impact on him. Punk felt a lump in his throat and fought letting his eyes go to Suzanne, but they did. Her face was raised to him, and he wished he could have read her eyes behind the dark glasses. He didn't want to talk anymore. "I'll miss him," he managed to get out, and then walked back to his seat.

At the reception in the hall adjacent to the chapel, Anita stayed close to Punk, holding tightly to his arm as he greeted the mourners. Eventually they found themselves alone, against a wall.

Anita pulled him close. She raised herself on her toes and kissed his cheek. "You did so good," she whispered in his ear.

He shrugged and tried to move away but she persisted. "No," she continued, "I've been to too many of these. You might not see it now, but you made a big difference to everybody, especially Suzanne."

They stood in silent embrace for a time. Anita drew back and twisted his arm and checked his watch. "I've got to go back to the health club," she said. "Will you be all right?"

"I'll be okay," he said.

"What are you going to do? Go back to the condo?"

"Probably. I definitely don't feel like heading back to the squadron. Maybe I'll just stay here for a few more minutes, make sure Suzanne's okay."

She kissed him good-bye.

"Thanks, Anita," he said.

With Anita gone he quickly grew tired of socializing. The mood was darker without her there, and suddenly he felt like he didn't know anyone in the room. He said his good-byes and wandered into the parking lot.

As he neared his pickup, he heard the rising roar of jets. He looked over the treeline across the street and caught sight of a formation of four Tomcats coming into the field. The lead fighter broke off sharply and passed directly overhead the chapel before rolling wings level and setting up to land. Punk tilted his head back and watched the three wingmen follow their lead through the landing pattern until he realized there were tears streaming down his face.

Punk slid behind the wheel of his gray pickup and rolled the window down. His keys were in his hand but he couldn't bring himself to start the car. He was a very small being in a universe controlled by forces beyond his control. Fighter pilots convinced themselves they owned their destinies until they were shown the ultimate truth behind their standing.

Whatever had kept him from folding in front of the crowd was gone. He continued to weep.

A hand reached through the window and grasped his shoulder, pressing the left shoulder board of his summer white uniform against him. He turned, startled, and saw Master Chief Callaghan's ruddy face. "Sir," the master chief said, "why don't we go for that run now?"

No words had been said between them by the time they reached the fenceline near the air station's back gate. The two men simultaneously tagged the chain-link fence and reversed direction, reestablishing in a single stride the brisk pace that had carried them from the base gym. It felt good to sweat, and Punk was tapping into a seemingly endless source of pent-up energy. Usually by the three-mile mark his legs would start to talk and the water tower next to the finish line in the distance would begin to move away. Not today. Today time was a pleasantly ill-defined dimension, and there was no room for physical pain in the lieutenant's mind as it fired with the insuppressible images of the day.

A sea of faces appeared as the horizon bounced before him. Punk replayed their expressions and their statements, and he considered those who'd reacted to the tragedy in unexpected ways. And then he thought of Anita, about how he'd doubted her in the past months. Anita deserved better. She understood that he was a naval aviator and naval aviators went away for long periods of time.

"How far you want to go?" Master Chief Callaghan asked.

"Let's take it out to POW Park," Punk replied, to which the master chief responded with an affirmative grunt. Punk had met the master chief during the first physical readiness test he'd done in the RAG. They'd run the mile-and-a-half course together and finished neck and neck with the respectable time of nine minutes on the button. But the fighter pilot enjoyed running with the master chief for a number of reasons beyond a shared finish time: The senior maintainer wasn't chatty. He didn't huff during the run as if his next breath might be his last. And he ran with an athletic economy of motion, especially for a big man. He'd polished his large frame during his years as a basketball star in high school.

Master Chief Callaghan was the pace horse in their pairing, and that appealed to Punk because he needed somebody to push him. And Punk sensed that today the master chief was ready to let the reins out even farther. From the start, he'd stepped it out at a varsity clip, and Punk knew the master chief was half expecting him to cry uncle. The cry would not come.

The pair passed through the front gate, four miles covered now, and continued down the bike path next to the main road and then along the four-lane boulevard that led back to the eastern portion of the suburban sprawl of Virginia Beach. After another half mile, they reached the Prisoner of War Park.

They touched the base of the Eternal Flame, the centerpiece of the park, and as they pivoted back for the front gate, Punk let out a yelp, and pulled up lame. He hopped over to the grass next to the monument and collapsed.

Master Chief Callaghan saw the lieutenant gripping the back of his left thigh and ordered him onto his back. The master chief began to stretch the twisted muscle by lifting Punk's leg to a near perpendicular level while Punk fought the overwhelming urge to scream.

"I knew I was pushing you too hard," the master chief said. "You officers aren't ready for that kind of pace."

"I'd give you shit back," Punk said between gasps, "but I hurt too bad."

The spasms eventually ceased, and the two men sat on the park's groomed grass with their backs against the polished stone memorial, looking across the field of corn that separated them from the runways of the air station. The sun was low in the western sky and transformed the jets over the base into rumbling black silhouettes. A gentle breeze from the east pushed the exhaust away and replaced it with the salt-tinged air from across the nearby ocean.

"You ever listened to rap music?" the master chief asked as he mopped his forehead with his T-shirt.

Punk raised his eyebrows. "Is this a trick question?"

"No."

"Well, it's not my cup of tea, but I've heard some of it."

"What do you think about it?"

The fighter pilot considered the question for a moment. "Honestly? It sucks. I'm not sure it takes much talent. They don't sing; they just talk. But I probably don't get it. Every time I think it's seen its day, it gets more popular."

"It's worse than popular," the master chief added. "It's dangerous."

"Dangerous? What, you mean the gangsta stuff?"

"Yeah. My oldest boy, Seamus, is into that. Check this out: I walked by his room last night and caught a line from one song about raping women and then blowing their brains out." As the master chief spoke, Punk noticed his brogue always seemed to grow less Bostonian and more Irish with his intensity. "That's what a teenager's supposed to be listening to? I just lost it, I tell you. I stormed into his room, opened his CD player and grabbed the disc and broke it in two right in front of his face. I told him if I ever heard him playing that stuff again I was going to smash his CD player."

"What did he say?"

"Nothing. That's what I'm worried about. A few years ago he would've thrown a fit, you know, started crying or thrown himself on the floor or something, but he didn't say a word. Not a word. He just looked me dead in the eye. I just wanted to grab the kid and shake some sense into him."

"Don't do that," Punk said. "These days you'll have family services on your ass in a heartbeat."

The master chief chuckled. "Not a problem, Lieutenant. No matter how much Seamus needs a good slug, that's not my style. It was my father's style, of course, but not mine."

Punk realized he hadn't been the only one running out his problems. "Has Seamus ever been in trouble?" Punk asked.

"Little things, you know, at school. Mary Kate and I always wrote that off as due to the fact I was never around. I mean, damn, before this tour I was on sea duty for more than ten years straight. This is the first time I've been around for more than five months at a time. But this is getting bigger than our family. I see it in the way he's dressing, who he's hanging out with, the way he acts around us. I guess that's why I lost my temper last night."

The master chief paused and allowed his eyes to follow one of the Tomcats as it took off and eventually disappeared into the sky over the Atlantic. "It's ironic, you know. Shore duty is supposed to be about getting to know your family again," he continued. "I'm getting to know Seamus, and now I don't like him. I mean, I love him and all, but I'm not sure I like him. I've got a bad feeling he's ready to do something really stupid, if he hasn't already, and I just haven't found out about it yet." The master chief wiped his face again. "It's hard to control stuff like that music . . . and TV. Have you seen some of these shows that are supposedly for kids? Every boy's a wiseass and every girl's a whore."

"I can't watch TV anymore," Punk said, "except for an occasional movie and news and sports, but even those drive me crazy a lot of the time. We should all just turn the damn things off."

"We do that, but he just goes over to his friends' houses and watches. All these kids have DVD players and collections of movies that would water your eyes, half of them R-rated."

"So make him pick better friends."

The master chief puffed a quiet laugh. "You mean pick a better gang. It's a lot easier to control sailors."

Punk pulled at the grass and silently mulled over the master chief's words. "Do you think Seamus would like a simulator ride?"

"What? You mean the pilot simulator?"

"Yeah. It's very realistic, like the best video game he's ever seen. We could get him in there for an hour; let him try to shoot down bandits and then land on the Boat. Might help to change his attitude a little bit."

The master chief thought about the offer, and Punk saw his face brighten. "That's worth a shot, but I've got to warn you, sir, you wouldn't be hosting a Boy Scout."

"I think I can handle it," the lieutenant said. "I'll get it scheduled tomorrow."

The enlisted man smiled broadly as he nodded a few times. "I thank you for the offer." He rose to his feet, stretched his massive freckled arms over his head, and changed the subject. "I know you probably don't want to talk about it, but just for the record, I thought you did a good job at the memorial service."

"Thanks. It wasn't easy to do."

"I don't imagine it was. During the service I counted how many of those I've been to over the twenty-five years I've been in the Navy. Twelve—ten officers and two enlisted men. The officers were all killed in jet crashes, and the enlisted guys were both killed working on the carrier's flight deck. One was blown over the side one night in the

Med and never heard from again, and the other was cut in two by an arresting wire that parted during a trap."

Punk slowly shook his head and blankly stared through the master chief contorting himself a few yards away. "This wasn't my first one, but it was the first one where I knew the guy well."

The master chief reached down, grabbed his shins and put his face to his knees, and then popped up again. "His wife seemed to be handling it, all things considered."

"Yeah, she's a sharp lady."

"Be careful, though. I've seen this before. The widow seems to be doing fine, and then she bottoms out later."

"Not Suzanne. In some ways her strength makes Crud's death even more tragic. She should've had a chance to focus on more positive things."

"You sort of put the ol' chaplain down, but he was right when he said everything happens for a reason."

"I didn't put the chaplain down."

"Sort of . . ."

"No I didn't, I just—"

Master Chief Callaghan silenced the lieutenant with a wave and a placid smile. "Let's head back to the gym. I've got to be a base coach for my younger son's baseball team this evening." He extended his arm down to the lieutenant. "Do you think you can make it back? We'll take it slow."

Punk grabbed the arm and vaulted to his feet. "You just worry about keeping up with me, old man."

CHAPTER FIVE

There really was a long green table. Punk had heard of it from the first day of flight school when instructors had counseled him to avoid being on the wrong end of it. The conference table was situated in the middle of the RAG's conference room with a green felt tablecloth draped over it. Punk realized that the instructors had never exactly specified which end was the *wrong* one, but as he looked across at the three senior officers in summer whites glaring at him, he was pretty sure he was on it now.

"Some aviators have a habit of being around when bad things happen," Commander "Slick" Slater said. Slick was at the RAG for refresher training on his way from a staff job to his command tour. He'd been guilty of having too much time on his hands while waiting to start his syllabus, so after the midair he was tapped to run the mishap board. He was known in the fighter community as a company man who put great effort into not looking like one. He had a round face, a quick disingenuous smile, and liked to wink a lot. "Are you one of those guys, Punk?"

"No, sir, I don't think so."

"It's a fair question, don't you think?" Slick continued. "In the past couple of years you've ejected out of one jet, had two crash around you, and you recently ran off the runway."

"It was the taxiway," Punk said. "And I wasn't at the controls. I was in the backseat of a FAM-1 student."

"You're a RAG instructor," Lieutenant Commander "Beaker" Ballard, a classic geek study of a RIO with thick glasses, sickly pallor, and spastic mannerisms, said. "It doesn't matter whether or not you're at the controls. When your replacement fouls up, you foul up."

"Did you brief midair contingencies before the flight?" Lieutenant Commander "Soap" McNabb said. Soap was a big black pilot who'd outlasted the infamy of dropping a last-second pass in the end zone that would've won the Army-Navy game his senior year.

"I went through the briefing guide."

"But did you specifically brief midair contingencies?"

"Did I tell them not to hit each other? No sir, I assumed they knew that already."

"I'm only going to request that you not be a wiseass once," Slick advised.

"What was your airspeed during the spacer pass?" Beaker asked.

"Three hundred and fifty knots."

"Did you brief ejection procedures?" Soap asked.

"I reminded them that three hundred and fifty knots was approaching the high end of the safe ejection envelope and any decision they would make about ejection would have to be made very quickly at the low altitudes we were working in the strafe pattern."

"But you didn't talk about ejection procedures in detail . . ."

"From what I remember hearing over the radio, those who had a chance to eject did so successfully, and the others never knew what hit them," Punk said. "With all due respect, I feel the board should concentrate on what caused the two airplanes to collide."

"What do you think we're doing here?" Slick said. "Besides, we'll worry about what we should concentrate on, thank you very much." He rifled through some papers in front of him. "You said your airspeed was three hundred and fifty knots during the spacer pass. How far back were your wings swept at that time?"

"I had them manually swept all the way back, sixty-eight degrees."

"What about the other jets?"

"I briefed that we'd do the spacer pass with wings at sixty-eight."

"But did everybody have their wings at sixty-eight?"

"I assumed so."

"You assumed so."

"Yes sir. I found out some time later that Dash Three never got his wings back."

"Some . . . time . . . later," Slick intoned. "Not during the flight."

"Well, sir, I didn't exactly have the luxury of staring at the other jets during that part of the flight. I was trying not to fly into the ground."

"What did I say about being a wise—"

Beaker patted the commander's forearm and said, "So you had no idea what your wingmen's configuration was during the spacer pass?"

"I had an idea, and my idea is that students follow the instructions given in the brief."

"That's a big leap of faith, don't you think?" Soap asked. "You've been an instructor for over a year now. Haven't you been burned enough to verify things firsthand when it comes to student performance?"

"I guess not. In my experience, students follow instructions and generally do the right thing."

Slick smiled greasily. "Like taxi into the mud?" He winked and continued without allowing Punk the chance for a retort. "Any more questions, gentlemen?"

"Yeah, I've got one," Beaker said. "Why did you sweep your wings back during the spacer pass in the first place?"

"For the same reasons we sweep our wings back when we come into the field," Punk said. "The airplane slows down faster with the wings back."

"Why would you care about slowing down when you're in the strafing pattern?"

"You need to slow down some."

"Yeah, but not as much as when you're about to land. What's the other reason for sweeping the wings back?"

"The other reason?"

"Yes, you said *reasons* before. I assume that meant there's more than one."

"Well, the airplane looks better with the wings aft. I guess you'd call it a pride-in-airmanship thing."

"Beaker," Slick said, "what's your point here? Tomcat crews have been coming into the field with their wings aft for nearly thirty years now."

"I'm trying to suggest this may have been one more thing

for a task-saturated replacement to deal with when maybe he could've been worrying about something else, like the fact that he was Dash Three and not Dash Two."

"You may have something there," Slick said. "Punk, did you have to have them sweep the wings aft for the spacer pass?"

"Have to?" Punk echoed.

"What does the briefing guide say?" Soap asked.

Beaker snatched a white-covered binder out of a stack piled next to the board members. He flipped through the tabs along the right edge and then opened the binder. "Okay, here it is," he said. "Spacer pass, speed three hundred to four hundred and fifty knots, wing configuration as briefed." Beaker looked up from the book. "So you didn't have to sweep the wings."

Punk let out a long exhale. "There are a lot of things I didn't have to do. I would hope a pilot in strike phase could sweep the wings, fly formation, and keep track of when it's his time to peel off all at the same time."

"Sometimes hoping don't get the job done," Slick said. He looked to either side. "Any more questions?" Both of the other board members shook their heads. "Anything you'd like to add, Lieutenant?"

"No . . . sir."

"Thank you for your time then." Slick studied his watch, and, with another wink, rediscovered his amiable veneer. "Unless I'm mistaken, it's Friday. Might I suggest a beer at the club?"

Punk passed along the officers' club buffet line and threw together two overstuffed burritos, the traditional Friday night dinner for many of the base's aviators, especially the bachelors. He pushed his way through the crowd that had swelled out from the main bar and returned to the table he was sharing with Flex.

"I don't know how you can eat that shit," Flex said, voice raised over the music pumping through the large speakers hanging in each corner of the room.

"The price is right," Punk returned. "Free food always tastes better. Besides, after the day I've had today, I don't want to worry about dinner."

A waitress deposited two bottles of beer on the table, and Flex coolly spun a five-dollar bill on her tray and waved her off as she tilled through her cash box. She gave him a come-hither glance that Punk found fetching but Flex ignored.

"Thanks," Punk said, raising his bottle.

"No problem," Flex said as he joined the hoist. "To better days."

"They can't get much worse." Each put a bottle to his lips, and in the time that Punk managed two gulps, Flex polished off his entire beer.

"Don't say that," Flex said between wipes of his mouth with the back of his wrist.

"Why not?"

"Because every time I think I know how bad things can get, I'm wrong."

"Superstitious?"

"No, experienced." Flex held his sunglasses up to the light from over the bar and wiped the lenses with the T-shirt under his flight suit. "My life's divided neatly now between B.E. and A.E.—'before ejection' and 'after ejection.' It's that simple."

Punk chuckled but considered the thought. As Slick had pointed out during the board's proceedings, Punk also had ejected once—on his last deployment, his Tomcat flamed out while he was attempting to divert from the carrier and into Kuwait. Spud had been with him for that, too. He'd never really thought about it in Flex's terms, but he knew what he was talking about. Even now, in spite of aviators' cavalier attitudes regarding the act, he was hit by the reality that walking away from an ejection was a miraculous occurrence.

He finished his first burrito, swallowing it nearly without chewing. Following the next swig of beer, he belched loudly. "Hey, was your interview with the mishap board as painful as mine?"

"Painful?" Flex said. "No. It was actually kind of mellow."

"I can't figure it out. They seemed to be focusing on me rather than the accident itself."

"Why would they be focusing on you? I don't know what you're worried about. I'm the one who's grounded right now waiting for this board to finish up, not you. And I didn't do anything. Last time I checked, the flight controls were in the front cockpit. That's fair . . . *not*."

"That's what they call 'crew concept.' "

"Well, it sucks."

"Sort of like taking the heat when your student taxis into the mud or being the flight lead and getting blamed for the fact that Dash Three never swept his wings back during the spacer pass, or that he was tasked with sweeping his wings at all." Punk took a bite of the remaining burrito and continued to speak with his mouth partially full. "Speaking of that: When during the spacer pass did you notice that the wings never came aft?"

Flex paused. "As soon as you guys brought yours back. I was pimping Pugsly, but he seemed like he had his hands full about then. I think he was task-saturated. But really when you get right down to it, wings forward, wings aft . . . what the hell, right? The jet rolled and we hit Lucky and Crud and that's it."

"That's not *it*, Flex," Punk said. "The jet—" He stopped himself. Throughout his years in the Tomcat, every time Punk had been about ready to give fleet-experienced RIOs full credit for understanding the nuances of the pilot's craft, statements like Flex's stopped him. Flex obviously didn't appreciate what it took to fly in formation, what effort was required to keep the beast in position. He could look through the canopy to keep track of where the wings were at any given time, but he couldn't feel the flight controls. Punk didn't have the endurance to broach the point. "And Pugsly still claims he didn't move the stick to the left?"

"That's his story and he's sticking with it. You think he's lying? We all know he can be a bullshit artist."

"I dunno. His ego worries me."

"I don't think it's his ego. I think he's a poseur. He's overcompensating for the fact that airplanes scare the shit out of him."

"What? He's the son of King Bellingham."

"Yeah, yeah, I know. You guys worshipped him over that in the locker room, remember? I'm telling you, the cone was never comfortable in the jet, even by replacement standards. In fact, I'll make you a prediction: Before this investigation is over, Pugsly will turn in his wings."

"You watch too many movies. No, let me correct that. You've watched the same movie too many times."

"That's my prediction. Anyway, the safety center's engineering analysis of the wreckage will show exactly what happened. Those guys don't miss a trick. And if they do, we've always got Corky to figure it out."

"Yeah . . . Corky." Punk ordered another round and mindlessly watched the waitress sashay away.

"Did you ever consider that maybe this is simply evidence that the Tomcat is just getting too old?"

"And you call yourself a Tomcat guy?" Punk said. "Look around you. This airplane is getting better with age. Precision-guided bombs; digital flight controls . . . the F-14's both more lethal to the enemy and safer to fly than it was a decade ago."

"Window dressing, shipmate. Just bells and whistles." Flex hoisted his bottle and then brought it down with a refreshed exhale. "We need to quit putting Band-Aids on dinosaurs and move on to the next generation of air warfare. Corky was showing me the data and specs on the Joint Strike Fighter. Have you seen what that thing can do?"

"Not in any detail, no."

Flex raised a balled fist and extended a finger with each point he rattled off. "Forget about a HUD. This thing has got helmet-mounted cuing for everything, even the attitude of the airplane. It's got health monitoring, a system that predicts failures and lets the crew know way ahead of time. The airplane pays for itself with its low cost per flight hour and maintenance man-hour requirement. It's stealthy. It's glass. Throw in a missile like the AIM-9X and air-to-mud stuff like the next version of JDAM and JSOW and you've got the next generation's kind of lethal. We need to get off our butts and make this thing happen."

"Who's 'we'?"

"Hell, I dunno . . . Congress, Democrats, other stupid-ass ignoramuses who've never spent Day One in the military but think they understand what it's all about because they read a couple of books while they were at Princeton or Yale."

Punk shifted the conversation back to the mishap. "Did Pugsly say anything before you guys hit the other jet?"

"Nope. Nothing. I watch my coneheads like a hawk, es-

pecially when we're close to other jets. And I didn't have
time to do anything but pull the ejection handle. If I'd
waited a split second longer we would've been Swiss cheese
like the other guys."

Punk winced. "Have you seen Pugsly lately?"

"Now that you mention it, no. Of course, I haven't been
looking for him either." The beers arrived, and Flex emptied his in another single toss of the head. He sat staring
blankly at the table for a time, obviously deep in thought.
"Maybe I was riding him too hard, you know. Maybe
you're right; maybe I should chill a bit." He checked his
watch, said, "I've got to run a ten K tomorrow morning,"
and got up and disappeared through the crowd.

Punk remained at the table in quiet observation, nursing
his beer and taking in the various people around him.
There was Fitz, another of God's gifts to flight instruction,
holding court with a group of awestruck replacements from
Class One, undoubtedly recounting the time he used his
big arms to wrestle his jet out of an irrecoverable spin. And
at the end of the bar was Corky McBride with the old
guard, the few real and other ersatz legends who'd helped to
transform Naval Air Station Oceana from a farmer's field to
a "master jet base." The elders had adopted that end of the
bar, and the snotnoses idling there without an invitation did
so at their own peril. The old guard was old, but they weren't
dead. They used their Friday happy hour sessions to preserve their ballsy past, and woe be unto the unsuspecting
lieutenant who, in their presence, might offer that he'd
done something noteworthy during his short flying life.
Baghdad? Kosovo? That youngster would be summarily
gang tackled and buried under a mountain of "first liar
don't have a chance" sea stories that got better with each
telling.

*Shit, try close air support over Hue. We had the entire
North Vietnamese army shooting up at us there. And see if
a woman can survive that.*

*Well, hell, Jasper, you wanna see shooting? Try Hanoi.
SAMs thicker than flies in summer and we didn't have no
radar jammers for your so-called "sanctuary." And I agree:
No fucking female could hack it.*

Half my squadron was killed on my first cruise.

ALL my squadron was killed on mine . . .

Punk inadvertently caught Corky's eye and the civilian came shuffling over to the table and sat down across from him. "Beer?" he asked, pointing at Punk's half-empty bottle.

"No thanks. I'm rolling out of here in a bit."

Corky hailed the waitress and ordered a scotch. He fired up a cigarette and took a manic draw. Punk could see from his movements and sagging face that he was a few drinks into his Friday routine.

"How did your interview with the board go?" Corky asked.

Punk narrowed his eyes. "You sure know a lot."

"I'm sorry. I don't mean to pry. Word gets around, you know." He grasped the cigarette between two fingers, and Punk noticed that his index finger was severed at the first knuckle.

"How did that happen?" Punk asked, pointing toward the finger.

Corky looked at it with mock surprise. "Oh, this? You've never heard the story, huh? I am getting old, I guess." He extended his arm across the table and held his hand up for Punk to study. "I was working in one of the hangars a few years back and had an F-4 canopy close on it. Hurt like a son of a bitch. Man, I howled. Don't think I could make that noise again if I tried."

Punk coolly considered the hand, like a pathologist might, and made a noise that signaled both amazement and sympathy. "I can't believe I've known you this long and never noticed that."

"My little sacrifice to national defense." Corky drew his arm back. "In any case, it's not something I brag about. Too many accidents like this can get a man fired."

"And I'm sure your wife wouldn't be too happy about that."

"Actually, it's been years since I worried about what a wife thought."

"Divorce?"

"Yeah . . . messy. I'm paying my ass off in alimony and child support."

"How many kids?"

"Two. A boy and a girl." Corky took another long drag on his cigarette. "I haven't seen them much over the years. Their mom sort of designed a program that guaranteed I wouldn't be a very big part of their lives." The thought took him somewhere else for a few moments, and then he changed the subject. "You know, I hate to ask, but this mishap has really bothered me. Did the board members give you any ideas about what they think happened?"

"No, other than Dash Three rolled into Dash Two. But that's not news."

"No idea about what caused the roll?"

"Not that they discussed with me. There wasn't a whole lot of discussion going on, period."

"So I hear," Corky said with a sly smile. Punk knitted his brow and Corky leaned forward across the table and spoke in an exaggerated whisper that barely carried over the noise around them. "I don't want to talk out of school because King Bellingham is an old friend of mine, but word has it the kid ain't exactly Dad made over in terms of his piloting skills."

"Word also has it that RDI is in financial trouble."

Corky lost the whisper. "I just think it'd be a shame to have your reputation as a good flight lead wrecked by a guy who choked in the heat of battle."

"That's a risk I take every time I launch with somebody on my wing."

"Yeah, but you would be off the hook if Pugsly found the guts to admit he screwed up, that he drove the jet into Lucky, wouldn't you? That's what I'm hearing anyway."

"How's that get me off the hook? We still lost a jet and killed two guys."

"Yes, but until somebody takes the blame, you get it all."

Punk stared blankly through the curves of his glass on the table. "You'll never get it, will you, Corky?"

"Get what?"

"Why do you keep asking me about the investigation? You work for the company that makes all the parts—until they go under, of course. Why don't you get out there and figure it out?"

"Well, that's not my job," Corky said. "And as far as the company going under, let me say this: Joint Strike Fighter. The company is not going under." He paused, and his voice became steadier. "Secondly, there was nothing wrong with either jet. The investigators from the Naval Safety Center are on the case and have yet to find anything. I trust those guys."

"As long as they come up with the *right* answer, eh?"

Corky stood up. "Look, Punk. I'm just trying to be sociable here. I may not be a badass fighter pilot, but I've been around for twenty-three years. I don't think they'd let me keep my job for that long if I wasn't an honest broker."

"It depends which 'they' you're talking about, Corky. Do you mean *they,* the Navy, or *they,* RDI?"

Corky took a final puff of his cigarette and then stamped it out in the ashtray. He looked as if he was going to say something else but instead just walked back over and rejoined the old guard.

Punk cursed himself under his breath for forcing the confrontation. He'd never been a big fan of the generally unctuous Corky, but he'd never argued with him either. The exchange nullified whatever decompression Punk had managed since he'd walked into the club. He finished his beer and decided he needed to find Pugsly.

CHAPTER SIX

Between series of raps on the door to Pugsly's apartment, Punk noticed a license plate, just visible among several rolled newspapers lying on the walkway a few feet away. He pushed the papers aside and saw it was a twisted and gouged Florida vanity plate that read NVY PLT, wrapped in a frame with "My other car is an F-14 Tomcat" across the top of it.

Punk continued banging on the door while trying to peer through an adjacent window covered on the inside with drawn blinds. He was about to give up and walk away when the door opened to the full length of the security chain. Pugsly's face slipped into the opening, highlighted only by the yellow-tinted lights of the third-story walkway.

"I need to talk to you," Punk said. "Can I come in for a second?"

Pugsly didn't respond.

"I'm not here to hassle you, I promise," Punk continued. "I'm here as a friend of Crud's."

The door shut. Punk heard the chain working out of the slide, and then the door reopened.

The apartment was dark, save a light in the hood over the stove in the small kitchen. The light barely traced what little furniture Pugsly had. The air was stale and tinged with cigarette smoke and burnt popcorn.

In the dim glow Punk studied Pugsly's silhouette as it crossed the room. His outline revealed him dressed in shorts and a T-shirt and barefoot. Punk could see his hair was a rat's nest. Pugsly slid into a recliner with his back to the kitchen light, which made it impossible to see his face. Punk took a seat on the couch across from him.

"I tried calling a couple of times from my cell phone on the way over here," Punk explained, "but all I kept getting was a recording that said your phone had been disconnected." Pugsly did not react although Punk paused, waiting for him to say something. "Did you know your car is sitting in the parking lot with a big dent in the driver's-side door, and your license plate was ripped off and bent to shit?" Still, the shadow offered nothing but silence.

Punk slid across the couch and felt his way to an adjacent end table and up the stem of a lamp. He asked if he could turn on the light and then clicked it on without giving his host the time to object. Pugsly grimaced like a prisoner facing daylight after weeks in solitary confinement. He'd obviously not shaved for days. Dark circles under his eyes were accentuated by the paleness of his face.

"You look like hell," Punk said. Pugsly shifted his gaze to the floor, and Punk changed the subject.

"I had my audience with the mishap board today." Pugsly's attention snapped back to Punk, and the lieutenant quickly pushed what he perceived to be his advantage. "I was a little surprised, I must say, by the board's attitude toward me."

Pugsly remained nonplussed, eyes impassively locked with the lieutenant's. As Punk took in the student's cold expression, he felt himself getting angry. "How does me taking the hit square with the Bellingham family's sense of justice?"

"I didn't touch the stick!" Pugsly shouted, flying out of the recliner. He moved against the kitchen counter with his back to Punk. "That's the only fact that matters: I didn't touch the stick. The jet rolled off by itself."

"Sure," Punk said. "And you just choked on the spin procedure in the brief that day." Punk leaned forward as the intensity of his voice grew. "You're a bullshitter, Pugsly. You're so busy trying to get out of your father's shadow, you'd say anything to keep the heat off of you."

"What do you know about it?" Pugsly seethed. "You don't know me or my father."

"This is bigger than your legacy, Pugsly. You can't hide

in your apartment all summer long. It's time to grow some balls and come clean."

Punk intended to elicit a response with his remark, but not as dramatic as the one he got. Pugsly wheeled around and glared at him with wild eyes. His face turned bright red as he started to shudder, and Punk got ready to dodge a charge like a matador across the ring from a rabid bull. Pugsly emitted a crazed wail and grabbed the first lamp he could reach and threw it across the room. It hit a wall with a flash of light and a crash of glass.

Pugsly crumpled back into the chair and began sobbing.

"Get the fuck out of here," he blubbered. "Leave me alone."

Punk stepped lightly around the shards of broken lamp on his way to the kitchen. He searched the cabinets for Pugsly's liquor cache and pulled out a half-finished fifth of young blond scotch. He filled two tumblers.

"Relax, Pugsly," Punk said as he reentered the living room. "I poured you a drink." He set one of the glasses next to the student's chair and retook his position on the couch.

"We're at the crossroads here," Punk said. "I've got a feeling something's going on behind this investigation, but I can't act on it until I'm sure you're telling the truth."

Pugsly silently stared at the floor, his appearance now even more disheveled than the ragamuffin who'd reluctantly answered the door. Punk started to speak again, but Pugsly silenced him with a raise of his arm. He reached over to the table next to the recliner and picked up his glass and took a swallow of scotch as a keynote speaker might sip water to clear his throat.

"I really don't care what you think about me," he said. "It's actually kind of funny. You're all just like my fucking old man. You guys crow about how self-confident a fighter pilot has to be to succeed, and when somebody demonstrates self-confidence, you break him down until he loses it."

"What are you—"

"*I'm* talking now!" Pugsly polished off his drink with a dramatic toss of his head. "I have nightmares. Every time I close my eyes I see them. I see my wing dragging through their canopy. They're looking up at me. Faces. Eyes." He focused on Punk. "Why should I lie? To protect my *profes-*

sional reputation?" A maniacal laugh shuddered his entire body. "I suffer a punishment worse than anything the Navy could do to me."

They sat in silence. Punk read Pugsly's expression for a minute or so and then showed himself out.

Punk leaned back in the chaise lounge and watched Anita strike a dramatic pose at the end of the diving board. She stood at attention, feet together and hands along her sides. She remained still for a few seconds, feigning concentration. She stretched her arms over her head and then slowly dropped them back to her side and simply stepped off the board into the water.

Punk applauded as she broke the surface, offering a champion's wave to the adoring crowd of one. "Ten-point-oh from the Swedish judge," Punk announced. "Very clean entry."

Anita climbed out and walked around the edge of the kidney-shaped pool, her bikini looking as if it had been designed just for her. Punk stood as she approached and wrapped her in a towel and nuzzled her neck. He looked up and noticed one of his male neighbors pretending to read.

"What do we want for dinner?" Anita asked as she reclined back in her lounge, absorbing the last of the day's useful sunlight.

"Dinner? Is it that time already?"

"We've been out here for three hours," she said. "So what do you want?"

"What do you want?" Punk asked back.

"I want whatever you want." She smiled, and he knew from her expression that she meant what she'd said.

Minutes later, as soon as the door to the condo closed behind them, he peeled her suit off and carried her to the bedroom. She smelled of chlorine, and he acted on the impulse to taste her. Afterward they showered together.

Punk threw two steaks on the kettle grill he kept on the small balcony off of the bedroom, and as the meat cooked the two of them sat and sipped from bottles of beer and looked out over the water. He reached over and took her hand and they relaxed in pleasant silence.

Over the last two weeks they'd seldom been out of each other's company. Since the memorial service he'd thought only of Anita, and all he wanted to do was spend time with her. She seemed to feel the same way about him.

After dinner they lounged on the couch and watched a movie. They'd stopped going out. Hopping between bars and chasing the nightlife felt unnecessary now. The movie ended, and as the credits rolled, Anita said, "Maybe I should stay at my place tonight."

"Why?" Punk asked with surprise.

"I haven't been to my apartment in two weeks. I don't even know why I'm paying rent. My roommate's going to think I've been kidnapped."

"Forget her. Stay tonight."

"You need your space."

"I need you to stay here."

"You'll get bored with—"

"Look, this is ridiculous." He paused and then nodded, convinced of the rightness of the next step. "Let's stop wasting time. Let's just get married."

"That's not funny," Anita said with brow knitted. "Don't even kid about that."

"I'm not kidding."

Anita studied him and when he didn't flinch she exploded off the couch, shrieking with joy. She spilled both of their beers on her way to wrapping herself around him and holding on as if she was never letting go—perhaps out of fear that he might retract the question. Punk felt her warm tears running down his neck.

"I guess that's a 'yes'?" he said.

"Of course, you big dummy," Anita said, and then gave him a deep kiss. "I love you, Rick."

"I love you." He realized it was the first time he'd ever told her he loved her.

Anita picked up the beer bottles and dabbed at the mess on the rug. "Can I call my mom?" she asked. "I've got to call my mom."

"Of course you can call your mom." Punk watched her walk into the kitchen and pick up the handset, and he felt a twinge of apprehension. It wasn't a test run. There was no taking it back. But then he fought that off with the idea that he was feeling nothing more than what every bachelor before him felt when he made the first moves to replace freedom with stability. Already he looked at her dialing the phone as Anita Reichert, and he saw their children around her, and the image seemed to work. She was informed and respected his chosen profession. She understood that there would be six-month separations. She lived for the idea of being in the wives club and making photo calendars and care packages and "guess whose legs these are?" videos to mail out to the Boat.

"Hello, Mom?" Anita called gleefully into the phone. "You'll never guess what Rick just asked me . . . YES!"

Shit, he thought, *now I have to go buy a ring.*

Punk was standing in front of the simulator building, enjoying the sun's warmth and marveling at the clear blue sky and wondering why he wasn't airborne or on the base golf course, as Master Chief Callaghan pulled up in the family minivan. The master chief emerged from the vehicle wearing an apprehensive expression as he stepped over to greet the lieutenant.

"You sure you still want to do this?" the master chief asked.

"Of course," Punk said.

"I read that boy the riot act on the way over here. He knows to be on his best behavior."

"Will you relax, master chief? This is supposed to be fun."

Seamus Callaghan appeared from behind the van. He stood nearly as tall as his father, but looked about fifty pounds lighter. He sported the sartorial finery of the modern troubled teen: a stocking cap pulled to his eyebrows with "Wretched" emblazoned across the front of it, and a headset with large padded ear cups. Punk had heard the thud of the heavy beat blasting directly into the boy's head even before he came into view. His neck was adorned with a variety of gold chains that spilled over a Boston Celtics jersey. In spite of the oppressive July heat, the jersey peeked out from under an oversized green stadium jacket that fell loosely over the boy's thin frame. The crotch of his black jeans hung nearly to his knees, and each pant leg was tucked into a gigantic unlaced hightop sneaker.

Punk offered his hand to the younger Callaghan. "It's good to see you, Seamus."

The teen considered Punk's extended arm and left him hanging for a few beats before averting his eyes and reluctantly meeting the lieutenant's firm grip with a weak one. The master chief snapped a few indistinguishable words of disgust, snatching the headset off of his son's head and horseshoeing it around the lad's neck.

"I'm sorry about that, Lieutenant," the master chief said.

"That's all right," Punk said with a laugh he hoped was disarming to both parties. "I like music, too." He motioned toward the glass double doors. "Why don't we go in?"

The petty officer behind the glass of the security badge issue station studied Seamus with concern before Punk stepped up and explained the situation. After another second's hesitation, the enlisted man placed two visitor's badges in the metal drawer and pushed it out to the lieutenant. Punk handed one badge to the master chief and, after the youth defensively recoiled a bit, clipped the other to the neckline of Seamus's basketball jersey.

Punk sat the father and son in the air-conditioned comfort of a classroom adjacent to the simulator control stations and reviewed some of the basics behind controlling a Tomcat with Seamus. As the pilot talked him through the use of stick, rudder, and throttle, the boy sat disaffected, barely nodding when prodded on his understanding. Master Chief Callaghan sat by his son with an intense expression, seemingly trying to absorb the material for the both of them.

Punk led the Callaghans into the dim light of the control room, where retired captain Fred Crowley sat wearing an old leather flight jacket covered with patches. The control room was colder than the rest of the building, almost uncomfortably so, and suddenly Seamus's jacket didn't seem like such a bad idea after all.

Crowley bathed in the glow of the displays as he worked a student pilot and RIO through their simulator period. He caught the group's approach out of the corner of his eye.

"Hop on out, fellas," Crowley passed into a thin mike sticking out from the console in front of him. "The next crew's here." He touched the nearest computer screen several times, bringing up a blank screen, and then stood to greet Punk and his guests.

"Captain, always a pleasure," Punk said as he shook the

paunchy man's hand and gestured toward the other two. "This is Master Chief Callaghan and his son Seamus."

"Punk, I told you not to call me captain," Crowley said. "It's Fred. And what self-respecting former fighter pilot doesn't know Master Chief Callaghan?"

"The captain and I go way back," the master chief explained as he returned the man's handshake. "We deployed with VF-74 together, on *Saratoga*. I was a brand-new petty officer and you were a brand-new lieutenant, if I remember right."

"You remember right, and you don't call me captain either," Crowley said. "I'm a civilian now, although I'm not too old to remember my roots." He brought both arms up in a body builder's pose. "The F-4 Phantom, yes, indeed. That was a real man's airplane, stuck together with rivets, wire, and a prayer. None of this fancy stuff these guys have now." He hunched his shoulders and gave Punk a playful jab to the chest. "Hey, I heard you just got engaged. Congratulations."

"How did you hear?"

"Oh, you know. Word spreads fast around these parts."

"I guess so. It just happened on Friday night." Punk briefly pondered the power of a single suggestion: *Let's just get married.* He smiled at the thought of Anita with the phone to her ear for the entire weekend. She'd only ventured away from the condo once, to buy an armload of bride's magazines that now littered his coffee table.

"Like I said, word gets around," Crowley said. "So what are we doing today?"

"We're getting the master chief's son Seamus psyched up to be a fighter pilot," Punk said with a gesture toward Seamus, who stood on the outskirts of the conversation with his head down and his hands shoved deeply into the pockets of his stadium jacket.

The master chief considered his son's body language and seethed, "Get on over here and meet the captain." The teen broke his lugubrious stance just long enough to shoot his father an indignant look before he reassumed his disaffected slouch and shuffled toward them. He greeted the trainer operator as unenthusiastically as he'd greeted Punk in the parking lot.

The other crew emerged from the simulator and, with a

wave and a call of thanks to Crowley, exited the control room, followed by one of Crowley's co-workers who would debrief their session in the classroom. Punk diplomatically suggested that Seamus remove his jacket and knit hat and, admiring the boy's clean-shaven head, led him to the white rectangular box, about the size of an eighteen-wheeler's trailer, that housed the cockpit mock-up.

Punk helped Seamus into the front cockpit and pointed out the stick and throttle, the airspeed, altitude, and attitude indicators, and reviewed some of the things he'd briefed in the classroom. As he placed a headset on Seamus he noticed that the teen's expression had gone from apathetic to apprehensive. Punk patted his shoulder and then positioned himself in the rear of the cockpit. He looked forward along each rail to ensure Seamus's arms weren't dangling, gave him a warning, and then lowered the canopy.

"Fred, why don't you start us at ten thousand feet," Punk requested through his headset. "We'll let Seamus get a feel for the jet."

"Roger, ten thousand," Crowley replied as he punched the keyboard in front of him and touched the computer screen a few times. "You're set. Ready to run?"

"Ready, Seamus?" Punk asked.

"I guess," the teen said.

"You're running," Crowley said.

The muted roar of engines was piped into the space, signaling the airplane was in simulated flight, and the horizon swung wildly around them as Seamus fought with the stick.

"Easy with it," Punk said. "You don't have to move the stick that much."

Seamus emitted a whimper as earth and sky repeatedly exchanged positions against the canopy. "I . . . I can't stop it."

"Hold the stick completely still," Punk commanded. The airplane—or the simulation of one—stopped rolling and held its attitude for the time being, twenty degrees nose low with the right wing slightly down. "Good. Now move the stick slowly to the left . . . slowly . . . okay, now center it again. Easy with it."

The jet continued its rapid descent as Seamus threw the stick from the inside of one thigh to the other. "This is bullshit," he muttered.

Punk continued his coaching, but Seamus didn't respond.

After another fifteen seconds of random inputs from the boy, the jet hit the ground and all motion stopped. A red light blinked above them, signaling their artificial demise.

"Well, you just tied the record for low flight," Crowley cracked. "Give me a second and I'll set you guys up again."

Punk looked around the left side of the front seat and saw that Seamus had his head down. "Don't worry, Seamus," he said. "That's why we have simulators. You'll get the hang of it after a little while."

"I don't want to do this," Seamus said. "How do you get out of this thing?" He pulled his headset off and began pushing on the canopy with both hands just above his head.

"What are you doing?" Punk called forward, pulling his own headset off at the same time.

"I want out of this thing." Seamus began pounding his fists on the Plexiglas.

"Hey, be cool, man. This thing isn't as solid as the real jet."

"Let me out."

"Look, Seamus, you don't strike me as a guy who'd quit so easily. I know you're tougher than that. Plus, you know your old man will hassle you till the end of time if you jump out of this thing now. You don't need that kind of aggravation. Let's give it one more shot, at least. If you still don't like it after that, we'll stop, okay?"

Seamus sat still for a time, and then shrugged and puffed, "Whatever."

"All right. Put your headset back on."

Punk watched the boy slip the headset back over his ears and then spoke to Crowley. "We're ready to go again."

"What are you guys doing?" Crowley asked. "We couldn't hear you for a bit there."

"Nothing," Punk replied. "We were just reviewing a couple of technique items."

"All right, you're running."

The simulator came alive again and the jet immediately began a slow roll to the left.

"Okay, counter the roll by smoothly moving the stick to the right," Punk said. "Good. Hold that right there." The nose climbed above the horizon, and Punk noted their airspeed: two hundred knots and decelerating. "We need to get the nose back down. Push the stick forward. Again, think *smooth*. Good. You're getting the hang of it. Now

take your left hand and move the throttles forward all the
way, until they won't go any more."

"Like this?"

"That's it. You're flying."

Seamus uttered a little whoop as the jet continued to
accelerate straight ahead.

"How does it feel?" Punk asked. "Are you in control of
this machine?"

"I guess so," Seamus said.

"All right. Let's see if we can't develop your scan. A
pilot has to be able to read his gauges in order to tell what's
going on with his plane. Find the airspeed indicator and
tell me what our airspeed is right now."

Seamus looked down at the instrument panel and
searched the dials for one that said "airspeed" on it. "I
can't find it."

"Keep looking. It's the first gauge left of your center
displays. And, at the same time, keep flying the jet. You're
starting a little dive here. Level off again. A pilot always
has to keep several things going at once."

Seamus gave the stick a little tug and continued to hunt
for the airspeed indicator. "Okay," he said. "I think I found
it. The speed is just over forty."

"Good. That's actually four hundred. The gauge is labeled by tens, so add a zero to whatever you read. That's
also in knots, not miles per hour."

"How many miles per hour are we going?" Seamus asked
innocently enough.

Punk fumbled with the conversion for a few seconds and
then just said, "About four hundred and fifty." He waited
for Crowley to come up and correct him, but he didn't, so
Punk figured he must've managed a guess close enough for
most career aviators' personal standards.

"All right, Seamus," Punk continued. "I think you're
ready to try some more advanced moves. Let's do a loop."

"I can't do that."

"Sure you can. First, you need to select afterburner."

"I'll crash again."

"No, you won't. Push the throttles all the way forward
again." Seamus did as Punk commanded. "Now move them
outboard, to the left, and then push them as far forward as
they will go again. That will give you full afterburner." The

synthetic roar of engines rose in volume and intensity around them, and the needles on their airspeed indicators passed across five hundred knots. "Pull back on the stick."

Seamus pulled the stick aft and seconds later had the nose knifing vertically into the artificial heavens. Punk thought he heard a hum of wonder from the front seat, and as the sky grew slightly darker around them, the boy asked, "Are we in space now?"

"No, not quite, but we're getting there. Keep pulling," Punk said. "We don't want to stall over the top. What's our airspeed?"

"Um . . . twenty. I mean, two hundred."

"Two hundred what?"

"Knots."

"What's our altitude?"

"Altitude? You didn't teach me about that one."

"It's right next to the airspeed. A pilot always has to know his altitude."

"I can't find it."

"You have to. Keep pulling here."

Seamus reacted to the fact they were now pointed straight down. "I'm going to crash."

"No, you won't. What's our altitude?"

"Okay, I think I've got it. It says thirty, no twenty-nine. Twenty-eight—"

"Those are thousands of feet. What's our airspeed? Keep pulling now."

"Ah, six hundred."

"That's too fast. When you start going downhill, the jet picks up speed quickly, which is a good thing sometimes. But the Tomcat doesn't turn that well at six hundred knots. Pull the throttles back to idle. And try to keep your wings level with the horizon."

The roar went away, and Seamus scribed the last quarter of the loop, stopping the pull once the jet returned to level flight. "Should we do another one?" the boy asked.

"No," Punk said. "That was damn good for your first loop. Let's try some turns now. Ready?"

"Yeah, I'm ready."

"Select full afterburner again. Roll left . . . stop there . . . now pull back. Keep the nose tracking across the horizon. What's our airspeed?"

"Three hundred knots."

"Good. Now to speed up we can do one of two things: The first is ease the pull on the stick. Go ahead and do that. What's our airspeed now?"

"Three fifty . . . three seventy-five . . ."

"What else do you think we could do to speed up?"

"Go into a dive?"

"Exactly. And to slow down?"

"Pull the throttles back or climb?"

"This guy's a natural, Fred."

"It looks like it," Crowley said in return. "I think he's ready to fight a bandit or two."

"My thoughts exactly."

The motion around the cockpit froze, and after Crowley continued tapping the appropriate places on his touch screen the crew was wings-level again. A few seconds later a MiG blossomed, seemingly several miles away, against the sky at their three o'clock position.

"Level one bandit, Fred?" Punk asked.

"That's affirmative."

"Before we start dogfighting, Seamus, we need to talk about your weapons," Punk said. "Because this trainer is set up to be unclassified today, we'll keep it really simple, 'sticks and stones' as we say. That means Sidewinder missiles and guns only. Look at the bottom of your heads-up display and tell me what it says."

Seamus squinted at the glass and said, "SW."

"Okay, that stands for 'Sidewinder.' That's your heat-seeking missile. Now click the toggle by your thumb on the stick down one notch. What's the HUD read now?"

"G."

"That's for 'Guns,' good old-fashioned bullets—a real man's weapon. What you select between the two depends on where we are relative to that MiG over there. Are you ready to try?"

"I guess. Will he be able to shoot back at us?"

"Unfortunately, yes."

"Like the cops, right?" Seamus laughed darkly.

"I'll talk you through it at first," Punk said. "We're ready to run, Fred."

"Okay, you're running."

The roar of the engines kicked in again and the horizon

wobbled slightly around them. "Roll right and pull," Punk commanded. "Keep it coming. Wings level now. We're nose on to this guy, one hundred and eighty degrees out. We'll take him down our left side. Do you have a tally?"

"A what?"

"Do you see him?"

"Yeah, yeah. I see him. I have a tally. What should I do?"

"What's your airspeed?"

Seamus had to force himself to look away from the dot coming toward them. "Uh . . . three hundred . . ."

"I want four hundred at the merge."

The boy pushed the throttles forward and focused on the airspeed indicator until Punk's saying, "Roll left and pull," broke his concentration. Seamus looked through the windscreen and realized he'd lost track of their foe.

"Where did he go?"

"Down our left side," Punk replied. "He's almost behind us. Roll more and pull harder."

Seamus tried to follow the guidance. "I still don't see him."

"At our long seven o'clock. I'll watch him for now. Keep the pull coming."

Seamus split his attention between the airspeed indicator and the horizon, making sure the nose of his jet stayed on it. After another ninety degrees of turn, he noticed the white glow of the MiG creeping into view across the top of the canopy. "I see him!"

"Put him right in the center of your HUD," Punk said. "I'll get you a radar lock."

Seamus saw a diamond superimpose over the bandit. "We're still a little too far away to shoot a Sidewinder," Punk said. "Give me full afterburner."

The boy pushed the throttles outboard and then fully forward and waited for further instruction.

"Okay, two miles," Punk said. "Make sure you have 'Sidewinder' selected."

"Yep, Sidewinder," Seamus replied as he squinted at the bottom of the HUD again.

"Get ready to squeeze the trigger. Ready . . ."

The MiG suddenly turned hard into them. Crowley's wicked laugh filled their headsets. "You didn't think I was going to let you shoot me that easily, did you?" he said.

The MiG passed down their left side again, nose low and in a left-hand turn. "Let's take him one-circle," Punk said. "Roll right this time, and let the nose fall a bit."

"I don't see him," Seamus said.

"Three o'clock low. Watch your speed but keep pulling."

"Now I see him. I've got my tally." The boy continued to tug on the stick until he'd filled his windscreen with the MiG once again. "How far away is he?"

"Just under two miles. Take the shot."

Seamus pulled the trigger. The sampled roar of a missile filled the space, and a white mass flew away from them toward the bandit. The boy watched it intently. After several seconds the Sidewinder hit and transformed the MiG into a cartoon fireball.

"Good kill," Crowley passed. "Splash one MiG."

A cheer erupted from the cockpit that put a wide grin on Master Chief Callaghan's face. "Must be in the genes, huh, master chief?" Crowley said.

"Sure," Callaghan replied, "but whose?"

"This guy's a killing machine," Punk said. "Set us up again, please."

A technician walked in and said, "Fred, we've got indications of a circuit board malfunction on Bus Number Two. We're going to have to shut the simulator down for a while."

Crowley frowned and then turned to the mike, "Bad news, fellas. The gremlins invaded the trainer, I'm afraid. We need you to climb on out."

Seamus moaned as Punk apologized and opened the canopy. The pilot got out of the rear cockpit and then helped the teen find his footing as he scaled back down the side of the mock-up. Once safely on the landing next to the trainer, Seamus let out a hearty "Damn right" and slapped Punk a high five.

Seamus followed Punk out the door and back toward the control room. "That was a blast! It wasn't easy, but at the same time it wasn't as hard as I thought it would be, once I got the hang of it anyway. Do you know what I mean?"

"I know exactly what you mean," Punk said.

"Did I do good for a new guy?"

"Better than that." Punk smiled and looked back at the boy and thought he seemed to be standing more upright than before, his gait surer. This outing had been a good idea.

Punk hit the control room and moved to the still-smiling master chief and extended his hand. "The kid's a quick study."

"Well, sir," Callaghan said, smile widening as he pumped the lieutenant's hand in return, "I thank you for the time and effort."

"Dad, did you see that?" Seamus asked, face glowing with his victory. "Could you see what was going on out there?"

"I saw it all, boy," the master chief replied. "I saw it all."

"Man, I wish my buds—"

"Ah, now you forget them, Seamus," Callaghan snapped, face quickly losing all hints of joy. "You'll never get here for real as long as you're hanging about with the likes of those boys. Don't you see that? You think the lieutenant here hung out in gangs when he was your age?"

An awkward silence followed. Punk broke it with, "Well, in any case, this flying stuff beats working, doesn't it, Seamus?" The lieutenant turned around to see that the upbeat lad born in the front seat of the trainer was gone now. In his place was the same slovenly delinquent who'd walked in the front door of the building nearly an hour ago. His shoulders slumped again, and the dark cloud over his head had returned. He shuffled over to the coat rack, put his stadium jacket and knit cap back on, and slipped the headphones over his ears again.

Master Chief Callaghan strode over to him and slapped the phones off much as he had in the parking lot. "You want to say thank you to the lieutenant and Captain Crowley?" he said.

"Thank you," the boy reluctantly muttered with his head down. And then he walked out.

The master chief watched his son exit and Punk could see the frustration, the hollow yearning, in the enlisted man's eyes—along with the anger. "There's a good man in there dying to get out," Punk said. "Just give him time."

"Time . . ." the master chief thought aloud. "I wonder how much he needs, and if we've got enough."

CHAPTER SEVEN

Once the fingertip of Florida disappeared under the Tomcat's nose, leaving nothing in view from twenty-nine thousand feet but the ocean and sky, Punk felt his mainland cares fade away. The next land he'd see, after about twenty minutes over the water, was Key West, land of Hemingway and hedonists, and land of RAG tactics detachments. The next two weeks would challenge the aviators of Class Two to the ragged edges of their abilities as they learned how to employ missiles at supersonic airspeeds against multiple maneuvering opponents.

They'd also learn to dogfight. Although the Tomcat had morphed into a multimission airplane and the replacements had already been through the basics of bomb dropping in the strike phase, the tactics phase dealt with the skills most aviation aficionados and Hollywood producers conjured up when they heard the words "fighter pilot."

Punk wasn't on the original roster for this particular detachment, but he wasn't complaining about the change in plans. A Key West det was understood in instructor circles as a very good deal. Key West in August was not as popular as Key West in January, but it was still Key West. So when Spud came to him with the last-minute opportunity to join the detachment, by virtue of the fact that another pilot's wife had gone into premature labor, Punk had readily accepted.

Punk was leading a two-plane formation with Spud in his backseat and Muddy on his wing. She was low pilot on the

Class Two flight-hour tally, exactly an hour and a half short of the fifty Tomcat flight-hour minimum required to start the tactics phase, so she was afforded the luxury of flying an F-14 to Key West instead of tubing it—riding in the back of a C-9 transport, with the rest of Class Two. Lieutenant "Hammer" Thomas was in her backseat, an instructor RIO and club rugby player with a habit of putting his head through walls.

"I can taste my Fat Tuesday's fruity drink now," Hammer said over the squadron common frequency, the one used for, among other, more official reasons, idle banter on logistics flights like theirs.

"I prefer to start my Duval Crawl a little farther down the street," Spud said, referring to Duval Street, Key West's bar-lined main drag. "The Bull is more my speed."

"Oh, I'll make it to the Bull," Hammer said. "I just need a little priming first."

"We old guys don't need priming," Spud said, "and those fruity drinks are for homos."

"When in Rome—" Punk added.

Ten nautical miles from NAS Key West, the approach controller had the two Tomcats switch to the tower frequency. "Key West tower," Spud transmitted, "this is Boxer one-zero-five. We're a flight of two, ten miles out. We have the field in sight."

"Roger, Boxer one-zero-five. Assume you want the break?"

"That's affirmative, tower." The break, performed only in weather good enough for the pilots to see the airfield from several thousand feet and a few miles away, was a classic military maneuver where airplanes flew over the runway and then peeled off one by one before dropping the gear and flaps and circling to land. In addition to looking good from the ground, the maneuver saved both time and fuel compared to a straight-in approach.

"Copy. Report three miles out."

"Roger." Punk checked the range from the field and realized they needed to lose some altitude. He looked over to Muddy, who appeared to be working hard to get into close formation, and gave her a signal with his hand that resembled a quacking duck's head. He then moved his head forward, and as he brought it back, he flicked a switch on the inboard throttle with his thumb, which caused the speed brakes to open. Muddy matched him with the configuration of her jet as she continued her attempt to get in the proper parade position. She hadn't flown around Punk since the dubious FAM-1 and was eager to impress.

"Tower, Boxer flight is at three miles," Spud passed over his radio.

"Roger, Boxer flight. You are cleared for the break, runway one-six. Report on final with the gear."

"Boxer flight cleared for the break," Spud replied. Punk closed his speed brakes, leveled off, and accelerated above three hundred knots. At that point, he looked back over to Muddy, noting that she was a bit too far below him, and raised his right hand above the canopy rail. He gave her the appropriate signals then flipped another switch on the inboard throttle, the one that commanded the wings to sweep.

Punk watched down his right wing and verified it was moving back. He looked over to Muddy's jet to check that her wings were sweeping as well and was shocked to see the top of her jet as she suddenly rolled in his direction. The last things Punk's mind registered before the other jet disappeared beneath his were the two white helmets of the other crew. He reefed back on the stick and grimaced, certain the two fighters were about to collide. He waited for the thump, slipping his left hand from the throttles to the lower ejection handle.

Spud had been focused out the other side of the jet and was surprised by the unexpected onset of several times the normal pull of gravity. Once he was able to separate his mask and visor from his thighs, wrapped in a fully inflated G suit, he raged over the intercom, "What the hell is going on?"

Punk didn't answer, but instead breathed a sigh of relief as Muddy's jet shot out their left side. Punk's pitch pulse and Muddy's too-low formation position had combined to keep the jets from smashing against each other.

"What are you doing, Muddy?" Punk asked over the squadron common frequency. There was no answer as the other jet continued to turn away from them. "Move the wings back forward and level your wings," he commanded. "Do you have it? Muddy, do you have control of the jet?"

She stammered something unintelligible, and Hammer

cut in with, "Standby, please." Moments later the wings came forward and the jet leveled off.

"Keep flying straight ahead and start climbing," Punk said on squadron common before keying the other radio. "Tower, Boxer flight needs to exit the pattern for a bit."

"Boxer, are you experiencing any problems?"

"We just need to check something out with my wing-man."

"Are you declaring an emergency?"

"Negative, tower. Not at this time. We're going to head out over the water for a few minutes and then we'll be back with you."

"Roger, Boxer. Contact departure control for flight advisories while feet wet."

"Roger," Spud replied.

"Muddy you have the lead," Punk said.

"Muddy has the lead," she returned, voice quavering slightly.

"Punk's fuel state is five-point-zero." Five thousand pounds of gas was plenty to make it through this unplanned side trip.

"Muddy has the same."

The radios were silent as the two F-14s flew over the sea and each aviator mentally replayed what had just happened. Punk broke the quiet as he brought his jet closer to the replacement's: "Muddy, did you lose the bubble there? What was that all about?"

"That wasn't me, sir," she said, her formality lending a strange air to the already awkward scene. "I didn't touch the stick."

"Oh, Christ," Spud said to Punk over the intercom. "Here we go again."

"All right. Let's climb up to ten thousand feet," Punk instructed Muddy. "In the meantime, we're going to look your jet over." He closed her right side while honoring the possibility her jet might maneuver without warning, in-specting the areas around the wing and right horizontal stabilizer. There didn't appear to be any leaks, none of the telltale streaks of maroon hydraulic fluid across the nacelle that might explain an uncommanded roll. He crossed under and took a look at the left side. "I don't see anything un-usual," he said. "What do your gauges show?"

"Everything's normal," Muddy said.

"How do the flight controls feel?"

"Fine."

"Get her to dirty the jet up and see how it does at slower speeds," Spud advised.

"Muddy," Punk transmitted as the flight reached ten thousand feet and leveled off. "Let's go ahead and drop the gear and flaps."

"Roger, we're slowing down," she said. As they decelerated through two hundred and fifty knots, she said, "Gear—now," and moved the handle to the down position. Punk followed suit, sneaking a quick peek at his landing gear indicator to ensure he had "three green" once he saw her gear fully extend. At two hundred knots she followed with, "Flaps—now," and matched the call with the flap handle, while again Punk mirrored her configuration.

"Try a few lazy turns," Punk recommended as he moved away from her a bit more. Muddy moved her jet slowly left and then right. "How's it feel?"

"Still fine."

"Any vibration? Cavitation?"

"No, sir."

"What do you think, Spud?" Punk asked over the intercom.

"Let's just get her on deck safely and sort it out," Spud replied, as shaken as the rest by their near miss. "We've been to enough memorial services already this year."

They headed back to the air station where Punk escorted the replacement pilot through a straight-in approach and landing before looping back around and landing behind her. Once parked next to Muddy along the squadron's flight line, he shut his jet down. Spud opened the canopy and a damp blanket of humidity immediately covered both of them. Punk looked past his plane captain and saw Muddy walking back to the hangar a few steps behind Hammer, her body language, distorted by the waves of Florida heat coming off the ramp, indicating that the hop had not gone well.

They'd been the last two jets assigned to the detachment to arrive from Oceana, so the place was already a flurry of activity. A handful of yellow-painted tractors rolled over

the concrete as resolutely as eighteen-wheelers on a turn-
pike, and technicians crawled over the majority of the
twelve Tomcats assembled. While the aircrews, even the
replacements, looked forward to a detachment full of hard
flying and occasional hard partying, the maintainers knew
their time in the tropics would be spent sweating over broken jets, punctuated occasionally by a few hours of down
time in the World War II–era barracks a half mile away.
They were working in two shifts and the senior enlisted
leaders reserved the right to go to three if the airplanes
weren't getting fixed in time to meet the demanding flight
schedule each day.

As soon as Punk passed through the door into the air-
conditioned comfort of the detachment maintenance control
space, he was hit by its unique odor of stale chlorine-scented
air, and it triggered memories of previous visits. He'd recounted dogfights and pondered the previous evening's
events while wandering around this hangar. But the scene
before him now flattened the wave of nostalgia.

Senior Chief Williams, enlisted head of the maintenance
effort in Key West, already harried though the detachment
had barely begun, grilled the female replacement on what
had happened and didn't buy her explanation. "I've worked
on F-14s for twenty-five years," the chubby black man said
past her toward where Punk was standing. "I've never seen
them move by themselves."

Lieutenant Commander "Scuzz" Venato was the RAG's
maintenance officer. He, like Spud, was assigned to the
RAG while waiting for assignment to command a fleet
squadron. Scuzz and Corky McBride, who was contractually
obligated to make all detachments, joined Spud, Punk,
Muddy, and Hammer in one of a handful of small rooms
adjacent to the ready room on the second floor of the hangar. Punk straddled a cracked wooden chair and stared at
a square yard of paint peeling from the wall above Muddy's
head, wondering if the Navy was ever going to rehab the
nearly dilapidated building. She swept the strands of sweat-
soaked hair from her forehead and reasserted that the airplane had rolled without her input.

Spud dismissed Muddy from the room. "What do we
think?" he asked the group after giving her enough time

to escape earshot. They exchanged glances but no one spoke, so he asked Hammer, "How did she do before the roll-off?"

"She's real quiet in the airplane," Hammer said. "It's hard to say."

"We're not asking for her qualifications as a mistress of ceremonies, Hammer," Spud said. "How was her flying?"

"That's my point, Spud," Hammer countered. "I could either interpret her quiet that she's behind the airplane or that she's—she's—"

"Quiet?" Punk said.

"Yeah," Hammer said, "quiet."

"Punk, you're batting a thousand with this girl, aren't you?" Spud said. "First the taxi deal, and now she tries to break into you. It's been a while since I was part of the dating scene, but we used to call that 'chemistry.'"

Punk methodically rolled the sleeves of his flight suit up a few turns to the middle of his forearms. "Today's problem wasn't her fault," he said before turning to Scuzz. "That jet should be impounded until we can get the systems engineers down here to give it a complete once-over."

"Our guys are looking it over right now," Scuzz said.

"No offense, but this is bigger than our guys."

"It's only happened twice, if that," Corky continued, "and each time there was a conehead at the controls."

"That's true," Scuzz said.

"Oh, come on," Punk shot back. "You're going to ignore the evidence because replacements were flying at the time?"

"What evidence?" Corky asked. "Let's be reasonable here. The Naval Safety Center investigators have been poring over the wreckage from the midair for months and haven't found a thing."

"How do you know, Corky?" Punk said, glaring at the tech rep. "The engineering investigation isn't complete yet, and until it is, the investigators' findings are classified."

"I told you before: It's my job to know."

Punk slowly shook his head. "You're shtick is wearing thin on me."

"I'm only here to help, Punk," Corky said.

"Fellas, fellas," Spud said while flapping his arms. "We're all on the same team here."

"Punk, the replacement wrote a down gripe on the jet," Scuzz said, "and we'll work it off."

"What do you think they'll find?" Punk asked, voice spiced with a hint of sarcasm.

"I don't know," Scuzz replied. "That's their job—and I trust them."

"I'll tell you what they're going to find," Punk said. "Nothing."

"If they find nothing, they'll sign the gripe off as A-799, nothing found, and then we'll put the jet back in an up status."

"That's . . . the . . . wrong . . . answer," Punk said. "That jet's broken."

"Then we'll find the problem," Scuzz said as he shifted in his seat and tore at the Velcro strips around the waist of his flight suit, obviously trying to keep the lid on his own anger.

"No, you won't," Punk shot back, doing his best to ignore Corky's pedantic snickering. "That's my point. You need—"

"Spud!" Scuzz shouted. "Talk to this guy before I lose my shit on him!"

Spud got up, ushered Punk through the door and a few more steps out of the room, and asked, "What are you doing, buddy?"

"This isn't about replacements fucking up, Spud," Punk said in a barely hushed whisper.

"Then let the system play out," Spud said. "That's all you can do."

"It's not all I can do." Punk paced and shot a few glances back into the briefing room. He lowered his voice further: "Something's not right here. Something's getting overlooked." He puffed an exasperated breath and ran both hands through his hair. "If they don't find anything wrong with that jet, I want to take it for a confidence hop before it's put back into the rotation."

"Punk, I'm the operations officer, not the maintenance officer."

"Broker the deal with Scuzz, Spud. I'm asking as a friend. I think I can recreate the regime that caused the roll-off."

"And if you don't?"

Punk stared blankly at the floor for a few seconds. "Then for starters I guess we'll have to give Muddy a down for her loss of situational awareness. But that shouldn't be a factor because I know something's wrong with that jet, the same something that was wrong with Pugsly's jet—the problem that killed Crud."

Spud studied the lieutenant's eyes. "All right, I'll talk to Scuzz. I doubt if your presence would help the situation. Wait over by the duty desk."

Punk started across the room, but stopped to glance at the detachment "hit board," a sheet of yellow legal paper taped to the wall with the list of informal transgressions documented throughout the detachment scribed on it. Each hit was punishable by a one-dollar fine that was tossed into a kitty funding an end-of-detachment keg party. He read the entry, fallout from another ferry flight that had arrived on the island from Oceana earlier in the day:

> 1. *Skids wrote gripe for broken clock in cockpit. Maintainer fixed gripe by winding clock.*

Punk smiled and continued over to the duty desk. He bellied up to the navel-high counter that bordered the edge of the six-inch elevated platform upon which sat the squadron duty officer's desk and chair. Behind the desk was the focal point of the room: a massive dry erase board that showed the day's flight schedule. Although the operations department made nearly one hundred copies of the daily flight schedule, authored the evening prior and distributed to every other department and work center in the squadron, the only accurate source during the course of an ever-changing fly day was the dry erase board maintained by the squadron duty officer. It was the same in every ready room throughout the fleet.

Only when the duty officer seated at the desk raised his head from making an entry in his log did Punk recognize who it was: Pugsly. It was the first time he'd seen him since he'd visited his apartment earlier in the summer. He looked better groomed than he had that night, but it was apparent that the stresses of sweating his future as a fighter pilot over the past several months had taken their toll. The pallor of his skin was unnaturally white, and he'd lost some weight.

"You look surprised to see me, Puke, er, I mean, Punk," Pugsly said. "Don't worry; I'm not flying. I'm still waiting for the results from this damn mishap investigation to get through the chop chain." His arm swept the wall behind him. "In the meantime, they've put me to work as the permanent squadron duty officer. I'll keep wearing nothing but khakis."

"You have the duty every day?" Punk asked.

"No, I'm going port and starboard with some guy from the class behind us who got nailed during his annual flight physical for an irregular heartbeat. We each work one day, sleep one day." The duty phone rang and Pugsly answered it.

Spud came up behind Punk and looked as if he was about to speak, but before he could, Pugsly thrust out the phone receiver and said, "Ops O, the skipper wants to talk to you."

Spud listened for a time, offering an occasional "yes sir," and then gave the phone back to Pugsly and asked him to transfer the call to the operations office. Spud said, "Don't go anywhere," to Punk before marching the fifty feet to his office, across the common area from the briefing rooms.

Punk turned back to Pugsly, who had just finished transferring Spud's call, and asked, "Any idea when they'll make the final ruling on you?"

"I heard the package was sitting with the admiral at AIRLANT," Pugsly said, "but they said he's waiting to make the call until the engineering investigation is complete."

"And what have you heard about that?"

"What have you heard?"

Punk paused for a second. "Nothing." He was hit with a twinge of guilt as soon as he said it. "I mean, Corky the tech rep was just saying something, but it was just a bullshit rumor."

"What did he say?"

Again, Punk paused. "He said the engineers hadn't come up with any findings yet."

Pugsly's expression turned lifeless, and he intoned, "I didn't touch the stick."

"I know you didn't," Punk uttered nearly subconsciously. Pugsly's eyes widened at the comment, and a hint of color came to his cheeks. Punk continued thinking out loud, blankly taking in the schedule behind the desk: "In fact, Muddy just had the same thing happen to her. This time I almost got hit."

"What are you talking about?" Pugsly asked. "What happened to Muddy?"

Punk snapped out of his daze and furtively glanced around them. "I guess it's okay to tell you. You'd hear about it through the rumor mill soon enough. As we were coming into the break, right as we were sweeping our wings, Muddy rolled into me. She says she never moved the stick."

Pugsly slapped the top of the duty desk and released a nervous laugh. "Don't you see what this means?"

Spud poked his head out of the operations office and said, "Punk, come in here, please."

"Don't you see what this means?" Pugsly said again loudly as Punk moved away.

"Shut the door behind you," the balding lieutenant commander ordered from behind his desk as Punk entered the room. "We've got a problem. That call was from the skipper. He wanted to know how the det was going, and, of course, I told him about your near miss."

"What did he say?"

"After he smacked the phone against his desk a few times he calmed down enough to talk to me. He's afraid Admiral Knowles at Atlantic Fleet is going to start micromanaging this situation. If that's the case, we're about to run into the classic 'leadership challenge' of gender integration."

"Leadership challenge?"

"There's a reason the Navy uses the word 'mishap' instead of 'accident.' 'Accident' implies elements out of human control, acts of God and whatnot. When taxpayers are paying more than fifty million dollars for an airplane, they're not going to accept 'shit happens' as the explanation for why we crashed or killed people. So, if they don't find anything wrong with Muddy's jet, like they haven't found anything wrong while sifting through the wreckage of Pugsly's jet, then the only explanation is pilot error in both cases. Of course, two guys were killed in Pugsly's mishap, but the only thing that kept the results of both mistakes

from being the same is you were paying attention to the
person on your right wing and avoided getting hit."

"And the person on my right wing was flying shitty
form."

"She still would've hit us if you hadn't pulled up. By the
way, what does that do to the tally of who's saved whose
life over the years between us?"

"I think you're still a couple up on me," Punk said, eyes
to the ceiling as he recounted. "The times you kept us from
getting hit in the tanker pattern overhead the aircraft carrier alone gives you the nod."

"Whatever. Allow me to say thanks."

"Do we hug now?" Punk stood and walked over to the
window, rendered semiopaque from condensation on the
inside and salt on the outside, and watched the maintainers
below as they scrambled over the jet Muddy had just piloted. "So what's the outlook for Pugsly?"

"Suffice it to say he doesn't have a senator interested in
his future."

"What about his dad, the famous ace?"

"Worth noting, I guess. But not the same horsepower—
not across this landscape, anyway."

Punk turned from the window. "If the jet rolled off by
itself, Muddy's not guilty of anything and should be applauded for saving it. If the jet simply responded to her
stick input, however unintentional, then she should down
the flight. Let me remind you, operations officer, that down
would be her second one and two downs during RAG
training is cause for a performance board to be convened."

"*If* Admiral Knowles allows us to convene a board on
her. Damn, this is already too hard." Spud drummed on
the desk for a few seconds.

Punk cracked open one of the dirty windows, hinged
along the top of the pane to swing outward, and peered
down on the ramp. The technicians had removed most of
the panels along the spine of the Tomcat, revealing the
control rods underneath. They'd also uncovered the actuators for the horizontal stabilizers and rudders, swept the
wings forward, raised the four spoilers on each wing, and
lowered the flaps. The fighter was torn to parade rest. Punk
saw a maintainer scurry from under the jet and figured
he'd been checking the hydraulic reservoirs and taking fluid

samples. "This situation gets much less complicated if those guys find something on that jet that would explain the roll-off," he said as he reclosed the window.

"Speaking of that," Spud said, "Scuzz has agreed to let you fly a confidence hop on the jet if they don't find anything wrong with it."

"I knew you'd make it happen. If they don't find it down there, I'm sure I can figure it out airborne."

"Who's the RIO going to be on this suicide mission of yours?"

Punk returned a hopeful expression and said, "It's not suicide; it's research."

"Does part of the testing involve flying low to attempt to create a roll-off?"

"Maybe," Punk replied. "Both of the roll-offs happened at low altitude."

"And if you recreate the regime too well, the airplane may not recover at all?"

"Perhaps . . ."

"You'll be needing my help then. It wouldn't be the first time I've had to eject us out of a jet."

The Bull and Whistle conjured up images of the grand old watering holes of colonial empires with its open-air, street-level view of Duval Street, its slow-moving fans that barely coaxed the humid tropical air across the patrons, and its weathered cement walls punctuated by deep cracks. The tables and chairs were made of oak and, over the years, had withstood the rigors of spilled beer and the occasional bar fight. The floor was hardwood, once the shiny pride of the establishment, now worn to the point where it looked unfinished. Entertainment was provided by a series of sun-bleached burnouts who'd haplessly tumbled as far down the coast as possible, strumming Jimmy Buffett songs with acoustic guitars in the far corner.

RAG instructors had long ago laid claim to the Bull and Whistle, or simply the Bull, as they called it. Its low-key vibe and unkempt graciousness meshed nicely with their aging sensibilities and their collective loss of appetite for the more prurient offerings of the city, aided by the Navy's intolerance for conduct that was once de rigueur, perhaps even viewed as a perk of a business that took its members away from home much of the time. The instructors' testosterone levels were down compared to the younger, mostly unmarried replacements', who patronized the more high-gloss tourist establishments like Sloppy Joe's and Hog's Breath Saloon, yearning to be part of the crowd surging to loud rock music and hoping for one-night love affairs with coeds on vacation with sorority sisters or divorcées down from Miami desperately clinging to the excitement of youth.

The first night of the detachment was a time for all to imbibe freely, as the flight schedule wouldn't start until the early afternoon of the following day. The base operations representatives would give a series of local-flying-rules briefs to the RAG's aviators in the morning. The rest of the days, including weekends, would be divided into three flying events with a variety of instructors and replacements briefing at 0630, 0930, and 1230 hours, and a classroom session for all the replacements at 1700 hours. After tonight, opportunities to hit Duval Street with any enthusiasm would be reserved for those whose next day started with the third flying event, and they wouldn't know who they were until late each afternoon when the flight schedule for the following day was published by the operations department.

Punk, Flex, Widget, and Hammer had formed the first wave of instructors on the town after getting cleaned up in the bachelor officers quarters, the tallest structure in Key West proper, and taking possession of *Sweet Belle,* a '72 Oldsmobile Cutlass that didn't require a key to start and had its top rusted down.

Painted a shade that Spud described as "jizz yellow," *Sweet Belle* was common property of sorts among the instructors, passed down from lieutenant to lieutenant, and matters of insurance and registration went blissfully unresolved. The car remained in Key West at all times and was kept somewhere between the airfield and the BOQ. It had a top speed of forty-three miles per hour (gauged from a Navy van trailing the car; *Sweet Belle's* speedometer didn't work) and got approximately six miles to the gallon. There were a couple of umbrellas on the floorboards of the backseat at any given time in case it rained, and the trunk was secured with a rope.

The lieutenants had found a parking place on the street a block away and captured their favorite table in the Bull, the big one in the corner that overlooked the intersection of Duval and Caroline streets.

"It's the Freemasons," Flex said from behind his wraparounds as the waitress delivered the first round. He reached for his wallet in the side pocket of his cargo shorts and produced a dollar bill. "You see this, that eye in the pyramid? That is the symbol of the Freemasons. And this, where it says 'Federal Reserve Note'? You think the Federal Reserve is a publicly held institution? *Not.* Foreign conglomerates own it."

"What the hell are you spewing about?" Widget asked in his Long Island accent between swallows of beer. His Nassau County–shaped proclivities made it nearly impossible for him to dabble in hyperbole. Life was too short, and traffic was backed up too often on the Throgs Neck Bridge to waste time embracing fringe group innuendo. "Where did you dream this shit up?"

"I saw it on TV a few weeks ago," Flex continued, intensity growing in his voice and gestures. "It made a lot of sense to me. Did you know that the Chinese now run both ends of the Panama Canal?" Widget's big head jerked with the statement.

"Not to mention the Massachusetts Institute of Technology," Hammer said.

"You're a funny guy," Flex said, leveling his finger at Hammer. "Laugh about this: They've gathered evidence that shows that Timothy McVeigh was brainwashed by the Army to be a domestic terrorist."

"What about the phantom roll-off, Punk?" Widget asked. "How long have you been a conspiracy theorist like Flex?"

"It's the Freemasons," Hammer said. "They're creating the roll-off the same way they brainwashed Timothy McVeigh into becoming a domestic terrorist."

"I'm serious, Hammer, don't kid about that," Flex said. "The McVeigh thing's not bullshit. Think about it. It's the perfect cover."

"Maybe Muddy was brainwashed by the Freemasons to be a terrible pilot," Hammer said.

"Muddy might not be fighter pilot material, but she is definitely doable," Widget said.

"Chicks in uniform have never done it for me," Flex said.

"Would you pork her if the situation presented itself, Punk?" Hammer asked.

"How would the situation present itself?"

"I don't know. You run into her jogging. You wind up spotting for her in the gym."

"You hide in her closet in the BOQ," Widget added before turning to Hammer. "You've written for *Penthouse* forum, haven't you?"

"Speaking of *Penthouse,* would you look at the size of those tits over there?" Hammer beseeched, focusing beyond Flex and across Duval Street. The others snapped their heads around. Widget rose out of his chair.

"In case you were wondering whether what you're looking at is obvious to the casual observer across the bar," Spud said, suddenly appearing behind them and putting his arm around Widget's shoulder, "it is."

"Where have you been?" Punk asked.

Spud pulled a chair away from the table and sat down. "See, I have this thing called *a job,* and I didn't get out of the hangar until a little while ago. And although I am the officer-in-charge of this detachment, budget cuts have prevented me from renting my own private car, so I had to wait for one of the vans in order to get back from the airfield, and then I had to walk from the BOQ to get here."

"Sorry, lieutenant commanders aren't allowed to ride in *Sweet Belle,*" Flex said.

"I'll remember that when you need a ride to the airfield and I've got the keys to the only van left. How does a guy get a beer here?" He craned around and caught the eye of the waitress across the room and pointed to one of the beer glasses on their table. She nodded and headed toward the bar. "Punk, maintenance found nothing wrong with Muddy's jet; they A-799'd the gripe. We've got a confidence hop immediately following the morning briefings."

"Of course there's nothing wrong with the jet," Flex said. "It's just another case of conehead-itis. Hammer, I guess you'll be filling out the down sheet for Greenwood after all."

Hammer looked to Spud who responded with a nod. Spud continued to deliver the news: "The skipper also called back again and relayed that the engineering investigation for Pugsly's mishap was just closed out. They couldn't find anything wrong with either jet, so the admiral at AIRLANT has accepted the board's recommendation to pull his wings."

"Does Pugsly know this?" Punk asked.

"I'm pretty sure he does," Spud replied. "The skipper had me forward the call to the duty desk once he was done with me. I think he wanted to break the news to him personally."

"How did he take it?"

"I don't know. He was gone by the time I walked out of the operations office."

"How did the admiral rule on me?" Flex asked.

"You've been cleared. They figured there was nothing you could have done to stop what happened. Plus, the board honored the fact that you were the one who initiated ejection and saved both of your lives."

Flex jumped up with his fists raised and let out a yell. "I'm back, motherfuckers!" The statement caused the rest of the patrons in The Bull to stop their conversations and glare at the group of aviators disapprovingly and the guitarist to halt his mediocre cover of "A Pirate Looks at Forty" mid-verse. The sudden and awkward silence remained until Flex waved a sheepish apology and sat back down.

Punk polished off his beer and asked, "Does anybody else need to get back to the BOQ?"

"We just got here," Flex said. "It's time to celebrate. I'm a fighter RIO again. I can fly tactics hops for the next two weeks, and I won't have to ride the transport back to Oceana with the coneheads when we're finished down here."

"I've got to go back for a second," Punk said.

"Why?"

"Uh, I forgot something."

"What?"

"Don't worry about it, Flex," Punk said, extending his hand across the table. "Look, I'm happy for you. I'll be back in a little bit." He scanned the group. "Last chance. Anybody else need to head back?" Nobody responded.

Punk started to walk out, but after two steps Spud grabbed him by the shoulder. "Did I hear you got engaged?"

"Yeah," Punk replied without making eye contact. "That's the rumor going around anyway."

"Congratulations?"

Punk smiled and shook Spud's extended hand. "Thanks." The lieutenant shrugged and strolled out.

As he hit Duval Street his cell phone vibrated at his hip. "Hello?"

"It's the future Mrs. Reichert."

"Wow, I've only been down here a couple of hours and you've already called me twice. You're going to use all my minutes in a couple of days at this rate."

"Then we'll buy more. You're an officer, remember?"

"I'm a poorly paid officer."

"Then I'll buy you more minutes. I can't go very long without talking to my fiancé, and I won't apologize about it. Plus I forgot to tell you some things before. Mom and I were out shopping today and I think I've settled on the china pattern I want. Oh, and we also looked at invitations. How many bridesmaids do you think we should have?"

"I don't know."

"I was thinking about six, but then I was working on the list and if we have six then Kim and Tammy get bumped and I know they'd freak and hate me for life, so I think we should have eight. Do you think you could get eight groomsmen?"

"Probably . . ."

When he got to where they'd parked, the car was gone, and he figured another group of instructors had taken it. That was the risk you took when using the peoples' transportation. "Anita, I've got to go. I'll talk to you later."

"When?"

"Soon."

"I need an exact time." She laughed.

"Soon."

"I miss you already."

"I miss you, too. I'll talk to you soon." He folded the phone up and toyed with the idea of a cab ride but decided to walk.

The sun was setting as Punk passed through the automatic sliding glass doors of the BOQ's main entrance, and he knew that soon the sword swallowers and contortionists and domestic-cat tamers and hundreds of tourists gathered across town in Mallory Square would be applauding the moment it completely disappeared below the horizon. He walked through the lobby and came upon Smitty standing next to a rack of brochures, studying one about "America's most challenging miniature golf course."

"Have you seen Pugsly?" Punk asked.

"No, sir," Smitty replied, spinning around, a bit startled, and stiffening his big frame to near attention. Punk sensed the rest of Class Two had defaulted to the same formality that Muddy had employed airborne. Each pair of wings pulled and each down awarded dealt a blow to instructors' efforts at instilling a sense of fighter community fraternity in the replacements.

But the mission of the RAG was to create fleet aviators, not to make replacements friends with instructors. A replacement's comfort was ultimately up to the replacement. Still, Punk had never liked operating with a wall between his charge and him. One of the appeals of naval aviation, to most junior officers anyway, was the notion that obligatory matters of rank faded in the face of professional competence.

"Where is everybody?"

"I don't know, sir. I'm just standing here waiting for Sinker to get dressed so we can go out and grab some dinner and maybe a beer or two."

"Stop calling me 'sir,' " Punk snapped. "It sounds fucking stupid." He stormed off toward the small bar beyond a pair of elevators.

The Three Wire—named for the arresting cable of choice out of the four that a pilot could catch with his tailhook when landing on an aircraft carrier—was a small, windowless place chock-full of plaques, photos, and other memorabilia haphazardly hung on the walls around neon-lit beer logos. It was the BOQ bar where the officers went for a drink when they lacked the time or energy to head for Duval Street.

Punk entered the dim light of the place and bade hello to Nellie, the sole bartender, an elderly fixture whose endurance and popularity in fleet circles was rivaled only by Ruthie in Fallon and Darlene in Oceana. The details of the diminutive Nellie's younger life were unclear, but during any one of her yarns spun from behind the bar she would drop a handful of famous names, mostly those of astronauts and politicians. She also was known for naming the variety of ill-fitting and strangely colored wigs she wore, names that often changed over the course of an evening.

Punk slid onto a stool, ordered a draft, and nodded politely down the bar to a pair of Florida National Guard pilots dressed in flight suits lined at the neck by black-and-white-checked neckerchiefs. Nellie plopped his beer down, cigarette dangling from her ruby red lipstick-caked mouth.

"Looks kind of dead in here," Punk said.

"Whadaya expect?" Nellie sneered in her permanently hoarse voice. "It's early in the det. You guys will come back to the Three Wire soon enough. Two weeks is a long time."

"We always come back to you, Nellie," Punk said with a smile. He pointed to the short strawberry locks she was modeling. "What's that one called?"

She worked both fists into the wig and tugged it against her head. "Blue Myrtle."

"Why blue? It looks kind of red to me."

"Blue as in the feeling, numbnuts." The long ash of her cigarette fell, and she wiped it off the counter with a damp rag. "And you're supposed to be an instructor?" She threw her head back and let out a close-lipped cackle that turned into a phlegmy cough, and then moved to recharge the popcorn machine at the other end of the room.

Punk spun around in the stool, leaned back on his elbows, and scanned the barely populated room. At one of the small round tables sat two old guys, tattooed and tanned as berries, former chiefs probably, each trying to out-gesticulate the other. In the far corner was a girl studying a book and writing notes. It took him a few seconds to recognize her.

He walked over and asked, "Have you seen Pugsly?"

"No, sir," Muddy replied without lifting her head. He studied her, having never seen her dressed in anything other than a flight suit. Her dark black hair looked better than it had after being mashed down by a helmet for a few hours. She was wearing a snug-fitting polo shirt that revealed that she was better endowed than Punk had previously realized. Her long athletic legs splayed out from under one side of the table.

"Do you mind if I sit down?" Punk asked.

She impassively extended an arm, still without lifting her head from the book.

Punk pulled a chair away from the table and sat down. "Is that the NATOPS you're reading?" The Naval Aviation Training and Operations publication was like an owner's manual for the jet. Replacements referred to it as "the blue pill" because of the color of its plastic cover and the fact that sleep quickly followed any time spent studying its contents.

She closed the fat book on her hand so that she wouldn't lose her place and looked at the cover as if she wasn't sure what she'd been reading. "Yes, sir, it's the NATOPS."

"Are you looking at anything in particular?"

Muddy finally looked up and locked Punk's eyes with hers. "I'm trying to figure out what might cause an F-14 to roll off by itself . . . sir."

"Well, like I told Pugsly earlier today, so am I." Her face softened, and her posture relaxed a bit. He leaned forward and crossed his arms on the table. "I'm flying a confidence hop tomorrow on the jet you flew today because I don't think you moved the stick, and I want to try and recreate the malfunction. Maintenance didn't find anything, so I'm now pretty much on my own—out of the box, as they say. If you've got any ideas, it might help if you told me what they were."

Muddy studied his face and then flipped the NATOPS around so that it was facing him across the table. He noted it was opened to the section titled "Flight Controls." She focused his attention with her index finger on a diagram that covered the bottom half of the right-hand page.

"This schematic shows the basic workings of the controls," she said, tracing her finger around the lines and boxes of the diagram as she spoke. "Now, if we want the airplane to roll, say, to the left, we move the stick to the left, which causes the horizontal stabilizers to deflect—left one trailing edge up, right one trailing edge down—and the spoilers to pop up on the left wing. We could also roll the airplane by moving the rudder pedals, but it would be at a slower rate than if we moved the stick." Muddy looked up from the page. "Am I good so far?"

"Good so far," Punk echoed.

"So there could only be a couple of reasons for a Tomcat to roll without pilot input," she said. "One is that the airplane has a mechanical or structural failure; you know, a flap falls off, an actuator breaks, a hydraulic seal bursts. Now maybe I'm naïve, but I would think the investigators would find those sorts of failures when they combed through the wreckage. That's got to be their bread and butter."

"It is," Punk agreed. "Those guys can figure out a lot with very little to go on."

"So if it's not a mechanical or structural failure, what is it?"

Punk raised his eyebrows and threw his hands up. "I give up."

She smiled demurely and scribed a circle with her fingernail around one of the boxes buried within the labyrinth of the schematic. "The computers. There's got to be something wrong with the digital flight control system."

"Why wouldn't the investigators check DFCS?"

"I assume they did, but what does 'broken' mean in the world of computers?" Muddy lifted her palm computer a few inches and dropped it to the table, then picked it up and clicked the power on. "That's not broken—or is it? It appears to be working, but how do I know for sure?"

"I don't know. I'm not a computer technician."

Muddy leaned back in her chair. "Obviously, pilots can't know everything," she continued, "but how far should our faith leap? It's easy to trust what you can see and feel. What about the rest of it? Where's your comfort zone? You've been a fighter pilot for, what, four or five years now? You must've thought about this."

"Well, DFCS is a new system. A few years ago, we didn't have—" Punk stopped and thought about her question, a bit embarrassed by how incomplete his attempt at an answer was going to be. "I want to know everything I can about the jet, I guess," he said, "but we have to trust a lot of people: maintainers, engineers, contractors. You'd never go flying otherwise."

"Is that trust assumed or earned?" Muddy asked.

Punk thought for a second, and then said, "Both, I guess."

"Not for me. Today I got the shit scared out of me and

a down for my efforts." She sighed, gathered the NATOPS under one arm, and stood up. "Good luck tomorrow, sir. I know Pugsly joins me in hoping you figure it out."

Punk watched her exit until she was passed by three of her classmates coming toward him. Smitty, Sinker, and Kosher strode up to the table, Kosher's shortness accentuated in the presence of Smitty. Kosher said, "You were looking for Pugsly?" He pointed toward the door. "Well, he was just spotted at the north end of town headed north in your old convertible."

"He was driving *Sweet Belle*?" Punk asked.

"Naked," Kosher added.

Punk shook his head. "We need to capture one of the vans," he said.

Kosher held out a set of keys. "Done."

"Let's go."

By the time they cleared the city the four naval officers had managed to hit every red light between them and the open road. Punk cursed and banged on the Navy van's steering wheel and mentally worked the time/distance problem they faced, like something he'd wrestled with years ago on his high school SAT: *If Pugsly heads north on the causeway at forty-three miles per hour and Punk starts on the same road at seventy miles per hour a half hour later, how long will it take Punk to catch Pugsly?*

"Are we sure he left Key West?" Smitty asked from behind the driver's seat.

"I've got a hunch," Punk replied. "He's got to be on this road."

It was dark by the time the van reached Marathon Key, and the road narrowed to two lanes. After another fifteen minutes without a sighting, the three replacements began to lose faith in the mission, like Columbus's men, convinced they'd never find a western passage to Asia.

"Maybe he turned around," Kosher offered from the shotgun position.

"Yeah," Sinker agreed. "He could have passed us going the other way and we'd never have known it. It's dark as hell out here."

"Maybe," Punk said, "but I don't think so."

"You don't *think* so," Sinker said sardonically. "Well,

that's good enough for me. Let's drive on this road all night. Hell, let's go to Miami. No, that's not far enough. Let's go to Maine or Canada."

"Damn, quit whining already," Punk said. "You guys are going to have to learn to listen to your instincts if you're going to excel in this business."

"Who's whining?" Sinker returned. "I just don't want to—"

"There he is!" Kosher said, jabbing an index finger against the front windshield. "That's a convertible in front of us."

Punk projected a self-satisfied smile to the riders and bore down on the car in the distance.

"He *is* naked," Kosher said as they closed, although the van's occupants could only see the back of Pugsly's upper torso and head from their vantage points. Slowing to forty-three miles per hour less than a van length from *Sweet Belle*'s rear bumper, Punk flickered the high beams on and off a few times and honked the horn but got no reaction. The car continued north, plying an unswerving path.

Punk focused beyond Pugsly, down the other side of the road, and saw no headlights. "Roll down your window, Kosher," Punk commanded. "I'm going to pull up next to him." He stepped on the accelerator and steered the van into the wrong lane, abeam the convertible.

"What should I say to him?" Kosher asked as he ground on the handle.

"Ask him where he's going," Punk said.

"Where are you going?" Kosher yelled across to Pugsly. No reply.

"Ask him why he's naked."

"Why are you naked?" Still no reaction.

"Tell him it's a breach of protocol for a replacement to drive *Sweet Belle*."

Kosher started to hail out the window again but then turned back to Punk and asked, "Is he still a replacement if he's had his wings pulled?"

"Headlights—" Smitty warned.

Punk tapped the brakes and eased back into the right lane snugly behind the convertible. An eighteen-wheeler passed down their left side followed by a steady procession of cars.

"Now what?" Sinker asked as Punk honked and flashed his lights at Pugsly to no avail.

"Ram him," Kosher suggested. "That'll get his attention."

"And damage *Sweet Belle?*" Punk said with faux indignation. He glanced down at the van's trip odometer. "We've gone thirty-five miles. He's got to be about ready to run out of gas."

"Maybe he filled the car up on the way out of town," Sinker suggested.

"I doubt he'd stop to fill up in his birthday suit," Punk said. "Besides, the fuel gauge is stuck at three-quarters full, and the last time I looked at the index card there were only about thirty miles left on this tank."

"Index card?" Kosher asked.

"Yeah. There's an index card strapped with rubber bands to the visor on the driver's side. Every time we fill the car up we write the odometer reading down on the card. One hundred and twenty miles later, we fill the tank up again. Pugsly probably thought he was fine on gas when he started, and now he either hasn't noticed the level isn't going down or he thinks that car gets awesome gas mileage."

Punk had no sooner finished his statement than the convertible's lights flickered and went out. Pugsly kept the car on the road until he was almost stopped but then used the last bit of momentum to move onto the right shoulder.

Punk parked behind the car, turned on the van's emergency flashers, and bathed *Sweet Belle*'s transom and Pugsly's pink upper back in the brightness of the high beams. The replacements started to bail out of the doors on the right side of the van, but Punk stopped them.

He approached the left side of the car like a lawman. "Pugsly, it's me, Punk. Where are you going?"

Kosher leaned out the passenger window and yelled, "Did he say why he's naked?"

"I'm not naked," Pugsly said without shifting his blank stare from the steering wheel. "I took my shirt off because I was hot."

Punk leaned against the driver's side door. "Where are you going?"

Pugsly let out a long sigh. "North, I guess. Away. They pulled my wings, you know."

"Yeah, I know."

"Now the car broke down—"

"It didn't break down, Pugsly. You ran out of gas."

Pugsly slowly moved his arm and tapped on the fuel gauge. "I have three-quarters of a tank left."

"The gauge is broken. I'll be right back." Punk walked back to the right side of the van and told Kosher to turn the van around and back it up to the car.

Kosher moved behind the wheel and did as the lieutenant ordered while Punk untied the rope securing the convertible's trunk. He fished around inside the compartment, barely able to make anything out with only the van's reverse lights to see by. After several seconds of feeling along the contours of the trunk, he produced a length of rubber hose and a wooden dowel.

Kosher shut off the van and jumped out as Punk twisted off the van's gas cap and ran one end of the hose into the tank. After removing *Sweet Belle*'s gas cap, he put the other end of the hose in his mouth and began sucking until he sensed gas was flowing then aimed the hose to the ground. Once fuel started pouring out he slid the end into the car's tank.

"You're stealing gas from a Navy van?" Sinker said.

"It's an emergency," Punk explained. "Besides, this car is almost an official Navy vehicle. It's not stealing; it's transferring."

"You're too good at that not to have done it before."

"I've learned it's best not to criticize a man for being good at something."

Every few minutes Punk ran the dowel deep through the tank's opening, next to the siphoning hose. Once he felt the stick hit the bottom of the tank he pulled it out and read it using the light from the van's cabin lamp. After several readings gas was licking at the "seven" notch carved into the dowel, so Punk pulled the hose out of the van's tank and ran the dregs through and into the convertible. "Seven gallons," Punk announced. "That'll get us back to Key West." He threw the hose and dowel back into the trunk and tied it shut. "The van's still fat on gas. You three drive it back to the BOQ. Pugsly and I will head back in the car."

"Do you want us to follow you?" Kosher asked.

"No. Just wait until I get the car started and then you guys can go ahead. If you don't see us at the BOQ in an hour or so, organize a search party."

Punk opened the driver's door. "Move over," he ordered Pugsly, who was still vegetating behind the wheel. "And put your shirt on. I don't want people to think I'm driving around with a naked dude riding shotgun. That's how rumors get started."

The convertible fired up on the second twist of the ignition. The replacements in the van saw the car's lights come on and sped off to the south in a cloud of dust. Punk did a U-turn, and by the time he was headed south, he could barely make out the van's taillights in the distance. A minute later he couldn't see them at all.

It was a great night for driving a convertible, even a dinosaur of a convertible, and Punk breathed the sea breeze and took in the stars from horizon to horizon. The engine tapped a sturdy eight-cylinder cadence, and the radio played old-time country, the only station the set's aging AM crystals allowed.

"What was your game plan, Robert?" Punk asked with the hope that using Pugsly's given name might calm him enough to engage in conversation. "Where were you going?"

Pugsly didn't answer. He rolled his head back over the headrest and exhaled with a whoosh in exasperation. Punk considered pressing him, but he remembered how the young officer had exploded that night in his apartment.

Pugsly finally broke what had been a ten-minute silence between them: "You know, my father actually answered the phone this afternoon. That was the first time since he found out about the midair. I called him from the duty desk after you told me Muddy's jet had rolled off by itself, and I was talking to his answering machine, telling how another pilot had the same thing happen to her that I had happen to me, and he suddenly picked up. We talked for a while, you know; activity around the duty desk had died down to nothing. No sooner did I hang up than the phone rang again with Captain Williamson on the line to tell me that I'd lost my wings. I wasn't sure what to do, so I called my dad back and got the machine again and relayed the news, and this time he didn't pick up."

"Maybe he'd walked out of the room," Punk suggested.

"No—no. He was there. He screens his calls. Done it for years. There are a lot of people he doesn't want to talk to, and now I'm back to being one of them." Pugsly reached down to his ankle and pulled a pack of cigarettes out of his sock. "Want one?"

"No thanks. I don't smoke."

"Of course you don't." Pugsly leaned in to the windshield and cupped his hands around the tip of the cigarette. His face glowed orange for a second, and then he leaned back in the seat and released a long plume of smoke. "My father smoked when it was in, and now he judges those who smoke. He's a *leader,* you know." He looked over at Punk for the first time during the southbound leg of this trip. "Have you read his book?"

"Yes."

"What did you think of it?"

"I enjoyed it. I read it while I was at the Naval Academy, junior year, I think."

"It's mostly bullshit, you know. I've combed through the official reports of all four of those flights. None of them mentioned the swirling dogfights portrayed in his book. All but one of the North Vietnamese MiGs didn't even know he was there. And this wives' tale about the showdown with the great Russian pilot Igor Nobolev, it's conjecture at best." He took another long drag on his cigarette. "Think about it. Four flights and you can spend the rest of your days as a keynote speaker and expert on military affairs."

"Yeah, but those were four pretty incredible flights. Especially the one where he bagged *two* guys."

"You can believe what you want. Everybody needs a hero, I guess."

"Who's yours?"

Pugsly looked away, out the right side of the car and over the scrub brush to the water. "I don't have any heroes."

"I thought you said everybody needs a hero."

"I should've said *most* everybody. After being force-fed a hero for my whole life I've developed a mental block toward the concept of them. Heroes are just people with good timing; goats like me are people with exceptionally shitty timing. Life comes down to being in the right or wrong place at the right or wrong time."

The conversation died. They rolled through the night and back into the outskirts of civilization, past the last chance sundries stores and the seafood shacks, the timeshares and the two-bit marinas. The lights of Key West crept into view.

Punk heard a noise, a high-pitched whine that sounded like air leaking out of a tire, and as he keyed on the sound, he realized that Pugsly was weeping. Punk feigned interest in the road painted by the convertible's dim headlights until the sobs grew so loud that it became impossible not to acknowledge them.

"What's wrong now?" Punk asked.

"Maybe I did move the stick," Pugsly moaned. "They didn't find anything wrong with the jet. Maybe I'm getting exactly what I deserve." He forced a wet, disturbed chortle through the tears. "Hell, maybe I'm getting off easy. Losing my wings? I should be charged with manslaughter."

With that, Punk swerved onto the shoulder and skidded the convertible to a halt. He threw his door open and flew out. "Get out of the car," he commanded, momentarily glowing in the headlights as he strode around the front of the vehicle toward the passenger side. "Get out of the fucking car, Pugsly."

Pugsly's eyes tracked him, but the younger officer remained in place. Punk reached in and balled one fist into Pugsly's right sleeve and the other into his left collar. The lieutenant pulled his junior out of the car, stood him up, and threw him across the door—an impressive feat considering the two men were nearly the same size, albeit Punk was made of more sculpted stuff. The emotion welling out of him at the moment was worth twenty pounds of advantage or more. Pugsly's cigarette was jarred from his mouth, and it tumbled across his shirt in small explosions of ash before hitting the dirt.

"Did you move the stick?" Punk asked, bringing his face toward Pugsly's while shaking him in time to the meter of the question. "Answer me! Did you move the stick?"

"No," Pugsly replied, reaching up defensively and grabbing Punk's wrists. "No, I didn't."

"Then shut the fuck up." He released Pugsly's shirt and took several steps away from the car. "You've got a lot of balls lecturing me about what life is. And I don't give a shit about you living in your dad's shadow and how he won't answer the phone. I'm not a social worker, Pugsly. I didn't run you down because I care . . ."

Punk paced and kicked at the gravel under his feet as he gathered his thoughts. "Here's life: We're joined in this thing whether we like it or not, you and me. We didn't choose this situation, but here we are. I lost my best friend; you lost a classmate. And now you've lost your wings. Can either of us do anything about it?"

"I guess not."

"*You guess not.* Well, I'll tell you one thing you can do: You can stop this victim routine. I know these last few months have sucked for you, waiting for the mishap to work itself out, but now that's over. You can't escape what's happened by driving into the sunset at forty-three miles per hour." Punk cast his index finger repeatedly at Pugsly. "Something tells me you're telling the truth when you say you didn't move the stick that day, but you make it hard for me to follow through with that instinct when you act like an irrational little shit.

"And now Muddy's in it, too. You remember Muddy, right? Your classmate? When she had the uncommanded roll-off, she cracked open the NATOPS and tried to figure out what might cause an airplane to roll off without a pilot's input. And her life's not all roses right now, either. She's going before a performance board in the next few days, a board that could recommend she be removed from RAG training. But regardless of that, tomorrow afternoon I'm flying a confidence hop on the jet that Muddy flew today to see if—"

Punk was interrupted by the clipped whoop of a siren, and the two naval officers were suddenly awash in a swirl of red and blue lights as a police car pulled up behind them. They shielded their eyes and watched a silhouette emerge from the cruiser and step toward them.

"Is there a problem, gentlemen?" the shadow asked in a deep voice with a southern accent.

"No, officer," Punk replied. "We just stopped to take care of something."

The shadow moved closer until it blocked the blinding light from behind it, and Punk was able to make out a portly man with a bushy snow-white mustache. He wore a dark uniform and a Smokey Bear hat that looked several sizes too small. "You know public urination is a crime in Florida."

"Oh, we weren't urinating, sir. We were just talking."

"Talking, huh?" He leaned down and studied the convertible's rear license plate. "This plate's expired."

"Oh, yes sir. We were going to take care of that tomorrow. You see, we just got back in the state from—"

"May I see your driver's license and the car's registration?" He pointed to Pugsly. "And sir, can I have you put your hands on the car while this gentleman produces those items?"

"Why?" Pugsly asked. "I haven't done anything."

"Just do it, dammit," Punk seethed as he reached for his wallet. He found his license and handed it over. "I think the registration is in the glove box."

The trooper followed Punk with his flashlight as the fighter pilot walked the few steps back to the passenger side of the car and opened the glove compartment. The box was empty, as Punk suspected it might be.

"I don't have the registration, officer," Punk announced matter-of-factly, as if that fact eclipsed the requirement that the vehicle have proof of registration.

The trooper ran the beam across each of them and then studied Punk's license. "I'm afraid I'm going to have to ask you two to sit in the back of my squad car while I run your plates."

Pugsly started another protest but Punk grabbed him by his biceps and ushered him into the back of the cruiser. Punk was struck by the smell of body odor, breath mints, and a slight hint of vomit. The trooper climbed behind the wheel and proceeded to tap on a keypad mounted in front of the center of the dashboard.

With fingers laced through the cage that separated the front and back seats, Punk attempted to peer at the small screen as the trooper typed and nodded and hummed, but the big man's beefy right shoulder blocked his view.

"Are you the owner of the vehicle, sir?" the trooper turned around and asked Punk.

"Ah, no, not really."

"Are you?" he asked Pugsly.

"No, he's not either," Punk said before Pugsly could get a word out.

"Do you know who the owner is?"

Punk gave the trooper a pained expression and then shook his head. "I'm not sure who the *owner* owner is. It's sort of jointly owned."

"Jointly owned, huh?" The trooper plucked the handset out of its bracket on the dashboard. "Dispatch, this is two-five."

"Go ahead, two-five," a static-laced female voice responded.

"I need a tow truck at milepost twelve for an impound. Tell Milo it'll be a light yellow convertible sedan. Older model. Looks like a Buick."

"It's an Oldsmobile," Punk said. "And you're impounding it?"

"Standard procedure. You're driving an unregistered car that you can't prove you own."

"Where will you take it?"

"Milo's Salvage in Key West. You can pick it up there once you prove the car belongs to you . . . and once you update the registration."

"Where are you taking us?"

"To Florida State Police station."

"Are we under arrest?" Pugsly asked.

"Did I read you your rights?"

"No."

"Then you're not under arrest. I assume you're headed to Key West and would rather not walk the rest of the way. Once we get through the paperwork you can catch a taxi from the station or get one of your *friends* to pick you up." Punk noted the strange emphasis the cop put on the word "friends."

The trooper pushed the accelerator to the floor and fishtailed back onto the highway. "You know, I can't say as I approve of your folks' lifestyle, but I've dealt with a lot of your type over the years down here; hell, it's impossible not to run into you guys around these parts. But my point is, even though you come down here and spend a lot of money and do your thing or whatever, you've still got to obey the laws of the state of Florida and the department of motor vehicles. There's no getting around that no matter which way your gate swings."

"I think you've got the wrong impression, sir," Punk explained. "We're not gay; we're in the Navy."

"Whatever you all are calling it these days is up to you. I tend to mind my own business except when it comes to enforcing the law."

Punk glanced over at Pugsly before putting his head in his hands. "I'd like to thank you for this."

"You should've let me go. I didn't ask you to chase me down."

"Don't start, Pugsly. Do not start."

They rode in silence for five miles, each staring out his respective window. Punk ran the events of a long day through his mind and then returned to the image of awakening next to Anita. Actually, he'd awakened *under* Anita, and thoughts of her pierced his melancholy just enough to keep him from choking Pugsly.

"Did you say you were flying a confidence hop tomorrow?" Pugsly asked out of nowhere, shifting his focus from outside his window to Punk.

"Yes."

Pugsly nodded his head slowly. "Not that it's going to change much," he said, "but did Muddy come up with anything after digging into the NATOPS?"

"She thinks it might have something to do with the digital flight control system, the computers."

"So how does that affect your game plan for tomorrow's flight?"

"My game plan?"

"Yeah. How are you going to check the computers?"

"The usual way, I guess."

Pugsly laughed hollowly and gazed back through the glass, eyes seeing but unfocused on the outlines of trees flashing by. "Good-bye, little ray of sunshine."

Before attending the mandatory course rules brief upstairs in the hangar's main briefing room with the rest of the squadron's aviators, Punk passed through the maintenance spaces searching for someone who might be able to elucidate the digital flight control system to him beyond what his cursory readings of NATOPS had afforded. If he were going to risk his reputation before the company men, he figured he might as well bone up on the only system to which the poorly marked and unofficial trail had led so far. Muddy's question of "How far should our faith leap?" kept replaying in his head, and he remained disquieted that he didn't have an answer.

He walked into the avionics shop and engaged the first man he came across, Avionics Electronics Technician First Class Pelligro Martinez, in a discussion about DFCS. "All I know is what the digital control panel readout tells me, sir," the diminutive petty officer explained in his thick Hispanic accent. "If the readout doesn't display abnormal fault codes during the built-in test on start-up, if I get a 'go' light, I assume the system's working fine."

"Do you guys have the ability to test computers here in the shop?" Punk asked.

Petty Officer Martinez grimaced as if the lieutenant was suddenly speaking in a foreign tongue. "No, sir. The software loads are installed at the factory." He went over to one of the many storage shelves in the space, grabbed a toaster-sized black box, and placed it on the workbench near where Punk was standing. "This is a pitch computer, but the system's the same for the roll and yaw computers. This sticker right here tells us everything we need to know at the squadron level about whether this box is ready to be put into a jet or not. You can see that it has OFP, operational flight program, four-point-five installed, which is the right software load, and that it's RFI, ready for issue. That's as good as it gets."

"Any chance that there could be a problem that wouldn't give you a fault code?"

The sailor winced again. "No, sir." He snatched a small manual off of an adjacent table and flipped through the pages. "Here is a listing of all the fault codes and what they mean."

"Is it the same list as the one we carry in the airplane with us?"

"Yep. It covers everything: wing rock suppression, spin suppression, roll rate gyro input, pilot strain force, stick strain force . . . everything."

Punk ran his hand across the smoothness of the top of the computer. "Who's responsible for developing and updating the software?"

"The manufacturer, I guess." The petty officer studied the label. "These computers are made by Raynotec Defense Industries."

"Corky McBride's company, huh?"

"Yeah." The sailor laughed. "He's always in here. Not a bad guy, though."

Punk smiled noncommittally. "How often is the software updated?"

"It depends. There's no special time frame, really."

"How do you know when it's been updated?"

"The Naval Air Systems Command puts out a message, an avionics change bulletin."

"When's the last time that happened?"

"DFCS is a new system. It's only been around a couple of years, and I don't think the software has ever changed." The sailor scooped up the pitch computer and returned it to the rack. "Have you ever had any problems with it, sir?"

"No, not really," Punk replied a bit defensively, thrown off guard by the sudden question in return.

"Then why all the interest, if you don't mind my asking, sir?"

"Just curious." Punk extended his hand. "Thanks for your time."

"No problem, sir," Petty Officer Martinez said as they shook. "I love talking about my specialty." Punk started to walk out of the shop, but the sailor stopped him. "Oh, sir, you know both shifts were here for a few extra hours last night working off the gripe that the female pilot wrote."

"Yeah, I heard. I'm sorry about that, but what are you going to do, right? The airplane rolled off without her moving the stick."

"Right . . . we didn't find anything wrong with the jet."

"I heard that, too."

"We tore that bird apart. Didn't find a thing."

"Okay . . ."

"Well, we got word that you wanted to do another flight on the jet to check it out."

"Yes, I do."

The petty officer's head dropped. "Sir, it's not that we think you don't trust us or anything like that . . ."

"This confidence hop has nothing to do with my trust in you guys," Punk explained.

"Yeah, I know that, I guess. That's not what I meant to say, really." He picked up the codebook again and studied it at close range. "Everybody's got to trust something, right, sir? I trust things like this book." He spoke slower now, picking each word very carefully. "This little book of codes . . . it's like my Bible."

Punk silently wrestled with the analogy before responding quietly, nearly to himself: "That codebook was put together by men, not God."

"*Smart* men."

"But men, all the same. And humans aren't perfect." The lieutenant moved toward the door again, offering one last comment before heading upstairs to the brief: "I promise you this: If I write a gripe after my flight today, I'll be loaded with a lot more evidence than Lieutenant (j.g.) Greenwood had."

Petty Officer Martinez smiled politely and rendered a cheerful wave, the sort that NASA scientists gave the first astronauts before they buttoned up the hatches over them. "That's all we can ask, sir."

"Go" glowed brightly from the digital flight control panel under Punk's right arm as he stepped through the poststart checks. The LED readout taunted him with its clarity, joining the chorus of naysayers and detractors echoing in his head. He stared at the readout as if that might change the result and was hit with the fact that he was disappointed the airplane was working right, an impulse that gave him pause. While waiting for Spud to finish prepping the rear cockpit for the mission, Punk reviewed the series of events that had allied him with not one but two coneheads, both with checkered reputations. He remembered the discussion he'd had with Scuzz, the maintenance officer, earlier in the day, immediately following the course rules brief.

"I know what I agreed to yesterday, Punk," Scuzz had said, "but now I don't have enough jets to support your little experiment. We lost two airplanes during the daily inspections this morning. We've got six sorties on the first event alone. I need every available jet to meet the rest of the flight schedule, and that includes the one you wanted to take on the confidence hop."

So Punk persuaded Spud to modify the flight schedule, switching the two of them for Widget and Smitty on a one-on-one air combat maneuvering flight, the first flight in the RAG's tactics syllabus, with Stormin' and Flex on their wing, before he persuaded Scuzz to assign them the jet in question in the name of compromise. Scuzz made it a point to say he didn't owe Punk a compromise but would accommodate his request anyway.

Punk fashioned a plan where he and Spud would launch ten minutes early and attempt to recreate the roll-off. If Punk couldn't recreate the roll-off, they were going to assume the jet was fine and meet Stormin' at the briefed rendezvous point to complete the syllabus event.

Now, two hours later, Punk patiently sat with his arms along the canopy rails and tallied the growing number of shit lists he was at the top of, including all the instructor lieutenants' for getting the convertible impounded during his humanitarian rescue mission. None of them had bought the idea that it was Pugsly's fault because everyone now knew that Pugsly was insane as well as self-centered and argumentative.

"Inertial nav is aligned; everything looking good back here," Spud passed over the intercom. "I'm ready to taxi."

"Here we go then," Punk replied. He waved at the plane captain and gave him the signal to pull the chocks away from the wheels, a hitchhiking motion with both hands, thumbs pointed outward. The enlisted man disappeared under the jet briefly and then reappeared, flashing a thumbs-up before waving his arms in the signal for the pilot to taxi forward.

After negotiating the maze of taxiways between the RAG's ramp and the active runway, they sat in the hold short for a few minutes waiting for a division of Florida Air National Guard F-16s to land. "Thanks for springing me out of the pokey last night, Spud," Punk said into the mask dangling from the right side of his helmet.

"Hey, don't thank me," Spud returned. "That was really *fun,* especially the part where the cop thought I was the matron of our little group." Punk laughed and strapped the loose bayonet fitting from his oxygen mask to the other side of his helmet as the tower controller cleared them to take off.

Half a minute later they were knifing through the cerulean early afternoon Key West sky, another example of why the RAG traveled so far south to conduct the tactics phase. Back in Virginia Beach a couple of summer thunderstorms could wreck flight schedules for days and get replacements behind training timelines. Two weeks in Key West would get the average-sized RAG class through tactics with a few ACM range periods to spare, although with Lucky losing his life, Pugsly losing his wings, and Muddy awaiting a performance board, there wasn't much of a worry about getting replacements enough time in the air. Class Two had dwindled to well below average size.

"Three pilots," Spud intoned over the intercom as Punk raised the Tomcat's nose a few more degrees above the horizon on their way to fifteen thousand feet. "This class is down to three goddam pilots."

"I hate to break you out of your funk," Punk said, "but I'm about to go through a series of steps that could send this jet tumbling out of control. Are you ready for this?"

"I guess. Although I have no idea what *this* is."

"That makes two of us." Punk pushed the throttles forward while bunting the nose level. "Lock your harness. Accelerating to three hundred and fifty knots . . . level flight . . . sweeping the wings back . . . now." He grimaced behind his mask and visor in anticipation of something extraordinary happening.

But nothing did. The wings swept fully aft and the F-14 didn't budge from where Punk had commanded it.

"You'll tell me once the jet starts to do something you don't want it to do, right?" Spud asked.

"Yes," Punk seethed. "I'm going to drop down low and try again. Pressure altitude might be a factor. Both of the roll-offs happened at fifteen hundred feet."

"We're at the rendezvous point, Punk," Flex reported over the squadron common frequency.

"We'll be with you in five minutes," Punk said. He moved the wings forward, rolled the jet inverted, and dove down to fifteen hundred feet.

"This is it, Spud," he said, leveling off and recapturing three hundred and fifty knots on the airspeed indicator. "All the variables from yesterday are matched: same altitude, same airspeed, same airplane. If anything's going to happen, it'll happen here." He took a deep draw on the 100 percent oxygen flowing into his mask. "I'm sweeping the wings . . . now."

He eased his grip on the stick hoping a lighter touch

might help him perceive what the gremlins might be doing to the fighter. Nothing. Not even the slightest bump of turbulence through the controls. He triggered the test on the digital flight control panel and was greeted by another bright "go" light, denied the satisfaction of even the most minor fault code. In his mind's eye he saw Muddy looking across the table at the Three Wire with enviable moxie, and that image morphed into Pugsly weeping about how he might have moved the stick after all.

"Are we done?" Spud asked cautiously.

"Punk is headed for the rendezvous point," Punk said, an indirect answer over squadron common to Spud's question.

"Roger," Flex replied. "How did your little test go?" Punk refrained from answering while in his head Pugsly's face was replaced with Flex's, complete with shit-eating grin. "Punk," Flex prodded, "anything wrong with your jet?"

"Punk is headed for the rendezvous point."

"All right," Flex said, getting the hint. "We're at fifteen thousand feet in a left-hand turn."

Spud thumbed the antenna into the correct piece of sky, then pulled the trigger on his joystick, locking the radar onto the contact, which caused a diamond to appear in Punk's HUD. Punk squinted through the shape and spotted a black dot above them, seven miles away but closing fast.

"Punk's tally. Stormin', go ahead and steady up to the west. Verify air combat maneuvering checks are complete."

"ACM checks complete," Stormin' replied.

"Remember, sticks and stones only on the first two engagements." Sticks and stones referred to short-range Sidewinder heat-seeking missiles and guns respectively. Limiting pilots to those weapons ensured the victor would have to work for the kill.

"Copy, sticks and stones."

Once they were two miles apart, Punk matched the other Tomcat's heading. He shot one last glance at the digital control panel before transmitting: "Speed and angels on the left."

"Speed and angels on the right."

"Fight's on."

Punk rolled sharply to the right while Stormin' did the same to the left. Both pilots pulled their sticks toward their laps while grunting against the onset of six-plus times the normal pull of gravity. After ninety degrees of turn by each F-14, they were nose on, closing at over eight hundred knots.

"Left to left," Punk said, defining how they should pass, left side to left side.

"Left to left," Stormin' echoed.

The merge was where a fighter pilot's mind fired at light speed and every synapse buzzed with the possibilities around winning and losing, like what a sprinter feels when he moved into the blocks before the gun goes off, except the fighter pilot has less time to consider his near-term fate. The two jets passed in a heartbeat, one hundred and eighty degrees out and five hundred feet apart, and all of the possibilities were reduced to the first move.

A good first move synthesized a host of variables including guessing what the opponent might do as a first move. Punk had informally studied the Class Two pilots since their arrival at the RAG, building a mental file of the likely direction each would go at the merge. Dusty Rhodes and Auto Ford were quiet, conservative types, guys who'd each hit the merge too slow to do anything but bury the nose straight down to get speed back on his jet. Muddy was indecisive due to her lack of confidence and usually a bit behind the situation; Punk's book had her first move as a simple horizontal turn.

A frenetic bundle of fret like Stormin', with darting eyes and birdlike mannerisms, was going to arrive at the merge with big knots and take his jet into the vertical—and so he did. Punk kept his eyes on the other Tomcat, twisting his torso against his right shoulder strap and throwing his chin over his left shoulder as the opponent raged past his wing line. Punk already had presaged the replacement's climb, putting his own jet on its back a second earlier and then pulling hard on the stick while pulling the throttles out of afterburner. "I'm on the gauges," he grunted over the intercom to Spud.

"Roger. I'm padlocked," Spud replied, head torqued backward like an owl's, straining but still seeing Stormin' and Flex climbing toward the sun as his own pilot swung the nose of their fighter across the water, now thirteen thousand feet below them and closing fast.

Experience gave instructors the dogfighting edge over the replacements they trained, but the odds on this particular event were even more skewed. The coordination between Punk and Spud was forged in the skies over southern Iraq and responsibilities fluidly passed between them. Spud continued to watch between the Tomcat's twin tails while Punk's eyes danced across the altimeter, the airspeed indicator, and the angle of attack gauge.

Spud was like a conscience as he fed Punk information just as he needed it, another bit of synergy gleaned from hundreds of hours under the canopy together. As the nose met the horizon after digging through the bottom of the loop and Punk pushed the throttles back to full afterburner, Spud started calling his pilot's eyes onto their opponent. "On the lift vector, plan form over the top."

"Blind."

"Keep the pull coming. Roll left. Stop. He's coming downhill now. No threat. Left of the sun."

"Tally."

When the two jets passed the second time Punk had an angular bite on Stormin' but not enough to take a shot. The replacement had already survived his first engagement longer than most. At the second merge both pilots duplicated their original moves, but as the second iteration continued, Punk was able to bring his nose to bear as Stormin' was still coming over the top of his loop.

"Out of burner. Flares, flares, flares," the replacement called over the radio, indicating he was both reducing the amount of heat pouring out of his engines and simulating the use of heat-seeking missile decoys. Although Stormin' obviously had mismanaged the first half of his second turn, Punk was impressed both that the replacement hadn't lost sight of him and that he recognized he was in a position to absorb a Sidewinder.

"Good flares," Punk said. "Continue."

Stormin' quickly squandered Punk's mercy, and after ninety more degrees of turn with the instructor saddled in behind the replacement, Punk called, "Knock it off; set up another one. Punk's gas is at seven-point-zero."

"Stormin' has nine-point-zero."

As they climbed back to fifteen thousand feet and got their jets back to speed, all four of the aviators drew diagrams and scribbled notes about the first engagement on cards tacked to the kneeboards strapped around their thighs. "Recall" was a graded item on the replacement's performance sheet. Though each Tomcat transmitted a signal that eventually turned it into a computer-generated shape on giant screens in the tactical air combat training range facility next to the hangar, replacements were inculcated in the art of dogfighting hieroglyphics. Instructors took great pride in what pilots could remember during the debrief based on a few squiggles and a little shorthand. The pilots interrupted their work every few seconds to look up and ensure they weren't about to fly into each other. Between peeks outside Punk scribed a couple of arrowheaded lines replicating the fight, labeled one "P" and the other "S" and wrote "arcing" under the spaghetti to cue him that Stormin' had been less than efficient with his last turn.

Both pilots checked their G meters to verify they hadn't overstressed their jets beyond the Tomcat's six-and-a-half G limit as they climbed back up to fifteen thousand feet. Punk also ran the DFCS system test yet again and was greeted by another "go" light.

"I think we've got enough gas for one more," Punk said. "Speed and angels on the right."

"Speed and angels on the left," Stormin' replied.

"Fight's on."

Punk entered the second engagement with an eye on Stormin's learning curve. Flex was certainly throwing in his two cents from the replacement's backseat, but dogfight execution was ultimately up to the pilot. "Right to right," Punk said, realizing that Stormin' had made a better turn this time.

"Right to right," Stormin' returned.

The replacement showed he wasn't married to the vertical move after the merge by throwing his Tomcat into a left-hand horizontal turn. Punk decided to take the fight "one circle" and slapped the stick against his right thigh until he was in a ninety-degree angle of bank. He pulled to six and a half Gs and raked the nose across the horizon while looking through the top of the canopy at Stormin', while Stormin' mirrored him, scribing an equal and opposite flight path.

"Three hundred knots," Spud said the moment Punk

wondered what his airspeed was. Punk eased his pull a hair, neutralizing his slight advantage on the replacement, testing the younger pilot's endurance. They merged again, neither with angles on the other, and then again after another one hundred and eighty degrees of crushing turn.

Stormin' was doing a good job moving his airplane, but as they passed the fourth time, he ran out of patience. Punk worked his best turn and craned over his right shoulder, huffing now like an athlete well into a contest, sweat running down his face and pooling along the edges of his mask, and he saw Stormin's jet suddenly go straight up. Punk knew what the younger pilot was trying to do; he also knew the conehead didn't have enough smack on the jet to make it work.

Flex barely had time to say "no" over the intercom before watching their airspeed bleed to zero. Stormin' jammed the throttles into full afterburner, kicked the rudders like a baby kicking the air, and put the stick against all four corner stops, futilely beating the stillness around the surfaces of the Tomcat, then succumbed to the fact that the jet had stopped flying for the moment. With Flex's call of "lock your harness," the replacement defaulted to the procedures ingrained over the course of a dozen periods in the simulator: He moved the stick to the middle, pulled the throttles smoothly to idle, and waited for gravity to do with them what it would.

Punk filled his windscreen with the other Tomcat and watched the jet swap ends a couple of times before regaining enough speed for Stormin's inputs to matter. Punk closed to twelve hundred feet and moved his weapons select switch to guns. Snakebit by the violence of the departure, Stormin' milked the stick, meekly attempting to mitigate his folly. He cried, "Flares, flares, flares," but those words gave him no sanctuary now.

Punk sweetened his solution and transmitted: "Trigger down—tracking—guns, guns, guns. Good kill. Knock this one off." He released one side of his oxygen mask from his helmet then made notes on his kneeboard card while turning the flight to the east.

Punk smiled slyly and keyed the radio again, but Spud interrupted him: "Hold it," the RIO said over the intercom. "You're not going to say, 'Here endeth the lesson,' are you?"

" 'Here endeth the lesson'? How many flights have we flown together now? When have I ever said, 'Here endeth the lesson' over the radio or anywhere else for that matter?"

"I don't know. I just had a feeling you were going to say it."

"Give me a little credit, please." Punk rekeyed the front seat UHF radio: "For the record, Stormin', flares don't work very well against bullets." Punk checked his mirror and saw Spud grimace and shake his head.

During the flight back to Key West, Punk didn't think to test the digital flight controls or worry whether the jet might roll without his input. For now it felt good to be a fighter pilot. Once on the ground that feeling was muted slightly when he was met back at the entrance to the hangar by Corky's client-pleasing visage.

"Well?" the tech rep asked.

"Well what?" Punk returned as he pushed by on his way to the maintenance counter.

"I assume the jet worked all right."

"Yeah, it worked all right."

"No problems?"

"No."

"No roll-offs?"

Punk stopped and turned back toward Corky. "No. No roll-offs."

"Good." Corky unfolded his arms. "So what do you think?"

"What do I think about what?"

"Are we on the same team again?"

Punk's eyes went to the tile around his flight boots. "You tell me."

Corky straightened up from his comfortable slouch against the doorframe. "What's that supposed to mean?"

"It means the jet didn't roll off this time. Maybe I'm overwhelmed by my new and growing sense of paranoia, but something tells me there's still a problem out there." Punk shifted his stare back to Corky's face. "Is there?"

Corky snickered. "You *are* paranoid."

"Then you have your answer. We're still not on the same team."

CHAPTER EIGHT

"He's not being committed," the little flight surgeon explained, slanted eyes peering over his reading glasses in an affectation that reminded Punk of the obligatory wise man in a kung fu movie. "He's being sent to Portsmouth for an evaluation."

"A *psychiatric* evaluation," Punk said from the other chair in front of Spud's desk in the detachment operations office, a space so battered and spartanly appointed it made their worn office at Oceana look luxurious by comparison.

"Yes. But let me remind you that you're not supposed to know about it."

"So you think he's crazy?"

"*I* don't think anything."

"So the doctors at Portsmouth think he's crazy."

"They don't think anything . . . not yet, anyway."

"Then why is he being sent to Portsmouth for a psychiatric evaluation?"

"Punk, you've seen it firsthand, better than anybody in this squadron," Spud said, bony hands aligning the edges of one of the stacks of paper that surrounded his coffee-stained blotter. "You've got to admit Pugsly's behavior hasn't been exactly normal lately. This is for his own good."

"Yes," the flight surgeon agreed. "In many ways his flight north last night was like a muted suicide gesture." Punk watched the "fighter Doc" opine and reflected on the gallery of doctors he'd dealt with over the years. To a man and one woman they'd assimilated into the culture, fashion-

ing themselves as aviators who happened to have medical
degrees. They'd stop by the ready room to scam backseat
rides and dispense eight-hundred-milligram Motrin tablets
like breath mints, assuaging the fears of aviators inherently
suspicious of those who could end a flying career with a
stroke of a pen across a down chit.

But during his two years as the RAG's flight surgeon,
Lieutenant Arnold Yee, United States Naval Reserve, Medical Corps, had shown he wasn't interested in a supporting
role on the fighter pilots' stage, and that was unsettling to the
fighter pilots. Instead of offering the wink that said his highest
calling was keeping aviators airborne, he obtusely interro-
gated them and tacitly broadcast that each of their ills was a
building block toward the breakthrough cure he intended to
find. They punished him by keeping him off the flight schedule as much as possible, but Doc Yee read the aviators' actions not as punishment but rather as respect for how
important his work around the medical spaces was.

"Taking flight in that car last night might seem like an
innocuous act," Yee continued, "but it's a textbook call for
help. However, we're very fortunate. I've arranged for him
to be seen by Captain Shaphanvaradin Dharghaman." The
doc paused as if that name would mean something to the
two aviators in the room. "He's the naval hospital's leading
mental health physician."

"Anyway, Pugsly's flying out on a C-9 in an hour," Spud
said. "He requested you by name to escort him over to
the terminal."

"Me?" Punk asked. "I'm probably the last guy he'd want
to see him off."

"Oh, no, quite the opposite," Doc said. "Your name
came up a number of times during my consult with him
this morning. In fact, you may be the only other officer he
trusts in this command. But, remember, you don't know
about his medical status."

"I don't? Good thing he trusts me . . ."

"He may trust you, but that doesn't mean that you
should trust him," Spud advised. "Have you ever been
trained in how to pat a guy down?"

Between Pugsly's trips to the smoking lounge, Punk and he
sat silently in the terminal's waiting area paging through

old magazines until a fireplug of an enlisted woman dressed in a flight suit strode among the rows of plastic seats bolted to the floor and announced that JR-119, the airlift to Norfolk with intermediate stops in Pensacola and Jacksonville, was manning up. Pugsly gathered his overnight bag and Punk joined him for the short walk across the hot tarmac to the C-9's rear stairway.

They were the last in the line of eleven passengers queued up to get aboard the transport. "I wonder if they'll give me drugs," Pugsly thought aloud, the first words uttered between them since Punk chauffeured him from the hangar an hour ago. "That might be kind of fun, don't you think?" Punk shrugged. Pugsly shrugged back, started up the stairs without any fanfare, but stopped after two steps and looked back down. "I would've made it."

Punk nodded. He wanted to say something upbeat and motivational but nothing came to mind. Pugsly shrugged one more time and continued up the C-9's stairs and into the fuselage. Punk watched him disappear and wondered if he would ever see him again.

"Excuse me, officer," a voice called from behind as Punk opened the door back into the terminal. "Officer? Officer, could you give me some information, please?"

Punk turned around and saw a man moving toward him, struggling under the burden of three pieces of luggage slung across his shoulders. As the man got closer Punk could see the shirt under his blazer was soaked with sweat right through to his bow tie. The bridge of his round-framed glasses had slid to the tip of his nose and threatened to fall off his face altogether. Punk thought he'd seen the man before, but he couldn't immediately place him.

The man winced as he worked the straps of his bags over his head before allowing the bundles to fall to the tarmac with a whack. He worked to catch his breath and pointed toward the C-9. "I just flew in . . . on that transport there. Can you believe . . . a two and a half hour flight . . . with no meal?" He paused for an amen from Punk, and when none came he continued his monologue, uninterrupted now by gasps for air. "It's unbelievable. Not only did I have to drive four hours to get to the base airport in Norfolk, I had to use my own car to get there. Next time I demand a flight out of Andrews Air Force Base or a commercial flight out of Reagan. Are you assigned to this base?"

"For the time being, I guess," Punk replied.

"Anyway, I was told to find . . ." He fished through his shirt pocket and pulled out a folded piece of paper. ". . . the operations officer."

"Which one?"

"There's more than one?"

"Well, yeah. Every squadron has one, and the base has one, too."

"Isn't that typical." The man reached to his hip and produced a cellular phone. "Hello, Myra? This is Ferguson. I'm down in Key West, and I'm not sure where I'm supposed to go. Is Senator Meyers in?"

Now Punk remembered where he'd seen the man before: It had been the day of Muddy's ill-fated FAM-1, and this was the guy who'd been glued to the senator at every turn. Punk put on a poker face as he took a few steps away and turned his back on the man while dialing his own cell phone. "Spud, it's Punk. Are you expecting a visitor from Senator Meyers's office?"

"No."

"I'm pretty sure you've got one."

Punk heard Spud cut the connection. A minute later Spud called back and said, "The skipper's bringing a Tomcat down here tomorrow. We're not starting Greenwood's board without him."

Punk reached the instructors' table in the Bull and Whistle, ushered the congressional staffer in front of him, and pointed his way around the group in a burst of introductions: "Ferguson, I'd like you to meet Flex, Widget, Hammer, Fitz, and Gordo. Gentlemen, this is Ferguson Platt. He's going to be with us for a few days."

The instructors nodded or waved from their seats graciously enough, but their muted enthusiasm told Punk they were already aware of Platt's presence in Key West. There were a couple of empty seats at the table between Gordo and Flex; Punk weighed the options and walked the man over to the empty seat next to the quiet and unopinionated good Protestant Gordo and then sat himself next to Flex.

Undaunted by Punk's subtle attempt at running interference, Flex leaned across him and addressed Platt: "Mr. Platt, what brings you down here?"

"Please," Platt said as he extended his hand in front of Punk toward Flex. "Call me Ferguson."

"Fergie, I'm Flex." Punk saw the staffer wince slightly as he hadn't anticipated one of Flex's bone-crushing handshakes.

"Ferguson," Platt corrected as he drew his hand back and massaged it. "And I'm down here just to observe a few things."

"What things?"

"How you conduct business."

"Oh, how nice." Flex leaned back and whispered, "Are you baby-sitting this guy?" in Punk's ear while Platt turned and introduced himself to Gordo. "Let me have him," Flex said. "I'll make sure he has a good time."

"Or you'll make sure *you* have a good time," Punk replied. "No, I'd better watch him like Spud asked me to."

"Suit yourself. I am allowed to talk to him, right?"

"As long as you mind your manners."

"I'm a fighter guy, Punk," Flex returned with a leer. "I'm not paid for my manners."

The waitress delivered beers to the newcomers, and Flex reengaged with their visitor. "What's it like working for a congressman?"

Platt wiped the foam from his lips with a paper napkin and said, "I don't work for a congressman; I work for a senator."

Flex's head shuddered, and he gave one exaggerated blink as if Platt had squirted him with a water pistol between the eyes. "Okay," Flex said sarcastically, "so what's it like to work for . . . a *senator*?"

Platt's eyes went to one of the ceiling fans hanging above them. "Rewarding and challenging."

"What do you do exactly?"

"I'm the military assistant to Senator Meyers." He immediately corrected himself: "Actually, I'm the assistant to the military assistant."

"Were you in the military?"

"No, not really."

"Not *really*?"

"Well, not at all. I was an intern for another senator while I was working on my M.P.A. at Georgetown, and Senator Meyers happened to read my thesis. She liked it enough to ask me to join her staff."

"That must've been some thesis. What was it about?"

"Women in combat."

The table went silent, and all attention shifted back toward the staffer. They looked at him like Indians, who'd heard of but had never seen a white man, coming across the Pilgrims for the first time, expressions evincing both trepidation and curiosity. The lieutenants had fielded rumors of the species, denizens of Washington—obtuse, naïve, self-absorbed—but until now they'd never seen one of them in real life.

Platt was ignorant of the confrontational air growing around him as he continued to speak, each word more animated than the last. "Anyway, the senator sensed we were kindred spirits once she read my work, and this was even before we realized that we'd both done our undergrad at Cornell. I started working for her, and I haven't looked back since. That was eight years ago, right about the time Senator Meyers first joined the Armed Services Committee."

"What's Senator Meyers's military background?" Widget asked from across the table.

"Very extensive. She started as a White House intern during the Kennedy administration."

"Yeah? What's that got to do with the military?"

"President Kennedy was in the Navy during World War Two." The aviators exchanged bemused expressions. "The senator also made a fact-finding trip to Vietnam during the Johnson years. And as a result of that trip she helped shape George McGovern's military policy during the seventy-two presidential campaign."

Punk studied the man as he spoke. His features were delicate, but at the same time he exuded a confidence that was forceful and intense. He may have been overeducated, but he didn't seem to necessarily suffer fools. He looked like he worked out. He had the rumpled, studied, Ivy League vibe down pat: well-combed, thick black hair, cuffed khakis and oxford shirt with sleeves rolled midway up his forearms—a somewhat affected look that Punk had first been exposed to during his summers as a midshipman gallivanting from one New England port to another, fêted by old money at yacht clubs from Manhattan to Marblehead. They'd all possessed the disingenuous graciousness of those who'd had the utility of the military explained to them with eat-your-peas-because-children-are-starving-in-Africa earnestness by their grandparents, but to whom the concept remained a distant reality.

"Then she worked for the National Security Council during the Carter administration for a while," Platt continued, "until she decided to run for the senate. She's been a senator ever since. Basically, when Eleanor Meyers puts her mind to something, it happens."

"What's her mind on now?" Punk asked.

Platt took a sip of beer. "Equality," he said. "A balance of opportunity."

"Is there some idea that there's an imbalance of opportunity here in Key West?"

Again Platt paused before replying. "Not necessarily."

"Then why are you down here?"

"It's a simple orientation trip." Platt smiled and spread his arms over the table. "And I'm on per diem. Please, allow me to buy the next round."

The aviators glanced at their watches to see where they were relative to the twelve-hour "bottle to brief" window and most nodded in acceptance. One beer was a check in the block after a hard day's flying. Two beers was the first step toward another booming night on Duval Street. As the waitress took their orders they subtly polled each other for first brief times to see who might be in for the evening's long haul. Of the group, only Fitz had the early brief. He took another look at his big watch strapped around his big wrist, yielded to the burden of his commissioning oath and Catholic rearing, and walked out of the bar.

Flex quickly sabotaged Platt's foothold on a congenial air at the table. "So, Fergie," he said, "what exactly did your thesis say about women in combat?"

"It suggested that on the modern battlefield there aren't too many places where a compelling argument can be made for the exclusion of women in combat roles."

"What's your idea of the modern battlefield?"

"Technology has mitigated physical requirements to the

degree that traditional notions of who should fight our wars
are outdated. Take what you guys do, for instance. It
doesn't take that much physical strength to fly a modern
fighter jet, does it?" The aviators' heads shook as if Platt
had simultaneously rabbit punched each one of them.

"It depends what sort of flying you're doing," Punk replied. "Air combat maneuvering takes quite a bit of
strength."

"What's air combat maneuvering?" Platt asked.

"Dogfighting."

"That's a perfect example of an outdated notion," Platt
said, pointing at Punk like he was the focus of a lab experiment. "When would you ever be in a dogfight on the battlefield of the future?"

"When the enemy sends his fighters up to get yours."

Platt chuckled patronizingly. "This is where I have the
advantage of time, access, and research. I would never want
to burden you with the reams of data and point papers I
had to pore through to get my thesis done, nor would I
wish upon you the hours of subcommittee meetings I've
endured with Senator Meyers on military procurement issues, but suffice it to say that modern weaponry will prevent enemy fighters from ever reaching our forces. You'll
never have to dogfight again."

"That's bullshit," Flex said. "Regardless of the technology, in a real war somebody's going to sneak through and
force us to get down and dirty. We prove it every day
in training."

"Then your training techniques are outdated," Platt returned. "In fact, just yesterday I sat through a brief by the
Chairman of the Joint Chiefs of Staff. Not only did he say
military readiness has never been better; he also said that
technology has made warfare a long-range affair."

"Who the hell is the Chairman of the Joint Chiefs of
Staff?" Flex asked.

"General Reginald Palko; you don't know that?"

"No," Flex replied unapologetically. "What service is
he in?"

"Army."

"Well, what the fuck does an Army guy know about
flying fighters? I don't walk around talking out of my ass
about tanks or artillery or whatever the hell else those guys

use." The next round of drinks arrived along with two platters of chicken wings, and the table was momentarily covered by a flurry of arms. "We're getting off of the subject of women in combat. Let me ask you a question, Fergie: Why do we need women in carrier-based squadrons?"

Widget took the floor from across the table. "Let me rephrase my squadronmate's question," he said, mouth already ringed with cayenne pepper sauce. "Does the introduction of the opposite sex into a previously single-gender organization change anything?"

"It shouldn't," Platt said.

"Never mind what it *should* and *shouldn't* do. Does it change anything? Be honest."

"No, not in my experience."

"You've never been in a single-gender organization, have you?"

"Yes, I have."

"Where?"

"Yale law school. When I was on the law review, the staff was all male for a few months. Two females joined us, and it didn't change a thing."

"Law school?" Flex cried. "You went to law school, too? Damn, Fergie, how many years have you wasted studying?"

"I'd hardly call a Yale law degree a waste."

"You've never done anything but study and read and sit in meetings. You call that a life?"

"I've done plenty of things."

"Oh, yeah? Name one thing you've done that would impress the guys at this table."

Platt turned Flex's question on its head: "Why don't you name one thing *you've* done that would impress me?"

Flex unflinchingly began counting accomplishments off on his fingers: "I've hit targets, received medals, broken sound barriers, converted natives, won wars, and cured virgins. You've never done any of that have you?"

"I have broken the sound barrier," Platt said.

"What?"

"I flew on the Concorde to Paris once."

"That counts . . . *not*. You were just a passenger."

Platt considered the logic. "Are you a pilot or a backseater?"

"I'm a RIO, a backseater."

"Then you're just a passenger, too."

"Being a RIO is much different than riding around in an airliner. When I'm in the rear cockpit of a Tomcat I—" Flex saw from the growing smirk on Platt's face that the professional subtleties of his role in the F-14 were going to be lost on the staffer, so he switched tacks. "You've never cured a virgin?"

"Of course I have."

Flex studied the staffer's eyes and shook his head. "I don't see it."

Platt was nonplussed; further, he blushed, which Punk knew was blood in the water for a ball-busting shark like Flex. "I think I hit a nerve," Flex said. "He's turning redder than that catsup bottle there."

"Shots!" Widget and Hammer cried in unison with raised fists as the waitress deposited on the center of the table a tray of small glasses each three-quarter filled with a bright-green liquid. Punk was relieved that the shift in focus spared Platt any more embarrassment for the time being. Widget took it upon himself to distribute the libation and propose a toast: "To dogfights. May they never end."

All remaining, including Platt, raised their glasses and hailed, "To dogfights!" The glasses were emptied with gusto, and as Punk brought his back down he cut a glance to Platt and saw his eyes cross.

The second round of shots was in place seemingly before the tears had dried from the first one. A new Platt, wholly different from the preshot one, rose and slapped the table a few times. "Gentlemen! Gentlemen! I'd like to propose another toast." Already unsteady, he plucked a glass off the tray and raised it. "I'd like to propose a—"

"I've got this one," Flex interrupted, raising his own glass. "I'd like to propose a toast to Fergie's virginity, soon may he lose it."

The other officers stood and echoed the toast: "To Fergie's virginity, soon may he lose it."

"Who s-said I was a v-virgin?" Platt said, fighting a couple of lurches somewhere in his digestive system.

"You did," Flex said. "Your theories scream it."

"You've obviously never partied around Ithaca. My frat did some outrageous things."

"Sure, sure." Flex turned to the others. "Boys, finish

your drinks and settle up. We're taking Ferg to the Pirates' Den."

Punk placed a hand on Platt's shoulder and held him in his seat. "I don't think Ferguson needs to go to the Pirates' Den. We'll just hang here."

"Punk, don't be a pussy," Flex said as he moved toward the staffer. "Few men have so needed to go to the Pirates' Den as Fergie." Before Punk could object further, Flex snatched the civilian to his feet and was out of the Bull with him. The rest of the aviators followed, stringing themselves over half a block between Flex in the lead and Punk as the reluctant final link in the chain.

Punk felt his cellular phone vibrate as he dodged people along the sidewalk. He answered it, knowing full well who was on the other end of the line. "Hello?"

"It's the future Mrs. Reichert calling," Anita sang. "I just wanted to see what you were doing."

I'm headed for a strip club. "I'm escorting this congressional staffer around that's visiting the detachment."

"Oh, that doesn't sound like any fun."

"I'm trying to make the best of it."

"Well, I won't keep you then. I just wanted to ask if you thought we could have the ceremony at the Naval Academy chapel."

Punk wondered when he'd feel the calm that was supposed to inevitably overtake his bachelor's anxiety. "Annapolis is four hours from Virginia Beach, Anita."

"Mom just brought it up, and I told her I'd ask you what you thought about it."

Mom . . . He saw the gaggle was getting close to its destination. "I've got to go. I'll try to call you later, but don't wait up."

"Well, don't be too bored. I love you."

"Love you, too."

The group was nearly rejoined by the time they reached the alley that fed to the entrance of the strip club. Flex lowered a shoulder and burst through the double doors at the entrance of the Pirates' Den with Platt under his other arm. A wall of sound hit them, a heavy metal roar with a low-end thump that could part hair, along with the redolence of stale beer and too-sweet perfume. A big Samoan bouncer waved Flex and Platt through with a bright smile but stopped the others and collected five dollars from each.

Punk noted that Flex seemed to know everyone in the dark place. He exchanged greetings with the patrons and waitresses who dotted the path between the front door and a line of chairs along the near end of the runway that split half the length of the small room. A longhaired biker sort called, "Howdy, Flex" over the din pushing through the house PA and waved from the DJ booth in the far corner, highlighted only by the spotlights that lit the runway.

Once he reached the stage, Flex swept his arm down the row of chairs like a maître d' and then sat down, but not before pulling a handful of bills out of his wallet. The music faded, and the DJ verbally ushered the dancer off the runway and cued the next girl with, "Gentlemen, put your hands together for Amber."

A new song started at the same volume as the last, and a moment later a bikini-clad woman appeared from behind the beaded curtain at the far end of the runway. She grabbed the first of two poles that ran the full height of the room and twirled around it several times, blond tresses flowing freely behind her. The third time around she let go of the pole and shot across the stage like an errant rocket. She leapt up and landed in a split directly in front of Flex, who promptly placed a folded bill in the side strap of her bikini bottom.

The dancer locked eyes with Flex through the volleyball shades he'd put on once they entered the club, and as Punk wondered how much attention five dollars bought, she stood and worked the knots that held up her bikini top, starting with the lower one. Punk furtively glanced over to Platt, and the staffer shifted his bleary eyes to him from the stage beneath the stripper's feet and then leaned over fighting heavy eyelids and slurred, "I shouldn't be here."

A moment among moments of truth over the course of an evening in the Pirates' Den arrived, and as the stripper's top fell, a few of the men raised their arms in praise. Punk's only thought was that the dancer had looked sexier with the top on. She'd obviously had surgery, a turnoff to him, and exceptionally sloppy surgery at that. Her breasts sat like two good-sized flesh-colored grapefruits attached to the front of her, unmoving as she continued to work the floor in front of Flex. The RIO rolled another bill into a tight cylinder and placed it between his teeth. She dropped to her knees, grabbed the money with her cleavage, and leaned over and gave him a closed-mouth but mildly passionate kiss.

Then she stood again and turned her back to the line of aviators and their guest. As her thumbs looped through the sides of her bikini bottoms, Punk noticed tattoos on either shoulder blade. Between the sweeps of her hair across her back and her gyrating, he couldn't make out whether they were moons or scimitars; and before he considered them further, his focus shifted south as she removed the balance of her clothing.

Her derriere suffered no evidence of medical meddling, and the group watched with interest as she backed into Flex to retrieve another bill, this one stuck to his forehead with a dab of saliva. Punk looked to Platt again, whose fuzzy gaze remained averted, a wobbly hand now shielding one side of his face, as she spread her cheeks and then clamped down on the money.

A cheer went up, and Punk studied the girl's impassive expression and wondered what series of events had landed her in a Key West strip club. She stared at the wall across from her like a sailor's widow looking over the ocean from the beach, miles away from this body with its ass pressed against the face of a misogynistic naval aviator.

Flex watched his bill sashay away and turned to Platt to gauge his reaction, fully expecting the staffer would be bathing in the light of the moment, marveling at Flex's prowess with currency. Once he saw the civilian's head down and realized that he'd intentionally missed the action, the RIO threw his hands up in exasperation and stormed off toward the DJ booth.

Flex returned to his runway seat a minute later with a shit-eating grin pasted to his sunglass-adorned face. He looked over at Punk, mouthed "roll call," and refocused on the dancer nearing the end of her routine.

The song ended. Amber gave one last come-hither pose and, accompanied by a smattering of applause, strolled with a feline strut through the beads.

"I've been told we have a special guest in the house this

evening," the DJ said through the speakers, "and you know we at the Pirates' Den like to treat our special guests right. Boys, help *Fergie* get to the stage, please."

Flex and Widget grabbed either side of Platt's chair and hoisted him onto the runway. The staffer sat on his elevated perch in confused disbelief as the DJ animated his voice like a fight announcer's and called: "Gentlemen, it's time for a roll call! Please welcome Mandy, Crystal, Lace, Brandy, Bambi, and Thunder."

Platt attempted to stand but was kicked back into the chair by a stiletto heel strapped to the foot of Mandy, the first dancer in the line of six that snaked through the beads. The women were on him before he could put up a fight, dividing their efforts with a wolf pack's efficiency.

The last dancer on the runway, Thunder, pushed Platt's knees together and stood straddling his lap. The amazon of a longhaired redhead towered over him, removed his glasses, and put them on herself. She removed her top, which earned another cheer from the aviators, and shimmied her shoulders in time to the beat, causing her pendulous breasts to slam against each of her biceps as they swayed from side to side before she leaned forward and slapped Platt across the face several times with them.

He grimaced with the beating and struggled to no avail against his tormentors. After delivering the flurry, Thunder turned her back to him, hauled her thong to her ankles, and held the pose as the rest of the dancers reduced Platt to his jockey shorts, tasseled loafers, and argyle socks. The bright spotlights caused his pasty white pallor to contrast sharply with the strippers' all-over tans.

Platt's shirt and pants were tossed to the aviators, and the redhead, facing away from him, plopped herself onto his lap, and sawed her hips across his crotch a few times. She stood and looked through her legs—a sculptor checking her work—and, seeing no yield, sat and sawed some more, longer and more vigorously this time. The dancers at either of his shoulders, Amber and Lace, placed Platt's reluctant hands on Thunder's surging orbs and guided them around in a series of circular moves that left a line of mouths agape along the edge of the runway.

At some point thereafter the momentum shifted. Over the course of a verse, Punk saw Platt's tortured expression relax and then contort in ecstasy instead of agony. Amber and Lace felt his resistance fade, so they let his hands go and moved away. The staffer began his own tactile journey about the abundant flesh of the stripper in his lap, and he started bucking in time with her movement against him. Thunder played along, throwing her head back so her hair cascaded over his face while mashing her hands against his on her chest. She moaned loudly enough to be heard over the music and grinded into him with enthusiasm. Punk looked at Platt's face again and saw that he too had gone to a distant place, a place where serious fucking happened and nobody was apologetic about it.

Without warning Thunder stopped bouncing and pulled Platt's hands off of her. She stood up and gazed down to where she'd writhed, and this time a prominent bulge in the staffer's jockeys greeted her . . . and the rest of the onlookers in the Pirates' Den.

"The circus is in town," Widget cried over the music. "Check out the *big top*."

"Hey, Big Top," Flex shouted. "Keep your pole under the canvas!"

As the aviators laughed to tears, rendered each other high fives, and chanted "Big Top," Platt sat still on the stage with his enthusiasm on cotton-covered display. They gave a standing ovation and slapped each other on the back, reveling in the fraternity of it all. The strippers got the civilian to his feet and escorted his hard-on, along with the rest of his body, down the runway and behind the beaded door.

He didn't immediately reappear, and the laughter stopped. Flex shot a concerned look toward the DJ booth, and the DJ shrugged.

"I've never seen that happen after a roll call," Flex thought aloud. "Usually the guy has to walk back into the crowd half naked while the dancers laugh at him."

The officers concentrated on the beads, Flex incredulous that his rite had gone wrong, and although they didn't know for sure what was going on backstage, each wished he'd been the one on stage instead.

"Objection," Platt said, fastening the upper two of the three buttons on his pinstriped, charcoal-colored suit coat as he rose out of his chair.

Captain Eagle Williamson, the RAG commanding officer, sat at the opposite end of the long rectangular table.
Punk had been surprised to find the table covered with a
green felt tablecloth, and he'd wondered if it was the same
cloth that had covered the conference room table used by
the mishap board back in Oceana or if the squadron had
a closet full of them. It seemed rather morose that someone
had thought to bring the cloth on the detachment, like
ground troops carrying body bags. But just as combat created casualties, RAG detachments created downed replacements.

Eagle was newly arrived from NAS Oceana, so he was
still garbed in his flight suit, although given the time to
change he probably wouldn't have. "Mr. Platt," he said
with an icy stare, "remind me of your role here."

The civilian adjusted his red and blue thin striped bow
tie and said, "Please, Captain, call me Ferguson. I'm here
as Senator Meyers's proxy."

Eagle rolled his eyes. "And that means, question mark?
I'm sorry, Ferg; I'm just a fighter pilot who never managed
to serve on the student council while he was growing up."

"*Ferguson.* And on behalf of Senator Meyers I've come
to ensure a fair and balanced hearing for Ms. Greenwood."

Punk, seated along the side of the table next to Spud
and across from Hammer and Scuzz, all dressed in pressed
khakis and waiting for their times to speak, cut his eyes to
the left and saw that Eagle was about to snap.

"Fine, fine," the captain said down his long nose, gesturing for Platt to retake his seat. "I'm already getting tired
of saying this: A performance board is an administrative
procedure, not a legal one. You can't object. In fact, I'd
prefer if you refrained from speaking altogether. I want
this board to be thorough but not last all day, if we can
help it." He returned his attention to Muddy seated on
Platt's left side. "Let me make my last request again: Please
walk us through the sequence of events that occurred the
day before yesterday when you arrived overhead the field
on Punk's wing."

Platt raised his hand. "May I briefly confer with Ms.
Greenwood?"

The skipper winced and threw his hands up resignedly.
Platt started to lean over to whisper into Muddy's ear, but

she blocked him with her forearm and addressed Eagle. "Skipper, my story's simple: I was joining up on Lieutenant Reichert's wing when the airplane inadvertently rolled off to the left. I didn't move the stick."

As she spoke, Punk focused on the single line of three ribbons pinned over the left shirt pocket of her khakis just below her wings. He was struck by the fact she'd already been awarded the Navy Commendation Medal and the Navy Achievement Medal and figured she must have earned them at some temporary duty station before starting flight school or just after she'd earned her wings before showing up for RAG training.

Muddy was certainly ahead of her peer group awards-wise. She seemed to be that type, the type that possessed a work ethic bordering on sanctimonious in the minds of the rest of the squadron unburdened by such impulses. Punk considered the intensity in her eyes as she continued her explanation around the event in question, and he knew she'd never quit the program on her own—and that both impressed and concerned him.

His concern had nothing to do with her gender. Ready-room anecdotes were filled with remembrances of pilots who'd attempted to compensate for marginal flying skills by being "great officers." In some ways, the label "great officer" was a euphemism for "crappy pilot" the same way "great personality" was code for "ugly chick." Some had managed the ruse for an entire career, doing nothing more permanently damaging than occasionally scaring their RIOs or wingmen in the air while impressing superiors with their administrative efficiency on the ground. Some were revealed and shown the door. The rest crashed. Airplanes were neither misogynistic nor politically correct, nor could they adapt their science to someone who lacked talent but tried really hard. But did Muddy really lack talent?

Once the replacement finished her statement, Eagle dismissed her along with Platt, but the civilian insisted that he remain in the room to hear the discussion about his "client." The skipper reminded him that he wasn't owed any consideration but could stay, provided he kept quiet. He then asked Spud to review Muddy's training jacket.

"She's toward the bottom of her class," Spud reported, "but above the minimum standard. Without the two downs she'd actually be in the middle of the pack, although Class Two is a pretty small pack."

"Punk," the skipper said, "you've been around her as much as any instructor. How would you characterize her potential?"

Punk thought for a moment. "There's a big difference in her two downs . . . you know, taxiing into the mud and rolling into me. I guess she's got potential, skipper. From what I've seen I'd say she's a straight shooter. She doesn't make excuses anyway."

" 'I didn't touch the stick' isn't an excuse?" Eagle asked.

"Maybe not . . ."

The skipper looked to the maintenance officer. "Scuzz, did you find anything wrong with the jet?"

"No, sir," Scuzz replied.

"I know that, skipper," Punk said. "I even took the jet flying to try and recreate the roll-off and I couldn't. But there's still some doubt here."

"What doubt?" Eagle said. "My experts tell me this airplane was working fine when—"

"Don't you see what's going on here?" Platt said as he jumped up and paced along the end of the table, periodically pounding his fist into his palm. "Whether this is a judicial procedure or an administrative one doesn't change the fact that right now, the accused has the burden of proving her innocence here instead of the prosecution—you all—having the burden of proving her guilt. I agree with Punk. This is nothing more than a kangaroo court."

Eagle knitted his brow toward Punk. "Did you say this was a kangaroo court?"

"He pointed out how illogical this proceeding is," Platt insisted before Punk could get a word out. "And I want to go on record as saying that—"

"You're out of here!" the skipper railed, casting an index finger toward the door like an umpire throwing an overzealous manager out of a ballpark. "I told you to keep quiet."

"I meant to," Platt said, gumption erased by the skipper's ire.

"You had your chance. Go."

"Senator Meyers will want to know why I wasn't in the room."

"Then you'd better tell her." The skipper rendered the staffer a little *bye-bye* wave. "Good-bye for now."

Platt slowly slinked out of the room. Once the door shut behind him, Eagle looked across the officers, splitting his gaze equally between the twosomes on either side of the table. "All right, gentlemen," he said. "This is what all great Americans signed up for. It's not all shooting missiles and dropping bombs; it's also deciding the fate of fledgling fighter pilots. So what's everyone's recommendation here? Scuzz, let's start with you: retain or separate?"

Scuzz raised his thick black eyebrows and nodded slowly. He fashioned his fist into a gavel and dropped it coolly onto the table. "Separate."

They waited for amplification but none came. "And?" the skipper asked.

Scuzz gave Eagle a double take like a tennis player who'd just had his best one-way-ticket serve smashed back into his side of the court. "And . . . what?"

"Why do you think she should be separated?"

"Because I think she's a shitty pilot." He folded his arms, broadcasting that his explanation was complete.

Punk started to say something to Scuzz but the skipper cut him off with a wave and shifted the discussion to the next junior officer. "Spud?"

"I'm a baseball man, skipper," Spud said, running one hand across his bald pate. "Ties go to the runner." He smiled contentedly and allowed his wisdom to sink in.

The skipper shook his head. "Great, we've got both Perry Mason *and* Yogi Berra here. 'Ties go to the runner'? What the fuck does that mean?"

"It means I agree with Punk. She deserves another chance."

"I haven't even asked Punk for his recommendation yet. How can you agree with him?"

"I'm fairly confident which way he's going to go. Plus, if I put on my operations officer hat, I have to be worried that Class Two is already too small."

"Well, comma, you've certainly milked all of the mystery out of it." Eagle shifted his eyes toward the lieutenant next to Spud. "Punk?"

"Retain for the reasons I stated earlier," Punk answered.

"Remind me what those were?"

"With all due respect to Scuzz, sir, I don't know how she can be characterized as a 'shitty pilot' at this point in her training. She had one major fuckup with her FAM-1, and that's it. I'm all about holding coneheads to standards, but I don't see a real trend yet. She bears watching, certainly, but not removal based on what she's done so far."

"You're pretty forgiving considering she almost killed you," Scuzz said.

"I'm still not sure *she* had anything to do with what almost killed me," Punk replied.

"Then you're ignoring the facts." Scuzz's eyes narrowed. "Why do you care so much about her?"

"Because I have a sense of fairness, maybe?"

"Do you care as much about the rest of the class?"

Punk felt his pulse pound in his temples. "If you're making an accusation, sir, why don't you just make it?"

"All right, you two," Eagle interrupted. "Cease buzzer." He leveled a finger at the maintenance officer. "I don't like where you were headed, Scuzz. That's all I ever want to have to say about that."

Scuzz mumbled a halfhearted, "Yes, sir."

Eagle looked over at Hammer and raised his eyebrows, and Hammer simply gave a thumbs down.

"None of you guys has made my job any easier," the skipper said. "I guess I get to be the tie breaker here." He tapped his fingers on the table and whooshed a heavy sigh. "Hammer, would you please bring Lieutenant (junior grade) Greenwood back in?"

Hammer rushed out of the small conference room and returned with Muddy half a minute later. The lieutenant was in the process of closing the door behind him when Platt wedged into the opening and squirted back into the space, immediately plopping into the same chair he'd occupied previously. He scanned the room, waiting for somebody to speak, and then realized that Muddy was standing at attention behind her chair and the officers were waiting for him to join her. He muttered, "Excuse me," and stood up, topping out several inches shorter than the replacement.

"Lieutenant (junior grade) Greenwood," the skipper said, "by a vote of three-to-two this board places you back in flight status. You will continue to train with Class Two."

Platt pumped his fist and hissed a muted *yes* and then extended his arms around Muddy to give her a congratulatory hug, but she took a half step away, eyes never leaving Eagle's face. The staffer wound up just patting her on the near shoulder. "Needless to say, we don't want to see you in here again," the captain continued.

"You won't, sir," she replied, and then added, "as long as the airplanes cooperate."

Eagle looked to Punk, who stared straight ahead, and then back to Muddy.

"This proceeding is adjourned."

As the group filed out of the room, Platt said, "Chalk one up for the visiting team." Muddy didn't respond. "You don't seem to appreciate the fact you're getting VIP attention here, Ms. Greenwood."

"I don't remember asking for it," she replied, expression only a hair more intense than the one she'd pointed at the skipper. "I'm not sure where Senator Meyers's efforts stop and yours begin, but I don't need your help. I got my wings on my own; I'll get through the RAG the same way." She started for the operations office to see if the skipper's ruling might have her back on the flight schedule for the following day, but paused in the doorway and shot a final line over her left shoulder at him: "And by the way, Big Top, it's not *Ms.* Greenwood; it's *Lieutenant (junior grade)* Greenwood."

Platt stewed alone in the conference room for a few seconds and then burst through the door into the common area. He rushed over to the duty desk, pushing his way past a handful of aviators gathered at the counter.

"Have you see Flex?" Platt asked the ensign seated behind the counter.

"Negative," the ensign replied, craning around to read the big flight schedule board against the wall behind him. "He doesn't brief for a few hours. He may not be here yet."

"No, he's here," Smitty said from in front of the desk. "I just saw him in the ready room."

"Where's the ready room?" Platt demanded.

"That way," Smitty said, pointing beyond the common area's double door main entrance and across to the other side of the corridor.

Platt rushed into the ready room and spotted Flex in the second row of the classic faux leather high-backed chairs with his feet propped along either arm of the chair in front of him. "Flex," he called down the line, "a word, please."

Flex casually lifted his eyes from the magazine he was paging through. "You still here? I thought you'd be off to tackle the next threat to political correctness somewhere else."

"No, I've been directed to stay here for a few more days at least."

"Where are you staying, by the way?"

"The Hilton."

"The one on the water?"

"Yes."

"Man, what a waste of taxpayers' money. I've got half a mind to make a hotline call."

"Would you please?" Platt said dryly. "Although I don't think it would do anything. Senator Meyers is also on the senate's fraud, waste, and abuse oversight committee."

Flex shook his head and refocused on the magazine. "So, what do you need? I'm kind of busy here, Big Top."

"That's what I want to talk about."

"How busy I am?"

"No." Platt scanned the few other aviators engaged in light reading or serious preflight review who dotted the chairs around Flex. "Could we chat in the back of the room?"

Flex let out a moan and tossed the magazine into the next chair. He rose like a prizefighter trying to get out of bed the morning after a punishing bout. Platt beat him to the rear of the long room and stood rigidly with his arms crossed. "This has got to stop," he hissed in a loud whisper as Flex reached him.

"What?" Flex asked.

"This 'Big Top' shit. You all have got to stop calling me that."

"Why? You call me Flex."

"Flex is your name."

"No, it's not. Jim is my name. Flex is my call sign."

"Well, I'm not in the Navy, and I don't want a call sign."

"Nobody *wants* a call sign. You think I like being called Flex?"

"I don't know. What's it mean?"

"It's kind of embarrassing, but I guess I can trust you. I was alone in my stateroom and one of my roommates walked in suddenly and caught me . . . you know . . ."

"What?"

"You know . . ."

"Masturbating?"

Flex contorted his face in disgust. "No, not masturbating. You really are obsessed with your dick, aren't you?" He hit his best Mr. Universe stance. "I was posing. I'd just finished my second workout of the day, and I was checking the results in the mirror when Steamer Stephano walked in and nailed me. I was Flex from then on."

"That's it?" Platt said. "That's not that embarrassing."

"Yeah, I guess you're right," Flex agreed. "Steamer got his after he shit himself trying to fart during a brief."

"I'm talking about compared to 'Big Top.' "

"Well, I'm sorry. You don't get to pick your own. I didn't happen to get a raging hard-on in front of a bunch of my squadronmates."

"I don't want to sound like I think I'm more important than you, but I work for a United States senator. If she knew what went on last night, I could lose my job."

"How's she going to find out?" Flex walked over to the magazine rack against the back wall and pulled out the front-page section of the day's edition of the *Miami Herald*. He began scanning the articles with the subtlety of a player in a Greek tragedy. "Let's see here . . . nope . . . nothing here . . . nothing here, either. I can't believe the paper missed such an important story." He tossed the paper on one of the chairs in the last row. "Relax. This ain't the Hill. You were with us, and we protect each other."

Platt retrieved the paper from the chair and looked over the front page just to be sure. "I guess I understand a little ball busting," he said, "but even Ms., er, Lieutenant (junior grade) Greenwood just called me Big Top."

"So?"

"So? She's female. She could nail me for sexual harassment or something." Platt paused as Flex grew a wide smile.

"It does make a difference, doesn't it?" Flex said as he walked the few steps to the coffeepot perched on a small table next to the magazine rack and poured a Styrofoam cupful. "Now you see what I was talking about at the Bull. For your sake, we'd better hope I was wrong, huh?" He took a swig of the hours'-old swill and grimaced at the taste of it. "Hey, Big Top, since you and I have this trust thing going on, how about telling me what went on behind the beaded curtain last night . . ."

In the middle of a dogfight, Muddy found herself inside someone else's body. The body looked like hers, and as Muddy looked through the eyeholes she saw the head was twisting around, desperately trying to keep track of several F/A-18s posing as the enemy, a wingman, the Tomcat's airspeed, altitude, attitude, angle of attack, and fuel quantity. *So many moving parts,* Muddy thought from inside the flesh shell. *So much to balance.* She watched the contortions; whoever was controlling the body was struggling. Muddy judged from the shape of the thin fingers wrapped around the controls that the body belonged to a female, a pilot like her.

Muddy felt sorry for her. The oxygen mask hose flailed with the jerky movement of the pilot's helmet, and she tugged against the straps of her harness, working hard to see the jets swirling about her, including the one flown by a married lieutenant commander who'd hit on Muddy the week before in the Hog's Breath Saloon on Duval Street. She had made the mistake of accepting what had seemed like a friendly invitation to dance, and then a slow song had come on and the handsome pilot—a reservist who flew for the airlines most days like the majority of the guys in the aggressor squadron—had pulled her close and grabbed her ass and whispered, "We could have a secret, if you wanted," and she'd pushed away from him in shock and disgust and run all the way back to the BOQ.

Muddy floated inside with peaceful clarity. She knew precisely what had motivated the hapless female pilot, the owner of this body, the one about to be blown to simulated bits by a simulated missile. Muddy had shown up for flight training in Pensacola under the same umbrella of equality, and though she couldn't say that the officially mandated notion of equality was missing from flight school, neither could she say it was embraced.

But flight school had been a model of gender neutrality compared to the RAG. Her presence in the cockpit of a fighter was still news and still generated interest from female senators with agendas, and those truths were depressing. That, and the fact that flying a fighter was turning out to be harder than she'd imagined it was going to be, and she hadn't even attempted to land an F-14 on an aircraft carrier yet.

A voice started to break through this inner world. She couldn't understand the words at first, but the meter of the speech sounded like the same phrase repeated over and over. She strained to make it out, and after a half dozen more iterations, each slightly louder than the last, she heard: "Do you see them?"

"Who?" she asked back.

"Punk, your flight lead, the bandits . . . call your tally."

"No tally. I don't see anybody right now."

"You've got to 'fess up then," the voice said with disgust. "If you lose sight I need to know immediately. Otherwise, I'm sitting back here fat, dumb, and happy, looking through the tails of the jet thinking you've got things under control up there."

Muddy recognized the voice as Flex's and with that she was flesh and blood again. *She* was the struggling fighter pilot. Muddy spent one more second marveling at the phenomenon she'd just experienced—a mental defense mechanism of some sort, no doubt—but then resumed her efforts toward not dying at the hands of the Hornet pilots.

"Bandit, nose on, seven o'clock," Flex cried. "Do you see him?"

"Negative," she huffed through her mask.

"Roll left." She snapped the jet to the left with Flex's command. "Stop roll. Hard pull." He keyed the radio: "Flares, flares, flares."

"Continue," the bandit pilot transmitted as he closed on them.

"Do you see him yet, Muddy?" Flex asked.

"Snap left, Muddy," Punk called over the radio. "I'm pulling for a shot."

"I still don't see him," Muddy said over the intercom.

"Goddam it," Flex said, "he's right there. Keep the pull coming or we're toast."

"Fox Two from Boxer One," Punk called as he pulled

the trigger on his stick. A loud *boop* saturated the frequency signaling that a simulated Sidewinder had come off of his jet. An electronic pulse from a missilelike pod on the jet traveled to towers in the ocean below that in turn fired the data to antennas on top of the Tactical Air Combat Training System building across the street from the RAG's hangar. The antennas fed the signal into a bank of computers that transformed the dogfight into a God's-eye view of shapes on two huge screens in a control room. There, a lieutenant acting as the range control officer and a civilian technician sat wearing headsets and monitored the war. The two watched the left-hand screen as a small dash moved away from the computer depiction of Punk's jet and traveled toward the computer depiction of one of the Hornets. After a few seconds the shapes collided.

"Good kill, Boxer One," the lieutenant said into the boom mike at his lips. "Bandit Four, you're dead."

"Bandit Four copies," the pilot returned. "Exiting the fight to the west."

"That's only one," Flex said. "We've still got three others out here."

Muddy rolled the Tomcat back the other way and searched the sky through the right side of the canopy, but everything was a blur now. Things flashed by but nothing registered. Flex continued to call moves, and she blindly followed his direction—not a steely-eyed fighter jock but a voice-activated autopilot. As Punk shot another bandit off of her tail, she struggled against the overwhelming urge to mentally detach herself again.

The schedulers had stacked the deck against her for her "graduation" tactics flight, hadn't they? Things had never gone well for her with Punk in the equation, and Flex was every replacement's nightmare. She'd managed the syllabus well enough since her performance board; however, those flights had been two versus two at worst, not two versus x—and in the case of this flight, x equaled four. She'd handled two bandits adequately enough—a one-for-you-one-for-me proposition—but this Battle of Britain–like scenario was overwhelming.

Flex momentarily stopped giving directions. Muddy knew that scribing a predictable path was the worst thing she could do, so she threw the jet into a series of hard turns.

"In the real world . . . you can't . . . wait for your flight lead to save your ass over and over," Flex said between grunts as he fought the onset of G she created with her stick inputs. "We need to . . . get a kill, Muddy. I won't let you get through the tactics phase without . . . at least one kill . . . on your graduation hop. Got it?"

Great, she thought, *I can't even keep track of my airspeed right now.* Only two bandits left, and she figured Punk was already saddled in on one of them. She torqued around looking for either of the Hornets but saw nothing but deep blue below and lighter blue everywhere else.

Why hadn't any of their long-range missiles worked before the merge? A dead bandit or two during the intercept before they got to the dogfighting arena would've certainly made their lives easier about now. They'd called the AIM-54 Phoenix shots around thirty miles away and heard the *boop*s, but the range control officer had come back with "missile failure" *four times*! And what was all that bullshit during the weapons lectures about the deadly Phoenix missile? What good was it if it didn't work the first time you needed it?

At once Muddy sensed this game was rigged, and that brought on the same feelings she'd always had when faced with the possibility of life conspiring against her: She obdurately resolved to beat the assholes or at least to go down kicking and screaming.

"Do you have a tally?" Flex asked again.

She didn't want to answer, and as she hesitated the radar-warning receiver on the right side of her forward instrument panel flickered with an inconclusive indication that another airplane directly behind them was trying to get a radar lock. From her vantage point against the ropes of this particular fight, that was all the evidence she needed to attempt a Hail Mary.

Muddy scanned her instruments: attitude, forty degrees nose high; airspeed, one hundred knots and decelerating; angle of attack, twenty units; altitude, fifteen thousand feet—but even in the time it took her to work her way around the gauges, their readings changed. She'd heard a couple of instructors sitting around the ready room talking about unorthodox moves with the Tomcat, and she remembered one of them saying how, at slow speeds and high angles of attack, putting the stick fully to one side and aft while booting in full rudder in the opposite direction would cause the jet to snap roll in the direction of the rudder input. What had further struck her about the exchange was the instructor had gone on to say that the digital flight control system was designed to prevent the effects of "cross-controlling" because those inputs had a history of causing Tomcats to go into flat spins, but that DFCS didn't seem to work.

She knew from her NATOPS study and Hollywood hokum that flat spins weren't good, but downing a flight at this point wasn't good, either.

"Muddy . . ." It was time to do something, anything, to make the noise stop. She booted the left rudder to the firewall and slapped the stick against her right thigh and then pulled it as far back as it would go. The Tomcat shuddered slightly, like a stallion fighting the reins, and then pirouetted so violently that Flex knocked his head against the right side of the canopy.

She neutralized the controls and fought overcorrecting for the oscillations of the nose as it wandered left and right, as far below the horizon now as it had been above it seconds ago. She focused on the angle-of-attack gauge and the airspeed indicator and saw that both showed the F-14 was flying rather than falling.

Her attention was diverted by an object parked in the center of her heads-up display. The bandit that had been on their tail and about to shoot was now several thousand feet in front of her. Without questioning her good fortune, Muddy uncaged the seeker head of her simulated AIM-9 Sidewinder strapped under her left wing and waited for a large plus sign in her HUD to superimpose itself over the bandit, indicating she had a good infrared lock on the F/A-18.

The Hornet pilot hadn't known what to think as his prey swapped ends in front of him, and before he could react, Muddy called, "Fox Two from Boxer Two," over the frequency. Another *boop* hogged the airwaves momentarily, and as the two jets passed, she waited anxiously for a ruling.

It was taking too long, and in her mind's eye she saw the boys club in session, huddled over the console in the control room laughing their balls off about another so-called missile failure. In the debrief they'd put on their best poker faces and intone, "Hey, this ain't no technothriller, Muddy. In the real world stuff doesn't always work. You have to be ready for that." And then Flex or Punk would hand her a down sheet, and she'd be done flying the Tomcat forever and would never be a denizen of the real world they spoke of. Never mind that she was sick of hearing about how much different life was in the real world and how nothing she'd experienced so far replicated it. This real world the instructors crowed about was a place right out of a Tolstoy novel, a hard land where man was inherently evil and life beat you into submission and only the tough survived—and some of them ultimately didn't make it.

She wondered why she couldn't suppress her desire to live there.

Muddy was about ready to yank the Tomcat into another defensive turn when the radio crackled: "Good kill, Boxer Two. Bandit One, you're dead." She smiled under her mask, but now she had to find Punk. The run wasn't over (and the results didn't count) until the fighters reestablished mutual support and were headed back in the direction from which they'd arrived at the fight, and the burden for maintaining mutual support during a RAG syllabus hop was on the replacement.

Just as the bandit had materialized in front of her, Punk appeared down her left wing, co-altitude about a mile and a half away—textbook combat spread formation. "Understand you're visual, Muddy?" Punk asked over the squadron common frequency.

"Muddy's visual," she returned, confidence belying the happenstance of the moment.

"Range control, Boxer flight is clear," Punk transmitted. "Knock it off. We're headed back to base."

"Bandits copy the knock it off," the Hornet lead said over the control frequency. "We'll see you guys in the debrief. Tell your conehead that last kill was an impressive one. I thought I had her."

"Roger," Punk replied before keying the other radio. "Muddy, bandit lead passes nice job on the last engagement."

"Muddy copies," she said, unsure of whether to admit it

had been mostly luck that had planted the Hornet in front of her. As she checked her fuel state, she decided that luck was part of the game sometimes, and just as she had been lucky this time she would certainly be unlucky in the future. Lucky or not, that kill had kept her from going to another board and sitting at the long green table with no one but Platt in her corner.

"Go ahead and join in a loose cruise for the transit back to base," Punk said. "You can close to parade position once we get in sight of the field."

"Roger." Drained by the flight, Muddy's mind wandered as she maneuvered her F-14 closer to Punk's, and she was hit by how tenuous her standing would be for the rest of her time in the RAG; the slightest misstep would bring her back to the wrong end of the long green table. What if the jet rolled off again? She realized there was no questioning luck during a struggle for survival. For now she'd lost the luxury of traveling the moral high road.

The first keg was tapped minutes after the last debrief was finished and the final grade sheet was signed. Officers and sailors shed their working clothes for beach togs and headed down to Tiki Beach, the naval air station's recreational area along the edge of a lagoon at the west end of the base.

The place looked nothing like most military recreational areas. Tiki Beach had a natural beauty, anchored by the clear blue water of the lagoon and the beach's sugar white sand punctuated by lush palm trees and complemented by thatched roofs over the gazebos and exotic hardwood veneers on the walls of the cabanas.

Punk stood at the edge of one of the volleyball courts with a few other instructors trying not to be obvious about ogling the female enlisted women in bikinis batting a ball around. "Dungarees certainly don't do them justice," Hammer muttered under his breath, which caused the others to nod.

Flex ran up behind the officers, peered over his sunglasses at the sailors, and said it was time to challenge the coneheads to the traditional end-of-det basketball grudge match. He asked Punk for his help, and the two of them jogged across the sand over to the kegs buried in the shade of a palm and attempted to goad the replacements onto the court.

"All right, losers," Flex said to the relaxed semicircle of ensigns and lieutenants junior grade, "the tactics detachment is not over until you prove your worth with the rock."

"The rock?" Smitty asked, seated Indian-style, plastic cup of beer in each hand.

"Yeah, the rock," Flex replied, gesturing toward the basketball court behind them. "Basketball. And you call yourself a black guy?"

"I've been a naval aviator so long that I'm pretty sure I can't legally consider myself a black guy anymore." Smitty stood up and looked around. "It doesn't look like we have enough guys. You need five, right?"

"Yeah." Flex smirked. "Five."

"You want to play, fellas?" Smitty asked the three members of Class Two comfortably seated in the sand.

"I guess," Kosher said. "Basketball has never really been my sport, though."

"Can't we just sit here and drink beer?" Smiles whined, sunscreen not fully rubbed into several parts of his sunvulnerable body.

"No," Flex said. "It's time to play hoops. Get a fifth guy and meet us over on the court, and that's an order. Tactics phase ain't over until you prove your worth with the rock."

"I love that line, Flex," Smitty said. "Can you keep saying it over and over?"

"Maybe I will, wiseass." Flex and Punk ran off, and they joined Hammer, Fitz, and Scuzz already clanging shots against the rim on the far end of the court.

A few minutes later Smitty, Kosher, Smiles, and T-dog sheepishly shuffled up courtside. "We can't find a fifth player," Smitty reported. "Want to go four-on-four?"

"Not," Flex snapped as he landed off a practice jump shot. "We're going full court. Where are your pilots? Are RIOs the only jocks in Class Two?" The replacements just shrugged. Flex pulled his shades off, letting them hang around his neck by the lanyard, and mopped his forehead with his T-shirt before scanning the group standing around the closest gazebo. "Look, I'll go ahead and bend the rules

here." He pointed through them. "You can have him on your team."

The replacements turned and saw that Flex was gesturing toward Ferguson Platt, who was standing by himself, beer in one hand, palm frond in the other as he stood studying the flora at close range. "Big Top?" Smitty asked incredulously. "I doubt he's any good."

"Neither are we; it'll be a fair game." Flex put his sunglasses back on and cupped his hands around his mouth. "Big Top! Get your ass over here!"

Platt dropped the branch and strode over, wincing at the call sign but happy to have been noticed. He'd tried to work the party and make small talk with some of the maintenance troops, but they'd quickly sniffed out his rulingclass demeanor and moved on.

"Yes, Flex?" the staffer asked as he stepped onto the court wearing a collared madras short-sleeved shirt and pleated silk shorts.

"Ever played basketball?"

"Damn right," Platt replied. "I was a guard on my fraternity's intramural team at Cornell for three years. We made it to the quarterfinals my junior year."

Flex looked to Smitty. "See? You're all set." Flex gestured for Scuzz to throw him the ball, and he began to dribble as he continued to speak. "All right, international rules of the game apply. Call fouls on yourself. First team to fifteen wins. Gotta win by two." Flex moved to the top of the key. "I'll shoot for first possession."

"Hold it," Platt said. "I'm wearing sandals."

"You'll be fine, Big Top. Those things give as much support as most sports shoes these days." Platt squared off with the backboard and dribbled twice. He brought the ball in front of his face and bent slightly at the knee and then sprang up and let fly. The ball arced into the hoop and cleanly kissed the net as it went through. "Get used to it, gentlemen."

The teams formed into two huddles and briefly kibbitzed to decide who would play what position. The players fanned out around the court, and Flex was about to pass the ball across the baseline to Punk, but Smitty waved his hands and said, "Hold it. This is going to be confusing. We need to go shirts and skins."

"All right," Flex replied. "We'll go skins. I could use the rays anyway."

"No, we'll go skins," Platt insisted. "I don't want to sweat on this eighty-dollar shirt."

"Eighty dollars for that piece of shit?"

"It's hand-combed linen."

Flex shook his head. "Fine. Hurry up."

The replacements peeled off their T-shirts and threw them onto the sand around the court while Platt unbuttoned his shirt, gingerly removed it, and held it in front of him. "Do they have hangars in the cabanas?" he asked.

"Goddam it, Big Top," Flex said, "just throw the fucking thing on the ground."

"No."

Flex let out an exasperated snort, stepped over to Platt, and tugged the shirt out of his fingers. He gripped the shirt with mock concern, pinkies dramatically aloft, and walked over to the palm tree that the staffer had been studying previously, and hung the item over one of the lower branches. "There," Flex declared. "Now let's play."

Flex bounced the ball across the baseline to Punk, who passed it right back and jogged to the middle of the key on the other end. Flex was stopped at half court by Platt, whose new farmer's tan made him stand out from the fledgling fighter pilots on his team who'd managed some hours sunning around the BOQ pool during the occasional down times over the last two weeks. Flex attempted a cross over dribble, but it hit his right knee and rolled across the tartan surface behind him. The RIO lost his balance and fell over in a heap as he twisted around, and Platt scooped the ball up and banked a layup off the backboard and through the hoop.

"One-zip," Platt said as he ran back to play defense.

The next time Platt met him, Flex made a nice behind-the-back move and broke free. Platt ran him down, and just before he was on Flex again, Flex pulled up short and threw up a long jump shot that swished through the net.

"One all," Flex said.

As the game's intensity ramped up, interest in other activities around the beach waned, and soon there was a throng ringing the court, including the bikini-clad sailors whose presence was not lost on the players cranking the machismo up a notch in response. Platt bombed in another jump shot over Flex's outstretched arms, and Punk saw the enlisted members of the crowd rave. He figured they'd naturally allied themselves with the contest's apparent underdog. The game was tied at five-all.

On the next possession Flex took a pass from Scuzz and, with a stutter step, left Platt flat-footed as the muscular instructor put a fake on Smiles and curled in a bank shot from directly under the basket. A cheer went up from the line of instructors, including Captain Williamson, who'd formed on the opposite side of the court from the sailors.

Platt responded by taking Kosher's in-bounds pass and going end-to-end for an easy layup, effortlessly blowing by Flex in the process. Flex came back with a head fake and a fadeaway from long range, and Platt answered with a similar shot from even farther away.

The duel between Flex and Platt ended when the civilian attempted a cutback move that his sandals couldn't support. He crumpled to the court with a yelp, curled into a ball, and grasped his right ankle with both hands. Doc Yee, who'd made it known that he'd done a stint as a sports physiologist at Bethesda, burst through the crowd and attended to the injured player while the others circled around with their hands on their hips and watched. The flight surgeon yelled for one of the squadron's corpsmen by the kegs to wrap some ice in a towel and bring it over to him. The corpsman quickly complied with the order, and after Yee fashioned a poor-man's compress around the ankle and ruled that it was just a minor sprain, a few of them helped Platt hobble to the shade where he sat, leaning against the trunk of a palm.

"I guess that's the end of the game," Smitty said with a shrug.

Flex pointed at the other members of Class Two along the far sideline. "What's wrong with them?"

"Nothing, I guess." Smitty looked toward his classmates. "Sinker, Auto, Dusty . . . any of you guys want to play?" All three averted their eyes. "Stormin', how about you?"

"I don't want to play," the thin pilot answered with a jerky shake of his prematurely balding head.

"Looks like you win by forfeit, Flex," Smitty said.

"Take a look, Mr. and Mrs. America," Flex declared

toward the gathered. "This is your next generation of war fighters—no, I'm sorry—war *forfeiters*."

Muddy emerged from the group and stepped onto the court. "I'll play."

"Sure, why not?" Flex snickered. "We'll spot you a few points to keep it fair."

"You'd better let us switch to shirts," Smitty suggested.

"No, I'll be fine," Muddy said. She pulled her T-shirt over her head, revealing a well-filled black sports bra, and walked onto the court while looking at Flex. "You don't need to spot us any points."

"What's the score?" Kosher asked.

"Eight to seven, our way," Flex replied.

"Whose ball?"

"We'll let you have it." Flex patronizingly rolled the ball across the court, and T-dog picked it up and threw it to Smiles, who bounced it across the end line to Kosher. Kosher dribbled a few times, casually moving toward the half court line when he saw Muddy wide open in the key. He sailed the ball overhand to her, much faster than the instructors figured he could, and she caught it and made a smooth hook shot for the score. The crowd erupted, louder than ever before.

Flex picked the ball off the court and, with a new determination showing on his face, passed it to Hammer. Seeking to silence the taunts from the sideline that Flex was being a ball hog, Hammer kept the ball and tried to drive the lane using his rugby instincts. Muddy blocked his path and, demonstrating how the two sports differed, poked the ball away and then passed it to Smiles, already headed up the court for an easy basket.

The instructors didn't score for the rest of the time Muddy was on the court. Her domination was highlighted by the three times she shifted from guarding Punk and stuffed Flex as he attempted to throw up jump shots, each block bringing down the house more than the last. She scored four times and assisted four more. She was comfortable on the court, the same kind of comfort anyone who's good at something possesses. Punk thought of how a high school friend had picked up a guitar once, and how he'd been able to tell just by the way the friend cradled it that he was a good player, even before he'd strummed a single note. The game ended with Muddy grabbing the rebound after another of Flex's increasingly desperate shots, and passing to Smitty on the run for the final point.

Punk congratulated the replacements on their win and marveled to himself at how the chemistry on the court had changed the instant Muddy'd removed her shirt. Was she just trying to be one of the boys or was she trying to be desired? Either way, she'd demonstrated a daunting combination of competence and physicality. The sailors in bikinis evoked animal lust with their curves and seductive expressions—a feeling momentarily crippling, perhaps, but overcome with reason by accomplished men. Muddy could fly their jets and kick their asses in pick-up basketball games. Hers was a remarkable if not scary mix, and he wondered how far she might get in the business of naval aviation if she eventually mastered the Tomcat.

"It's like you've said for the past two weeks, Flex," Smitty jeered as they all made their way past the still-recovering Platt and over to the keg. "Know the threat." The bulky black replacement raised Muddy's arm over her head. "This girl was a two-time all-conference center at the Naval Academy." Punk saw her blush as her arm dropped, and she looked all at once very beautiful, and that perception was unsettling. He shifted his thoughts to Anita and the pleasures of his upcoming return to Virginia Beach.

Flex pulled his sunglasses off and glared at the replacements. "This was a setup," he said.

Smitty casually looked up from drawing a beer. "We'll just call it a victory." He raised his plastic cup and swept it over the heads of the rest of Class Two gathered around him. "In accordance with Flex's rules, by a score of fifteen to eight in favor of Class Two, this tactics detachment is officially over."

By the time the August sun crested on the horizon across the lagoon, all of the squadron but a handful of instructors and the skipper had headed into town for one last night on Duval Street. Punk and Flex planted tiki torches in a circle and lit them to keep the bugs at bay, and the rest of the group gathered folding beach chairs and placed them inside the protective ring of fire. The sun seemed to quickly disappear, and the flames from the torches sent across the scene an orange light that danced with shadows on the faces of the officers now seated facing one another.

"I missed the first couple of days, Ops O," Eagle said to Spud directly across from him, "but all-in-all, comma, I'd say this was a pretty good detachment."

"We didn't lose anybody else, skipper," Spud replied, exhaling cigar smoke as he spoke. "My standards may be falling, but when it comes to Class Two, I'll take what I can get."

"We didn't lose any replacements," Hammer said from the skipper's right side, before turning toward Punk seated next to Spud. "But we did lose *Sweet Belle*."

"*I* didn't lose it," Punk said. "And we could've got it back."

"Yeah," Hammer returned, "for one hundred and twenty dollars. That's about three times what the car's worth, not to mention they were actually going to make us buy insurance for the damn thing."

"Is Class Two that bad?" Eagle asked.

"Grade-wise I guess overall they're no better or worse than other classes. They certainly have a flair for the dramatic, though." Spud took another long drag on his cigar. "I will say I'm relieved Muddy squeaked through."

The skipper scanned the area. "Speaking of Muddy, where did Mr. Platt go?"

"He went out with the replacements, skipper," Punk said. "I think he got tired of Flex."

"He got tired of me?" Flex said, straightening up in his chair, shades across his face reflecting the small fires around them. "I was tired of that toolbox way before he had time to get tired of me."

"Well, comma, just between amigos," the skipper said, "I'm relieved Muddy got through, too." He emptied his cup, shook the dregs into the sand, and started to rise but was stopped short by Fitz, who was on his way to the keg already and happy to oblige a refill. "Let's just say Platt has powerful friends," Eagle continued, "including some who wear stars."

"And they have the balls to call themselves warriors?" Flex said. "They're nothing but goddam pawns. Why don't we take a stand?"

"About what? Muddy made it over the bar, right?" He panned the group. "Am I right?"

"So what are you telling us about Big Top's powerful friends, skipper?" Flex asked. "Be honest with us, sir. Remember, it's just us amigos here. Regardless of whether she made it or not, did they pressure you?"

Eagle thought about the question and then offered Flex a placid smile. "Pressure? That's what you make it, gents. I've gotten better at picking my battles lately." Punk sensed less passion from the skipper compared to the first time he'd heard him broach the topic in his office months ago. Eagle gazed over the heads of the officers across from him, momentarily mesmerized by the flicker of one of the torches. "You great Americans don't worry about that shit. Just make sure the replacements are ready to fight wars once we send them to the fleet. Nobody's asking you to lower any standards . . . at least, *I'm* not asking you to lower any standards."

"Is somebody else asking us to lower standards?" Punk asked, half attempting to conjure up the old ire.

The skipper paused and looked to the flame again. "No," he replied cautiously, as if he wasn't sure how the answer would sound until he heard it for himself. "No. Nobody's asking you to lower standards."

Fitz returned to the circle, and Captain Williamson quietly nursed his beer and listened to the observations of the junior officers around him. Punk studied Eagle furtively as the skipper leaned back in his chair and threaded his fingers behind his head, nearly half of his face hidden by the wide shadow cast by his beak of a nose. His manner suggested he had nowhere he'd rather be than right where he was, exuding infectious comfort around his boys. Eagle would be up for command of a carrier-based air wing after this tour, and Punk thought the captain's future charges lucky.

Eventually the group broke the circle, some heading into town for dinner, others returning to the BOQ for a full night's sleep in preparation for tomorrow's return to Virginia Beach and their personas as husbands and fathers. As they stood and fashioned their game plans, Spud turned to Punk and asked, "Is something wrong?"

Punk tried not to look surprised by the question. "No,

I'm just thinking about what it's going to be like going home tomorrow."

Spud smiled. "It never gets old, does it? That's one of the reasons I've stayed in this business as long as I have. The lows can be pretty low, but the highs are very high." He chuckled. "Remember when we were sitting around the fire in Bahrain on the last cruise, bitching about how bad life was on the Boat, and saying how we couldn't wait to get back where everything would make sense and be so simple?"

Punk nodded with the memory. "I guess we were wrong."

CHAPTER NINE

The good luck with weather continued as they ferried the jets back to NAS Oceana. That morning, high pressure fronted by thunderstorms had pushed the gloom that had dominated the region for a week out to sea. From the night sky over Cape Hatteras, Punk could see the entire string of lights that marked the Hampton Roads Bay Bridge-Tunnel, that long, man-made miracle connecting Virginia Beach to the Eastern Shore.

As Punk lined up with the runway for his approach, he realized he hadn't landed a jet at night for weeks, if not more than a month. In spite of that fact, he managed to keep the meatball centered on the Fresnel lens and nailed the pass, and as the runway markers passed every thousand feet, each one more slowly, he finally allowed himself to think about the pleasures of watching his wide-screen TV and sleeping in his own bed.

Punk followed the plane captain's signals and parked the Tomcat between two others that had arrived from Key West hours before. He shut the engines down, and Hammer threw down their hanging bags, stored for the flight in the only available spot behind the rear ejection seat in the canopy.

As Punk opened the door to maintenance control, he saw Master Chief Callaghan seated at his desk behind the counter.

"Welcome home," the master chief said as he extended a big arm toward the lieutenant. "I've got to admit I've been a wee bit lazy about maintaining my running schedule during your absence."

"Let's get back into it tomorrow," Punk said, shaking the enlisted man's bear-sized paw.

"Deal."

Punk went upstairs to the parachute rigger shop and removed his harness and G-suit and hung them on his assigned peg before putting his helmet directly above on a ledge that ran the length of the fifty sets of flight gear along two of the crowded cinderblock walls. He then fished his cell phone out of one of his G-suit pockets, and as he slipped it into the left chest pocket of his flight suit, it went off.

"Hello?"

"It's me." *Anita.*

"Who's 'me'?" he jibed.

"You're expecting a phone call from another scantily clad vixen breathlessly awaiting her future husband's return?"

Punk felt himself start to stiffen. She'd always given good phone, but after two weeks of it he was ready for the real thing. "Where are you?"

"I'm still at my place."

"Why don't you head over to my condo and I'll see you there in a little bit." He clicked the phone off, grabbed his hanging bag and a helmet bag, and made his way out.

Punk passed the guard shack stationed by the gate bathed in floodlights, through which he had to pass to get to the parking lot. "Have a great evening," he said to the young black sailor inside the phone-booth-sized shack. The guard rendered a salute, and Punk returned it.

His pickup wasn't the gunmetal gray showroom gem it had once been, but in the dim light of the lot he was happy to see it hadn't been towed or otherwise screwed with during his time away. He finally started to decompress once he got on the main drag leading off the base. As he waited at the last red light before he'd clear the base, he noticed over to his right that the parking lot of the officers club was filled. It was Wednesday night, a *club* night, and he felt the tug.

The light turned green and he slowly drifted into the intersection, wrestling with his options. If he went straight he'd be wrapped in his fiancée's pleasure within the half hour. If he turned right, he'd be laughing and scratching with the boys over a cold one or two, essentially the same thing he'd been doing in Key West for the last two weeks.

Punk resolved to stay at the club only a short time. He called Anita and told her that he had some things to finish up, and walked through the automatic sliding doors and funneled into the main bar.

The first group to catch his eye was a collection of Air Force pilots in town with their flying machines on cross-countries, other service rivals testing the turf firsthand to see if the tales of women and revelry were true. Punk counted four of them, noting the F-16 patches on their flight suits.

The group surrounded a dark-haired women like hyenas, cutting their prey off from the rest of the herd. Punk watched her and could see from the clumsy movement of her head that she was drunk. One of the pilots produced a camera and another propped the woman's head up and put his cheek next to hers in a pose documenting just how wild their night in Navy Fightertown had been. After the flash went off, the pilot returned his to his drink on the bar. The woman's unsupported head flopped backward. As her hair fell from around her face, Punk realized it was Suzanne.

Punk elbowed his way through the crowd, pushed through the Air Force gauntlet, and grabbed her. She sloppily wheeled around but didn't seem to recognize him. He slipped his arm around her waist and got her to her feet. Her knees buckled several times, but he managed to keep her upright.

He started to escort her through the throng, but one of the Air Force pilots stepped in his way.

"What the fuck do you think you're doing?" he asked. Punk looked up from monitoring Suzanne's wobbly gait and saw he was in the middle of a showdown. The Air Force officers stood with arms crossed, elbow-to-elbow around him.

"I'm going to take her home," Punk explained, and started to push between them.

"Bullshit," the nearest one returned, grabbing Punk by a lapel of his flight suit. "We've been working this one, pal, and drinks ain't free."

Punk grabbed the man's wrist and pulled his arm away, careful not to lose his grip on Suzanne in the process. "Look, fellas, she's—"

"She's spoken for, asshole," another of the Air Force guys said as he took hold of Punk's flight suit with both hands. Punk saw from the insignia sewn about their shoulders that they were all captains, the Air Force equivalent of his rank. None of them was any bigger than he, but he was outnumbered. He looked for some help from his servicemates but couldn't see beyond his opponents.

Another of the visiting pilots dug his grip into Punk's arm, and Punk winced and used both arms to parry the man's hand away. Suzanne fell to the carpet, and as he reached for her, he was stood up by three of them and pushed against the bar. His arms were pinned, and the one directly in front of him drew his fist back. Punk tucked his chin down and braced for the shot.

Suddenly the man cried out. Someone had grabbed his arm from behind and twisted it against his back. Another arm slinked around his neck, and Spud's face appeared across his shoulder.

"I always thought you Air Force knobs were smarter than this," the lieutenant commander said. The man kept resisting, so Spud pushed the twisted arm farther up his back, which caused the pilot to cry out again. "Now we can go two ways here, friends. You guys let my favorite fighter pilot take the lady home, and I'll get you all a drink, or you guys get your asses kicked all the way back to your tiny little jets by me and my band of Navy brothers here."

The other three pilots looked past Spud and saw that he was accompanied by a handful of respectably-sized Navy guys who looked ready to rumble, including Smitty.

"Relax, Murph," one of the captains advised the guy Spud held. "We're outgunned."

Spud felt the man's body slacken, and he released his grip. "Go ahead, get her out of here," he said to Punk, who gathered Suzanne off of the floor, threw her arm around his neck, and made for the side exit. Just before the door shut behind him, he heard Spud call out, "Beer all around!"

"My car's this way," Suzanne slurred as Punk guided her across the asphalt toward his pickup.

"You're not driving anywhere," Punk said. "I'll take you home."

"I'm fine," she insisted. Her knee buckled and she nearly fell again but Punk tightened his grip and caught her.

Suzanne fought getting into Punk's truck like a racehorse balking at the starting gate. On the third attempt he managed to synchronize her flailing limbs and wedge her into the passenger seat. He quickly strapped the seatbelt around her and shut the door.

They rode in silence for three miles. Suzanne craned across the headrest and occasionally moaned as her head lolled from side to side. Punk divided his attention between the road and Suzanne, and he thought of Crud. What would he think if he could see her?

"Stop the car," she suddenly demanded. "I'm going to throw up."

Punk pulled onto the shoulder, and she opened the door and loudly yielded to the nausea. He was afraid she might fall out so he gripped her sweater with one hand while rubbing her back with the other. After the third convulsion she wearily pulled her body back into the pickup and shut the door.

"My mouth tastes terrible," she groaned.

"We'll stop and get you something to drink," Punk said.

Punk pulled into the drive-thru lane of the first fast-food place they came to. "What do you want?" he asked as he approached the festively colored but poorly lit menu board.

"A soda," she replied, hand against her forehead.

"What kind?"

"Whatever . . ."

A perky female voice crackled through the little speaker mounted in the center of the menu: "May I help you?"

"A large orange soda, please," Punk said.

"Orange?" Suzanne said with disgust. "Not orange."

Punk almost snapped back at her, but instead he leaned through the window and said, "Change that to a cola."

"Diet," Suzanne said.

"Diet cola," Punk said, edging still closer to the speaker.

"One large diet cola," the distorted voice said. "Anything else?"

Punk arched his eyebrows at Suzanne, and she shook her head.

"No, that'll be it," he said.

"A dollar twenty-nine. Please drive around."

The drink kept Suzanne both awake and silent for the rest of the trip. Punk could see from the sloppy motion of her hands and head that she was still pretty drunk. As Punk pulled into her neighborhood, he thought about the time during his last deployment when he'd received an E-mail from Crud announcing that Suzanne and he had just become what they'd always feared: working stiffs with a mortgage. Crud had loved the house and reveled in the little projects that gave it personality, bragging at work about a new router, or how he'd mounted shelving above the washer/dryer.

Punk worked the doorknob and before he could get the door open the baby-sitter, a bespectacled curly-haired lass who looked to be in her mid-teens, cracked it and peered through. Suzanne suddenly put her hand to her mouth and pushed into the house, brusquely barreling past the sitter.

"She's okay," Punk said as the girl watched Suzanne sprint through the living room. "I think she ate something that didn't agree with her." He stepped inside accompanied by the twice-repeated sound of violent retching from the bathroom. "Is Jason in bed?"

"Yeah, he was a little cranky, but he went down after a while. I let him watch a little more TV until he calmed down. I hope that's all right."

"Sure, that's fine. How far away do you live?"

"Just a couple of houses down. I can make it home by myself."

Punk held the door while the girl stood by like a bellhop waiting for a tip. After a moment, he got the hint. "How much do we owe you?"

She looked to the ceiling and performed the mental gymnastics. "Let's see . . . three hours . . . eight dollars an hour . . . that's twenty-four dollars."

"Eight dollars an hour, huh?"

She smiled wryly. "I'm very good."

He opened his wallet and found a ten and two twenties. "You wouldn't happen to have change?" The sitter shook her head, and he resignedly handed her thirty dollars. She took the bills and hurried out of the door.

Suzanne had not reappeared, so Punk walked to the

kitchen to get something to drink, stopping along the way to look at the photos of Crud on the wall. He'd been in that hallway many times, and it felt weird not to hear Crud's jovial voice echoing throughout the house.

He searched the kitchen cabinets until he found a glass and was about to dispense some ice from the refrigerator door when he heard Suzanne throw up again. He waited until the noise subsided and then padded to the hall bathroom and furtively peered in. Suzanne was sitting on the vinyl-tiled floor in front of the toilet with her back against the wall.

"Are you going to make it?" he asked in what he hoped was a calming voice.

She looked startled at first, but then offered a weak smile and moaned.

"Can I get you anything?"

She mumbled something and shook her head.

"Why don't you try a shower?" he suggested. "That always makes me feel better. Can you get up?"

Suzanne nodded and waved him out.

"Okay. You take a shower," Punk said as he backed out. "I'll go watch some TV in the den. Call if you need me. You sure I can't get you anything? Water? Coffee?"

"No," she said.

He pulled the bathroom door shut and went back to the kitchen to make a pot of coffee.

About fifteen minutes later, Suzanne entered the den dressed in shorts and a T-shirt, with her wet hair wrapped in a towel. She curled up on the couch with a mug of coffee Punk had poured for her cradled in her lap. Punk noted that her movements seemed more deliberate than they'd been when he'd wrestled her into his car. The shower must have done her some good, although her eyes showed the lingering effects of the evening.

"What are you watching?" she asked.

"It's an old B flick," Punk said. *"Cheers for Reggie."*

"You guys and your cruise classics. How many times have you seen this one?"

"Hundreds, but it's impossible to look away."

She smiled and sipped the coffee. The silence between them was contrasted by the loud slapstick humor of the movie. Punk sat in the recliner, staring at the TV screen, mindlessly running his fingers over the keys of the remote control like a blind person reading braille.

Punk grew tired of the tension. "What were you doing at the club?" She didn't reply, so he turned toward her. "Did you hear me?"

"Yes," she answered with eyes unfocused on the table in front of her.

"And?"

"And . . . what do you care?"

"What's that supposed to mean? Of course I care."

"Really? You care like the squadron wives care, right?" She spilled coffee down her wrist and forearm. "You've all disappeared from the face of the earth."

"I've called you," he offered, unsure of what to say.

"Called me? That's very generous, Rick." As she dabbed her arm with a napkin the towel around her head unraveled and fell. She rubbed it against her wet locks a few times and then threw it to the floor. "You haven't been by the house since the day you came by to tell me that Cal was dead." Tears welled in her eyes as her voice broke. "That was almost two months ago."

He grew even less sure of what to say. "I guess I was afraid that I'd bring bad memories."

"Bad memories?" she echoed with a sardonic laugh. "Rick, those were the happiest days of my life. I loved being a Navy wife. But now I'm a leper."

"You're not a leper."

"Yes, I am. I see it in the faces of people when I walk into a room. I'm damaged goods. My identity is lost, and I'm trying to find where it went. That's why I was at the club tonight. Nobody invited me to go, so I went by myself." She began sobbing. He felt the urge to go over to her but was unsure if that was what she wanted, so he didn't. "And then when I got there," she continued through the tears, "nobody talked to me . . . so the Air Force guys thought I was unattached . . . and started buying me drinks. I'm not sorry to tell you the attention felt good."

"Yeah, but—"

"But what? But I look like a boomerang girl? Like a club whore? You can't judge me until you've walked in my shoes. I don't fly your jets, but I'm not a museum piece for everyone to ignore and then display when it suits them. I'm a real person." She reached down for the towel and dabbed her eyes with it.

"I'm sorry, Suzanne," He rose out of the chair. " I *am* here for you."

"Oh, yeah? You're here for me? You're too busy getting engaged. What are you going to do for me?"

He extended his arms and smiled. "I could give you a hug."

Her face brightened and she got off the couch with a sigh and put her arms around him. She buried her face in his chest and tried to laugh but instead began to cry again. "I didn't think it would hurt this bad," she said. "I loved him so much."

"Me too," Punk added as he stroked her damp hair. "Me too."

He held her until the tears stopped. She raised her head and saw she'd left a good-sized wet spot on the front of his flight suit. "I've drenched you."

"That's all right," he said. "This bag needs to be washed anyway. I don't know how you can stand to be close to me. I've got to stink."

"You do," she laughed between sniffles, "but I miss that sort of thing, too."

The last thing Punk needed to see as he opened the door to his condo was a woman sitting on his couch in a terrycloth bathrobe crying. He glanced at his watch, and only then did he realize how much time had passed since he'd talked to Anita on his cell phone. He threw his bag on a kitchen stool and went over to her.

"What's wrong?" he asked, hoping his voice delivered a sincere ignorance about why she might be upset.

Anita wiped her eyes with the backs of her wrists, smearing the already smeared eyeliner farther down her cheeks. "Nothing," she blubbered.

He sat down on the couch and wrapped his arms around her, but she didn't reciprocate. "No hug, huh? Something *is* wrong."

Anita recoiled to the far arm of the couch. "Where were you?" she asked without facing him.

He'd long since lost the endurance it was going to take to tell the truth, so he tried floating a white lie: "I told you; I had some things to finish up around the squadron."

"For three hours?"

Punk was going to have to give her something of substance. "Well, I was working with the master chief, and that took a long time; then I had to stop by the officers club to find the operations officer and get him to sign a form."

She finally looked at him. "The officers club, huh? Isn't that convenient?"

"That's where Spud was. I can't help that. It's where most guys go on Wednesday night."

She sat up straight and drew the bathrobe's collar around her neck. "So how long did you stay at the club?"

"Why the third degree?"

"I asked a question."

Punk paced toward the kitchen. "Well, this certainly is a delightful homecoming."

"I could say the same thing, couldn't I? How long were you at the club?"

"I don't know. I didn't really pay attention. It took me a while to find Spud, and then he bought me a beer and we started talking. Then I left."

"Who did you leave with?"

Punk snapped his head around toward Anita. "One of your fucking little friends called you, didn't she? That's what this is all about." He marched back to the couch, anger growing along the way, and stood in front of her. "I'll tell you who I left with: Suzanne Workman, that's who. She was drunk and getting hit on by some Air Force jerks, so I drove her home. I stuck around her house until I was sure she wasn't going to die of alcohol poisoning or hit her head on something." He threw his arms out. "There, you've got me."

"Why didn't you tell me that in the first place? Why did you lie to me?"

"I didn't lie to you."

"You didn't tell me the truth, either." The corners of Anita's mouth jerked downward as she weakly waged a battle against her tears.

Punk attempted to comfort her by moving behind the couch and massaging her neck and shoulders, but she stiffened at his touch and flew off of the couch. "What do you want from me?" he asked exasperatedly.

She abruptly stopped crying. "Not a thing, Rick. I'm leaving." She moved toward the bedroom and he followed her, wondering what he could say at that point to salvage the evening.

"Why are you doing this?" Punk asked as she stuffed clothes into an overnight bag on his bed. She tried to work the zipper closed, but it didn't budge. She cursed and threw the bag across the room and flopped backward onto the bed and began to cry again, more violently this time. Punk remained unsure of what to do, so he simply leaned against a dresser and waited for her to calm down.

Her cries subsided into whimpers, and eventually she was composed enough to sit up. "You want to know what I want from you?" she asked as she stared blankly at a framed America's Cup print on the wall.

"What?"

She locked his eyes with hers. "I want to be the one you rescue. I'm your fiancée, after all, Rick."

He moved over and kneeled at her feet, taking her shaking hands in his firm ones. "You *are* the one I'd rescue, if you needed it. Tonight Suzanne needed rescuing. She's my best friend's widow. What would you want me to do, walk off and leave her to the wolves?"

Anita's expression relaxed. "No, of course not."

"You should thank God you're not in her position. You're playing the victim here, but think about what she's going through. She's a wreck."

"I know . . ." She sighed. He felt the fight leaving her and sensed the advantage was shifting in his favor. In the time they'd dated they hadn't fought very often, and when they had she hadn't seemed willing to sustain discord for very long. "A phone call would've been nice, though."

"You're right; you're right." Punk rubbed his palms along the tops of her thighs. "It's been a long day. Why don't I get us a couple of drinks and we'll go to bed." He moved his hands up and undid the knot tied in the bathrobe's belt and then cupped her breasts and kissed her deeply. Her lips were salty from the tears.

"I'm glad to be home, doll," he said. She'd always been a sucker for that word.

"I need you, Rick," she replied in a way that sounded wholly more earnest than what he'd said.

As she took the bathrobe off and crawled naked under the sheets, he slipped out of his flight suit and walked to the kitchen dressed only in his blue-and-gold-striped boxers. He pulled a bottle of white wine out of the refrigerator and filled two glasses. He threaded his fingers around the stems with a single hand and switched the lights off one by one on the way back to the bedroom. As he reached under the last lampshade he caught a whiff of something foul. He torqued around and realized the stink was coming from his underarms, so he decided to grab a quick shower before joining Anita in bed.

He stood under the stream of hot water inside the smoked glass stall and thought about Suzanne. The idea of her being some Air Force puke's one-night stand made his skin crawl, and he cursed himself for allowing her to feel abandoned. She deserved better from him. Crud's memory deserved better from him.

He toweled himself dry and remembered he had a living pinup nude and waiting in the next room. He grabbed the wineglasses, and by the time he made it through the threshold of his bedroom he was fully primed.

But not for long. As Punk started to climb onto the bed he saw that Anita was fast asleep, smeared makeup giving her the look of a disheveled mime in repose. He entertained the notion of giving her a nudge, but her sad face stole the impulse. He slid across to the other side of the bed and crawled under the sheets. He was asleep before his head hit the pillow.

CHAPTER TEN

The replacements sat in the dark behind several rows of long tables, watching the large monitor in a front corner of the classroom. The screen was black save for a set of white crosshairs across the length and width of it in the foreground and a series of digits, some constant, some constantly changing, along the top of the picture. Two dots of light appeared in the background, moving slowly apart across the middle of the screen and growing larger. The dots continued to track outward, superimposed along the horizontal axis of the crosshairs, before sagging and then disappearing. A few seconds later a bright flash washed out the screen. The monitor went black.

"Class Two, welcome to the carrier qualification phase of your RAG syllabus," Lieutenant "Creepy" Morgan said as he clicked the classroom lights on. "You all know me by now, so we'll dispense with the formalities where I tell you about my amazing life. I am the CQ phase leader. For the next five weeks it's my job to make sure you don't wind up planting yourself on the ramp of the aircraft carrier like the Tomcat pilot in the PLAT tape we just watched did." Creepy gestured toward the monitor. "As you can probably guess from the size of the explosion, neither of the guys in the airplane survived."

Creepy was an extremely strange-looking human being. He was tall and thin with limbs that bent at odd angles when he moved and fingers as long as carrots. His face was gaunt and pale and his eye sockets were dark caves in which his beady eyes hid. His hairline had receded nearly to the crown of his head and he parted the tuft of curly brown hair that remained down the middle in a style seemingly created by the single swipe of an ax. Fleet lore had it that one time during his first deployment, Creepy had gone down to the ship's library to read and had eventually fallen asleep. When the enlisted librarian walked in and caught sight of the pilot slumped in a chair—pallor of cadaver gray, body motionless with hands folded across his chest—he'd assumed Creepy was dead and hailed a medical response team.

Creepy moved to the podium and raised a thin, blue-covered book. "This is CV NATOPS, not to be confused with the regular NATOPS, which is about five times as fat. But just because CV NATOPS is skinny doesn't mean it isn't important. You guys have to know every number in here." He pointed at Stormin' in the front row. "When do you slow to approach airspeed in the Case One pattern?"

Stormin' fumbled with the answer for a few seconds and then threw his hands up and guessed, "At the one-eighty?"

"Wrong!" Creepy returned, maniacally delighted by the gaffe. "The right answer is once you reach the bow on downwind." He leveled another finger at Dusty. "At which of the four points that define the low-holding circle overhead the carrier do you descend into the break?"

"Point four," Dusty said, phrasing his reply more like a question than an answer.

"Wrong!" Creepy sang out again. "The correct answer is point three." He focused on Muddy. "The air boss owns the airspace within a what-mile radius from the carrier?"

"Ten," she said without hesitation.

"Wrong . . . er, that's right." He smiled sheepishly but quickly recaptured his stern demeanor. "Obviously, many of you have studying to do." He placed the CV NATOPS back on the podium. "All right. You guys have come a long way. You made it through FAM; you made it through Basic Weapons; you made it through Strike; you made it through Tactics. But guess what? None of that is going to matter if you can't land on the Boat.

"You see, you all are in the Navy, not the Air Force. We don't flare our jets and gently touch down on our one-million-foot-long, ten-thousand-foot-wide runways. We start our flights by hooking our jets up to a catapult and throwing all sixty-seven thousand pounds of them into the air in two-point-two seconds, and when we're done we slam down at a seven-hundred-foot-per-minute rate of descent, catch a wire with our tailhooks while our jets are at full military power and stop within a couple of hundred feet. And, oh, by the way, our runway moves around in the angry sea. And we land at night and in bad weather."

Creepy walked over to the far end of the front row and put his long fingers on one of Smitty's big shoulders. "And RIOs, you guys need to pay attention during this phase, too. This is where you put on your copilot hats and back your pilots up all the way to touchdown. I'd never want to be you, quite frankly, but if I was you I'd make damned sure I wasn't just along for the ride. If your pilot drives the jet into the ramp, you're going to die a microsecond after he or she does."

The instructor moved back behind the podium. "I am the RAG's senior Landing Signal Officer. The squadron has two other LSOs, Fitz and Gordo, whom you all know already, as well." Creepy looked at Auto. "Stand up."

Auto raised his eyebrows and asked, "Me? Stand up?"

"Yes, stand up!" Creepy shouted, shocking the rest of the class and jolting Auto to his big feet. Creepy scanned the room. "Didn't I just say I was an LSO? Auto, sit back down." The doughy pilot compliantly slid back into his plastic chair. "Pilots, when an LSO tells you to do something, you do it without question. Muddy, if I say, 'Wave it off,' what do you do?"

"Wave it off," she replied.

"Right. Stormin', if I say, 'Power,' what do you do?"

"Add power."

"Very good. You guys are getting the hang of this. Dusty, if I say, 'Drop your trousers,' what do you do?"

"Drop my trousers," Dusty replied with more confidence than he'd mustered for his previous response.

"No," Creepy railed, "you call the JAG. You're not gay, are you? No, wait; I can't ask that . . ." The class laughed, and Dusty turned beet red. "There are limits to my power, but not many. The point is, when an LSO gives you pilots a mandatory call on the radio, you comply with it immediately; no questions asked. We can debate whether you thought the call was necessary in the debrief if we need to.

"This is how the carrier qualification phase is going to go in a nutshell: Replacement pilots will be crewed with the same instructor RIO for the duration of the phase. Replacement RIOs will be crewed with the more senior pilots who happen to be coming through for a quick refresher on their way back to the fleet. Now, we've got six RIOs in Class Two and we're only going to have two refreshers, a future skipper and a future department head. The top two RIOs grade-wise will get to fly with them. The rest of you will just have to wait until you hit the fleet for your first taste of carrier action. Trust me, there's a good reason we don't put replacement pilots and RIOs together for their first CQs. I wouldn't have wanted to be in my backseat for my first catapult launch.

"Now, to qualify, pilots have to complete ten arrested landings during the daytime and six at night. But before we send you to the Boat, you're going to practice your buns off down at Fentress, our auxiliary landing field twelve miles south of here in the middle of a swamp. We call it 'field carrier landing practice,' 'FCLPs,' or 'bouncing.' You'll learn to hate Fentress like we all do, except you guys are going to hate it worse because of the hours you'll be flying down there. You see, the RAG is lowest priority on the scheduling side of things and right now there are two fleet air wings getting ready to go back to sea, so you'll be flying somewhere between two and four in the morning for most of your ten bounce periods. Each bounce period consists of launching out of Oceana, flying down to Fentress for ten touch-and-gos, all graded by an LSO, and then returning to Oceana. Are we having fun yet?"

Creepy went to the front of the classroom next to the dry erase board and removed one of the four plastic models on dowels that were hanging from hooks drilled into the wall there. He held up the miniature Tomcat on a stick for the replacements to see. "Here's another rule to drill into your heads right from the get-go: When an LSO tells you to wave it off, your natural inclination is to attempt to climb right away and therefore your first reaction might be to pull the stick back to get the nose up." He tilted the model in concert with his words. "The Tomcat is nearly sixty-three feet long, so when you bring the nose up the first thing that happens is the tail goes down, and that means the tailhook goes down. Now if you get a late wave off call and do this as you cross the ramp you might catch a wire while you're trying to fly away. That's called an 'in-flight engagement.' The Tomcat has a lot of thrust but it doesn't have enough to take an aircraft carrier flying with it, so the wire will stop the jet in midair and slam it onto the deck. If this happens, at best you'll blow a tire. Usually the damage is much worse. I know of a couple of jets that were struck from the inventory following in-flight engagements. Suffice it to say your landing grade for that pass won't help your average."

Creepy canted the model back to near level again. "There's only one right move when you get the call to wave it off: Hold the attitude; I repeat, hold the attitude, and advance the throttles to military power. Do not raise the nose."

He hung the model back against the wall. "Any questions yet? Anybody need a break?" The replacements didn't move for fear of the Dusty treatment. Creepy shrugged and silently snatched a remote control from the podium, aimed it at the monitor, and pushed the Source button a few times, switching the display from the VCR's output to that of the computer. "All right, let's get into the weeds here and start talking about the Case One pattern . . ."

The third time he heard Flex exclaim, "You've got to be shitting me," Punk shut the water off, pulled the plastic curtain back, and asked, "What are you talking about?"

"This article in today's paper," Flex explained, dressed only in gym shorts and seated on the wooden bench that ran the length of the lockers in the instructors' locker room. "Listen to this: 'When asked how she enjoyed the demanding training in Key West, Lieutenant (junior grade) Greenwood said, "I'm not going to lie to you; it's fun shooting an instructor." ' "

"That's in today's paper?"

"Sure is. Check out this headline: 'Female Fighter Pilot Is Real Top Gun.' "

"When did Muddy have time to give an interview? She just got back yesterday afternoon."

"They must have been waiting for her right as she walked off the transport. There's a picture of her here and everything."

Punk wrapped a towel around his waist and slapped his wet feet across the tile floor to Flex and studied the photo over the RIO's shoulder. The shot showed Muddy dressed in khakis, a polite, understated grin on her face, flanked on one side by the same lieutenant commander PAO with whom Punk had exchanged words the day of her first attempt at a FAM-1. On the other side was Ferguson Platt, who was the only one of the three looking at the camera. In the background was part of the fuselage of the C-9 transport with the words "Spirit of Jacksonville" written on it in script.

Punk started to read the article but Flex grew bothered by his hovering and folded the paper in a huff and said he was late for his weight lifting session at the base gym. After throwing on a sleeveless T-shirt and sparring with several lockers, Flex flung the locker room door open and jogged out.

Punk sat down on the bench and read the paper:

FEMALE FIGHTER PILOT IS REAL TOP GUN

By Melanie Gravasso, Staff Writer

The student pilots stride across the ramp at the Naval Air Station Oceana with a new swagger following a two-week period in Key West, Florida, spent honing their skills in aerial combat. These are the real Top Guns, cookie-cutter models of those who have previously made the grade and demonstrated the right stuff behind the controls of a supersonic fighter jet.

But one among them is noticeably different. Instantly distinguishable by the flowing brown hair over the collar of her uniform, Lieutenant (junior grade) Evelyn Greenwood has joined the ranks of the traditionally all-male community of naval aviation, and her success in the training program so far speaks volumes about how far the military has come with gender integration in the past decade.

"The fact that Lieutenant Greenwood is female is not an issue with us," Lieutenant Commander Hank Sparza, spokesman for the Atlantic Fleet, said. "The Navy has been in front of this from the very beginning. It's a success story."

Greenwood, who goes by the nickname "Muddy" because she likes to take her jeep off-road on weekends, said she was initially intimidated by the sheer size of the F-14 Tomcat but that she overcame that concern.

"It's really no different than any airplane I've ever flown when you get right down to it," she explained. "Now that I know what the Tomcat can and can't do, I'm very comfortable with it."

Greenwood's fighter pilot status is the culmination of years of dreams and hard work. She was raised near a small airport in Illinois and enjoyed watching the airplanes fly over her house. That interest drove her to the Naval Academy in Annapolis, Maryland. During her senior year when it came time for service selections, she had no doubts. "I took an honest look at all my options, you know, ships, even the Marine Corps. None of those came close to matching my desire to fly airplanes."

But she discovered it takes more than just desire to succeed. "It's extremely challenging and rewarding when you accomplish the mission," she said. "It does beat having a real job, though."

When asked how she enjoyed the demanding training in Key West, Lieutenant (junior grade) Greenwood said, "I'm not going to lie to you; it's fun shooting an instructor."

Punk glanced at the photo again and clucked a laugh over the last quote. To his knowledge she'd scored only one kill during the entire detachment. Operation Greenwood Press was obviously still in full swing.

Once dressed, Punk negotiated the several dozen stairs in a handful of strides and then stepped into the hangar bay, which was a hotbed of activity, being a post-detachment no-fly day—a chance for the air force to get healthy. He stood and watched a team of aviation machinist mates attempt to drop a huge turbofan engine out of the starboard nacelle of one of the Tomcats and onto a dolly. Punk passed around the opposite side of the now single-engine Tomcat and continued past the large hangar doors into the oppressive humidity of post–rain squall August. He decided to say hello to a few of the plane captains, who were grooming the jets parked in several neat rows on the flight line.

"Hey there, Airman Powolski," Punk called up to the young sailor straddling the pilot's ejection seat while cleaning the inside of the canopy on the first jet in the row of a dozen or so. "Welcome back from Key West."

"I'd say it's great to be back, Lieutenant," the ruddy-faced Powolski replied, protective helmet with built-in "mouse ears" causing him to speak louder than he needed to, "but I found out my girlfriend moved in with another dude while we were gone." His normally pink cheeks were crimson with the heat, and he wiped the Plexiglas with such intensity that Punk feared it might crack. "That's what I get for hooking up with a chick who works at a massage parlor, I guess."

Punk wasn't sure what to say back, so he offered a friendly life's-a-bitch wave and moved on. The next jet on the line was one-eleven, the jet with Punk's name on the side of it. His name had been on a number of jets between his fleet squadron and the RAG, moving up in each inventory as he rose in seniority, and he'd never grown tired of seeing the letters neatly stenciled down a canopy rail. He admired the right side for a while and then moved under the belly behind the nose gear to admire the left. Once he threaded his way around the boarding ladder and stood erect again, he suddenly found himself face-to-face with Corky McBride.

"Punk," the weathered tech rep said with pseudo warmth, "I've been looking all over for you."

"Oh, really?" Punk responded, trying his best not to look taken aback. "What's up?"

"Let's go for a walk." Corky grabbed Punk at the elbow and moved with him toward the far end of the flight line, away from any activity.

"Where are we going?"

"To talk in private. This needs to be just between you and me."

They walked all the way behind the ordnance shack, a low-slung building at the far reaches of the flight line where the ordies kept their arming pins and snoozed between loading drills, just before the ramp turned to taxiway. There wasn't a soul around, and Punk was reminded of the sorts of locales where hits were carried out in gangster movies. There was silence between them for a short time. Corky put a cigarette between his lips but didn't light it. "No smoking zone," he explained.

Punk scanned the area and grew impatient. "What do you need, Corky?"

Corky studied the pilot. "You're a golfer aren't you?"

Punk grimaced in confusion. "What?"

"I heard you were one of the better golfers in the squadron. Is that true?"

"Well, I'm okay, I guess."

"Good." He looked to either side. "I'm in a bind here, and I'd really appreciate your help. My boss is in town, the big boss from corporate headquarters. He asked me to find him a young gun for his outing today."

"You dragged me all the way over here to ask if I wanted to play golf?"

"Yeah," Corky said. "I didn't want to ask you in front of the troops. They're convinced you officers do nothing but goof off as it is. So can you play or not?"

"Today? What's the tee time?"

"One thirty."

"Where's he playing?"

"Oak Tree."

Punk raised his eyebrows. Oak Tree was as exclusive as golf got this side of Augusta. He'd tried to wrangle his way onto that course since he'd moved to Virginia Beach nearly five years ago but hadn't ever come close to succeeding. Plus, he felt agreeable since he was more than a little relieved that Corky's topic was as innocent as filling a golf outing for his boss. He checked his watch: quarter to twelve. It was a slow day around the squadron. He could run home and change into his golf togs and be on the driving range within the hour. "How much are the greens fees?"

"RDI's got you covered."

"Is that legal?"

"We do it all the time." Not an answer, really, but close enough for Punk's standards of conduct.

"Who else would I be playing with?"

"Mr. Rainno and two others. It's just a casual get-together. The boss likes to talk to fleet operators to keep his finger on the pulse."

"Just a casual little get-together, Corky?"

"Don't worry about it. I'm sure it'll just be an older version of the boys in the ready room. Are you in or not?"

Punk shrugged. Free golf at a signature course was hard to turn down. "Sure. Why not?"

"All right. I owe you. I'll call the course and let them know you'll be coming."

"I'd better get moving, then." The lieutenant started to walk away.

"Hold on," Corky said. Punk saw him slowly reach into his blazer, and again his mind briefly registered the image of an assassin and his hapless victim. "You'll be needing these." Corky produced a sleeve of golf balls. "I don't know how good they are, but they do have the RDI logo on them. As long as I'm around that'll be worth something."

"Rick, is it?" the big man asked as he extended his arm toward the lieutenant. "Lafayette Rainno; call me Laf." Punk was immediately struck by his sheer size—neither muscle-bound nor flabby, just *big*—and his dark tan. Under a white silk polo already soaked with sweat, he wore a solid gold rope chain with a missile-shaped medallion hanging from it. His full head of golden blond hair was slicked straight back. He reminded Punk of a professional wrestler. Rainno jabbed a thumb over his shoulder. "Do you know these guys?"

"Ah, no, sir."

The two other members of the foursome stepped from behind their host. The first guy to reach out was a short, thin gent with immaculately groomed white hair and a complexion that looked as if he hadn't seen the light of day all summer. Punk was sure they'd met before, but he couldn't remember when or where. "Grayson Knowles," he said without fanfare as they shook.

Admiral Knowles, Commander in Chief of the Atlantic Fleet. "Good to see you again, sir," Punk replied, immediately searching for the appropriate balance of reverence and golf-style camaraderie. The admiral's faded blue golf shirt was too small and at least twenty years out of fashion with sleeves that barely made it halfway down his bony biceps and stayed collars that came to dramatic points.

The other man threaded in his introduction behind the admiral's. He was of average height and build and had a sharp jawline, a long neck, and seventies-length hair that was too black and so tightly permed that it didn't look real. His choice of clothing was more up-to-date than the admiral's, although the combination of a red shirt and blue slacks with a white belt was a bit much to Punk's sartorial eye.

"Rick?" the man confirmed, grip noticeably softer than what had been offered during the previous two handshakes. "I'm Marty Long."

Congressman Long. Well, that explained the campy ensemble. Although Punk had never met the man, he did know, based on the comments from some of his more politically astute squadronmates, that Long was a promilitary conservative, which didn't seem like a stretch since he represented an area that included both the largest naval station and shipbuilding complex in the world.

A CEO, an admiral, and a congressman, Punk thought. *Just a casual get-together, huh, Corky?*

Two caddies came over—short, sweaty Latinos each humping a couple of bags—and one of them announced in broken English that the group was due on the first tee.

The starter, wearing knickers and showing his advanced age, seemed unimpressed with the august standing of the individuals in the group, and he sternly reviewed the local course rules with them. Once his speech was complete he paused as if waiting for questions. Their body language—arms crossed and eyes averted—suggested they didn't have any. So, with an elegant gesture toward the white markers, the starter bade them happy golfing.

Rainno took to the tee box and announced that the bet was a round robin, six holes paired with each of the other members of the foursome, five dollars to the winner of each hole. Punk tallied the potential losses, happy that he'd stopped at the ATM on his way to the course.

Rainno took the four players' golf balls in his hands and tossed them into the air. When they came to rest on the grass, Punk was paired with the congressman.

Rainno then flipped a tee, which landed with the pointed end facing him. "I guess we're up first, Gray," he said to the admiral. "Why don't you do us the honor?"

The admiral teed up his ball and went through his preshot routine, which involved three runs through his cantan-

kerous swing while he stared at his hands. He finally
addressed the ball, let out an audible exhale, and took the
club back, slower than he had during his practice swings.
He paused at the top and then lashed at the ball so hard his
right foot came off the ground during the follow-through. It
was an ugly, angry motion, and Punk was amazed to see
the ball sail respectably over the fairway, tracking slightly
left to right, and come to rest about two hundred and
twenty-five yards away. The admiral purposefully plucked
his tee out of the ground as if he wasn't at all surprised by
the shot; he even let out a little moan as if he was disappointed by the result.

Rainno was next. He swiped at the golf ball with the same
intensity Punk figured he applied to any of his undertak-
ings, but unfortunately golf was a sport that didn't necessarily respond to smash-mouth desire. His wild follow-through
twisted his body, and he almost fell over as the rest of the
group watched his drive duck hook into the left rough less
than one hundred yards from them. Rainno caught his balance with an awkward splay of his right leg and a timely
plant of his driver. He looked at his palms before tossing
the club to the caddy and directing him to keep the grips
dry.

"You can still make par from there, Laf," the admiral
offered as Rainno stormed off the teeing ground and the
congressman took his place.

The congressman's swing was a by-the-numbers arrange-
ment that Punk figured was the product of breeding and
several visits to expensive schools run by high-profile PGA
Tour svengalis in Florida or Arizona. Punk thought he
heard the lawmaker counting to himself as he swung at the
ball. The shot flew nicely, though, and wound up just beyond the admiral's.

The mental side of the game had always plagued Punk,
which is what kept him off the traveling squad at Annapolis
despite the fact that he consistently fired scores in the low
seventies during friendly rounds on the Academy's course
across the river from the main campus. Once the scores
began to count, however, like during tournament qualifying
rounds, he always found a way to take himself out of contention. Now as he bent over to stick his tee into the
ground, he was gripped by the notion that he could fuck it

up. These were not just the buds from the squadron; these were important men. They'd look at his nice clothes and top-of-the-line equipment and marvel at his practice swing and then laugh as he shanked one.

He looked down the fairway at the lush greenness and the white sand traps and the old trees and mused about what a crime it would be to dishonor the grounds with a crappy shot. *Don't think,* he thought as he took his stance and waggled a few times. *Just keep your head still and swing.*

And so he did, and he was delighted to hear them wax awestruck even before he'd had a chance to take his eyes off the ground over which his ball had just been perched. He looked up and caught sight of it, still climbing, and he held the follow-through like a pro, as if he'd intended everything after all.

"Holy shit," Rainno exclaimed. "I've played here for years and never seen anybody clear that bunker with a drive. That's got to be over three hundred yards out there." He stepped over and eyed the logo on Punk's yellow shirt. "Naval Academy Golf Team? No fucking wonder. This guy's more than a ringer. The bet's off."

"Oh, no, Laf," the congressman shot back. "This bet is definitely not off, at least not for the first six holes."

As they walked down the fairway, they split into two groups led by their caddies. The congressman gave Punk a pat on the back and congratulated him for a great shot. Punk felt obliged to warn him that he hadn't picked up a club for a few weeks and anything could happen with each swing, but the congressman wanted good ol' American can-do from his strapping young men and didn't seem to want to hear it.

On the second hole Punk stood by the caddy and watched Rainno agonize over the course architect's conspiring against him by placing a sand trap in the path of his thinned approach shot out of the rough.

"Why don't they cut this damn grass down some?" Rainno yelled toward the others in his group. "They ain't hosting the U.S. Open here."

"It's long, all right," the admiral agreed. Rainno had already used the U.S. Open metaphor five times this round.

After executing what had felt like a decent swing, Punk

watched his own approach shot fall miserably short of its target, and he feared the first hole magic had disappeared. He humbly handed his six iron back to the caddy, who offered an "almost" while the congressman put his own shot right next to the pin.

As they continued toward the green, the lawmaker, buoyed by his success, asked, "So, how are things in the Navy?" painting Punk with the same broad strokes he might the flag officer in the group. Punk tried to give a thoughtful answer, but the congressman seemed to lose interest about three-quarters of the way through it, and the lieutenant figured he'd been revealed as the big-picture poseur he was. He resolved to keep his remarks brief if he spoke at all.

Punk and Congressman Long won all of the first six holes, which caused Punk to relax enough that he thought he might be able to play well for the day. Rainno took a ball from each on the seventh tee and continued to grouse about what a ringer Punk was, in spite of the fact that most of the wins had been on the congressman's scores. The balls were tossed and Punk wound up paired with Admiral Knowles for the second third of the course.

They played on in silence save the occasional rant from Rainno, and the admiral didn't acknowledge Punk until the tenth hole when he walked over between shots and asked, "Do you know Lieutenant (junior grade) Greenwood?"

"Yes, sir," Punk replied. "She's a student of mine, in fact."

"She's really doing well," the admiral said without acknowledging the fidelity of Punk's answer. "Did you see today's paper?"

"Yes, sir."

"That was a *great* story." Admiral Knowles walked away and didn't say another word to him. They wound up winning four of the six holes they played together.

Punk was paired with Rainno for the last six. There was a backup at the thirteenth hole, a par three over water, so the two of them sat on a bench next to the tee box while the admiral and the congressman chatted in the shade of one of the course's signature oak trees.

"Hot enough, isn't it?" Rainno said as he mopped his big head with a towel. "This weather makes me glad I live in California most of the time."

"It doesn't get hot out there?" Punk asked.

"Not like this. It's desert heat; no humidity."

Punk hummed his understanding, and the conversation abruptly died. As they sat in awkward silence, Punk saw that the foursome in front of them still had a bit of a wait as the group on the green had just started putting. He wondered what Rainno would say if asked about the Tomcat's roll computer but attempted some small talk instead: "How long have you been with RDI?"

Rainno answered as if he'd just been handed the mike at a business luncheon: "My father started the company in 1964 after ten years in the Navy as a supply officer. He was a good man, a man with the dream that a business should be about more than mere bottom lines and getting by. He had a dream of excellence, and damn if he didn't see it through. People think RDI was always a big company, but it wasn't. It took a lot of work to get us where we are.

"When he died of cancer eleven years ago I was promoted to CEO from senior vice president in charge of foreign military sales. I've done what I can to keep Dad's dream alive."

Rainno paused and Punk figured he should say something to preserve the cadence of conversation. "That's all you can do, I guess."

"Yeah, but in many ways Dad's job was easier than mine."

"How's that?"

"Well, the Soviet Union loomed large for the duration of his tenure, and the Department of Defense had deep pockets." He stared blankly at his seven iron while working his thumbnail along the grooves in the face of it. "RDI operates on pretty tight margins these days. One contract can make or break the company. Even a rumor could kill us."

Rainno's tone changed, as if he'd caught himself being too negative and wanted to shake off the funk. "We'll be fine. I won't allow us to do anything less than thrive. And it not just me, either. Every employee of RDI is committed to the success of this company."

The foursome ahead of them cleared the tee box, and as Rainno stood he lost the thoughtful, shareholders-meeting veneer and returned to the role of boorish exec at play. He called over to the oak: "Are you two girls ready to get your asses kicked by me and my fighter pilot buddy here?"

Punk and Rainno won the first three holes of their pairing, and in the middle of the sixteenth fairway the CEO leaned his massive frame on a club and out of nowhere said, "I like you, Rick."

Punk wasn't sure how to respond. "Thanks for hosting me. This is a great course."

"No, I mean I really like you. You're a good guy. Corky chose well; better than usual." He made a couple of half swings while waiting for Admiral Knowles to hit out of the woods on the far side of the fairway. "Are you happy in the Navy?"

"Pretty much . . ."

"That's not an answer."

"I love flying jets."

"Yeah, who wouldn't?" Rainno said. "I had a backseat ride a few years back. Made me wish I'd decided to be a pilot. But that's life, right? Somebody's got to fly the jets, and somebody's got to make the stuff that makes the jets fly." He put his hand on Punk's shoulder. "At some point the flying stops and the making starts. That's when you need to be in the making business."

Once they'd holed their final putts, the others compensated their caddies as Rainno stood behind the green scribbling on a scorecard. The caddies scurried off to the storage room to clean the group's golf clubs, and the guests formed a semicircle around their host.

"All right," Rainno announced as he referenced his card, "Rick gets sixty dollars; Gray owes forty; Marty owes nothing and gets nothing; I owe twenty." He reached into his wallet and handed a crisp new bill to Punk. "I knew you were a ringer."

"At least it's going to a Navy guy," the admiral said as he handed Punk two twenties. "Lord knows you already get enough from me, Laf."

"Hell, I'm giving the Navy money for once," Rainno returned before pinning on a salesman's smile. "Gray, next time you talk to the Pentagon tell them I'm going to have to jack up prices a bit to make up for what your fighter pilots hustled out of me."

A lieutenant dressed in khakis, identifiable as the admiral's aide-de-camp by the aiguillette about his left shoulder, strode up and handed Admiral Knowles a cellular phone. Punk considered the aide's broad chin and intense manner, and he thought he recognized him. As the admiral walked a few steps away to conduct his conversation, the aide came over and asked, "Academy guy?"

"Yeah."

"I think we might have been in the same Weapons class first year. What are you doing here?"

"Playing golf," Punk replied as if there was nothing unusual about his presence in the foursome.

"Well, you must be doing pretty well if you're playing golf with Mr. Rainno and the admiral. Congratulations." He looked over his shoulder and saw Admiral Knowles was done with his phone call. "I've got to go do my thing. Great seeing you." The lieutenant took the cell phone back from his boss and jogged off toward the sedan he'd left idling at the curb near the entrance to the clubhouse.

Punk wanted to stop him and ask him what he'd meant by "congratulations." Congratulations for what? Worse still, was he winning something and didn't realize it? He watched the aide climb behind the wheel, unsure of whether he was envious of or repulsed by his peer's conception of success.

And he hadn't even caught the guy's name. That was how most chance reunions went, at least around the fleet between academy grads. A couple of hooks, a "Beat Army" or two, and practical strangers became long-lost brothers for a few seconds before they disappeared from each other's lives . . . until the next unplanned encounter when they'd make a big deal out of the coming-of-age events they'd shared.

"Laf, I've got to run," Admiral Knowles announced. "Five hours away from this job is more than I can get away with. Thanks for the round." He shook hands with the others and marched into the backseat of the sedan, and the aide sped off like there was a war to fight.

As the three remaining members of the foursome watched the admiral drive away, Congressman Long was suddenly hit by the impulse that he too was a busy man who couldn't stand around after the round was over. He pulled a slim cellular phone from the right front pocket of his pants, pushed the two-way button, and summoned his driver. Seconds later another sedan showed up in a cloud of dust. The congressman shook hands with Rainno and Punk and followed the admiral off of the club grounds.

"I could buy and sell both of those guys and I don't have a driver," Rainno observed. "How about you?"

"I don't have a driver," Punk said.

"No, do you have to rush off, too?"

"I'm not important enough for that."

Rainno laughed and said, "Neither are they, but that doesn't keep them from acting like they are." He gestured toward the massive Tudor-style building behind them. "Let me buy you a beer."

Rainno remarked that golf shoes weren't permitted in the clubhouse, so they went through a side door on the lower level into the men's locker room to change back into their street shoes. As he sat in a leather chair with his feet on soft carpet and slipped on his tasseled loafers, surrounded by lockers made of the finest cherry and paneled walls adorned by dramatically lit photographs of golfing greats, Punk was struck by the difference between his present surroundings and the locker room at the hangar where he'd showered earlier in the day.

The attendant, a guy who looked older than the starter and introduced himself to Punk as "Jack," reminded Rainno that jackets were required for gentlemen in the Grille Room after five P.M. Rainno had one for himself in his locker. Punk had to borrow one from Jack's stash of those left behind by visitors over the years. The tartan wool blazer was an inch short in the sleeves and out of season but fit well enough that it would get the fighter pilot into the Grille Room.

"Let me give you a quick tour of the place," Rainno said. He led Punk out of the locker room and up the wide stairs toward the brightness of the main entryway. They stopped in the foyer, just inside the revolving door that fed members in from the circular driveway, and admired the large wood-and-glass chandelier hanging from the high ceiling. Punk admired the grand light fixtures, ornate twists of brass and crystal that grew out of the glossed mahogany walls, the leather couches and chairs in the adjacent sitting area. There was lots of greenery about: sprawling figs in

wide pots on the fine carpet, lush ferns in planters mounted
on the walls, and arrangements of flowers at the center of
every table. The air had a pleasant scent, a blend of the
fragrances of tapestries, Persian rugs, and a hint of wood
smoke. The club receptionist, an elderly white-haired
woman who Rainno addressed as "Miss Garland," sat behind a huge colonial desk at the center of one wall and
nodded gracefully as the two men passed on their way into
the next room.

"Nothing too spectacular about this," Rainno said as he
went through the doorway. "Just your standard conference room."

"Standard, huh?" Punk said, marveling at the large
room. He knocked his knuckles against a massive oak table
with green-shaded banker's lights at each place. "I could
land a Tomcat on this."

Jammed bookcases ran the full height and width of two
walls. Punk pulled down a copy of John Updike's *Golf
Dreams,* one of his favorite books, and opened it to the
frontispiece and saw that the author had inscribed it to the
members of Oak Tree. He then inspected a copy of Steven
Pressfield's *The Legend of Bagger Vance* a few books over
and was amazed to see it was also signed by the author.

"You a reader?" Rainno asked, looking over Punk's
shoulder.

"Yeah," Punk replied, "especially when I'm on deployment." He pulled Ben Hogan's *Five Lessons of Golf* from
the shelf and gently brushed a finger over the signature as
if he might absorb some of the legend's magic from it.

"I love books," Rainno said as he swept an arm across
the two walls. "They're all signed first editions."

"There must be thousands of them," Punk gushed.
"That's got to be worth millions."

Rainno offered a shrug and moved across the room and
pulled back the drapes, revealing the eighteenth green
through a large bay window. The CEO stood with his hands
on his hips and took in the bucolic scene. "That's why I
don't do meetings in this room," he quipped. "It's impossible to pay attention."

Punk followed Rainno through a small side door and up
a staircase. As he negotiated the tight creaky stairs, Punk's
nose caught a faint whiff of mothballs. The temperature in

the narrow hallway at the top was a few degrees warmer than the rest of the clubhouse but not unbearable.

"This is sort of the secret part of the place," Rainno explained, "like a little hotel that some of the members don't even know about."

He twisted the first knob he came to and pushed the door open. Inside were a small raised bed, a chest of drawers, and a rocking chair. A finely framed picture of what looked to Punk to be the early days of Scottish golf adorned the wall above the carved oak headboard. The broad wooden beams of the roof cut an angle overhead giving half the room very low headroom. There was a window in the center of the slanted ceiling and through it the treetops were just visible. The feel of the place was cozy and permanent.

"Arnold Palmer lived here for two weeks before the U.S. Open in '62," Rainno said. "Or was it '63? No, it was '62. Anyway, nonresident members are allowed to stay in these rooms, if they want, although it's generally considered bad form to do so, for some reason, so nobody ever does. But there are four of them up here."

Downstairs in the Grille Room they were greeted by the captain who sat them at a table near a large bay window, much like the one in the conference room, overlooking the first tee. Rainno ordered two of the house lagers, and the corpulent, dark-skinned man in the short jacket nodded and hurried away.

"The club has its own brand," the CEO explained. "Our brewmeister was brought over special from Germany just to make beer for Oak Tree."

"This is an impressive club," Punk said, "but I don't understand why you're a member. You live in California. How many rounds do you play here in a year?"

"Five . . . ten, maybe. I'm a member of a lot of clubs around the country: this one, Baltusrol in New Jersey, Medinah in Chicago, Olympic Club in San Francisco, and Riviera in Los Angeles. It's a hobby, like collecting stamps."

Pretty expensive stamps, Punk thought.

"You've got a good game," Rainno said. "What club do you belong to?"

"None. I just play the military base courses around here." The big man shook his head in disgust. "Dog tracks all."

The beers arrived in tall slender glasses. Rainno raised his in a toast: "To new friends."

Punk matched him. "New friends." The beer tasted good, rich and a smidge dry, the way Punk liked his beer. "One of those beers," as Crud used to say. He remembered how Crud had tried his hand at home brewing during their RAG days and how he'd made their class choke down bottle after bottle at the beach house, sediment and all. Then he remembered that, last night, he'd promised Suzanne he would mow her lawn once the day cooled down. He snuck a peek at his watch. A few hours of daylight left.

Rainno lowered his glass with a refreshed sigh. "So what are you going to do with your life, Rick?" he asked. "You've obviously got your act together—handsome, tall, well-spoken, jet pilot. Married?"

"Not yet."

"Good. Take it from me; it's not something you want to rush into. I'm in the middle of getting divorced from my third wife. You think I'd learn." He took another swig and said, "I'm sure you've got a foxy girlfriend, though."

Punk raised his eyebrows and nodded.

"Yeah," Rainno continued, "guys like you and me love the good-looking ladies. Isn't fucking great?"

Punk tried to seem unfazed by Rainno's prurient shift, intrigued, as he'd been on the course, by the CEO's two vastly different personas: civic-minded tour guide and profane frat-boy cocksman. "Sure," Punk said agreeably, "fucking is really . . . fun."

"Yeah, it's great," Rainno restated. Punk saw that although Rainno was facing him he wasn't actually focused on anything, but he suddenly snapped out of it. "But it's not the greatest. Do you know what is?"

"What?"

"Financial freedom." He directed a finger at the lieutenant. "You don't get something for nothing, Rick. You've got to understand that early on. You think Admiral Knowles is a big deal? Commander in Chief of the Atlantic Fleet? I own that guy. I walk into town unannounced and he clears his calendar. He canceled an awards ceremony to come play golf today, for shit's sake."

"You're in the defense business. You must've spent some time in the military."

"Nope. Never did. I saw the lay of the land early on."
Rainno looked over to the captain and gestured for another
round. "Just look at Congressman Long. I scare the crap
out of him, too. If RDI walks out of his district we take
hundreds of jobs and thousands of votes with us." Punk
didn't quite get the math but figured it had something to
do with the size of RDI's families. "So it gets back to my
original question, Rick. What are you going to do with
your life?"

Punk nodded to the captain as the man placed another
beer in front of him. "Try to be happy?"

"It goes by fast, Rick. Look at me; I'm fifty-one." Punk
would've guessed older. "I've probably only got thirty years
left." Punk would've guessed fewer. "But I could stop
working today and be well off for the rest of my life.
That's happiness."

"Is it?"

"Wait, don't tell me. Money doesn't buy happiness. Job
satisfaction buys happiness; no, serving the country buys
happiness; no, leading men buys happiness." Rainno
laughed and rendered a mock salute. "That's all the junk
gold-flaked also-rans like Knowles have fed you to keep
you down on the farm. The sooner you realize that, the
happier you'll be in life.

"Just look at something like that library in the conference room upstairs. You guys talk about how much trust
you have in the military. Try keeping several million dollars' worth of books in plain view, not under lock and key,
on an aircraft carrier or someplace like that. You'd be
robbed blind in minutes."

"Well, we could keep the carrier at sea until we found
whatever was stolen," Punk joked, trying to avoid a showdown of ideals, as Rainno grew ever more animated.

"I've been around, Rick. I know your type. You've got to
find your own people. You're nothing more than a glorified
warden out there right now. And loyalty? You think you'd
ever have a front-page scandal if you really had loyalty?
The problem is the Navy demands loyalty to too many
things." Rainno began ticking points off of his fingertips.
"Loyalty to the Navy, loyalty to the country, loyalty to the
Commander in Chief, loyalty to the Constitution, loyalty to
your squadron. Jesus, how confusing. There's only one

place for loyalty and that's the company. When people focus their loyalty on one thing there are no problems."

Punk checked his watch again. "I've got to take off. I promised a friend's wife I'd mow their lawn."

Rainno formed a lurid smile. "Mow the lawn, eh? Where's her husband? On cruise?"

Punk released a dark sigh and said, "No, he died in a mid-air collision between two Tomcats a few months ago."

"Damn." Rainno put his knuckles against his eye sockets for a few seconds and then let his hands fall to the heavy wooden table. "I'm sorry."

"That's all right. You didn't know."

"Was that the one where the student hit him?"

"The student's *jet* rolled into him, yeah."

Punk's semantics were lost on Rainno. "Corky told me that student had his wings taken away. Good thing, eh? He won't be doing any more damage."

Punk didn't reply but stood and extended his hand. "I've got to run. Thanks for a very memorable outing, Mr. Rainno."

"Laf," he corrected as he rose as well and they shook. "You're not going to finish your beer?"

Punk shook his head. "Better not; I'm about to operate heavy machinery."

"Oh, that's right. You don't have a driver."

"I was talking about the lawn mower."

Rainno chuckled and pointed at Punk's torso. "I know that jacket you're wearing fits you like a dream, but you'd better leave it with me."

Punk looked down at himself, surprised he'd forgotten he had the wool coat on. He slipped it off and handed it across the table.

"The fastest way to the parking lot is out that door there," Rainno said.

They shook hands again and Rainno slipped him a business card. "Find your people, Rick. Give me a call when you're ready to make the move into the making side of things."

As Punk pulled off the hallowed grounds and onto the common roads of the proletariat, he glanced into his pickup's rearview mirror and, through a glint of light, thought he saw the gates to Oak Tree slamming shut.

*   *   *

Punk pulled the grass catcher off the mower and dumped the final load of clippings into a green plastic bag that was already half full. He tied the bag and took in the cut grass smell and proudly surveyed his handiwork. It had been a long time since he'd mown a lawn, and he'd forgotten how completely satisfying it could be.

He laid the bag on top of the mower and wheeled it toward the front entrance to the house, and there he stopped and sat on the cement stoop and drank iced tea from a plastic mug. The sky behind the vinyl-sided houses across the street was reddish orange at the rooflines and gradually blackened to onyx around the waxing moon. Fireflies flew patrol over the yard, and children on BMX bikes chased down the twinkling bells of the ice cream truck as the notes from its chimes floated over from the next block. Through the front door he could just hear Suzanne in the kitchen singing along with the stereo as she put the final touches on dinner. It was good to hear her singing. He felt his stomach rumble with the thought of her casserole.

Jason did laps around the driveway on his tricycle, little legs pumping the pedals in a blur and face gripped with the same look of determination his father used to wear. Jason was three now, and he looked more like Crud every time Punk saw him.

The boy went around and around, solid rubber tires grinding loudly against the cement, until he detoured up the sidewalk and purposefully rolled to where Punk was seated. Jason came to a quick stop, dismounted the tricycle, and marched the rest of the way to Punk's feet. He was wearing sneakers with Velcro straps, baggy, knee-length shorts, and a Villanova tank top. His hair was a cute black mess and there were streaks of dirt under his left eye and on his chin.

"You're really doing great on that bike, Jason," Punk said brightly.

"My daddy's in heaven," the boy announced. "I won't see him until I die." He spun on his heel, climbed on the tricycle again, and sped back to his driveway circuit.

Anita shook Punk awake. "Rick. Rick, wake up."

Punk sluggishly turned over. "What?"

"I hear something . . . banging." Dressed in T-shirt and panties, she rose up in bed, covers across her lap, listening intently. "Did you hear it?"

Punk sat up and tilted toward the bedroom door. "No, I don't hear anything."

"Shhh," Anita commanded. "There it is again."

Punk heard it that time; someone was knocking on the front door to his condo. The air-conditioning kicked on and caused both of them to jump a little. He threw the covers off and retrieved a T-shirt from the carpet next to the bed.

"Wait here," he said. He stepped out of the bedroom and shut the door behind him.

There was another series of pounds on the front door as Punk entered the den. He switched on a light next to the couch and pulled a nine iron out of the golf bag he'd left leaning against his wide-screen TV. He grabbed the portable phone out of the kitchen. As he walked to the door he looked back toward the bedroom to make sure Anita hadn't followed him.

He peered through the lens in the door, golf club in one hand, phone in the other, but there was no one there. The air-conditioning shut off, and the condo was suddenly too still.

"Who is it?" he said.

"Seamus," a voice returned quietly.

Punk didn't recognize the name at first. "Who?"

"Seamus Callaghan."

"Stand in front of the door so I can see you." A hooded figure moved into the fish-eye. "Take your hood off." The hood was pulled back and Seamus's shaved head shone in the light of the second-story walkway. The boy stood facing the peephole, motionless with eyes averted like he was standing along a police lineup.

Punk opened the door and gestured for Seamus to come in. The boy stood for a second as if he wasn't sure that Punk meant it, and once Punk waved him in a second time he shuffled through the doorway.

As he shut the door behind the boy, Punk caught a whiff of cigarettes and beer. He saw that Seamus's jacket was torn midsleeve and had a clean slash across the back of it, too clean to have been made by hand. Punk stuck the phone back in its cradle and returned the nine iron to the bag. "You want to take that off?" he asked, pointing toward Seamus's damaged jacket. Seamus incoherently mumbled something that Punk interpreted as his preference to leave it on. "Can I get you something to drink? A soda or something?" The boy shook his head.

Punk led Seamus to the couch and then sat in the adjacent recliner. In the light of the lamp Punk could now see the teen had a three-inch scab on his forehead and a bruise across his left cheek. He looked thinner than before, wore a pissed off expression that seemed welded to his face, and sniffed frequently as if he was fighting a cold.

"You don't look so good," Punk said.

"I'm fine," Seamus quietly insisted.

Punk went to the kitchen and grabbed a box of tissues and put them on the coffee table in front of Seamus. The boy muttered thanks and gave his nose a healthy blow.

Anita cracked the bedroom door and poked her head out. "Is everything all right, Rick?"

"Yeah, we're just going to talk for a while, babe. Go back to sleep. I'll join you in a little bit."

She took a disdainful look at Seamus then compliantly slipped her head back into the darkness and shut the door.

"Aw, man, I'm sorry," Seamus said, rising off the couch. "I didn't know you had your lady with you. I don't want to wreck your evening."

"No, it's no big deal. Sit down." The boy shrugged and fell back deep into the cushions. "What happened to you? Were you in a fight or something?"

"Something like that."

"Was it a knife fight?"

Seamus didn't answer.

"Did you know your jacket is slashed in the back?"

Seamus shrugged, and Punk wasn't sure whether that meant the teen didn't know or didn't care about the damage.

They sat in silence for a minute. "Are you sure I can't get you a soda? Water, maybe?" Punk asked again.

"No." Seamus reached into a coat pocket and pulled out a pack of cigarettes. "I could really use one of these. Do you mind?"

"Actually, I do," Punk replied. "Can it wait?"

"I could really use one right now. They stop my nose from running for some reason. I guess the smoke dries the snot up." He blew his nose again.

Punk stood and stepped across the room and slid on some flip-flops that were sitting on the carpet in front of the television. He motioned for Seamus to get off the couch. "Let's go for a walk."

The air was as hot and thick as it had been during the day. Punk felt the humidity wrap itself around him and checked the time. It was nearly three-thirty in the morning. They walked, and from the second-story vantage point Punk looked across the parking lot toward his car. He thought he saw movement in the tree line just beyond it, but as he stared longer there, he saw nothing.

Punk ushered Seamus down the stairs to the ground floor. They followed the path that wound around the pool to the beach, and once they got there they commandeered two beach chairs left in the sand.

They sat facing the water, and as Punk wondered whether any of the lights on the water were coming from Navy ships, Seamus managed to defeat the warm breeze coming off the Chesapeake Bay and light his cigarette after several attempts. The wind made it at least five degrees cooler by the water than it had been on the other side of the condominium.

"That's a dirty habit, you know," Punk counseled, noting that the moon had moved a long way across the sky from where he'd spotted it at Suzanne's house. The light from it was bright; it reflected off the water and blanketed the sand and both of them with a dreamlike, otherworldly glow. "You should quit while you're young."

Seamus turned his head and blew smoke with the wind. "I should enjoy it while I'm young, you mean." He suddenly seemed more lucid and relaxed.

"When's the last time you were home?" Punk asked.

Seamus took another drag. "I've lost count. Five days ago, maybe."

"Your parents are worried."

"I'll bet they are. They're worried they're going to run out of champagne celebrating that I'm gone." He laughed at his own joke.

"It's not funny, Seamus. You need to go home."

He shook his head. "No. No way. I'm never going back there."

"Why not?"

He'd already sucked the cigarette to the filter, and he flicked what was left into the sand. "It just won't work. I don't want to talk about it, either." He pulled out the pack and fired another one up.

"Why did you come to my condo? Better than that, how did you know where I live?"

Seamus smiled slyly. "We're very familiar with the area."

"What does that mean? And who's 'we'?"

The boy stood up and brushed the sand from his warm-up pants and oversized jacket. "Man, I could use a beer. There's a minimart across the street over there. You want to go with me and get a six-pack?"

"You're too young to buy beer."

"That's where you come in. Or I could use my fake ID. Usually we don't have to, though. There's always a wino near the Dumpsters looking to make a quick buck."

Punk stood and dusted the sand from the back of his calves. "You do what you have to do, Seamus. Your dad is concerned about you, but it's your life, I guess; wreck it however you see fit. I'm going back to join my girlfriend in my nice cozy bed. You have fun sleeping in the Dumpster." He trudged a few steps through the sand toward the walkway and then paused and called back to the teen—a sticklike silhouette from fifty feet away. "Oh, one more thing: If this condominium complex has a crime spree in the next few days or weeks, I'm going to be sure and tell the police where to start their search."

Punk continued for home. There were more lights on in the units than the last time he'd looked, and he wondered if their voices had carried that far.

"Wait," Seamus yelled after him. "I need to talk to you."

Punk reversed direction and signaled for Seamus to keep his voice down. "Then talk," he said in an exaggerated whisper. "Knock off the bullshit gang-banging stuff. Talk." He retook his place in the beach chair.

Seamus stood facing the water with his back to the pilot. He fired up another cigarette, his third in the last ten minutes, and said, "I know my dad and I got in a fight after that time in the simulator, and I know I was an asshole when I walked out. I just wanted to tell you I had a good time in there, and appreciate the time you took out of your day to try and help me."

The boy's sudden sincerity surprised Punk. He sounded much older than his sixteen years. "It was my pleasure," the lieutenant said.

Seamus turned and faced him. "You told me I was a good pilot. Were you serious?"

"You showed natural ability in the simulator. It's not a big stretch for me to say you've got the makings of a good pilot."

The teen recaptured his hangdog slouch. "Too bad guys like me wind up as enlisted guys."

"What are you talking about?"

"My father's an enlisted guy; he doesn't fly the jets, he just fixes them."

Punk patted the chair next to him. "Come over here and sit down for a second. You're making me nervous." Seamus complied with Punk's request, and Punk shifted his chair a quarter turn in the sand and made sure the boy was listening. "My father was an enlisted guy."

Seamus's focus snapped from his feet to Punk's face. "*Your* father was enlisted?"

Punk nodded. "He was in the Marine Corps for twenty years. He retired as a sergeant major, the Corps' equivalent of your dad's rank. I grew up on bases all over the world, went to three different high schools. We never lived anywhere longer than two or three years." As he spoke his mind fired with random images from his rearing: He was looking at the back of his father's shaved head from the rear seat of the family's station wagon filled to the gills along a desert highway; a bear hug from his father at home plate faded into an argument between them before the senior prom about hair length, which morphed into a memory of a brief fistfight over an empty beer bottle adrift under a car seat, and that scene became a vision of a salute from a sergeant major in dress blues directed to a new ensign in dress whites at an Annapolis graduation.

Punk threw his hands up. "But getting a life is up to you, Seamus, not your father. You can't walk around for the rest of your life blaming your sorry state on your father's job. It seems like a cool thing to do now, but in a few years it'll bore the hell out of your friends, if you have any by then.

"I grew up under the roof my father provided, and I didn't fully appreciate what he did when I was your age any more than you appreciate what your father does. I wasn't the easiest teenager in the world to get along with, but I sure didn't cause my parents as much trouble as you're causing yours right now.

"So I'll let you in on the truth a decade earlier than I figured it out: Without men like your father, guys like me are nothing. I'll give you an example: On my last deployment I was awarded the Distinguished Flying Cross for keeping the bad guys off of one of my squadronmates who'd been shot down over Iraq. It was the greatest flight of my life, and I may never have another one like it, but without the help of the flight deck chief, Chief Wixler, now Senior Chief Wixler—a good friend of your father's, by the way—I wouldn't have even left the flight deck that day.

"And Senior Chief Wixler is no Master Chief Callaghan. Your dad is an icon, known throughout the Navy. I don't know a single officer who's as popular, admirals included. He didn't earn that respect by being a glory hound or thinking about himself; he earned it by taking care of his men and cocky pilots like me. I'm sure he's a hard-ass when it comes to you, but that's how fathers are when they give a damn about their sons.

"You can make it big if you want, fly jets, whatever, Seamus, but first you've got to go home. Cut your old man a break here."

Seamus stared blankly at his large shoes half buried in the sand. "He's going to be pissed when I walk in," he said quietly.

"I bet he will be, but that's not all bad."

Seamus produced another cigarette, lit it, and smiled. "That's not all bad," he said to himself. The boy gave Punk a little wave and headed across the sand for the lights of the city. Punk hoped that while Seamus was on his way home he'd avoid stopping to bribe the wino.

CHAPTER ELEVEN

If Punk'd had a sense that his return to proper running form would be a linear process, it was gone by the time he flopped across several rows of the bleachers behind the home team dugout of the softball field just beyond the finish line of the running trail.

Master Chief Callaghan had prodded the lieutenant along in the usual way, but the pain in Punk's lungs and shins had nearly eclipsed the master chief's ability to motivate. And the noontime heat of early August hadn't helped any.

"Don't lie down," the master chief counseled as he walked off his own fatigue. "You'll cramp up again."

Punk sat up and feared he might vomit, but after several deep breaths the feeling subsided. "That . . . run . . . truly . . . sucked."

A Tomcat in a landing pattern flew over them and for a time the world was an excruciatingly loud place. The two of them plugged their ears and put their heads back and looked at the same airplane but saw different things. Master Chief Callaghan probably focused on the puckering exhaust nozzles and the landing gear and heard the grinding of metals and the flowing of fluids and imagined the problems to come. Punk looked at the pilot's white helmet and mentally followed him through a sequence of movements and thoughts: reviewing the landing checklist with his RIO, scanning his instruments, looking through the canopy.

The decibel level eventually returned to where conversation was possible again.

"You're sure Seamus didn't come home last night?" Punk asked.

"Positive," Callaghan said, wiping the sweat from his freckled face with his T-shirt. "Even when he does a touch and go he leaves a sign of some sort."

"I should've called the cops; they would've taken him right home."

"Or right to jail. Don't beat yourself up over it, sir; you did the right thing. Mary Kate and I decided a while ago to keep the police out of it."

"I'm not as good a judge of character as I thought. I would've bet big money by the look on his face when he walked off that he was headed home."

The master chief got up and took a long drink from the fountain and then looked back to the bleachers and saw the lieutenant was deep in troubled thought. "Social work isn't as rewarding as you thought it was going to be, is it?"

Another fighter flew over and they yielded to the noise for another fifteen seconds or so. "Where were you ten years ago?" the master chief asked once the rumble died off.

"Ten years ago? I was just entering the Naval Academy."

"Ten years ago Seamus was six years old. His life revolved around his bike and Pee-wee soccer." Callaghan kicked at the infield clay that had migrated under the backstop and collected in front of the bleachers. "I was just a petty officer then, and I used to bring him to the squadron in these little coveralls his mom had sewed for him. He'd grab a wrench and put it to a wheel like he was working on the jet. All the guys used to laugh. I was so proud of him I could have burst." The master chief shook his head sorrowfully. "So what the fuck went wrong?"

"What's your other son like?"

"Completely different. Liam is a year younger. He's a good kid, good student, great athlete—he's heavier, you know—and he's low maintenance. He sees how much hell his brother's putting us through. He sees his mom crying every night."

Master Chief Callaghan wore a somber countenance but quickly shook it off. "It's got to be genetics, best I can figure. I wasn't around any more during Liam's life than I was for Seamus's, so it ain't my influence that's made any difference. Seamus has that outlaw gene, the one that got the Callaghans thrown out of the old country." He laughed to himself and scooped up a handful of the dusty clay under his feet and held up his fist. The dirt ran out of the bottom of it like an hourglass. He stared at where the stream hit the ground, mesmerized by the microcosmic destruction he wrought. When the flow stopped, he rubbed his palms together and stood back up. "But what the hell. At least for now we know he's not dead."

"Good day, future defenders of the American way," Creepy said from behind the podium in his own netherworldly fashion. "Let's pick it up where we left off yesterday." He moved his arm like an insect and clicked the remote at the television. The introductory slide of the Landing Grades presentation brightened into view on the screen.

"Pilots, this might just be the most important lecture of your naval aviation career. You see, from now on, every landing you make as a RAG student will be graded, whether you're doing practice carrier landings at Fentress or actually landing on the Boat. And this pressure doesn't stop once you finish the RAG. You'll be graded on your landings throughout your career. It never ends and nobody's immune. I've seen department heads, skippers, and even air wing commanders sidelined or even grounded for life because of their landing grades."

Creepy clicked to the next slide. "I know we all had a glimpse of the Boat in flight school, but that's all it was. Eight passes in broad daylight in a docile, dinky airplane like the Goshawk does not qualify as fleet-carrier experience. Now we're going to demand that you take an airplane with a sixty-seven-foot wingspan and put it down at one hundred and forty knots in a landing area that's only eighty feet wide. And we'll also need you to do it at night.

"So let's review the grades, and I say 'review' because you were all exposed to these during the carrier-qualification phase of flight school, but I know you'd be hard pressed to spout off the definitions here and now if I asked you. Anyone want to give it a try?" The class members looked at each other without giving any indications they were interested in taking Creepy's challenge; they'd learned from the mild level of abuse he'd dished out the day before.

"Fine. We'll start with the best grade a pilot can get, an

OK underlined, worth five points. You'll see this grade maybe once or twice in your career . . . maybe. An OK underlined is an OK pass flown with some kind of emergency or when a captain gets his one-thousandth arrested landing and the LSO wants to kiss his butt and the PAOs have demanded something slick for the base newspaper." Creepy moved against the dry erase board and pulled the cap off of a red marker lying in the trammel and scribed on the board the abbreviation for an OK underlined: the letters "OK" with a line under them. "At this point you shouldn't even worry about an OK underlined. I just bring it up to let you know that they exist.

"Back on Planet Earth we strive for the OK pass, worth four points." He wrote "OK" under the OK underlined. "This is an above-average pass flown with small or no deviations and the pilot giving appropriate and timely corrections. Below the OK is the Fair pass, which differs from the OK in that the deviations are *acceptable* rather than small in magnitude, and the corrections from the pilot are still appropriate and timely." Creepy wrote an "OK" with parentheses around it, the abbreviation for a Fair pass. "A Fair pass is worth three points.

"Now if you fly a Fair pass and your tailhook doesn't happen to catch any of the four wires strung across the flight deck, usually because you land beyond them, the pass will be graded as a Bolter." He scribed a "B" on the board. "A Bolter is worth two and a half points."

Creepy clicked to the next slide and moved from behind the podium. "Here we get to the grades carrier pilots want to avoid. Enough of these and they'll find themselves in another line of work—if not dead—before too long." Next to the "B," Creepy drew a dash. "The No Grade is a below-average but still safe pass and is worth two points. *Excessive* deviations and a pilot making inappropriate corrections or no effort to make corrections will earn you a No Grade.

"Just below the No Grade is the Pattern Wave Off, worth one-and-a-half points." He wrote "PWO" under the No Grade dash. "As the name implies, an LSO will give you a Pattern Wave Off if your landing pattern is so gooned up that he just wants you out of there before you even attempt to land.

"Which brings us to the Technique Wave Off—a one-pointer." Instead of adding to the smattering of abbreviations that were starting to clutter the board, he simply erased the "P" from PWO. "Technique Wave Offs are the result of a *gross* deviation, an inappropriate correction, or because a pilot failed to respond to the LSO's calls." Creepy looked at Auto. "We don't have to go over that again, do we?" Auto shook his head emphatically, and the rest of the class chortled.

Creepy mashed the remote several times with a skinny index finger, and a grainy videotape appeared on the screen showing a Tomcat in a left-hand turn approaching a carrier during the daytime. He paused the tape, freezing the fighter in midair.

"Every aircraft carrier has a series of cameras around the flight deck, the pilot landing assist television—PLAT—system, that record all of the takeoffs and landings," Creepy said. "So if you crash, especially if it's a violent one, you'll live in highlight reel infamy for decades to come. For instance . . ." He hit Play.

The view was through the camera mounted in the middle of the flight deck that showed the view aft. The F-14 slid from the upper right side of the screen to the center and leveled its wings as it continued down the glide slope. It looked like a beautiful day at sea; the sky was clear and the flight deck appeared rock steady. Creepy tweaked the volume of the television up a notch.

"A little power," a voice on the tape said, presumably that of the LSO waving the pass. Twin hints of exhaust puffed behind the jet in response but the Tomcat remained below the crosshairs as the approach continued. "You're low. Power," the LSO coaxed, voice more forceful this time. He didn't have time to unkey the mike before it captured the sound of engines unwinding. The Tomcat fell relative to the crosshairs, straight down, as if it wasn't traveling forward at all. *"Power! Power!"* voices screamed, the backup LSO joining in the demand that morphed into a plea, words distorting as they came through the television's speakers. *"Wave it off! Wave it off!"*

The Tomcat hit right behind the intakes against the ramp of the flight deck, and the resultant explosion cracked the jet in two. The view switched to the camera mounted on the carrier's island and captured the front half of the F-14 careening down the flight deck trailing a line of flame. *"Eject! Eject!"* somebody commanded over the frequency but neither ejection seat fired before the nose section slid off the flight deck and into the water, making a splash that crested just high enough to be seen by the camera.

Smitty leaned over to Muddy and whispered, "I think Creepy learned his instruction methods from my high school driver ed teacher."

Creepy clicked the screen back to the slide show. "That was a dramatic example of the last grade, the lowest grade, known as a Cut pass," he said. "Zero points. *Unsafe* deviations." In the middle of the other letters and symbols he'd left just enough space to add a large "C" with an arrow horizontally through the center of it. "The operative word here is 'unsafe.' You don't have to crash to get a Cut but anytime you do—you know, you stop without all the big pieces still on the jet—you should plan on getting one. Basically, if you scare the shit out of an LSO you're going to get a Cut. If you fly a Cut pass during carrier quals you'll definitely be sidelined and maybe worse than that."

Creepy moved back behind the podium and took a cleansing breath. "Those are the grades, quick and dirty," he said. "Care about them. Your landing grade point average will follow you around like your academic grade point average did in college." Several of the class members tittered and quietly murmured that if that was the case, then they were screwed. "Contrary to what you might hear from some of the salty members of our staff here, landing grades matter, not just for blind achievement's sake, but for safety. I don't want to sound like those geeks who are always handing out occupational safety posters and telling you to buckle the strap to your helmet and roll your flight suit sleeves down, but the higher the landing grade, the safer the pass.

"Before we move on, let me say one more thing." Creepy walked to the center of the classroom and leaned against the first long table, silently scanning the faces of the replacements for dramatic effect. "Pilots: Auto, Muddy, Dusty, Stormin'," he said, "I've been doing this CQ phase leader thing for a while now, and I'm going to make a prediction." He backed away from the table and began to pace, seemingly tortured by what he knew about the future, like Christ at the Last Supper. "One of you will qualify, no problem at all, a natural-born ball flyer. One of you will raise some eyebrows but make it. One of you will take a while to get the hang of it and wind up with a disqual this time but will be able to try again with Class Three, six weeks down the road." He stopped and looked each pilot in the eye. "And one of you will do something that scares the shit out of me and never fly again."

Creepy let that thought hang in the air for a short time. The replacement pilots sat stone still, afraid that the slightest twitch would reveal who they were among the LSO's vision. "Now let's move on to ball flying techniques . . ."

Punk pushed the throttles to the military power stops and then moved them outboard and forward until they would go no farther. Full afterburner. The nozzles of each engine opened to its full aperture and spewed a twenty-foot-long cone of flame behind the jet.

Spud had volunteered them for this postmaintenance check flight at the last minute, and Punk had readily accepted, very much in need of an escape from the surly bonds. It was a gorgeous day, and a maintenance check flight was generally a low-impact hop, especially compared to a syllabus event, unless maintenance forgot something in the process of fixing the jet. The aviators had quickly briefed in the parariggers shop while putting their flight gear on, and now it was just a matter of going through the profile checklist and filling in the blanks with whatever readings they came up with. And the best part of the deal was the required check to see just how fast they could get the fighter to go—a license to speed.

Punk watched the airspeed grow and within a dozen seconds the jet blew through the sound barrier, a phenomenon quite transparent to the crew except for the needle on each airspeed indicator moving past the mach one-point-zero tick mark. No huge thumps, no reversing of the flight controls, no heavenly spectral light shows, just a reading on an instrument.

"I'm betting we'll get no more than one-point-five," Spud said into the mask strapped across his face.

"No, this jet's a rocket ship," Punk replied. "I can feel it. One-point-six easy."

"Bet a beer? It is Friday, after all."

The airspeed passed mach one-point-two. "I'll take the bet, but I think I'll pass on the club this afternoon. I got in Dutch with my significant other after Wednesday night's little fiasco."

"These are sad times that single fighter pilots allow their significant others to drive them around like yard ponies."

Mach one-point-three. "These *are* sad times, but she doesn't drive me around like a yard pony. What's a yard pony?"

"You are."

"No, I'm not."

"Then why wouldn't you join your fellow aviators for some obligatory fraternity this afternoon?"

Punk didn't answer. He quietly divided his scan between the sky in front of the jet and the airspeed indicator. Behind him Spud stared at the airspeed indicator, willing it to stop creeping clockwise.

Punk broke the silence between them several moments later: "Are we satisfied that there was never a problem with the jet?"

"What?"

"The roll-offs. Were they just caused by a couple of cone-heads being stupid?"

"Maybe . . ."

"Maybe? Crud's dead, Pugsly's lost his wings, and Muddy's barely hanging on by the ragged edge thanks to Senator Meyers. And we just keep flying like lemmings off the cliff."

Spud moved his helmet against the left side of the canopy and looked down the rail and into one of Punk's mirrors, hoping to make eye contact with his pilot, although eye contact was basically impossible with visors down. "Lemmings, huh? I guess that's what makes me such a good RIO. I don't dwell on the fact that I don't control everything in the universe. Leap of faith, baby, leap of faith."

"Leap on this: We just passed mach one-point-five. You lose the bet."

"Beers are on me then."

"Yes, they are."

"So you are going to the club after all?"

"Hey, nobody's driving me around like a yard pony."

Spud scanned his instruments and saw that, along with reaching mach one-point-six, they'd deviated slightly from their assigned course. "Let's come left to a heading of one-two-zero."

"Coming left to one-two-zero . . ."

After settling the beer bet at the officers club's main bar with Spud, Punk walked into the back bar and saw that most of the Class Two replacements had congregated along the far wall next to the pool tables. He was their sole remaining class advisor with Crud gone and felt a twinge of guilt for having not paid closer attention to their progress.

Crud had always been better with advisor duties, reviewing training jackets daily and going sidebar with coneheads before bad trends got worse. Aside from being force-fed Muddy's problems and eavesdropping on the occasional ready room anecdote, Punk was fairly ignorant of how the rest of the class had performed over the long haul. He'd flown with most of them on his wing or in his back seat, but those events had been episodic at best. *Spud would've told me if somebody was falling behind,* he thought as he approached the group.

Three of the four class pilots were standing in a circle beside a pool table talking intently while the class RIOs gathered around the juke box a few feet away and argued about how to best spend the dollar Smitty had just fed into the slot. "We get six songs," Kosher said. "Don't waste any of them."

That's what usually happened during the carrier-qualification phase: Pilots and RIOs went their separate ways for the time being. The RAG syllabus through tactics had been about fighting the machine as a single unit, pilots and RIOs working closely together, roles flowing seamlessly between cockpits. But CQ introduced a different game. Pilots began to realize that landing the jet was something they ultimately had to do by themselves, and RIOs began to realize that the pilots ultimately had to land the jets by themselves. RIOs could pay attention, as Creepy suggested, and do what they could to keep their pilots ahead of the airplane—cheerlead, perhaps—but there was only one set of flight

controls in the Tomcat and those were located in the front
cockpit. The only flight control a RIO had was an ejection handle.

As Punk got close, Stormin', Auto, and Dusty stopped
talking and greeted him with formal, polite smiles.

"How's life with Creepy going, fellas?" Punk asked as
he worked his way through them, shaking hands.

"Interesting," Auto said.

"He's scared the hell out of us for the last two days,"
Stormin' said.

"That's okay," Punk said. "You've got to respect the
Boat. But your class advisor is here to help make the
boogeyman go away. What can I help you with?"

"I forgot we had a class advisor," Dusty said. "Well, we
were just talking about night approach techniques. What's
yours?"

"Meatball, lineup, angle of attack," Punk said. Meatball:
glide slope, high or low. Lineup: azimuth, left or right.
Angle of attack: speed, fast or slow. In theory that was all
a carrier pilot needed to know to land safely.

"Yeah, yeah, we know that," Auto said in response to
Punk's boilerplate. "But what do you do beyond that?
What are your little tricks that make a night pass easier?"

Punk considered the three of them—big Auto the smart
one, Dusty the wallflower, and the nervous bird they called
Stormin'. He knew at this point information was a dangerous thing. Their heads were like sponges ready to take in
every bit of knowledge without discrimination until they
could hold no more.

He looked in the replacements' eyes as they spoke and
he didn't see fear, which almost surprised him until he remembered that he hadn't felt fear during the carrier-
qualification lectures, either. Now it all made sense and
seemed double to them. Fear would come later.

They didn't know fear yet. For all of the replacements'
experience and pseudo mastery of the Tomcat to date, they
still hadn't been hit with the realization that the simple act
of landing an F-14 on an aircraft carrier at night was the
scariest fucking thing they'd ever have to do with the jet.
Punk had dropped bombs on a hostile SAM site in southern Iraq with more calm than he'd been able to muster
when trying to land later on that same hop. Even now the

mere mental image of the pattern of lights seen through the HUD from a Tomcat plying the dark skies a mile behind the Boat filled him with a sense of foreboding. In spite of his static surroundings he felt his heart race and his fists clench. He wanted to channel his fears to the replacements, to let them feel what he'd felt before it mattered, but he knew the same sense of invulnerability that had gotten them this far wouldn't allow it. They'd learn by burning, just as he had.

"No tricks," Punk answered Auto. "Only basics. Meatball, lineup, angle of attack."

"Fitz was saying that after the ball call he comes in and flies the needles to half a mile and then comes back out and flies the ball to touchdown," Auto said. "He said the ball definition isn't really good enough at three-quarters of a mile to try and fly it from that far out at night. He said by the time you see movement you're already way behind."

"What do you think of setting the fuel flow at twenty-five hundred pounds a side, and then using DLC or working the nose for speed control?" Stormin' asked. "That's what Scuzz was saying he did sometimes."

"Are any of you guys golfers?" Punk asked. All three of them sort of shrugged in nonanswers. "There are a lot of parallels between ball flying and swinging a golf club. What's the first lesson of golf?"

"Wear stupid clothes?" Auto said.

"Bring enough cigars for everybody in your group?" Stormin' said.

"It's keep your head still," Punk said. "Now you can drive yourself absolutely crazy thinking about hand position, knee flex, elbow angle, swing plane, wrist cock, weight shift, and grip pressure. You can employ all kinds of visualization mechanisms: ring the bell, throw the horseshoe, shake the hand, and point the rifle. You can read books and magazines and watch TV instructional shows and videotapes. You can pile it on until your golf game has gone completely to hell. And then the clouds will part and it'll strike you to just think one thought when you take the club back: Keep your head still." He looked down at his beer bottle and saw it was empty. "Meatball, lineup, angle of attack, gentlemen." *Here endeth the lesson.* "I need another beer."

Punk knew he was a hypocrite, like parents who tell their kids not to drink underage or have premarital sex know they're hypocrites, but that was part of being an instructor, he figured. During his time as a replacement and throughout his first fleet tour he'd glommed onto every little ball-flying technique tidbit he'd heard about and invented a few on his own. He'd tried monitoring fuel flow, spotting the deck, moving only one throttle, cracking the speed brakes slightly open, raising his visor, lowering his visor, focusing on the TACAN needle, even momentarily closing one eye when flying the ball. He'd never made the top ten list for his landing grades during a line period in the air wing, but he'd never crashed either, not when trying to land on the carrier, anyway. Running out of gas during a divert to Kuwait was another story.

He noticed Muddy behind him, in the same general vicinity as the rest of Class Two but seated by herself at a small round table instead of standing with the group.

"Nice article," Punk said as he pulled up a chair across from her. "Tell me again how you enjoy shooting instructors."

She rolled her eyes. "I swear I had nothing to do with that. That was totally a creation of that PAO guy."

"Sure . . ."

"I didn't say any of those things. I barely spoke five words to that reporter. They ambushed me right as I got off the plane."

Punk noticed her bottle was empty. "Can I buy you a beer?"

"Okay," she said, spinning the bottle around so he could see what brand she was drinking.

He went to the bar and a minute later plopped two cold bottles on the table and sat back down. "So, what do you hear from Senator Meyers's office?"

Muddy grimaced and looked down at herself. "Am I wearing a sign that says 'Give Me Shit' or something?"

Punk flashed her his palms. "Just making conversation."

"Well, how about questions like 'how's it going?' or 'what's new with you?' " She snatched at the beer and emptied it halfway with a single tip. "I'm sorry," she said as she set the bottle back down. "I guess I've got a lot on my mind." She stared into space for a few moments and then looked over at Punk. "I haven't talked to the senator for a while."

"I wasn't really serious—"

"She used to call me all the time during the FAM phase," Muddy continued. "Around dinner time. She'd call me at home and ask how things were going and tell me what she intended to do for womankind." She saw Punk avert his eyes. "No, I didn't have anything to do with Big Top coming down to Key West. Like I said, I haven't talked to her for a while. I'm sure that fact hasn't stopped the rumor mill around here, though."

"I don't think it's possible to stop that," Punk said. "You shouldn't worry about it, though."

Muddy shifted her gaze back to the bottle. "You'd think I would've learned to do that by now. I was introduced to that lesson early in plebe year. One moment of spontaneous passion and the next thing you know I'm sneaking into the men's bathroom in Luce Hall trying to remove my name from the list of 'WUBAs who love hard dicks' scrawled on a stall wall." She polished off the rest of the beer in the second hoist of the bottle, and Punk realized he hadn't even touched his yet. "But you've got to love the rumor mill, right?" she said. "In fact, rumor has it that you're engaged."

"That's an old one."

"How old?"

Punk checked his watch for the date. "Three weeks today, as a matter of fact."

His cell phone went off in his chest pocket, and he ignored it. "Aren't you going to answer that?" Muddy asked.

"No," Punk replied. Their conversation paused until the phone grew quiet again after the fourth ring.

"When's the wedding?" Punk simply raised his eyebrows in response, and Muddy followed with, "You don't seem very excited about it."

"Enough about me," Punk said. "What's going on in *your* life? Have you had time to meet Mister Right during your RAG training?"

"Mister Right? I don't think he exists, at least not in this stage of my life. I have started seeing this guy, a lawyer I met working out at this gym near my apartment, but I'm afraid our days are numbered already. Lately he's been saying he wants to get to know me better and meet the guys I fly with."

"So bring him out here," Punk said.

"Right. You think I'd embarrass myself in this wolf's den? A normal guy would be ripped to shreds by you ball busters here. No thank you."

"So why don't you date Navy guys?"

"No way. I dated a couple of mids when I was at the Academy and a couple of fellow ensigns in flight school. The relationships never lasted very long, and the breakups were always ugly. And right now I don't think I want a scorned fighter pilot throwing out details about my private side."

"Interesting how you assume the guy's going to be scorned."

"That's the way it has always worked with me. Hell, I had one guy break down and cry in Pensacola when I told him it was over. But if that happened around here, the facts would get warped into something bad about me, I'm sure." Muddy picked up her empty bottle and shook it. "Are you ready for another? My round this time . . ."

She got up and went to the bar, and as she passed a hint of her perfume floated past his nose. Punk again was caught a bit off guard by his attraction to her. He'd known a handful of female pilots in his time and they'd all seemed to fit into three categories: emotionally damaged goods, the son Daddy never had, or men trapped in women's bodies. Muddy nibbled at the first one, but she had a confidence about it that he'd never seen before. He turned and furtively watched her at the bar and suddenly had a vision of her on the basketball court in Key West, and then he imagined himself testifying before Congress, telling Senator Meyers that she should just butt out, and he felt shallow for ever voicing opposition to female integration, even in the most informal quarters. He wondered if even Flex would have the guts to look Muddy's parents in the eye and say, "She's female; she's out."

"Are you ready for carrier-qualification phase?" Punk asked when she returned to the table with the second round. "I am your class advisor, you know."

"We have a class advisor? Oh, that's right." She pointed across the table at him and chuckled. "*You're* our class advisor. To be honest, I'm not sure if I'm ready for carrier quals or not. Creepy sure has a way of getting our attention, though."

"He's a different kind of instructor, all right. But he is a great LSO. He's known fleet-wide for the accuracy of his eye."

"What do you remember about your RAG carrier quals?" Muddy asked.

Punk thought back to those days for a few moments. "It was all kind of a blur. I do remember that I became really superstitious, sort of the same way I used to during finals at the Academy. I'm talking about playground shit like not stepping on cracks in the sidewalk and not using the Lord's name in vain, stuff like that. I started touching parts of the airplane during preflight that I never had before, useless parts like the nose gear door and the wingtip light covers. It got very weird. But I qualified, so what the hell, right?"

Muddy leaned forward and lowered her voice: "I've been having this dream the last couple of nights. You won't think I'm losing it if I tell you about it, will you?"

"Hey, I'm your class advisor."

"Okay. I ride this mountain bike off of a cliff. It's really dark and, all of a sudden, below me is an aircraft carrier. The LSO says, 'Wave it off,' but I can't. I just keep falling. I look back at the meatball and it's going down. The LSO tells me to wave it off again. 'I don't have a throttle,' I scream at him, but he can't hear me. There's no way my momentum is going to carry me far enough to make the landing area. I know I'm going to smack into the back of the carrier but at the last second I reach up and grab the railing around the edge of the deck. I'm swinging there for a while, high above the water. My grip is slipping; I'm waiting for someone to help me. Then Creepy looks over the flight deck and says, 'Now you have to try again.' Then he reaches down and peels my fingers off the railing and I fall." She took a swallow of beer and asked, "What do you think?"

"You can remember all of that from your dream?"

"Yeah. Like I said, I've had that same one a few times now."

Punk could see from her expression that she wasn't just making light conversation. "I'm not a psychologist, but all

I can say is any dream that has Creepy in it has got to be clinically classified as a nightmare." She laughed politely but her eyes didn't lose their plea. Punk leaned closer and paternally patted her forearm. "I'll give you the same advice I just gave your classmates: Keep it simple. Meatball, lineup, angle of attack. Beyond that, you, more than any other pilot in Class Two, need to keep your head right. I know the board down in Key West was a blow to your confidence, but I also believe that roll-off wasn't your fault." He saw the wheels turning in her brain as she focused on his hand against the sleeve of her flight suit. "Of course I can't prove it, not yet anyway. And I'm certainly not getting any help from RDI, but that's another story, I guess." Punk paused until Muddy looked up at him. "Don't worry about anything that happened to you in the RAG before now. Just concentrate on flying the jet."

Muddy nodded and offered a slight smile, and the atmosphere at the table suddenly felt too intimate.

"I've got to go home and plan a wedding," Punk quipped. As he got up to leave, he noticed the rest of Class Two and a few others around the back bar quickly shift their eyes away from the two of them. He had an impulse to convene a lesson in dealing with dated social attitudes, but instead he just walked out and left the rumor mill to its own production.

That following Monday, Punk paid his first visit to an aircraft carrier since the end of his last deployment more than a year before. He'd been volunteered by Spud, the officer-in-charge of the upcoming carrier-qualification detachment, to be the assistant officer-in-charge, so the two of them along with Creepy walked aboard for the presail conference a few days before the ship was scheduled to put to sea. The carrier was tied to the pier in Norfolk, which was a forty-five minute drive from Oceana. Spud was the only family man of the three, so they'd all piled into his SUV for the trip.

Aircraft carriers had a smell unique to that category of vessel. In spite of the crew's efforts, there was no suppressing the odor. The unique redolence—a years-old blend of salt water, salt air, fuel oil, grease, exhaust, deodorant soap, burnt food, and humanity, a smell that took several washings to erase from clothing—gave him the impression that his excursion into the real world had been no more than a vivid dream he'd had on cruise while catnapping in his rack in his eight-man stateroom between dinner and the brief for the night go. As the three naval aviators cleared the quarterdeck and ducked through the first hatch and into the hangar bay, the underlying pungence made Punk's nose wrinkle, and he was struck with an overwhelming sense that he'd never left the environment even though this was his maiden visit to this particular carrier.

Spud led the aviators, comfortably dressed in their flight suits, through the empty hangar bay, vast without airplanes in it crammed wall to wall, and down the ladder to the officers' wardroom on the second deck.

"Something about the Boat," Spud called over his shoulder as he worked the second of four hatches they had to pass through to reach their destination. "I'm already hungry, horny, and tired."

The wardroom was half full of people when Spud pushed through the door to the large room that served as the ship's officers' lounge and cafeteria most of the time. The textured tiles that made up the low, false drop ceiling hid the maze of pipes and wiring in the overhead. Framed prints of American naval battles dotted the rice paper–covered walls. Fake trees stood in every corner and artificial flower arrangements sat atop the white table cloths on every table. The mess specialists had closed the lunch line that ran along the adjacent kitchen more than two hours before, but the smell of tuna casserole still hung heavily in the wardroom's air.

Punk scanned across the various informal gatherings scattered about and saw a handful of faces he recognized, but before he had a chance to greet anyone a commander dressed in a long-sleeved khaki uniform stood and announced that the presail conference was about to begin. The three nearly late arrivals each scrambled to draw a glass of iced tea from the dispenser next to the now-empty salad bar and took their seats around one of the dozens of circular tables, facing the rectangular head table behind which were seated the event's organizers and principals.

The most notable was the ship's captain, Captain Carl "Midnight" Cooper, a tall black man with a broad chin and clean-shaven head.

The captain stood, motioned for silence from the group, and said, "I'd like to kick off the meeting by welcoming everyone aboard the greatest warship in the greatest navy in the world." His thick mustache across the middle of his chiseled features gave him a camera-friendly, action-hero look that the Navy had exploited throughout his career. He'd been the first black skipper of an F/A-18 Hornet squadron and then the first black commanding officer of the Blue Angels, although rumor had it he'd been relieved a few months ahead of schedule because he'd had trouble keeping the four-plane diamond over the air show venues. Apparently the coup de grace had been a show in Florida, where he'd started at a military base and after a loop or two was so disoriented that he'd nearly landed at a civilian airfield four miles away. True or not, the experience obviously hadn't hurt his career too much, and all he had to do now was keep his head down and he'd be a shoo-in for admiral like most of the naval aviators who survived command of a nuclear-powered aircraft carrier. "We're looking forward to a great detachment," he finished and sat down.

"That was really *great*," Punk quipped just loud enough for Spud and Creepy to hear.

The executive officer, the carrier's second in command, Captain "Herder" Shepherd, a short, chubby guy who'd spent most of his career flying helicopters in circles just off the starboard side of the carrier, waiting for fixed-wing aviators to eject into the water so he could rescue them, followed the captain. "I'm in charge of heads and beds around here, so if your local commode doesn't flush or you need a pillow, let me or a member of my staff know."

The executive officer turned the floor over to Lieutenant Commander "Longo" Longoria, seated in the crowd across the room from the Tomcat guys.

"Oh, Christ," Creepy muttered as Longo strutted toward the head table. "What's he doing here?"

"You know him?" Punk asked.

"Of course I do. Longo's the AIRLANT LSO, the head LSO on the East Coast."

"Longo?" Punk said. "What a stupid call sign. It's just a takeoff on his name."

"He's one of those assholes people never liked well enough to put the effort into coming up with a real call sign. But now he reports directly to AIRLANT himself, the three-star who, in turn, reports directly to the four-star at CINCLANTFLT."

"I've seen him in action before," Spud added from the other side of Punk. "I agree with Creepy."

Longo stood between the CO and XO, flight suit contrasting with the senior officers' khakis, and addressed the gathering: "Captain, Captain"—he nodded to each—"thanks for having me aboard this beautiful ship. On behalf of both the Commander of the Atlantic Fleet, Admiral Knowles, and the Commander of Naval Air Forces Atlantic Fleet, Vice Admiral Griffin, I'd like to say we're very proud of the accomplishments of this crew this year."

Punk winced at the mawkish line and the idea of a lieutenant commander acting like he wore the stars of his bosses. "We've got a lot to get done in a short time," Longo continued. "The first deck periods will be dedicated to the Tomcats followed by the Hornets, and then we'll finish up with the Hawkeyes. Remember that all of your pilots require ten day and six night arrested landings to qualify. Also remember that the maximum number of traps replacements can get in a single day is ten, so it's going to take at least two days to get them completed. Now, I have already talked with the captain about this, and he is willing to grant waivers to pilots who are doing well, so in that case guys could finish up all the night requirements on the first night and just have four more traps to get the following day. We'll take a good look at those as they come up. It's not a hard-and-fast rule. It's definitely case by case."

Longo simultaneously grasped the near shoulder of both the CO and XO, as if he were about to speak in honor of the new couple at a wedding reception. "During this detachment my job will be to support these men in ensuring that we conduct operations successfully and safely." He swept one hand over the room. "I'm looking forward to working with all of you to make that happen."

After Longo disappeared back to his table and a few

more people stood and forwarded their agendas—including the ship's public affairs officer who said he was in the middle of a campaign to "brand" the carrier and pleaded for whatever human interest stories the squadrons might happen to bring aboard—the presail conference was adjourned.

As they queued up to leave, an arm suddenly wrapped its way around Creepy's shoulder. "Greetings, my friend," Longo said, pulling Creepy into his armpit and giving him a chummy shake.

"Hello, Longo," Creepy returned dourly without turning his head from the floor at his feet.

Longo extended his free hand toward Punk without letting go of Creepy. "Longo Longoria from AIRLANT . . ."

"Punk Reichert," Punk said as he worked to match the man's firm handshake. "I'm the Tomcat RAG's assistant officer-in-charge for this det."

"Oh, I've heard of you; you're the war hero, right?" he asked with a hint of satire before immediately returning his attention to his fellow LSO. "You and I are going to be working very closely together on this thing."

"What thing?" Creepy asked.

"Your thing. I think you know what I'm talking about, shipmate."

"No, I don't. Maybe if you stopped talking like a mafioso I might be able to get it."

"We'll chat later, my friend."

Punk watched Longo as the gaggle of conference attendees squirted one by one through the port side entrance to the wardroom. Longo's surname and thick black hair suggested Hispanic bloodlines but his light complexion and angular face complicated the picture. And he had a strange looking head. The distance from his chin to his eyebrows was only about one-third of the way between his chin and his hairline, and his forehead bulged out like a vast, windswept flesh desert that appeared to house a twice-normalsized brain. He had an average build but carried himself like a bodybuilder: shoulders pinned back and arms away from his sides.

"Why are you even going out with us, Longo?" Creepy asked as he extricated himself from the just-bigger man's clutch. "Isn't this replacement training stuff beneath you? I've never seen you on a RAG CQ detachment before."

"I care about the performance of all pilots, even replacements; plus I've never been ordered to go on one of these before." A higher-ranking officer caught Longo's eye from across the room. "I'll catch you guys later." Just before he whisked off he winked and pointed two hand pistols at them and dropped his thumbs like hammers while making a clicking sound.

"He sure is a friendly guy," Punk said quietly out of the corner of his mouth as Longo was engulfed by the green wave of flight suits behind them. "I hate him already."

"That's a smart move," Creepy said. "It'll save you time later."

The moment they made it back into the cloud-tinted afternoon light of early fall, Punk's cell phone vibrated. He grabbed it from his pocket with one hand while using the other to help negotiate the brow from the quarterdeck down to the pier. "Hello?"

"It's the future Mrs. Reichert calling," Anita sang as his feet left the steel ramp and hit the concrete. "I need to ask you a question about the rehearsal dinner. Do we want to open it up beyond the wedding party? I know some of our friends are going to feel left out otherwise."

He wished he hadn't answered the phone. He didn't want to talk about numbers of bridesmaids, china patterns, rehearsal dinners, the wedding. He didn't even want to hear her voice. Punk had never been good at holding his tongue, whether discussing grades with professors at the Academy or arguing with his old skipper about squadron morale.

"I can't do this, Anita," he said and then grimaced like a Marine who'd just accidentally pulled the pin on a grenade.

"Can't do what?"

He immediately wanted to take it back. This was the wrong way to have this discussion. "Let's talk about it later."

"No, Rick," she shot back with a sudden pithiness, "let's talk about it *now*."

Punk fell back a few steps from Spud and Creepy as they continued down the pier. "I just think we should slow things down a little between us," he said.

"Slow things down?" she shouted into the receiver.

"I've got a lot going on right now, and I think it would be better if—"

"*Ohhhhh Gaaawwwddd!*" she screamed with Shakespearian agony and then broke into sobs. "I knew it. I knew this was too good to be true."

Why had he asked Anita to marry him in the first place? But, no, it might have worked, right? It might *still* work. She just needed to relax and give him some room, like before he'd proposed to her. That was the Anita that he'd loved.

He saw Spud look back and he waved the other two on. "Anita, this doesn't affect how I feel about you. This is an insane time."

"So what are we, dating again?" she asked.

"No," he replied. "Let's just slow things down."

"That's a step backward, don't you think? We were supposed to be *married,* Rick." He winced every time she used his given name, as if she was shining a bright light on him in front of the world. He heard the gears of the rumor mill start to grind. The officers club would be a busy place soon.

"I really think it would be better if we talked about this face-to-face later," he said.

"You're a self-centered son of a bitch asshole dickhead!" she railed. "You think you deserve better than me, well, *you're not better than anybody and you'll never find anybody better than me!*" He heard her crying. "No, that's probably not true," she muttered between sniffles, barely loud enough to be heard over the industrial din around him. "I'm sorry I screamed."

"We'll talk later—"

"No, we won't," she said, voice now very calm. "I've got to go somewhere to think, somewhere by myself. But don't worry. By the time you get home you'll never know I was ever here."

"Anita, just—"

"The funny part is I would've made you a good wife."

"Anita—"

"Good-bye, Rick." And the line went dead.

CHAPTER TWELVE

Punk and Creepy stood in the aft catwalk on the starboard side of the aircraft carrier, enjoying the warmth of late summer and watching the skyline of Virginia Beach's resort strip slowly disappear below the horizon. Punk felt mixed emotions as he gazed at the white sliver of the tallest building, the Ramada hotel, the last visible connection to land-based civilization, which promised freedom and options and creature comforts and relief from stress, standing in contrast to life on a carrier at sea. But dry land was also where his problems were, and it felt good to simply get on a boat and sail away for a few days. He couldn't remember ever being relieved to put to sea before.

"Nice day," Creepy said.

"I hear a hurricane is bearing down on the Virgin Islands," Punk said. He looked down at the waterline and watched the sea foam trail off into the wake. He pondered the depth of the ocean and thought about what it would be like to scuba dive fifty feet down and watch the carrier float overhead. Then he looked down on the missile launcher mounted below and wondered how long it had been since it had been fired. He looked at the deck around it and wondered how long it had been since it had been painted. A mind could wander in the catwalk when there weren't jets roaring all around.

"A hurricane in the Virgin Islands won't affect us for a week or so," Creepy said. "I checked the weather on the computer in the ready room, and we should be fine for the next couple of days."

"I just wonder if—"

"Punk!" a voice called from the flight deck above them. "Punk, is that you?"

Punk shielded his eyes against the early afternoon sun high overhead and saw Ferguson Platt, dressed in an off-white golf shirt and dark slacks. His normally too-combed hair was a windblown bush.

"Big Top, I didn't know you were coming out with us."

"I'd kill for the ability to plan my life more than twenty-four hours in advance," Platt said and then pointed at them. "How do I get down there?"

"There's a ladder over here," Punk said.

Platt negotiated the stairs and stepped with some trepidation across the catwalk. Before shaking hands with Punk, Platt looked through the grating under his feet and marveled at the fact he could see the ocean churning around the carrier's hull. "This must be what it feels like to be a trapeze artist."

"Big Top, this is Creepy," Punk said.

"Still with the Big Top stuff, huh?" Platt said with eyes narrowed. He turned and pumped Creepy's arm. "Ferguson Platt."

"Nice to meet you, Fergie," Creepy said. "Welcome aboard."

"*Ferguson* . . . and thank you."

"Is this your first time on an aircraft carrier?" Punk asked.

"Yes, it is, in fact. When do the airplanes start landing?"

"In about two hours. Are those the only shoes you've got?"

Platt raised one knee. "These are Italian loafers."

"You're going to trash them. Didn't you bring any running shoes or something like that?"

"No. I'm only here for two days."

"We're *all* only here for two days. What size do you wear?"

"Nine and a half, medium."

"Too small for me," Punk said. "Creepy, what size do you wear?"

"Thirteen extra narrow."

Punk gave the LSO a double take before turning back to Platt. "Come with me."

Punk pried open the first hatch and then cranked it shut again once Platt had come through. Down the passageway, Punk opened a door on his left, which was the back door to ready room number eight, a space occupied during the last extended deployment by the Demonslayers, a Hornet squadron, but now home to the F-14 RAG for the next few days. The ready room was perpendicular to the line of the ship's keel and ran nearly the full width from one main passageway on the 0–3 level to the other. The floor was tiled in a blue-and-yellow checkerboard scheme in concert with the Demonslayers' colors, and their emblem—a fist gripping a decapitated devil's head by the hair—was everywhere, but most prominently painted across the entire surface of the sliding corkboard in front of the dry erase boards that covered the width of the front wall. Rows of ready-room chairs filled two-thirds of the space.

Fitz and Gordo, the other two RAG LSOs, were seated in the front row of chairs watching the news on the uppermost of three televisions mounted against a steel beam in the front left corner of the room. The middle TV showed the PLAT camera picture, which currently featured the view down an idle flight deck, and the bottom television hosted the weather forecast in the form of several paragraphs of abbreviations that made little to no sense to the untrained eye. Behind the duty desk in the other front corner of the room was Kosher Kaplan, the replacement RIO, who'd earned the dubious distinction of having the lowest grade point average among the RIOs in Class Two and had therefore been awarded the duty officer job for the first day at sea. He'd be relieved the next day by Ben Dover, another backseat underachiever.

The LSOs greeted the staffer with no more enthusiasm than they'd displayed when they'd first been introduced to him in Key West. "Nice Afro, Big Top," Fitz tossed out. Platt followed Punk out of the front door and into the adjacent maintenance control space.

"Good afternoon, Petty Officer Dietrich," Punk said to the curly-red-haired clerk seated behind a computer at the far end of the small room. "I need some boots. How hard would those be to get out here?"

The clerk, who looked no older than fifteen and was waging a barely postadolescent acne battle on his cheeks and forehead, scratched the back of his neck under the collar of his light blue dungaree shirt and gave the lieutenant a pained expression. "It'd be real tough, sir. I'm not sure what's up with the Boat's supply system out here yet. I don't even know if they're planning on doing anything at all for this det besides keeping the jets up."

"How are you fixed for Tomcat patches?" Punk asked, well schooled in the art of wampum in these circles.

"I could use a few," Dietrich said with a sly grin growing on his pimpled face.

"And the guys in supply?"

"I'm sure they could too."

"All right then. Please see about getting the boots."

The petty officer thought about it for a moment, and then asked, "Are they for you, sir?"

"As far as you know," Punk said.

"What size?"

"Nine and a half, medium."

Dietrich looked down at Punk's boots. "Those look bigger than nine and a half."

"They stretch after they're broken in. Can you get them for me or not?"

"I'll have to make a few calls. Give me twenty minutes or so."

Punk said thanks and backed out of the space and into Platt, who was reading a long-since-expired ship's policy instruction taped to the bulkhead.

"We've got some time," Punk said after shooting another glance at his watch. "Why don't I give you part of the grand tour?"

"Fine," Platt said tersely, apparently still a bit put out that his loafers weren't the right shoes for life underway.

On their way toward the stainless-steel stairway that traveled into the carrier island superstucture like a spine, they were stopped by a voice behind Platt. "Lieutenant, excuse me. Excuse me, Lieutenant."

Punk turned and saw the ship's public affairs officer hurrying toward them. "Lieutenant, I am Lieutenant Vickers, the carrier's PAO," the thin officer with a sparsely haired mustache and no chin explained from a few steps away.

Like all the officers assigned to the ship's crew, he was dressed in the long-sleeved khaki uniform, and his was simply ornamented with the railroad tracks of his rank on his collar, a nametag over the right pocket, and a gold surface-warfare pin over the left. "Are you with the Tomcat squadron?"

"Yes, I am," Punk replied around Platt.

"You're the squadron with the female pilot, right?"

"*The* female pilot? I guess . . ."

"I have direct orders from Lieutenant Commander Sparza, the CINCLANTFLT PAO, to write a press release on her carrier qualification."

Punk started to lose his temper, but he caught himself. "Let's make sure she qualifies first, shall we?"

"Is she aboard the carrier now?" the PAO asked.

"No."

"When will she be?"

"I'm not sure. Why are you asking?"

"Are you in charge of the detachment?"

"I'm the assistant OIC."

"Who's the OIC?"

"Commander O'Leary."

"Is he on board?"

"Of course."

"Where is he?"

"Right this minute? I'm not sure." Punk felt his patience waning. "Are you trying to go over my head on this?"

"I'm just trying to get my job done."

"So am I," Punk said. "I'm sure I speak for my boss when I tell you to stay away from her until she qualifies. Otherwise you may never have access to her." Punk stormed off with Platt in trail, leaving the PAO standing defiantly in the middle of the passageway.

"This isn't for me," the PAO said toward their backs. "This is for the Navy!"

"Boy, that guy was a real pain, huh?" Platt said as they moved on.

After trudging five flights up into the island they came to the bridge, a wide space with a panoramic view through large windows that wrapped around all sides and currently as quiet as a library. The carrier's Captain Cooper was seated in his elevated chair on the far left where he could both keep an eye on the flight deck below and, to his right, the officer of the deck conning the ship in front of the helmsman. The OOD occasionally put the binoculars hanging around his neck to his eyes and then broke the silence with a rudder order issued with no more emotion than a guy telling a waiter what he wanted for lunch.

The captain wore a pair of reading glasses that gave him a distinguished air as he rifled through a stack of papers on his lap. He caught sight of the bridge's new arrivals out of the corner of his eye and peered over his glasses at them expectantly, certain that they were there to brief him on some problem; that was usually why people who didn't normally belong on the bridge came there. Small problems were briefed over the phone. Big problems were briefed in person.

"Just giving a quick tour, Captain," Punk said, reading the knitted brow on the man's face as he extended his hand toward him. "Lieutenant Reichert, sir. I'm with the Tomcat RAG."

"Oh," the captain said, sounding a bit relieved as he met Punk's handshake.

"And this is Ferguson Platt," Punk added.

"Yes, of course. I met Mr. Platt in Admiral Knowles's office yesterday."

"Good to see you again, Captain," Platt said as he shook hands.

Punk pondered how Big Top had intimated that he'd had less than twenty-four hours notice about the trip but hadn't mentioned anything about hanging out with Admiral Knowles.

"You know, Ferg, I didn't get a chance to tell you I'm a big fan of Senator Meyers," the captain said. "I was assigned to the Navy's Office of Legislative Affairs in the late eighties and worked with your office quite a bit. What ever happened to Bill Reese?"

"Ah, he was . . . he moved on," Platt said.

"He was a great guy. Well, you let us know if there's anything you need, Fergie, anything at all."

"Thank you, Captain," Platt said.

Captain Cooper looked at Punk. "You take care of this guy, now."

"Yes, sir," Punk said and started off the bridge.

"Say hello to the senator for me, Fergie," the captain called over his shoulder. "And also Bill Reese, if you happen to see him." He returned his attention to the papers on his lap as the OOD calmly gave another command to the sailor at the helm.

"Bill Reese?" Platt wondered aloud as he followed Punk up one more flight of stairs toward primary flight control, home of the air boss. "I haven't heard that name for a few years."

"Who's Bill Reese?" Punk asked, working the handle to yet another hatch.

"Bill Reese was the military advisor to Senator Meyers before me," Platt explained. "He was charged with selling information to the Russians, but he plea-bargained—if you can call it that—and managed to stay out of prison."

"How did he plea-bargain?"

"He used the race card."

"The race card?"

"Yeah, Bill Reese is a black guy. He was the highest-ranking minority on Senator Meyers's staff at the time. So after the FBI busted him—and they nailed him dead to rights; caught him by a dirt road in Maryland with a trash bag full of documents—he got a high-profile black lawyer and they started playing the race card. As usual, it worked. You cry 'racism' in America, doors fly open; you cry 'sexism,' people plug their ears."

Punk heard Senator Meyers's voice as Platt spoke. "I wonder if the captain knows about that little chapter in Mr. Reese's life?"

"Of course he does," Platt opined. "The women of America could take a lesson in support networking from those people."

Punk decided not to attempt a hot-button discussion as he ushered Platt into primary flight control—"pri-fly"—the uppermost space on the ship, six levels above the flight deck. Pri-fly was not as large as the bridge but had the same sort of windows and panoramic view, like a Florida room suspended nearly a hundred feet in the air. Straight across the space from the hatch, in front of a wraparound console of knobs, switches, dials, and handsets, were two elevated ready room–style chairs perched side by side facing the port side of the ship, thrones from which the entire flight deck was visible.

Currently lounging in the chairs and noshing on box

lunches were the normal occupants: the air boss, the man in charge of the action on the flight deck, and the miniboss, the air boss's assistant and eventual successor. If the captain was king at sea, the air boss was one of his handful of brothers who had the misfortune of being born other than first in the family. He'd never be king, but he still had power over his part of the kingdom.

The boss and mini were engaged in a lively conversation and didn't hear Punk and Platt enter behind them.

"I was the command duty officer last night and I'm making my rounds, right?" the air boss, seated on the left, recounted, mouth half-full of ham-and-cheese sandwich. "I walk into aft berthing and there's this little white female hard body and this huge black guy, both totally naked. She's on one of the bottom bunks on her back with her legs up in the air and this guy's on his knees just going to town on this girl's snatch, I mean his face is totally buried. So I say, 'Sailor, what do you think you're doing?' and he looks up and, without missing a beat, says, 'Eating pussy, sir.' " Both men broke into raucous laughter.

"Howdy, boss," Punk said and cringed.

The two jerked around in their chairs. "Fuck, Punk," the air boss said after he wiped his mouth with a napkin. "You scared the shit out of us."

"Sorry . . ."

"God, I was afraid you were our female combat systems officer. That bitch is always spring-loaded to—"

"Boss, let me introduce you to Ferguson Platt," Punk interrupted. "He's the assistant military advisor to Senator *Eleanor* Meyers."

"Oh . . . oh, right," the boss said while shaking Platt's hand. "Ah, don't mind my story. I was just telling the mini here a bad joke. It was 'off the record' as you guys say in DC." The air boss had been the commanding officer of the EA-6B Prowler squadron in Punk's last air wing. The fact that the boss had gone from the sea-based squadron to sea-based ship's company was evidence that as officers got more senior the opportunities for shore duty were fewer, a phenomenon they labeled as the "Hotel California" Effect: *You can check out any time you like, but you can never leave.*

The boss introduced the mini, a dumpy former S-3 naval

flight officer with glasses, who looked like an accountant rather than a guy who'd spent his adult life flying off of aircraft carriers.

"Are you ready to do this?" the air boss asked Punk, happy to change the subject.

"You mean are the replacements ready?" Punk said. "We'll see pretty soon, won't we? I'm just giving Ferguson the nickel tour before things get busy around here."

The boss now had a mouthful of sandwich, so he just nodded and gave a thumbs-up before Punk pressed up against the glass that overlooked the bow. He directed Platt's eyes to the flight deck with an index finger. "You see all of those guys on the flight deck with colored jerseys on? Most of them work for the air boss. Yellow jerseys are the catapult and arresting gear officers—the 'shooters'—and the taxi directors, enlisted petty officers. The blue shirts are the tractor drivers and the worker bees who chock and chain the jets. The green shirts are the deck apes, the guys who make sure the catapults and arresting wires are working right, a dirty business as you saw from the gunk that's already on your loafers. The purple shirts fuel the jets. The brown shirts are squadron guys, plane captains mostly.

"During carrier quals the boss will control the movement of jets around the deck. Each squadron will have a representative up here to make sure pilots are being sequenced in properly and working toward their quals as fast as possible. With every replacement getting sixteen traps in two days it can get kind of confusing." Punk looked at his watch again. "Why don't we swing back through the ready room, and then we'll walk around the flight deck."

Punk bade the boss and mini farewell and led Platt back down through the island and aft along the starboard side passageway and through the back door to ready room number eight. Fitz and Gordo hadn't budged from lounging in the front row. Punk opened the front door and peeked around the corner into maintenance control and saw that Petty Officer Dietrich had a brand new pair of boots on the floor next to his desk.

"Are those for me?" Punk asked.

"Yes, sir," Dietrich replied. "Only the price went up a bit."

"How much?"

"Two ball caps."

"Damn. Two patches and two ball caps, huh?"

"Four patches . . ."

Punk ran a finger over an eyebrow and walked over and grabbed the boots from the floor. "Pleasure doing business with you," he said, wryly.

"Likewise, sir," the petty officer replied with a flea marketer's wink. "Oh, when can we expect delivery?"

"Tomorrow. I'll have the stuff put on the COD with the mail."

"That should be satisfactory." Punk started to walk out, but Dietrich stopped him. "Aren't you going to try them on?"

"You lost your right to be a wiseass with the fourth ball cap," Punk said.

Punk pushed back into the ready room and tossed the boots at Platt's feet. "Try these on."

"Wow," Platt exclaimed. "Are these the official aviator's model?"

"Punk Reichert autographs, dude," Punk said. "As official as you can get."

Platt pulled his loafers off and slid the boots on and quickly laced them. He stood and walked around with his arms out like he was trying out new legs along with new boots. They fit," he pronounced. "How much do I owe you?"

"On the house."

"I can't accept. These are certainly worth more than twenty dollars."

"Then we'll trade you." Punk gathered up the loafers and studied them for a second before sticking them behind the duty desk. "These look like good ones," he said. "What did they cost, one hundred bucks or so?"

Platt snorted a laugh and said, "More like three hundred . . ." The three officers exchanged amazed shakes of their heads and agreed they'd be happy to never pay three hundred dollars for a pair of shoes. ". . . I won't trade them."

"I was kidding," Punk said. "We'll consider the boots loaners while you're out here."

With the civilian suitably shoed, the familiarization tour continued, now focusing on the flight deck. "Let me show

you the catapults on the bow," Punk said over his shoulder
as he led Platt onto the nonskid. Walking the several hundred yards to the near end of catapults one and two took
some effort as the two of them were buffeted by a stiff
breeze across the flight deck caused by the carrier making
twenty-five knots through the water as it rushed to build
enough sea room to conduct flight operations in a couple
of hours.

Punk had to speak loudly to be heard over the wind
roaring in their ears. He pointed aft toward the waist catapults and then back to the bow cats. "The carrier has four
catapults, but we'll only be using these here, cats one and
two, during carrier qualifications because we'll have jets
taking off and landing at the same time all the time."

Punk walked along the greasy track for catapult one until
he came to a notched piece of steel jutting out of it. "This
is the shuttle," he explained. "This is what a jet hooks up
to, like a slingshot." He swept his arms down the length of
the catapult. "What you see of the shuttle is the tip of the
iceberg. Beneath the deck are two long cylinders that get
pressurized with steam. Once the pressure is great enough,
the steam is vented down these tubes and that drives the
shuttle, and then the airplane slings off the deck."

Punk walked two dozen paces aft and stepped across
three large squares of thick steel laid flush with the flight
deck. "These three panels are the jet-blast deflectors. When
a jet's on the catapult, these things spring up and keep the
exhaust from blowing everything over the fantail."

Punk guided Platt several hundred feet aft along the centerline of the landing area. About halfway down the angle
deck Punk took a hard right toward the port side of the
carrier. Perched on a platform mounted in the catwalk was
a huge device that looked like a prop—a director's conception of a time machine, perhaps—out of an old sci-fi movie.
The contraption had a big box for a body with a line of
square white-lensed lights on one side vertically down the
center and a line of round green-lensed lights horizontally
across that hung out beyond either side of the body like
wings or branches. "This is the Fresnel lens. This is what
gives the pilot glide slope indication, you know, tells him
whether he's high or low." He moved his hand up and down
and side to side around the center of the lens. "The goal is

to keep the 'meatball,' or 'ball,' lined up with this horizontal line of green lights here, known as the 'datums.' "

"Seems easy enough," Platt said.

"Keeping the ball centered is only one of several plates the pilot has to keep spinning during an arrested landing. He has to make sure that he's not flying too fast so that he doesn't pull the wire out too far, like I explained down below in the arresting gear engine room, and he has to make sure he lands the jet on the centerline of the landing area so he doesn't roll over the port side or take out parked jets with his wingtip."

"Or *her* wingtip," Platt added.

"Let's hope not," Punk said as he pushed away from the lens and moved inboard to the nearest arresting wire. "As you can see, there are four arresting wires, four chances to stop. They're numbered one to four, starting aft. The target wire is the three wire, generally. That's the one pilots want to catch for the best landing grade."

"Who grades them?"

"The LSOs, landing signal officers, like Creepy." Punk guided Platt from the four wire outboard and aft to the LSO platform on the port side nearly to the stern. "This is where the LSOs stand and help the pilots get aboard. As the planes come in, they watch them and talk to them through these handsets. They also control the lights on the lens using this thing." Punk grabbed a device hanging next to the radio handsets that looked like a tennis racket handle with a trigger on the end of it. "This is the 'pickle.' The LSO uses it to control the wave-off lights." Punk slapped his palm against a thin wall between the LSO platform and the Fresnel lens. The barrier had a cloudy Plexiglas window inserted into it at eye level. "This barrier is here so the LSOs don't get blown away when the jets go to full power in the wires."

"Full power? Don't they want to stop?"

"If the jet doesn't catch a wire with its tailhook then it has to get airborne and try again. To get airborne, the airplane needs to be at full power. A lot of pilots over the years have assumed they were stopped only to wind up trickling over the angle deck because they missed or spit the wire and weren't going fast enough to fly again. The LSOs will be watching the replacements like hawks over that. A pilot needs to go to full power and stay there until he's sure the jet has caught a wire."

Platt looked at the padded ramp that funneled down into the port catwalk. "What's that?"

"That's where the LSOs jump if somebody's about to crash into the deck." Platt smiled but stopped once he realized Punk wasn't trying to be funny.

"Let's hang out in the ready room until the fun starts," Punk said before launching himself backward into the padding and sliding below the port catwalk. Platt looked down at Punk through the steel grating of the catwalk like a child afraid to go off the diving board at the community pool.

"C'mon, jump," Punk prodded.

"I'm not sure how to do it right," Platt said.

"Just flop onto your back and slide down. It's not that tough."

"I'll pass," Platt said tugging at his shirt. "This is a silk polo. I don't want to wreck it."

"Fine," Punk said, chuckling as he pointed farther aft of where Platt was standing. "That ladder over there goes right down to where I am."

Platt worked his way down the narrow stairway, and they headed back to the ready room. Punk and Platt joined Fitz and Gordo, who still hadn't moved, in the front row of ready room chairs, and the four of them watched the news at the top of the hour and waited for the jets to arrive.

"Is there anything else to do?" Platt asked after a few minutes. "This is kind of boring."

"Welcome to life at sea," Fitz replied. "Multiply this moment by several million more just like it and you have a deployment."

The air of anticipation was heightened as the ship heeled slightly with its turn and the wind across the flight deck picked up to the twenty-eight knots straight down the flight deck. Groups of jets circled overhead waiting for the deck to come ready. With just about ten degrees of turn to go before the Boat was squarely into the wind, the first four Tomcats passed eight hundred feet over the starboard side in a right echelon, matching the ship's course. Punk looked

up at them and saw their wings were swept and half expected that one would roll into the other.

A mile in front of the Boat, the first jet rolled into the
break. After ninety degrees of a sharp left-hand turn, the
wings swept forward and the gear came down. The second
jet matched the lead twenty seconds later, and then the
third. They were all headed on a reciprocal course from
the carrier now, established on the downwind portion of
the landing pattern at an altitude of six hundred feet in
two-mile intervals. One by one they slowed to one hundred
and fifty knots. Abeam the bow they slowed to their final
approach speed, which at the Tomcat's max arrested landing weight was one hundred and forty knots.

Abeam the LSO platform, just over a mile off the port
side, the lead jet picked up the final turn to landing. The
Tomcat's descent was more pronounced now. After ninety
more degrees the fighter was at five hundred feet; another
forty-five degrees, three hundred and eighty feet.

The platform had quickly become a crowded place with all
the RAG LSOs and Longo eager to see how the latest crop
would fare. Creepy was the controlling LSO and Gordo was
the backup. Longo had no active role at the moment, but
was poised to judge the others. Punk and Platt stood with
their backs against the thin wall, Platt waiting for Punk to tell
him what to do. The LSOs sported sunglasses of various
styles, and all of their faces were well tanned except for
Creepy's, which was slathered with zinc oxide in a way that
gave him the look of a child on the beach just emerging from
under the hand of a protective mother. Platt, the only one on
the platform besides the enlisted spotters wearing protective
headgear and goggles (LSOs just wore "foamies" in their ears
so they could hear the pitch changes of the approaching jet's
engines), looked over the fantail at the Tomcat approaching,
and Punk could see from the staffer's expression that he'd
just realized that the behemoth was hurtling toward a landing
that would take place mere feet from where he was standing.
Probably the closest he'd ever been to a landing before had
been the terminal of an international airport a mile or so
away from the runway.

"This should be Slick," Creepy said to Tex, the LSO
next to him who was acting as the "writer," the guy who
took dictation as the LSO spouted out the details of each

pass. Tex was a mild fellow for an Aggie, short and slight, and the head LSO from the E-2 Hawkeye RAG.

The two controlling LSOs stood on the flight deck just off the platform, each with a handset to one ear and the pickle in the other hand. Their pickle hands were raised over their heads to remind them that the deck was currently fouled. The guilty tow tractor drove out of the landing area and the lights at various places around the flight deck went from red to green.

"Clear deck!" one of the enlisted spotters cried.

"Roger, clear deck," Creepy replied over the wind as he dropped his pickle hand down to his side.

"One-zero-seven, Tomcat, ball, nine-point-zero," Smitty called on the radio from three-quarters of a mile away once Slick, his pilot, told him he had the meatball in sight. Smitty had finished at the top of the Class Two RIOs, so he got the good deal of bagging traps with a senior pilot going through refresher training on his way to assume second in command of a fleet F-14 squadron.

"Roger ball, Tomcat," Creepy sang back over the frequency after making a mental note that the jet had nine thousand pounds of fuel left—plenty of gas. "Twenty-eight knots of wind straight down the angle."

Punk thought briefly of his time in front of the mishap board as he focused his eyes on Slick driving ever closer to the Boat. He remembered how the commander had warned him about being a wiseass and how he'd nurtured the tension in the room. But as Punk watched him fly as if on a rail, jet unwavering down the chute, he knew he owed the man credit for being an awesome ball flyer. That was worth something—not *everything,* but something—on the junior officer scale.

Slick gave the jet a burst of power through the "burble," the turbulence that hovered aft of the Boat and was caused by the disturbed air flow around the carrier's island, and nullified its attempt to settle the jet below the proper glide path. A second later he and Smitty passed by the LSO platform and a moment after that their jet was at full power stretching out the three wire. The jet made a high-pitched shriek before it went by, like a million tortured sparrows. Once it passed, the noise instantly turned into a baritone rumble that shook rib cages all over the deck. There was a thwack at hook impact then the metallic whine of the wire pulling out of the holes in the deck on either side of the landing area. Platt turned to watch through the Plexiglas, but it was too scratched to see through, so he craned his head around the inboard side of the barrier and was hit by the acrid smell of burned rubber and the taste of nonskid as flecks hit his teeth. He jerked back behind the barrier, and Punk laughed and recommended he not do that again.

After being pulled back slightly by the recoil, Slick pulled the throttles to idle, expeditiously raised his tailhook, and swept the wings aft.

Creepy turned to Tex and said, "Questions?" Tex looked back with pen poised, waiting to log the comments. "I guess he'll be expecting something, won't he?" Creepy asked rhetorically. "OK pass. Little high at the start, a little low at the ramp. Three wire."

Tex nodded and scribbled on the screen of the hand-held computer.

"What is he writing?" Platt asked, rising up on his toes to see over Tex's shoulder, voice raised beyond what it needed to be as he fought to hear himself through the mouse ears integrated into his protective helmet.

"He records Creepy's comments in this pass log using standard LSO shorthand," Punk explained. "The LSOs use the comments to debrief pilots on their landings once the flying's done."

Forward of the LSOs, Slick taxied out of the landing area and followed the director's signals across the deck and over to catapult one where he was handed off to another yellow shirt who lined the jet up for launch as one of the green shirts mated the Tomcat's launch bar with the shuttle. As Smitty was still trying to recage his eyeballs from the arrestment, Slick saluted the catapult officer and just over two seconds later, after going from a dead stop to one hundred and fifty knots, they were hurled back into the sky.

Dash Two of the four-plane flight, Muddy with Flex in her back seat, rolled into the groove, and Creepy rogered Flex's ball call. A few seconds later Creepy called, "You're high," over the frequency. She stayed high through the middle position of the pass, just inside a half-mile from touchdown. The LSO waited to hear the pitch change of the engines, and when it didn't come he rekeyed the handset and said, "You're still high. Ease power."

The shrill whine of the motors remained constant until just before the jet cleared the round down at the edge of the flight deck. At that point Muddy pulled the throttles almost to idle. The jet was too quiet for Creepy's ear as it passed the LSO platform on its way toward engaging the four wire with its tailhook. "Power back on!" he called. As Muddy's jet smacked onto the deck she pushed the throttles against the military power stops and the arresting wire paid out and quickly brought the Tomcat to a stop. Sure the wire had done its job, she pulled the throttles to idle and raised her tailhook and followed the taxi director's signals out of the landing area. The first yellow-shirted director handed her off to another and she wound up behind catapult one's jet blast deflector where she waited for her turn to get thrown back into the sky so she could do it all again.

"No grade," Creepy dictated to Tex. "Too much power on a wrapped-up start. High in the middle to in close. Underline fly through down at the ramp. Three wire."

As Tex wrote in the logbook, Creepy keyed the radio: "One-zero-one, paddles . . ." There was no reply. "Muddy, paddles . . ."

"Go ahead, paddles."

"Yeah, Muddy, I need you to start reacting to my calls. You were overpowered that entire pass. Make the ball go where it needs to be on the lens right at the start. Don't be satisfied with it other than in the center."

"Roger."

"Watch riding her," Longo said, dispassionately. "That was only her first pass."

Creepy cut his eyes toward Longo but said nothing.

"Who's 'paddles'?" Platt yelled at Punk.

"He is," Punk said, pointing at Creepy. "The LSO is 'paddles'—you know, like the old days when they actually used paddles to wave airplanes down to the deck."

The radio crackled with the next ball call: "One-zero-three, Tomcat, ball, four-point-eight."

"Roger ball, Tomcat." The jet was already lined up too far to the right and drifting away from the extended center-line. "Come left," Creepy said. The fighter responded with

a little wing dip, but not enough of one to fix the problem.
"Wave it off, wave it off." Creepy triggered the wave-off
lights with the pickle, and the Tomcat flew over the deck.

"Dusty makes the first bid to be the problem child!"
Creepy sang in a sportscaster's voice before turning to Tex.
"Wave off. Too much power on high wrapped-up start.
Underline high drift right in the middle."

Twenty seconds later Boxer 112 called the ball with
Stormin' at the controls and Beaker in his back seat. The
F-14 came down the glide slope on a rail much like Slick
did: wingtips rock steady, indexers—lights mounted next to
the nose gear to aid the LSO in determining the aircraft's
speed—burned solid white with an on-speed indication. The
jet flew past the LSOs and snagged the three wire.

"That didn't suck," Creepy said to Tex once the jet qui-
eted to idle power in the wires. "OK. Little high start to
in the middle. A little fly-through down in close. A little
low at the ramp. Three wire."

Another two Tomcats in formation came into the break
over the carrier and dirtied up to land. There were six
Tomcats in the mix now, including all of the Class Two
pilots.

The flight deck crew was in large part comprised of veterans of the carrier's last extended deployment, and the Tomcats were taxied out of the wires and hooked up to the
catapults with wartime efficiency. The landings and takeoffs
came so fast that Muddy had trouble assimilating all the
feedback. Flex was jabbering over the intercom and Creepy
was throwing out motherhood over the radio and the air
boss was telling her to follow the director's signals and not
blow people over by coming up on the power too much
and puckering the exhaust nozzles and the captain came on
the freq and told Dusty he never wanted him to do that
again on his carrier (she figured he'd pulled power too
quickly in the wires following a trap). She wanted to
laugh—except it really wasn't funny—that bouncing at Fentress hadn't really prepared her for this. There was no possible way to prepare for this. This was one of those things
in life that you just did and hoped you survived so you
could do it again with the benefit of experience the second
time around. And then she thought about doing this
again—and again—year after year and cruise after cruise,

and she wondered why she was trying to do this. She suppressed the thought and watched a green shirt disappear under the left side of the Tomcat's nose making sure the jet was hooked up properly for launch.

With Boxer 101 poised in the shuttle for the fourth time this CQ period, Muddy stirred the stick to ensure the flight controls were free, gave one last check of her instruments, and saluted the catapult officer. The cat officer returned her salute and touched the flight deck. A second later the nose strut compressed with the shuttle's forward movement, and she and Flex were riding fifty thousand pounds of accelerating fighter down the bow. This time she kept her wits about her enough to actually look at the airspeed indicator during the shot, and upon getting airborne, she realized another small victory by dropping the tailhook before Flex told her to.

Once she rolled wings level on downwind she raced through the landing checklist: "Wings are twenty degrees forward and auto, wheels are down and locked, flaps are full, DLC is engaged and working, trim is set, speed brake is out, hook is down, harness is locked. I'm showing six-point-three on the gas. Speed should be one hundred and thirty-seven knots."

"Roger, concur," Flex replied as they passed abeam the bow and Muddy worked to slow the jet down another thirteen knots. "How are you feeling?"

"Fine, I guess."

"Let's try and work the ball into the center earlier this pass. You've done the same thing all four passes so far: nursed the high until in close and then came down like a ton of shit to snag a wire. That may seem like a nice, conservative way to go, but actually you're setting yourself up for trouble that way. Just fly a centered ball all the way."

"Roger," she replied. Flex's demeanor had surprised her so far. He wasn't Mister Rogers, but he wasn't *Flex* either. She wondered if the Boat scared the hell out of him, too, or maybe it was just the idea of the hurtling at the Boat with a replacement at the controls.

They were abeam the carrier's stern now, at the "one-eighty" position of the landing pattern, one hundred and eighty degrees left to turn to match the carrier's course. Muddy banked the fighter to the left and started her final turn. *Hit the numbers,* she thought. *Keep the scan going. Thirty degrees left angle of bank, passing through three hundred feet per minute on the vertical speed indicator. Ninety degrees to go to final course . . . working a little fast, a little high . . .*

Dusty called the ball in front of her and moments later was waved off. *He's fucking up worse than me,* she thought, and for a moment she bathed in the perverse calm of the fact.

"Keep your turn in," Flex coaxed.

Scan, dammit; move your eyes around. Muddy saw she was going to overshoot the final course, so she wrapped the jet into a harder turn and worked her focus between the attitude indicator in the middle of her instrument panel and the Fresnel lens on the left edge of the flight deck, now three-quarters of a mile away.

"I've got a ball," Muddy passed over the intercom to her RIO as the white light on the lens crested into view.

"One-zero-one, Tomcat, ball, six-point-two on the gas," Flex said over the radio.

"Roger ball, Tomcat," Creepy replied. "Twenty-eight knots of wind down the angle."

Muddy thought about Punk's advice back at the officers club—meatball, lineup, angle of attack—but that seemed, although empirically sound, overly simplistic now. There were gauge readings and instrument indications and noises and sights and cues . . . and smells. She was sure she could smell the oxygen flowing into her mask and wondered if all the stimulation had given her superhuman senses, the kind that could smell oxygen.

"You're overpowered," Creepy said.

Her last thought as she crossed the ramp was not to come down like a "ton of shit" as Flex had put it. She saw the ball was a cell high but decided not to make the same play she had before at that point and hoped for a four wire.

As they hit the deck Muddy went to full power and this time her shoulder straps didn't dig into her collarbones. The tailhook missed the wires and now futilely bounced across the flight deck doing nothing but ripping up ticks of nonskid wherever it hit.

"Bolter, bolter, bolter," Creepy called on the freq as Boxer 101 continued off the end of the angled deck and back into the air.

"A Bolter's worth a half-point more than a No Grade," Flex said as Muddy continued to climb to six hundred feet before picking up her interval and turning downwind. "But too many of either of them ain't gonna do it for us."

"Us," huh? Are your wings coming off with mine?

"One-zero-one, paddles."

I know, I know. I boltered. "Go ahead, paddles."

"Muddy, you need to get your pattern squared away. Your overshoot killed you that time, and in general you're working too hard because of your starts. It's messing up your power setting as you roll into the groove. Hit the numbers all the way around and life will be a lot easier."

"Roger."

From behind Creepy, Longo said, "Your voice inflection didn't help matters on that one."

"She was overpowered," Creepy said, turning around and facing the other LSO.

"I know that. But it's the way you said it."

Creepy extended his hand with the pickle in it. "Do you want this?"

"It's nothing personal, paddles." Punk always thought they sounded like doctors when they called each other "paddles." "It's just an observation."

Dusty called the ball again and in the pattern behind him, Muddy started to run through the landing checks over the intercom when she was drowned out by the chorus of both Creepy and Gordo screaming, "Power, POWER," on the radio and then "WAVE IT OFF! WAVE IT OFF!"

Muddy looked to the flight deck just over a mile to her left, half expecting to see a fireball like the ones in the black and white PLAT videos Creepy had used during CQ ground school, but all she saw was Dusty's jet rolling out in the landing area hooked to a wire. Judging from the short distance he traveled down the flight deck before coming to a stop, she figured he'd snagged the first available wire, a one wire—never a good sign.

The voices of the LSOs echoed in her head as she stepped through the landing checklist. As she reached the one-eighty a voice came on the radio and said, "Sideline him, boss. Don't taxi that guy to the cat."

"Sounds like Dusty's a disqual," Flex said, thinking to himself but actually talking over the intercom.

"Already?" Muddy said.

"Hey, this is like an audition for a Broadway show," Flex said. "You've got to have your shit together as soon as you hit the stage."

Muddy pictured Flex spotlit on a stage, wearing a leotard and counting out steps: "Two and three and four and *twist* and two and three . . ." and then she realized she'd already passed through the ninety and was high and fast and had eased the jet's angle of bank too much again.

On the platform Creepy turned around and preempted any criticism from Longo over Dusty's disqual: "Five passes: a Wave Off, a Bolter, a Fair, and two No Grades. I've seen all I need to see."

Longo nodded congenially. "You made the right call, paddles."

Creepy looked at Longo with mild surprise as Flex called the ball for Muddy. The LSO sighted up the glide slope and saw that, once again, she was struggling at the start. He rogered the ball call and then talked to the wind: "Dusty might have some company before long."

The wardroom was packed with hungry officers during the dinner hour. Seats were hard to come by and those who'd completed their meals were hustled along by expectant looks from newcomers burdened with food-laden trays. The clanking of silverware against plates joined the din of conversation, but the place seemed quiet compared to the chaos that had surrounded some of them on the flight deck for the last two hours.

"Does it get any better than beanie-weenies?" Flex asked with his shades dangling and spoon poised over the bowl full of steaming shades of brown and red. "*Not.* It's the perfect at-sea meal."

"Flex, you've got to get Muddy to start flying the ball," Creepy insisted as he shoved a french fry into his face.

"You don't think I'm trying?" Flex said with eyes wide. "I think she's got rampitis right now. All she can think of is not hitting the round down."

"Then she'll disqual. She's got to center the ball. She's already on the bubble and we're not even into the first night yet."

"Disqual?" Flex said mockingly, mouth now full of food. "Don't say that around Big Top. She can't disqual with him here. The senator would get *mad* at him."

"Hey, you do what you have to do," Platt said, defensively. "I'm just observing things. It's very hands off."

"Sure," Flex shot back between chews. "Just like everything associated with this so-called second wave of female integration." He shoveled another mouthful of beans and chopped hot dogs into his face.

"Table manners aren't part of your training, huh?" Platt said as he considered Flex across from him.

"Fuck you, and don't change the topic," Flex returned. "What are you planning on changing anyway?"

"Upward mobility," Platt explained, genteelly wiping his mouth with a cloth napkin. "We need more females in the higher echelons."

"Why?" Flex asked. "Why do we *need* more females in the higher echelons? We got other problems to worry about right now."

"Like what?" Platt asked. Before any of the officers at the table could respond, he continued: "I told you before, gentlemen, your notion of war is over. Globalization makes it impossible. Technology makes it impossible. You want to talk about pressing issues? Talk about equality in the workplace."

"You know, this really is bullshit," Flex said. "You blame the male majority for keeping women from moving upward in the Navy. That has nothing to do with it." He took a swallow of iced tea to clear his mouth out, a signal that he was getting serious about the conversation. "There were two females in my last squadron, one pilot and one RIO. The pilot married a Hornet guy in the air wing and dropped her resignation letter and the RIO, who was already married to a helicopter pilot, an Academy classmate of hers, got pregnant and dropped her resignation letter."

"And?" Platt asked.

"And their leaving the Navy had nothing to do with the attitude of the Navy. The competitive fires died off and the maternal instincts kicked in. That's all there is to it. It's like resident software. Even if our skipper had begged them to stay in they would have left."

"Did you ever think that those sort of personal choices, choices every normal female will face, force women out of the Navy?"

"Well, you can't have babies and fly jets at the same time."

"Exactly. Not the way the system works now, anyway."

"What the hell are you talking about?"

"Currently women are punished professionally for taking time out to start a family. The system needs to be changed so that a female pilot can get married, get pregnant, give birth, and nurture the child until it reaches day care age and then return to the job as if she'd never left."

"You mean as if she'd been building flight hours the whole time she was gone?" Flex asked.

"Exactly," Platt said.

The aviators exploded into a chorus of pshaws. "You haven't been out here long enough, Big Top," Flex said. "Watching night flight ops might modify your opinion. This job doesn't get any easier or any safer for those around you if you go away for years at a time having babies."

Spud rushed up to the table and grabbed Punk by the shoulder. "We've got a meeting to go to up in the operations office. They want to review our game plan before we start the night work."

"Flex, can you escort our guest back to the ready room?" Punk asked as he slid his chair back.

"No problem," Flex said with a wry smile and a nod toward the civilian. "Maybe we'll take a detour through the engineering spaces along the way—let the snipes give him the initiation." He made the "okay" sign, then sawed his other index finger through it.

Punk followed Spud out of the port-side door, and as they turned the corner out of the wardroom, Punk ran headlong into an officer wearing khakis and a ship's ball cap. The officer, a lieutenant (junior grade), had his head down, and the brim of the cap covered his face from view as he rushed down the main passageway. After they collided, Punk excused himself and backed away and then realized whom he'd smacked into: Pugsly.

"What are you doing out here?" Punk asked as he backed against the bulkhead in an attempt to stay out of the traffic pattern.

Pugsly lined the wall next to Punk. "I've been reassigned here for the time being," Pugsly explained, eyes darting as if he couldn't dally for long. He looked healthier than when Punk had put him on the plane in Key West: trimmer, and his face had some color to it. Gone, too, were the circles under his eyes. Also gone from over his left pocket were his pilot's wings of gold. "I'm working for the supply officer."

"How long are you going to be with the carrier?" Punk asked.

"Just a month or so. I report to Surface Warfare Officers School in early November."

"That's great," Punk said with less sincerity than he'd intended.

Pugsly shrugged and took a step back into the flow of humanity through the passageway, but Punk grabbed him by the biceps before he passed. Punk opened his mouth to speak but Pugsly offered his palm and said, "Don't say it. I don't need to hear it. It was never in the cards." He was silent for a moment, looking down at his black chukka boots, and then he mumbled, "Besides, they tell me the Navy needs ship drivers, too." He looked up and smiled as if he'd liked the way that had sounded and all at once seemed comfortable in his skin. "Now, if you'll excuse me, I have several thousand corn dogs to attend to." Pugsly urbanely put thumb and forefinger to the brim of his ship's ball cap and then melted into the crowd down the passageway.

Muddy anchored her jet in a holding pattern at five thousand feet between twenty-two and thirty-two miles behind the Boat. The bright moon, the one all the instructors always raved about, didn't seem to change anything. It was still dark. She looked up at it again, willing it to be brighter.

The rules required that replacements had an hour of "comfort time" in the air before attempting their first night landings, but from Muddy's viewpoint there was nothing comforting about it. She didn't want any time to think because her mind was usually on its own program with the images it conjured up.

Their push time was twenty-five past the hour, and Flex reviewed the game plan for hitting the holding fix, the place in the sky from which they'd start their approach: "Five minutes to go until push time. We'll drive out for another minute, do a two-minute turn, and then drive back in and hit the fix right on time."

"Copy," she replied. Five Tomcats were out there with them. She and Flex would be the third to push, behind Slick and Stormin'. Bathed in the red lighting of the cockpit, Muddy thought about Stormin' at dinner and how jovial he'd been, a regular pain in the ass, especially with a dejected Dusty at the table.

Dusty had tried to put on a good face. He'd reviewed his passes over his untouched bowl of beanie-weenies like Ulysses recounting his trials. "In five tries I only had one Fair," he'd mused, which had caused Muddy to consider that in six tries she'd had only *three* fairs. She thought about Creepy's debrief in the ready room and steeled herself once again to following his guidance. But it was dark . . . she wouldn't be able to see the ramp, but she knew it was lurking out there.

There were jets all around them, punctuating the ink above and below at one-thousand-foot altitude intervals. "One-zero-seven is com, uh, commenting . . . er, *commencing*," Smitty said awkwardly, as Slick started down for the Boat twenty miles away. *Smitty's nervous about talking on the radio?* Muddy thought. *Oh, to be burdened with nothing but talking on the radio.* A minute later Beaker announced that Stormin' and he were on their way, and Muddy suddenly felt the same tension she'd dealt with when the referee held the ball aloft just before tip-off. She'd always managed to fight it off and play the game. "How are we looking on the hitting and holding fix?" she asked Flex over the intercom.

"What?" Flex asked incredulously. "You're quizzing *me*?"

Please, don't be a dick now. "Let's see . . . one minute, just over four miles . . . I think we're okay."

"We'll know pretty soon, won't we?"

With thirty seconds left until the push time, the digits on the range readout seemed to hold up; the damn thing wouldn't change from "23.0." She goosed the power to speed up the jet. As a result they hit the fix on time but were thirty knots fast. The approach pattern was based on all parties involved traveling at two hundred and fifty knots, and the last thing she wanted to do was drive up Stormin's ass and get waved off for interval after working her own butt off for an entire approach. She had four traps to complete tonight, and she could already feel that she was working on nothing but raw adrenaline. She'd tried to nap in her stateroom after dinner during the hour and a half she'd had to herself before the brief, but she'd done nothing but stare at the bottom of the upper bunk for twenty minutes before throwing her boots back on and joining Auto and Stormin' down in the ready room. The normally frenetic Stormin' had been one cool cat at dinner as he bathed in the light of his first day-period success, but as the night brief approached he seemed more jumpy than any of them.

"One-zero-one's inside of twenty miles," Flex reported over the radio.

"Roger, one-zero-one," a warm female voice said from the air traffic control room about one hundred hull frames forward of ready room number eight. "Contact approach on button fifteen."

"Switching." Muddy saw her backseat radio frequency readout go from 16 to 15. "Approach, one-zero-one's checking in at eighteen miles."

"Roger, one-zero-one," a man's voice replied. "Base recovery course is two-seven-five."

"Copy," Flex said. "We're steady two-seven-five."

Muddy kept the descent coming until they reached twelve hundred feet and then she leveled off. Once they reached ten miles away the controller said, "Call your needles."

The pattern for approaching the carrier at night (or during days with poor visibility due to weather) was much different than the visual pattern used when the sun was out. On clear days the jets flew down the side of the ship, went into the break, and circled around to land. At night, they held in racetrack patterns dozens of miles behind the carrier and then pushed at one-minute intervals for a straight-in approach. When pilots got close enough, the automatic carrier landing system (ACLS), akin to the instrument landing system used at civilian fields, assisted them. The ACLS antennas were fixed to the aft side of the carrier's island and projected "needles" that appeared on the pilot's attitude indicator, which in the case of the Tomcat was a large video screen in the center of the instrument panel. The needles were nothing more than two white lines, one vertical and one horizontal. The vertical line represented the correct azimuth for the approach and the horizontal line represented the correct glide slope. The trick for the pilot was to keep the two lines crossed right in the center of the screen, like the symmetry of a plus sign.

And that's exactly what Muddy had when the needles appeared on her display. "Good needles," she transmitted to the controller. "Showing on and on."

"Roger," the controller replied. "Fly your needles."

And so she did for the next eight and a quarter miles. She found herself staring so intently at the display that the needles started to vibrate, so she forced herself to look outside, but her eyes didn't stay long as she caught sight of the small pattern of lights floating in the middle of nothing that she would soon be attempting to land on. She decided not to look outside until after the ball call. Again she wondered what the moon hype was all about. She'd been promised a horizon and there was none.

The flight deck was poorly lit at night by design, with dim yellow lights on the island barely showing some of the highlights of the dangerously sharp objects all around them. The glow of the control panel along the aft edge of the platform, which was actually in front of them since they were facing aft watching jets land, washed the LSOs in red light like Boy Scouts around a fire—except for Creepy, who looked like anything but a Boy Scout, more ghoulish than ever in the darkness.

"One-zero-one, three-quarters of a mile," the controller said, at the point he would pass control of the approach to Creepy, the controlling LSO. "Slightly high, slightly left, call the ball."

"One-zero-one, Tomcat, ball, nine-point-zero."

"Roger ball, Tomcat," Creepy said. "Thirty knots, slightly axial."

Axial. That was the first time she'd heard that today. She thought back to CQ ground school and remembered that Creepy had said axial winds came straight across the bow instead of down the angled deck and had a tendency to take jets left of centerline. He'd also said that the burble was greater with axial winds.

No sooner had she finished the thought than Creepy said, "Right for lineup." Muddy nudged the stick against her right thigh and the right wing dropped slightly as she worked to get the fighter back on centerline, and at that moment her jet was hit by the burble. The combination of the lineup correction and the disturbed air caused the jet to sink well below glide path.

She shoved the throttles a fistful forward as Creepy demanded, "Power," and she wasn't sure if he meant power beyond what she'd just added or if she'd accurately presaged his call. In that moment of indecision the jet remained below glide path as it crossed the ramp and landed into a two wire.

"Lights off on deck," the air boss ordered over the radio as Muddy had forgotten to switch hers off after she'd stopped moving, which was the procedure. She cursed herself for falling into another conehead trap that Creepy had warned them about.

"No Grade," Creepy dictated with evident ire. "Lined up left at the start. Not enough power in the middle to in close. Two wire."

As soon as Tex was done writing, Longo snatched the book out of his hands and moved into the light of the control panel to study it.

"I'll give her one more look this evening, Longo," Creepy said, "and if she shows me something like that again, she's done."

"Whoa, whoa, whoa," Longo returned. "She's done? Don't you think that's a bit premature?"

"She hasn't responded to my calls all day, and she's throwing a lot of ugliness at us."

"Ugliness?" Longo ran his finger around several of her passes in the logbook. "Three Fairs out of six passes in the first day period . . ."

"And two No Grades and a Bolter," Creepy said, finishing the thought on a different note than what Longo had intended. "And now she's started the night period with another No Grade. I think I'm being generous by giving her another try, to be honest."

Longo gave the logbook back to Tex and then snatched the pickle from Gordo. "I'm now the backup LSO," he announced.

"Why?" Creepy asked. "If you're doubting my ability why don't you relieve me instead?"

"I'm not relieving Gordo," Longo insisted. "And I'm not doubting your ability. I haven't agreed with all your calls, but I don't doubt your ability."

"Really? Then you won't make a snide comment if I go on the radio and talk to her as she taxis back to the cat?"

"What are you going to say?"

"See?" Creepy said, throwing his arms out and petitioning the others on the platform. "He's doubting my ability."

The exchange ended as the next jet called the ball.

On the bow Muddy was having a tough time keeping track of which set of wands were signaling to her. More than once she had to stop to sort it out, and at that point one of the sets would start flailing, so she'd follow those until she became confused again. Eventually the jet was in the shuttle and set to launch back into the night. One set of wands passed her off to another and after wiping out the controls and checking the gauges again, she flicked the external lights on with the pinky switch on the outboard side of the left throttle. The shooter's flashlight went to the deck and then was thrust rapidly forward, and a second later Muddy and Flex were on yet another horizontal roller-coaster ride into the abyss.

Now that they had their hour of flight time under their belt there was no need for the holding pattern. Instead of flying twenty or so miles away from the Boat, the pilots followed the approach controllers' directions and drove aft of the ship until they were hooked into a left-hand turn in for the final portion of the straight-in approach, usually only about five or six miles away from the ship.

Things flowed quickly, not as quickly as they had during the daytime, but faster than what Muddy had expected. She felt like she was at least doing well enough to qual, although Creepy had given her a number of calls each pass and had talked to her twice just after she'd cleared the landing area. But he'd also talked to Auto. And even Stormin' had received the occasional "power" call.

As she intercepted the final course for her fourth and final approach, she heard a new, authoritative voice on the frequency: "One-zero-three and one-twelve, do you guys feel like getting two more traps this evening?"

"Yes sir, Captain," Slick said.

"That's affirmative for one-twelve also, Captain," Stormin' said.

"All right, then. We'll get you both back on the cat."

The exchange confused Muddy. "Don't those two already have four night traps apiece?" she asked Flex.

"If things go well enough for a pilot the LSOs will call up to the bridge and ask the captain to grant a two-trap waiver to the ten-trap-a-day rule," Flex explained. "If the captain grants the waiver, which he usually does if the LSOs ask for it, then the pilot can get another two and complete the night work in one night," Flex explained. "Tomorrow both of them will just have four day traps left and they'll be done."

Muddy thought of finishing night traps tonight. One less brief, one less man up, one less nerve-frayed evening. She was already out here—might as well suck it up for another twenty minutes and bang out two more traps. But were things going well enough for her to be offered the option of two more traps? She wanted to ask Flex what he thought her chances were but didn't as she was sure he'd tell her to not worry about it and just concentrate on flying a good pass next time down the chute.

The needles appeared and she chased them for five miles, convinced the ship was jinking on her and trying to make the approach as hard as possible. The approach controller handed her off to paddles at three-quarters of a mile, and she transitioned her focus from the display inside the cockpit to the light pattern against the black world in front of her.

You're just landing the damn jet, she thought between the cadence of meatball, lineup, and angle of attack. *You're not dropping bombs; you're not dogfighting; you're just landing the jet. Stop making it harder than it has to be.*

Then something clicked, like when she took a three-point jump shot and knew it was going to go in from the moment it flicked off her fingertips. With one slight addition of power she made the jet behave like a trained animal until touchdown, nodding at the burble as she passed through and grabbing a three wire like she meant it and even switching off her lights just as her forward momentum stopped on the rollout. Creepy didn't say a word.

Muddy kept waiting to hear the radio key, waiting for the captain's paternal voice to ask her if she wanted two more night traps tonight. She had never thought she'd embrace the notion of more night traps, but now was sure the light had come on and wanted to capitalize on it. This zone was surely a fragile place, easily destroyed. But after she cleared the landing area and taxied around the flight deck a bit, a circuit that included a teasing pause behind catapult one's jet blast deflector that made Muddy think she might be about to get airborne again, she got the signal to shut her engines down. Unlike her classmate Stormin', she was going to be flying around in the dark again the next night.

"Four people live in this room at a time?" Platt asked as he spun a slow circle in the middle of the stateroom's common area.

"Six, actually," Punk said. He sat in one of the padded metal chairs and pulled down a fold-up desk in the middle of a wall of drawers, lockers, and other fold-up desks that covered the entire wall of the stateroom. "This layout isn't too bad though," he said as he leaned back in the chair and looked around. "On my last deployment we had eight guys in our stateroom."

"Eight guys?" Platt said. "That's like living in prison."

"Prisoners get more space," Flex said as he hung his flight suit on a hanger that he'd found in one of the lockers. "It's a well-known fact." He walked over to Platt. "Hey, Big Top, can you do you me a favor?"

Platt recoiled a bit, suspiciously eyeing the muscular RIO. "What?"

"Something's stuck here." Flex extended his right index finger. "Tug on this, will you?"

Platt blindly complied, and as he did Flex loosed a thunderclap of flatulence.

Platt yanked his arm back and regarded Flex with an expression of absolute revulsion. "That's got to be the grossest thing I've seen in twenty years," the civilian said, voice dripping with disgust. "What are you, twelve years old?"

"Hey, man," Flex replied with a straight face, "you're the one who pulled my finger. And besides, I wanted you to get the full experience of being on deployment."

As the occupants of the room coughed and gagged and fanned themselves, Punk asked Platt where his belongings were.

"I don't know," Platt said. "I thought they'd be delivered to my room."

"Delivered to your room?" Flex said with a laugh. "What do you think this is, the Four Seasons? Do you have a wad of bills in your pocket to tip the bellhops with?"

Punk waved for Flex to shut up. "Where was the last place you had your bag?"

"The little room off to the side, right as you walk onto the ship."

"I think I know where you're talking about," Punk said and stood up. "Come with me."

Punk led Platt along the nearest cross passageway and then aft a few frames down the main starboard passageway on the 0-3 level and then spun down several sets of stairs to where the quarterdeck was set up when the ship was in port. At sea the spaces, with little utility away from the pier, were like a fairground the day after the fair has ended. Platt pointed to one of the alcoves and said he thought that was where he'd left his hanging bag, but he wasn't really sure. Punk decided they should go back to the stateroom and make a call to the supply department.

Minutes later back in the stateroom Punk hung up the phone and reported that the supply department principals were on the case, and he added that he was confident it would turn up soon.

"I hope you're right," Platt said. "Everything smells like jet exhaust, and I probably stink, too."

"You do," Flex said. "But I, for one, am too polite to mention it."

"I can lend you some soap if you want to shower," Punk offered, catching a whiff of his own body odor. "I know I need one." He pointed behind the wall of lockers to the other half of the room, the sleeping chamber—three sets of bunk beds in metal frames. "There's a towel on your rack on top of the folded sheets and blanket. If for some reason your bag doesn't show up by tomorrow morning, I can take you down to the ship's store and you can buy whatever you need to tide you over for a day or so, and I'll lend you one of my extra T-shirts and maybe we can

even draw you a flight suit." Punk looked over to Creepy.
"What size would you say he was?"

"Hmm . . . forty-two long, maybe," Creepy said.

Platt's expression brightened just a bit. "A flight suit,
huh?"

Punk had fallen asleep to the sounds of Flex and Platt
debating how to fix the welfare system at just after one in
the morning. Some time later Punk's eyes shot open. For
a few moments, as he lay in his rack contemplating the
shadows made by the traces of white light that snuck
through the ventilation screens and the bulkhead from the
ever-bright passageway cracks, he feared he was on cruise
again. He checked his watch: two A.M. He'd only been
asleep for an hour.

He tossed for a while, now fully aware of every noise coming from the flight deck just over his head, past the pipes and
wires that lined the ceiling of the stateroom that were just
visible now that his eyes had readjusted to the dark. He heard
the tapping of small hammers and the grinding of sanders
and the rumble of tow tractors—all the familiar sounds of
the Boat and ones that he wouldn't have thought twice
about after a month at sea. He felt a sense of nostalgia for
the innocent days of his first two deployments, days before
Crud's death.

His mind turned to happier things, and he suddenly wondered how Suzanne was doing. Her face popped into his
head, and he saw her smile and he wanted to talk to her.
The intensity of the desire shocked him a bit. He flopped
from one side of his body to the other and the feeling
didn't go away.

He slipped down from the upper bunk, careful not to
step on Creepy, who was doing his best Nosferatu imita-
tion, on top of the sheets and blanket with his arms crossed
over his chest. Punk padded around the corner from the
sleeping area over to the phone against the far wall, past
the desks and lockers, wondering if it would dial to shore.
Only a few phones could on his last carrier but that had
been a year and a half ago and shipboard technology was
certainly better now. But as he dialed 9, he got nothing but
a busy signal.

His desire did not wane in spite of the failure. He slipped

his flight suit and boots on and walked aft to ready room number eight.

Punk passed by maintenance control, currently manned by one black petty officer who was watching a movie on a small television in the corner, and entered the dark and abandoned ready room unnoticed. He switched on the lights and took a seat behind the duty desk. He reached for the portable phone and pushed 9.

He got a dial tone but just sat there with the phone to his ear, fighting his doubts. Would Suzanne be upset at him for waking her? Would she wonder why the hell he was calling from the carrier? He dialed her number, a number he'd dialed many times before.

The phone rang four times before she picked it up, and he was certain he'd wakened her. "Hello?"

"Hi, Suzanne."

"Hello, Rick."

Her voice sounded warm, and he was relieved that she didn't seem surprised that he'd call. "Hello," he said again, like a sixth grader calling a girl for the first time.

"Where are you?"

"In the ready room on the Boat. Did I wake you up?"

She chuckled. "No, unfortunately not. What time is it?"

Punk gazed over his shoulder at the clock mounted against the bulkhead behind the duty desk. "Ten after two in the morning."

"I don't sleep as much as I used to."

"Oh." He wasn't sure what to say next. "You should . . ."

"What?"

"Sleep more."

"I would if I could."

"Try to think good thoughts."

"Like what?" There was suddenly a playful, fetching quality to her voice.

"I don't know," he replied. "Think about me taking you to dinner and a movie when I get back."

"I guess I could try that one. I don't know if it'll put me to sleep though."

"Give it a try."

"I will. When are you getting back?"

"About nine in the morning, day after tomorrow. The COD is flying into Norfolk."

"How are you getting to Virginia Beach?"

"I'm not sure," Punk said. "The squadron duty van, probably."

"I'll come get you."

"You don't have to do that, Suzanne."

"I want to. I'll meet you at the terminal."

"It's a pain driving all the way over there."

"No, it's not. I can easily do it. Like I said, I want to."

His mind's eye developed a pleasant image of her waving from the terminal's observation deck. "Okay. Okay, I'll see you there."

There was another moment of silence, but it didn't feel awkward this time. He pictured her curled up on the couch with the phone to her ear. "I'm glad you called, Rick."

"Me too. Now go to sleep."

"Barbasol?" Platt wondered aloud as he read the shaving cream can label. "I didn't think this stuff was even made anymore." He slid a few feet down the aisle. "And do they have anything in stock besides dandruff shampoo? This stuff will fry the hair off of my head."

Punk called across the small store to the clerk at the register who was currently ringing up a sailor buying what appeared to be a lifetime supply of beef jerky: "Is this the only kind of shampoo you carry?"

"That's it, sir," the pudgy seaman with a shaved head said. "The supply officer wants to keep inventory low because we have a big inspection coming up."

Platt shook his head and muttered something about the power of dissatisfied customers as he added the bottle of Head & Shoulders to his basket and approached the counter. The sailor rang up the shampoo, shaving cream, plastic comb, disposable razor, deodorant stick, toothbrush, toothpaste, and bar of soap for a total cost of five dollars and ninety-five cents, which mitigated Platt's grumping a bit.

"That's a lot of stuff for less than six dollars," he marveled as they headed back to the ready room from the second deck where the ship's store was located. "And no tax."

Platt was proudly sporting the flight suit Punk had procured early that morning, even before Platt woke up, from

Petty Officer Dietrich for the bargain price of two more ball caps. Punk had requested a forty-two long, but all supply had in stock was a forty regular. The staffer didn't seem to mind the fact that he looked like a kid who'd gone through a growth spurt a bit faster than what his parents could keep up with; in fact, Punk sensed a new swagger in his gait. Platt was a quick study, and at the start of day two on the Boat, he'd zipped on his flight suit and laced up his boots with the confidence of a midcruise nugget. Punk knew he needed to keep an eye on him. The Boat had a way of showing neophytes that they knew just enough to be dangerous—and they were usually dangerous to themselves.

When they got back into the ready room, Ben Dover, the duty officer for the day, reached behind his chair and produced Platt's black leather hanging bag. "Thank God they found it," the civilian said with his eyes to the heavens and hands to his chest, relieved enough not to complain about just wasting nearly six dollars on souvenirs from the Museum of American Hygiene. He unzipped the bag and combed through it before looking at Punk with a serious countenance. "This doesn't mean I have to give my flight suit back now, does it?"

It was an elusive thing, this zone. Whatever had clicked for Muddy on the last pass the previous night was gone the next day. She felt gawky as she taxied clear of the landing area after her third trap of the morning—nothing was instinct, even the movement of her eyes was conscious and deliberate, and she wished she'd been able to get more sleep last night. The yellow shirt flashed two closed fists, and she pushed down on the tops of the rudder pedals with her feet and brought the fighter to a stop behind catapult one.

Muddy focused out the left side of the Tomcat, over the top edge of the raised jet-blast deflector, and watched the vertical stabilizers of Stormin's jet shimmy as he moved into the shuttle for another cat shot, and then she looked to her right and saw Slick sidelined with a broken jet on the elevator in front of the island. Brown and green shirts scurried under, around, and on top of the stricken machine like trainers tending to a punch-drunk boxer between rounds. The radio keyed, a prompt of sorts, and she knew it was for her.

"One-zero-one, paddles," Creepy said.

"Go ahead, paddles," Muddy answered.

"Remember what I said during the brief: We've got a lot more wind out here today, so getting your pattern squared away is even more important. Start your turn earlier at the one-eighty. If you wait until you're abeam the ramp you'll get blown long in the groove. Start the turn abeam the LSO platform instead."

"Roger," she replied robotically.

"And I've got to get you to start flying the ball from the start. Center it and keep it there."

"Roger." *Center it and keep it there.* It sounded so simple, like "find the Titanic and raise it" or "land on Mars."

On the LSO platform Creepy glanced over his right shoulder at Longo and sarcastically said, "I apologize for taking the liberty of talking to your protégé."

"It's your program, paddles, not mine," Longo returned, dispassionately.

The air boss's voice boomed through the 5MC, the flight deck loudspeaker system designed to be heard over jet noise: "Paddles, pick up the phone!"

Creepy reached over to the console and put the phone to his ear and then motioned to Punk. "Spud wants to talk to you."

Punk slipped between Fitz and Gordo and relieved Creepy of the receiver. "Hello?"

"I'm back in pri-fly," Spud said. Punk twisted around and looked up to the top of the island and saw Spud pressed against the glass waving down at him.

"I'm not waving back," Punk said. "Nothing personal."

"We just got a weather update. It looks like a front is coming through this afternoon."

"What kind of front?"

"Let me look . . ." Punk heard the rustling of paper through the earpiece, and then Spud began reading to him. "Cold front passage in the coastal waters of southern Virginia and northern North Carolina at approximately eighteen hundred hours local time. Some precipitation likely on either side of the front. Rain could be heavy at times. Expect wind speeds of eighteen to twenty knots with higher gusts. Skies will be overcast and layered between fifteen hundred and twenty-five thousand feet."

"Damn," Punk said. "Where the hell did this come from?"

"Out of nowhere, apparently. Give paddles a heads up."

"Will do."

"Another thing: I was just down on the bridge talking to the captain. He expressed some concern about how Muddy was doing."

"Standby . . ." Punk took the handheld from Tex and did some quick mental gymnastics. "She's doing about a No Grade plus."

"Sounds like she's on the bubble."

"I think that's safe to say."

"How many traps does she have left?"

Punk looked at the kneeboard card he'd been using as a Class Two tally sheet. "Three. One more today and two tonight."

"She'd better post Fairs or better from here on out."

"Yep."

"He was also wondering how Mr. Platt was getting along."

Punk glanced back at Platt standing against the barrier in his high-water flight suit with the sleeves cuffed to hide the fact they were several inches too short. He'd refused to wear the protective headgear today, insisting it was for the weak, and had convinced Flex to lend him his wrap-arounds.

"If you want something from the Senate Armed Services Committee you'd better ask him now," Punk said. "I think he's ready to tell the senator to support you."

"Just keep him from wandering into the landing area."

"Will do." Punk looked up to the top of the island and gave a simple wave.

After following Stormin' off the catapult and around the first half of the landing pattern, Muddy approached the one-eighty for what she hoped would be her last day pass in the RAG. She had been seeking the click, that thing that hit you once you entered the zone, but had been unable to find it.

Just as she finished going over the landing checklist with Flex, the radio buzzed with the first transmission of its kind for this detachment: "Stormin', you're a qual. Congratulations."

She forced her scan around the cockpit and fought off envy. Who would've picked Stormin' to be the first among Class Two to carrier qualify—the first to finish the RAG? Then she saw Lucky in her mind's eye, laughing and scratching in the ready room the morning before he was killed, and she remembered how they'd all sensed he was the Top Stick. *Watch your angle of bank. Keep the vertical speed moving toward seven hundred feet per minute.*

"One-zero-one, Tomcat, ball, six-point-five."

"Roger ball, Tomcat. Thirty knots down the angle."

Down the angle. Muddy again noted the absence of a wake behind the Boat as she rolled into the groove and remembered what Creepy had briefed about higher natural winds and a proportionally slower ship's speed through the water. She leveled her wings just as she got to centerline, and felt the click, a small one but a *click* nonetheless. With that one move she knew she'd already solved the lineup portion of meatball, lineup, angle of attack. Even the high winds weren't going to change that.

"Don't touch a thing," Flex coaxed over the intercom two seconds before they crossed the ramp and slammed onto the three wire. She shoved the throttles to military power and held them there until convinced they'd trapped and then pulled the thrust to idle.

"Power in the wires!" Creepy commanded over the radio, but before Muddy could honor him her jet had already stopped. She waited for the tongue lashing that was sure to come as she cleared the landing area, knowing that pulling power prematurely in the wires would result in a cut pass. She also was sure that at this point she wasn't in a position to absorb a cut pass into her landing grade average.

"Did it seem like I went to idle too fast to you, Flex?" Muddy asked over the intercom.

"Not really," Flex said. "But maybe Creepy saw something we didn't."

Across the landing area from Boxer 101 Creepy was about to put the radio handset to the side of his head but Longo reached around the others and stopped his arm before it got there. "She was fine, paddles," Longo said over the gusts. "That wasn't a cut in the wires."

Creepy considered Longo with eyes narrowed. "What do you think, Fitz?" Creepy asked.

Fitz shrugged and said, "Longo's probably right."

Longo extended a hand toward Creepy like a baseball manager about to take the ball from a pitcher he'd just relieved. "Take a breather, paddles. Let's let Fitz wave a few." Longo turned to his right. "Gordo, you be the backup LSO for now." He looked forward and saw that the broken jet was now fixed: Slick was at full power on catapult one, throwing out a soot ball that deflected around all sides of the jet blast deflector, and another jet was behind the blast deflector eating a portion of the exhaust while waiting to go next. "We still have a couple of guys to finish up here."

The LSOs shifted positions on the platform in concert with their newly assigned roles and Longo dictated to Tex, who'd been trying to coax Muddy's last grade out of Creepy: "Fair pass. Little high start to in close. Little come down at the ramp. Three wire."

Creepy took station between Punk and Platt against the barrier and listened to Longo's take on the pass and shook his head. Punk furtively studied the LSO next to him. Creepy hung his head and more than once muttered, "Unfuckingbelievable."

In front of the island a blue shirt hooked a tow bar to Muddy's nose gear, and a tractor eased the Tomcat back into the spot where it would be chocked and chained for nearly ten hours before the night go. Muddy felt another jolt of envy toward Stormin', and she imagined the radio crackling with, "Muddy, you're a qual," but then defensively shifted her thoughts to something else. She focused over the starboard side of the bow and took in the white caps pursing on the water, and she thought about sitting on the beach and not giving a shit about anything. And then she noticed a line of clouds gathering on the horizon.

As soon as the final day trap was completed Punk convened a powwow in the six-man. Now most of the squadron instructors afloat, the Death Boxer principals—Spud, Punk, Flex, Creepy, Gordo, and Fitz—sat in a circle in the middle of the stateroom's common area and wrestled with how to proceed.

"Slick and Stormin' are qualified," Spud said with his

eyes down to the notebook in his lap. "Auto and Muddy each have only two traps left. Creepy, I need you to shake it off and be the controlling LSO tonight."

"Only if you keep Longo off the platform," Creepy said.

"I can't do that," Spud returned. "Besides, even if he handled it poorly or hurt your feelings, he wasn't wrong. Muddy didn't take a cut in the wires. I was watching it; the air boss and the captain were watching it."

"That's exactly what I'm talking about, Spud," Creepy said. "I've never made such a bad call on the platform. He's shaken my confidence . . . thrown off my game."

"Okay, I'll talk to him and tell him to chill out a bit. Stop worrying about him."

"Yeah," Punk added. "Creepy, he's been under your skin since the presail conference. Ignore him."

Creepy puffed a sorry laugh. "Yeah, right. We have too much history for me to ignore him. He was my nemesis in my last air wing. Plus he's got some kind of agenda out here involving Muddy."

"He's right about that, Spud," Punk said. "Longo's working for Admiral Knowles, and Admiral Knowles is working for Senator Meyers. That's why Platt's out here."

"Why are you guys always so spring-loaded to create a conspiracy?" Spud asked. "Of course Longo's working for Admiral Knowles; Longo's attached to AIRLANT; AIRLANT works for CINCLANTFLT."

"So where does Senator Meyers fit in?" Punk asked.

Spud raised an index finger and with the other hand produced a pamphlet from one of the lower leg pockets of his flight suit. "Before you drop your letters, you might want to take a look at this: the Constitution of the United States. I know this sounds corny to you young hard dicks, but it's like my American Express card: I don't go anywhere without it. I use this to remind me of where I fit in the big picture." He flipped the pamphlet open and ran his finger along a page and began to read to the assembly: *"Article One, Section Eight, Clause Thirteen: The Congress shall have power to provide and maintain a Navy."* Spud scanned the room with an erudite smile.

"And that means?" Flex asked.

"Did you take the commissioning oath?" Spud asked back.

"Of course."

"Then you understand that Senator Meyers gets to poke and prod you as much as she wants," Spud explained. "So quit bitching about it. Your peace lives with Eagle's guidance not to lower the bar." He looked over at Creepy. "Have you lowered the bar out here?"

Creepy shrugged and muttered, "I guess not."

"Well, don't lower it tonight, either," Spud said. "Be true to your standards and everything will work out fine. And do what Spud said: Ignore Longo. I need you on the pickle tonight. You're the CQ phase leader and our head LSO. If Muddy happens to disqual, Eagle's going to want to hear that you waved her."

The ship lurched, the first motion any of them had really noticed since they'd cleared the channel by Chesapeake Light the day before. "Seas are building with the wind," Spud said as he gripped the arms of his chair. "Let's keep an eye on the forecast. We can handle a few drops of rain, but we need the clouds to stay above fifteen hundred feet to keep the CQ going. I, for one, don't feel like staying out here another day if I don't really have to, and I know the Hornet RAG guys behind us are chomping at the bit to get going tomorrow."

Spud took the LSO logbook from Creepy and thumbed through it for a short time. "Muddy's going to need a couple of decent passes . . ." He smiled again. ". . . or some help from Longo." He looked at Creepy. "Just kidding."

On the way out of the room he grabbed Punk's biceps. "Put on your assistant officer-in-charge hat and come with me."

Spud figured that Longo, an F/A-18 pilot by trade, was probably cooling his heels in ready room number six with the rest of the Hornet Mafia onboard awaiting their replacements' entry onto the carrier's stage tomorrow, so that was where he headed with Punk after they left the six-man. Spud's hunch proved to be correct as they walked in ready room six and found Longo napping among a few others in the second row of ready room chairs.

"Longo," Spud said as he reached across another guy and gently tapped him, "can we go sidebar with you for a second?"

"What?" Longo said as he jerked awake. He blinked at

Spud until the haze cleared then silently rose out of the chair, stretched, and, after excusing himself across the legs of the pilot next to him, followed Spud to the back of the room. Punk fell in behind them.

Spud took a seat in the chair against the wall in the last row and patted the chair next to him. "Sit, please."

"What's up?" Longo asked innocently as he flopped into the chair with his palms up and eyebrows arched.

"I need Creepy to wave tonight," Spud said.

"Sure, sure," Longo said compliantly. "That's what I was planning on."

"Okay . . ." They both sat looking at the back of the chair in front of them and nodding. "I also need you to stop riding him."

Longo snapped his face toward Spud. "Riding him?" He was fully awake now. "Where did you get that? I simply stepped in when he made a bad call."

"That's fine," Spud said. "I just want to ensure you're letting my man do his job, that's all."

"I'm helping him do his job, Spud," Longo said and lowered his eyes to the leather nametag on Spud's flight suit, concentrating on the naval flight officer wings etched into it. "Besides, I wouldn't get too concerned if I were you. This is a *pilot* problem."

Spud bit his lip. Punk knew there were few things that would send him off the deep end like the "single-seat mentality." Just as during the Vietnam era, when Skyhawk and Corsair II drivers had looked down on those who rode in the rear cockpit of the Phantom, Hornet pilots would now crow about how they'd rather have the two hundred pounds of gas and label the RIOs as "nav bags."

And it wasn't that Spud was thin-skinned. He understood and embraced the ball-busting culture of naval aviation; it was that beneath the jabs some of them, like Longo, tacitly refused to acknowledge the utility upon which Spud had built his flying career, a profession that would soon place him in command of a Tomcat squadron. It was one thing to joke about how he didn't have a control stick in his hand; it was quite another to suggest his life was a waste. Besides, Spud often pointed out that he'd known enough task-saturated Hornet drivers who'd flown into the ground and kept enough Tomcat pilots, including Punk, from doing the same thing to abide by the sentiment.

"Longo, God love you," Spud said, reaching over and patting the LSO's shoulder, "in the Tomcat community we don't have pilot problems and RIO problems. We've just got problems, and I like to deal with problems before they get out of hand."

"Me t-too," Longo said with a small frog in his throat, apparently a bit uncomfortable with Spud touching him.

"Good, good. Is Muddy disqualing a problem?"

Longo snapped his face toward Spud again. "She hasn't disqualed."

"No, but she could." Spud searched Longo's expression for his reaction to the very idea of it.

Longo nodded his head slowly. "Sure, she could still disqual."

Spud put his long skinny arm around Longo's neck and pulled the LSO nearly cheek-to-cheek. "You know what I've always liked about this business, Longo?"

"What?"

"We can speak plainly to each other. Do you like that?"

"Sure, I guess . . ."

"You're a kiss-ass. I've never cared for kiss-asses, but they seem to thrive in the Navy, probably because we're a business that doesn't have to turn a profit. But we do have a job, and the same natural law that is unforgiving of a company with a weak sales force is unforgiving of a navy with weak warriors. This isn't a pilot thing. This isn't a Tomcat thing. On your next deployment America may be at war, and Muddy may be on your wing. Make sure you're happy with that."

Spud released Longo and stepped over him and shot back one last line: "Please say hello to Admiral Knowles for me."

Shot clear of the dark and wet flight deck, Muddy went into the clouds at two thousand feet and didn't break out of them until just before she reached her holding altitude of twenty thousand feet. Stormin' had wished her good luck in the passageway before the launch, but now she knew he was sitting in the ready room watching the rain hit the PLAT camera and clucking about how he was glad he'd finished his night traps on the moonlit evening before.

The full moon was out there, taunting her in holding, but it would be gone when she dove back into the clouds on her approach to the Boat. She checked the clock on the instrument panel. Five minutes until push time. *One minute outbound, two minutes in the turn, two minutes inbound.*

She thought about how Smitty had bragged about having ten traps under his belt and how Fitz had slammed him by saying that a RIO bragging about ten traps was like somebody going to ten porn flicks and telling people he'd had sex ten times. She chuckled into her mask.

Over the intercom Flex said, "One minute 'til push."

The LSO platform wasn't the pleasant spot for watching flight operations that it had been the evening prior, but Platt had insisted on being up there anyway, in spite of the fact that the captain had invited him to watch the action from his chair on the bridge. There was a steady rain beating on the flight deck now and the wind was howling, making the temperature at least twenty degrees cooler than it had been the night before. Platt looked at Punk from under the rainhood of a borrowed foul-weather jacket and gave him a toothy smile. Punk, feeling a little green around the gills himself with the slight rolling of the ship that had started over the last hours, had feared that Platt would become seasick, but he'd seemed impervious to the motion. In fact, he seemed to enjoy it. His only response in the ready room each time the ship had surged through a wave was to say, "Yo-ho-ho."

A light appeared out of the clouds miles behind the Boat and then another, like cars down a desert highway. As they came into view, Longo decided he needed to take over as backup LSO. Without any warning, he moved two steps across the platform and relieved Fitz of his pickle.

Creepy didn't notice at first, but as Muddy called her needles over the radio he turned to say something to Fitz and wound up looking into the red-tinted glow of Longo's huge forehead. "What's going on?"

"I've just declared this a high-risk evolution," Longo explained. "I'm backup LSO now."

"What does a *high-risk evolution* mean?" Creepy asked.

"A lot of beams are crossing," Longo said. "Weather, sea state, replacement pilots—"

"Your designs on power."

Longo glared at Creepy. "Watch it, mister. Remember I outrank you."

"My point exactly."

Five miles away at an altitude of twelve hundred feet and approaching the Boat at one hundred and forty knots, Muddy concentrated on keeping her needles crossed in the center of her display and again attempted to look outside as little as possible. The rain was lighter than it had been when they'd penetrated the clouds, and the rain removal system was doing a good job of keeping the view through the front of the canopy clear.

The Tomcat bumped around in the turbulent air and with each jerk Muddy worked to steel herself for the challenge before her. *Just two traps,* she thought. *You can do this.*

She reviewed the landing checklist in her mind for the one millionth time since she'd gone through it out loud with Flex ten miles out. Gear and flaps were down. Hook was down. Those were the big tickets.

"Remember what Creepy briefed," Flex said. "The winds are going to be higher out here tonight. You've got to stay up on the power. You'll drop like a rock with any power off corrections."

"Roger, I've got it," she said.

"One-zero-one," the controller transmitted, "slightly high, slightly left of course, at three-quarters of a mile, call the ball."

"Do you have the ball?" Flex asked over the intercom.

"I've got it," Muddy said.

Flex keyed the radio: "One-zero-one, Tomcat, ball, eight-point-five on the gas."

"Roger ball, Tomcat," Creepy returned. "Thirty-eight knots, axial."

Thirty-eight knots? The ship must be dead in the water.

Muddy forced her scan to work between the big three variables and waited to feel the click. She wanted to lead the effects of the burble but the bumps all the way down the chute made it impossible to discern, so she guessed and nudged a knuckleful of power and when the ball didn't sag she figured she'd guessed right.

It was a varsity night for a replacement, Punk thought, dividing his attention between the PLAT monitor on the LSO console and Muddy's jet, now just several hundred yards away. It looked like a decent pass from his vantage point, and the radio was silent.

As Muddy crossed the ramp a handset keyed—a subtle power call—and a second later the fighter hit the deck. Ball dead center at touchdown, she proudly noted. *That's got to be a Fair, at least.* She went to full power and waited for the tug, but it didn't come.

On the frequency a voice cried, "Bolter, bolter, bolter."

Bolter? She couldn't afford a Bolter now. "How did we bolter?" she asked Flex as she continued to climb. "We were in there." She quadruple-checked that the hook handle was in the down position.

On the platform Longo shouted to Creepy: "Hook skip!"

"I agree," Creepy said with less excitement in his voice, miffed that Longo didn't seem to give him credit for seeing the same thing. Creepy turned to Tex and said, "Hook skip OK. Little high start to in close. Little come down at the ramp."

When Creepy said, "OK," to Tex, Punk saw Longo nod dramatically and pump his fist.

Muddy turned downwind, still wondering what the hell had kept her from stopping and convinced that she was now a disqual when Creepy came on the radio and said, "One-zero-one, that was a hook skip bolter." She whooshed a sigh of relief and replied a roger.

"Sometimes you do everything right and you still don't stop," Flex explained. "That was a good pass. Let's give 'em one more of those."

"I'll try," she replied.

"Don't try; just do it."

Widget called the ball for Auto, and after a hard power call by the LSO, Muddy saw the jet stop on the deck and disappear as Auto switched off the external lights. It hit her that she would finish first between the two of them, and she thought about how he'd feel envious when Creepy announced that she was a qual on the radio. And then she thought how they'd all wonder what was going on if the call didn't come.

The controller hooked her out of the downwind leg at seven miles, a bit farther than the night before, and after one hundred and eighty degrees of turn, she had the jet aimed back at the Boat for what she hoped would be her final approach as a replacement. The needles came up, and she saw that she'd leveled her wings well left of the proper course, so she made a play to the right. The turbulence seemed worse this time.

She feared there would be no click on this pass, and before she was ready the controller informed her that she was high and left and told her to call the ball.

"One-zero-one, Tomcat, ball," Flex said. "Four-point-three."

"Roger ball, Tomcat, thirty knots down the angle . . . you're high."

I know that, Muddy thought. She meekly tweaked the throttles back and waited for the ball to move.

"Right for lineup," Creepy called.

Damn, don't stare at the ball; keep the scan going. Meatball, lineup, angle of—

"You're still high; start coming down, Muddy."

"We're five knots fast," Flex said over the intercom. "Get it on speed."

I'm trying. She walked the throttles back a little more but immediately thought it was too much and pushed them back forward. Her dream crept in, and she saw herself hanging off the catwalk. *Go down, damn ball . . .*

"You're high!" More forceful, almost angry this time.

Muddy felt herself detaching, just like she'd left her body during the tactics graduation hop, and she lost control of her left arm. She fought to stay in the present; she had to. *Land this pass,* she thought. *Stop and you could be all done.*

"Center the ball, Muddy," Flex said. "A Bolter ain't gonna hack it."

He was right. She couldn't afford to bolter. She wrestled to control her left arm and managed to get the power back and at the same time urged the stick forward slightly. The ball started downward . . . *too fast now!*

"Wave it off!" Creepy screamed. "WAVE IT OFF!"

She jammed the throttles forward to the stops as the jet crossed the ramp. The jet wasn't climbing yet. She eased the stick back, hoping that would stop the descent. There was a slight lurch and then the aircrew felt the jet stopping, although they hadn't touched down on the deck yet.

"Fuck!" a voice cried over the radio, and Muddy wondered who'd cursed on the frequency and whether he'd be reprimanded for it. The Tomcat slammed onto the nonskid and Muddy figured they'd crashed and all she could think to do was jam the throttles into full afterburner. She focused on controlling nothing but her left arm and didn't notice that they'd caught the four wire and stopped.

"Power back, one-zero-one," the air boss transmitted. "Power back. We've got you."

Muddy pulled the throttles to idle and sat for a second staring blankly at the instrument panel. "Follow the director's signals," Flex coaxed, snapping her out of the daze. She looked over at the yellow wands waving at her and raised the tailhook, swept the wings back, and taxied out of the landing area.

"Cut pass," Creepy said to Tex. "Not enough rate of descent start to in the middle. High in close. Fly through down at the ramp. Four wire. And make a note about the inflight engagement."

"Hold on here, paddles," Longo said, pushing his way between the other two. "Cut pass? No way. I'd buy a No Grade but not a cut. Where are you getting that from?"

"She just had an in-flight engagement, Longo," Creepy shot back. "Were you watching or not?"

"*Minor* in-flight," Longo corrected, "if one at all." He pointed through the light rain toward the bow. "Real inflights, the kind that deserve a cut pass, break jets. She's taxiing out of the landing area just fine."

"Pick up the phone, paddles," the air boss's voice hailed over the 5MC.

Creepy reached for the phone but Longo grabbed it first. "Yeah, boss . . ."

"Yeah, Creepy?"

"No sir, this is Longo."

"Longo, the captain wants to know who said 'fuck' on the radio."

"Ah, yes sir. Tell him I'm dealing with it, please."

"I don't know if he'll buy that. He was really pissed." The air boss changed the subject. "So, what are we doing with one-zero-one?"

"Well, that wasn't a pretty pass, but she's a qual. Park her and we'll hot switch an instructor into the front seat and then shoot the jet to the beach."

"Okay, that works for me," the boss said. "The sooner

we get these folks qualified and out of here, the easier my life will be."

Longo hung up the phone and looked forcefully at Creepy through the dim light of the platform. "The captain was upset about your choice of words on the radio."

"I'm sorry; it was an involuntary reaction to an in-flight engagement. Did the captain state an equal concern about the crash?"

"It wasn't a crash and stop calling it an in-flight. That's an order."

"Oh, an *order*," Creepy said with a sardonic laugh before his face turned angry. *"It was an in-flight engagement and a cut pass."*

"That was a No Grade, not a cut."

Creepy ran a hand over his rain-soaked face. "Understand that you're changing the grade I gave her?"

"That's a start. I'm not sure I agree with the comments about the pass either. That wasn't a fly-through down; hell, she didn't drop her nose that much. She was just starting the jet down."

"Not that much?" Creepy said with another laugh. "Spoken like a true Hornet pilot."

Punk saw Longo's posture stiffen. "Don't get parochial, Creepy. Just give her the No Grade . . . and the qual."

"No."

"I'm willing to let the profanity on the radio thing pass. Just give her the No Grade."

"You have a problem with profanity? Here's one: *Fuck you.*"

"I'm warning you, Creepy."

"I don't know what you've got going on here, Longo, or whose pocket you're in, but I'm not playing this bullshit game." He pointed across the darkness toward the yellow-tinted outline of the Tomcat now pivoting a tight circle in front of the island. "She isn't ready to go to the fleet yet."

"That's your opinion, and I disagree with you. I'm the senior LSO here. Give her the No Grade."

Creepy returned the pickle to its hook and pushed his way past Longo over to the outboard side of the platform. "You give it to her. I'm not giving her shit." With that he vaulted into the padded ramp and disappeared into the night.

Longo stood in the wet darkness, left side of his face barely lit by the lights from the console, and awkwardly absorbed the stares of everyone left on the platform, including Platt, who wasn't sure what was going on but was enthralled by the heat of the debate. Longo looked at Tex and started to speak, but Tex shook his head slowly in disgust and handed Longo the PDA and then followed Creepy's route into the ramp was and gone.

"What is this, a mutiny?" Longo asked as Auto called the ball for his final pass. Longo waved him off as he realized that he had become the de facto controlling LSO and that the situation on the platform was currently a mess.

"Paddles, pick up the phone!" blared through the 5MC. Longo reluctantly put the receiver to his head. "Yes, boss?"

"What's going on down there? We had a ready deck. Why did you wave him off?"

"We're in the middle of shifting roles on the platform here, boss," Longo said. "You know, trying to spread the LSO training around. My bust on the wave off. It won't happen again, sir."

Longo slammed the phone down and hastily deleted what Tex had scribed as Muddy's last grade and then wrote new comments on the next line. He keyed the radio: "One-zero-one, paddles."

"Go ahead," Muddy said, fearing what might be said next.

"You're a qual."

"Congratulations, Muddy," Flex said over the intercom as the deck crew chained their jet to the deck. "You're fleet meat now."

Muddy was surprised that she didn't feel like a celebration was in order, having imagined such joy at this point. She was exhausted—mentally and physically exhausted. She looked down to the deck on the left side of the nose and saw somebody in flight gear, Gordo maybe, waiting to hot switch with her. *Cat shot to the beach,* she thought. *Another good deal for the instructors.* That was fine, though. She didn't much feel like flying anymore this particular evening. She shut down the left motor, unstrapped from the seat, and waited for Flex to open the canopy so she could climb out.

Longo fixed his gaze momentarily on Fitz. "You're now the backup LSO," he said and then looked past Fitz to Punk. "Get over here. You're the writer." Both hesitated, which caused Longo to snap, almost pleading: "We've got another jet to land!" Fitz and Punk exchanged looks, and Fitz reluctantly shuffled across the platform and grabbed the other pickle off the hook.

Just before the final ball call, Platt leaned over Punk's shoulder and said loudly: "I'm glad I blew the captain off. I wouldn't have seen any of this!"

Passing maintenance control on their way back to the ready room, Punk and Platt, both soaked, ran into Muddy, who was filling out her flight time summary. She looked over and saw Punk and immediately cut her eyes back to the counter in front of her. Punk saddled up next to her, careful not to drip on the paperwork, as Platt continued into the ready room to find a towel.

"Congratulations," Punk said.

"Thanks," she replied quietly, without looking up from the form she was filling in.

Punk stood quietly for a time, unsure of how exactly to approach a topic he felt compelled to address. "You know, you're done with the RAG, but nothing is over for you," he said. "Nothing is ever over for those who wear wings and fly off of aircraft carriers. They never build up an excess of good landings they can use during a slump. The pressure never ends. This is what you've signed up for, no more glamorous than landing the jet safely after every flight. Nothing Hollywood would ever care about."

He was silent again until she finally looked up at him. "Out there," he said, "it's just you. No senators, no four-stars. Just you."

"I never wanted their help."

"But you got it." Punk rapped his moist knuckles against the stainless steel counter and walked behind Muddy. He opened the ready room door before turning back toward her. "It's going to be up to you to outlast it."

CHAPTER THIRTEEN

Early the next morning Punk sat between Spud and Platt in the crowded air transport office aboard the carrier waiting for the word to man-up the C-2 Greyhound transport plane spotted behind catapult one. The C-2, commonly known as the COD for "carrier onboard delivery," had just trapped and dumped off several bags of mail and some spare parts. Within the hour it would launch again with Punk, Spud, Platt, and a mix of sixteen others bound for Naval Air Station Norfolk, another base about twenty-five miles from NAS Oceana.

Most of those waiting sat watching an action movie on the television perched on top of a weathered metal filing cabinet in one corner of the cramped space. The others read months-old magazines or fiddled with the flotation devices around their necks. The vibe in the place reminded Punk of a very small bus station.

"What does the catapult shot feel like?" Platt asked, still dressed in the flight suit and boots for the trip home. Punk wondered if he'd ever take the stuff off. "I've heard it's really intense."

"A car crash and an orgasm rolled into one," Punk said.

"You know I've heard that analogy a million times," Spud said, "and I have no idea what it means."

"Me either, now that you mention it," Punk said before turning back toward Platt. "The seats in the COD are facing backward, and for the cat shot, the crew chief will have us all grab our shoulder harnesses and lean forward against our thighs. It's not that big of a deal."

"No orgasm?" Platt said.

"That's up to you, I guess," Punk said. "I'm not helping, anyway."

An out-of-breath sailor burst in and shouted across the space: "Buckhaltser, turn to the news, quick!"

The thin sailor behind the small counter looked up from the manifest he was reviewing and said, "I like this movie."

The first sailor heaved an exasperated sigh and excused himself across the legs of those seated in the fiberglass seats bolted in a line. "An airplane just crashed into a building in New York." He pushed a button on the front of the television set a few times and then moved behind the counter with Seaman Buckhaltser to watch.

"Is that the World Trade Center?" Punk asked. "What the hell kind of airplane hit it?"

"Hey, keep it down in here, please," Spud said, twisting his head around. "We can't hear the report."

Buckhaltser pointed the remote at the television and tweaked the volume up a few notches. "We don't know what could've caused such a horrible accident," a quavering female voice said. The view showed the north tower of the World Trade Center smoking like a massive industrial chimney through the gaping holes the airplane had made when it hit. "One can only guess that perhaps the pilot of the plane had a heart attack, or perhaps the air traffic controller who was in charge of routing the plane gave the pilot incorrect instructions."

"Incorrect instructions?" Spud said. "That can't be it. It's a clear day up there. What kind of a dumb ass would follow a controller's instructions into a building?"

"Maybe it was a suicide," Punk said. "You know, some airline pilot at the end of his rope or something."

"What about the passengers?" Platt asked.

The room grew mostly silent, and all sat transfixed watching the television. Those who'd been waiting in the passageway crowded into the hatchway to see the screen. More views were coming in now: pictures from street level below, helicopters above, boats on the Hudson River, and other skyscrapers around town. The female anchor continued to offer hypotheses, joined now by a growing troupe of reporters scattered around lower Manhattan. Punk checked the clock on the wall: it was just after nine o'clock.

Then the mystery of whether or not the crash had been an accident was solved: Through the sometimes perverse miracle of live TV, a roomful of people sitting aboard an aircraft carrier seventy-three miles off the East Coast of the United States joined millions of others across the world in watching as another airliner smashed into the World Trade Center's south tower, transforming itself and a dozen or so floors of the building into a mass of shrapnel and fire.

"Terrorism . . ." Platt muttered under the expressions of shock, horror, and disbelief around him. "It's terrorism."

Another sailor, this one wearing a cranial with goggles down and a white float coat with "ATO" stenciled across the back of it, apparently unaware of the events on the news, pushed his way through the gathering in the hatchway and announced: "We're ready to man-up the COD. Form a single file line in the catwalk outside the hatch and follow me up to the flight deck."

"We'd better hurry up and get airborne," Spud said. "If Big Top's right, the FAA just might shut down all air traffic and then we'd be stuck out here."

Punk shuddered with the thought. The carrier wasn't scheduled to pull in for another four days, and even if they canceled the rest of the carrier quals it would take them a day or so to get back into port. He wanted to see Suzanne as soon as possible. There was no telling what this shock would do to her.

An agonizing fifteen minutes later Punk was relieved to lean forward in his aft-facing seat and grab his shoulder straps as the catapult fired and the COD was pulled to flying speed. During the half hour trip back to Norfolk the crew chief patrolled the aisle, shouting news tidbits over the noise of the C-2's twin turboprops:

"All the airports in New York have been shut down . . ."

"The Port Authority has ordered all bridges and tunnels into the city closed . . ."

"The President said it was a terrorist attack . . ."

"Another airliner just crashed into the Pentagon. First reports estimate hundreds killed . . ."

The Pentagon? Spud and Punk looked at each other,

both performing a mental inventory of who they knew was assigned there. "Smoke," Spud said, referring to Commander "Smoke" Stackhouse, his roommate during their last deployment, a pilot who'd also screened for fighter squadron command. After his tour in the *Arrowslingers*, Smoke, the consummate overachiever, had requested one of the tough jobs in the Pentagon and had been rewarded for his efforts with a billet in the J-3 shop of the Joint Staff.

"This wasn't just a one-time terrorist attack," Spud shouted over the din. "This was an all-out assault on the continental United States. It's worse than Pearl Harbor!"

The COD touched down and Punk peered out the little window across from him to make sure they'd landed in Norfolk. At first nothing looked familiar and he feared they'd been diverted, but then he made out the line of warships' superstructures in the distance and breathed a sigh of relief.

Suzanne was waiting with Jason in the terminal lobby, and as she caught sight of Punk she took her son's hand and hurried across the well-waxed floor. She hugged Punk tightly and kissed him on the lips for a few beats longer than friends kissed. Punk gathered Jason in his arms and the three of them started to walk off.

"Punk," Platt called out. "I may not see you for a while."

"Probably not," Punk said as they shook hands. "I'm sure you're about to get real busy."

"I'm afraid we're all about to get real busy," Platt said. "Especially you guys. Good luck. Kick some ass for me."

Platt's cell phone went off, and he bade Punk farewell one more time and stepped away to take the call.

"They've evacuated the Pentagon," Spud announced as he walked up. "I tried calling Smoke, but there was no answer. I just heard on the TV that over two hundred people are missing. The current operations cell was wiped out. I think that's where Smoke works."

"I'm sure he's all right," Punk said. "He's probably out on the lawn with everybody else. It's got to be crazy there." Punk conjured a vision of a smiling Smoke, the best pilot in their old squadron, blond hair flowing, mustache licking across the width of his face as he burst through the ready room door after a flight. His glass was always half full, the kind of guy a squadron needed around during the dark days of an extended deployment. He had to be all right. Smoke was earmarked for greater things.

Spud muttered, "You're right; Smoke's fine," and rubbed his face. "Need a ride back to the squadron?"

Suzanne patted Punk's arm and said, "I'll drive you." He saw in her eyes that she needed adult company.

"No, I've got a ride," Punk said to Spud, "I'll see you over there in a little bit."

Suzanne seemed dazed but increasingly calmed by Punk's driving as the ride went on; for now she was the minivan's co-pilot again, and that had always been her position of choice. At the back gate of NAS Norfolk they had to weave around several cement barricades to exit the base, and Punk noticed the line of cars on the other side of the road waiting to get in. Marines in full combat gear now manned the gate's guardhouse and several others were stacking sandbags around a machine-gun emplacement.

They drove the interstate toward Virginia Beach. There was an eerie order about things, as if the population was in collective denial. But the talk on the radio made denial impossible. They listened to the news, each report more dire than the last, and from his car seat in the back Jason repeatedly stated, "An airplane flew into the building. A big crash."

After a long wait in traffic headed for NAS Oceana and a car search at the main gate, Punk pulled in front of the hangar and hopped out of the minivan. Suzanne slid behind the wheel and gave him another kiss, just a peck this time, and he told her to call him if she needed to talk. She smiled and looked at once strong and beautiful.

The ready room was abuzz with heated discussions as Punk walked in. Aviators crowded around both the small television above the duty desk and the larger one mounted against the front wall. Punk looked at the main flight schedule board behind the duty officer and saw that the word "canceled" had been written across it in large letters.

"Take a look, gentlemen," Flex said as the television showed Tower Two crumbling for the twenty-fifth time this hour and then switched to a street scene that framed people fleeing like extras in a B-horror movie. But it wasn't a movie. "This is what happens when you don't have the balls to deal with your problems."

"Which one?" Hammer asked.

"Iraq. We should've kept the tanks rolling to Baghdad while we had the chance." The television coverage switched to the Pentagon, and Flex grew even more enraged. "Fuck all those countries," he said. "We need to go at them like the Roman Empire used to: Go in there and lay waste and then say, *'We didn't do this, you did.'* That's the only kind of logic those camel jockeys understand."

"Emergency all-instructors meeting in five minutes!" Widget cried from behind the duty desk. "The skipper's coming down to talk to us."

The gatherings dispersed as the television continued to display the horrific reality. The coneheads were ushered out of the ready room and the instructors made their way to their chairs. Spud and Scuzz walked in with PDAs in hand, and Spud, after muting the volume on the nearest television, addressed the group. "We'll dispense with the usual meeting formalities and just let the CO have the floor once he walks in. Keep it to a dull roar until then, please." Spud took a seat in the front row next to Scuzz.

"Fuck this shore duty shit," Flex said from the chair next to Punk. "I'm calling my detailer right after this meeting and requesting an immediate transfer back to one of the squadrons at sea. I'm not going to miss this war without a fight."

Eagle stepped in and the room came to attention. "Carry on," he instructed, and walked to the podium at the front of the room. As the officers retook their seats, the skipper studied the split-screen view on the television, lower Manhattan on one side and northern Virginia on the other. "That sums it up, doesn't it?" he said. "As you all know by now, the Fighter Wing commander has ordered that all flight operations be curtailed, so we've canceled the rest of our flight schedule." He looked at Spud. "Did that final event land yet?"

"Yes, sir," Spud replied. "They just did."

"CINCLANT has put the entire region in Threat Condition One. Right now, barricades are being moved in front of every gate at every base. All cars are being thoroughly searched. Traffic onto the base is already backed up about a mile. Get used to it. These procedures are going to be with us for more than a day or two."

The skipper saw that the officers were all focused on the

screen over his shoulder, so he grabbed the remote from the podium and clicked the TV off. "I need your attention for a few minutes, please."

He scanned the room to ensure the officers' eyes were on him. "There are two carriers on station: one in the Persian Gulf, one in the North Arabian Sea on the way to relieve the first one. The one in the Persian Gulf was supposed to be headed home tomorrow. As you might guess, they're not going anywhere. The one in the North Arabian Sea is staying there and not moving into the Gulf." Eagle pointed in the direction of a rumble emanating from the active runway. "The aircraft carrier some of you were just on has been turned north to patrol off the coast, and right now a skeleton wing of fleet airplanes is being flown aboard. And the tasking isn't just going to the fleet, either. The flight schedule has been cancelled, but we're not done flying. You're going to be among the few allowed back into the skies over the United States.

"For the next days or even weeks you need to stop thinking of yourselves as instructors—you're war fighters again. The general at Langley Air Force Base is working on a homeland defense plan that draws assets from all the fighter bases between Maine and South Carolina. We're going to be strapping real missiles to a few of our jets and flying real combat air patrol hops over New York and DC around the clock. Everyone in here is on a two-hour tether until further notice."

Eagle focused on the blank television screen and was silent for a time. He shook his head and said, "Words fall short. However, I take solace in the fact that we're in a business that'll be part of the response . . . whenever and wherever it happens to take place. I'm afraid I won't be participating, but some of you will. If you get the nod, count yourself among the blessed. Trust me, life goes by fast and opportunities to do your nation's bidding don't come around that often." He tossed his hands up. "Any questions?" There were none. "Let's get to work."

The radio was silent save the occasional administrative transmission between the ground controller and the handful of fighters under his charge. The silence across the frequency taunted Punk as much as he was taunted by the weather, weather that would've afforded fighter pilots twenty-mile tally-hos, a chance to decisively commit missiles at range.

But there were no airplanes around to shoot. For now, the enemy had vaporized in the crash or was grounded. The intercepts that should have happened never did. A section of F-15s were scrambled after the first airliner plowed into the north tower of the World Trade Center, and when the second one hit the south tower, the Eagles were still over one hundred miles away. And while the focus was on New York, the continental defense network got side-doored by the airliner that had flown into the Pentagon.

In the backseat of the Tomcat, Spud was silent as Punk orbited over Manhattan and looked down on the billowing ash that the wind swept over Brooklyn and Long Island. He wondered what it would've been like to consummate the intercepts that would've saved the buildings and thousands of lives. In his mind's eye he filled his HUD with commercial jet and pulled the trigger and saw the terrorists in the cockpit, ignorant of the heat-seeking missile raging toward them.

But the satisfaction of the thought was muted by the deaths of civilians aboard the airliner, and he wondered what would've really gone through his brain at the time. The scenario was like something out of his military courses back at the Naval Academy: *You're ordered to kill innocent people. Should you carry out the order? CAN you carry out the order?* His classmates had rolled their eyes and sneered and agreed that those sorts of case studies were a bunch of hackneyed, unrealistic crap invented by officers with overactive imaginations.

Besides, the theoretical "would you kill civilians if ordered" matrix was still theory. All the nation's fighters hadn't been enough to stop the attack. But like a boxer who puts his hands up after he's been hit square in the face, here the tactical jets were ready to pounce on any airliners aimed for one of the most prominent landmarks on the East Coast—only there weren't any airliners flying, and the most prominent landmark wasn't there anymore.

Punk banked the Tomcat to the left and started his race-track pattern back to the south. He glanced down the can-

opy rail and caught sight of Yankee Stadium and wondered
if things like a World Series pennant race would ever seem
important again. His rage grew, and he tried to squeeze
black juice out of the control stick in his right hand. Fuck
those assholes with their faux-religious horseshit and their
destructive zealotry. So they liked to see things fall down,
huh? He looked under his left wing at the tip of the Sidewinder missile strapped to his jet. He wanted to flame
something right now. He moved his weapons select switch
on the stick from "Sidewinder" to "Guns" and fingered the
trigger. They'd scatter as he walked the rudders and
sprayed bullets across the desert, wouldn't they? They'd
scream for Allah's mercy as the twenty-millimeter rounds
tore into them. And they'd die . . .

Payback. That's something Americans knew about. They'd
seen their heroes dish it out in the cineplexes and on their
widescreen televisions. The concept of payback was embed-
ded into the national psyche. An eye for an eye. But would
that instinct alone see them through?

The rhetoric was already flying: The war would be a clash
of ideals, a fight for freedom. But what was freedom? What
were Americans willing to fight for, willing to *die* for?
Cheap gas? Bigger SUVs? Shorter drives to the mall?
Ready access to the latest DVDs at the local movie rental
store? How many in the heartland could find Syria or
Yemen or Sudan on a map? And were the gentry of
America ready to send their progeny to war?

Maybe this disaster was the wake-up call the United
States had been subconsciously daring the rest of world to
make. This attack didn't just happen overnight. The terrorists had been patient and calculating. Early reports had
some of them living in the U.S. for nearly two years. They'd
exploited the weaknesses in the system. Three of the four
airplanes hijacked had hit their marks. Few of the strikes
during Desert Storm had posted that sort of result. They
may have been radicals, but they certainly couldn't be dismissed as complete idiots. And hatred for all things American had not died with them. Crowds were dancing in
Middle Eastern streets.

But the more Punk thought about it, the more he realized he didn't care about Islamic extremists' opinions or
resolve. America's egalitarian naïveté had been its greatest

weakness, and he felt a fool for even considering another point of view. Flex was right. The terrorists, whoever they were, were the enemy once and for all. No talking now; just action.

He focused across the canopy rail again, and in his head he heard the voicemail that was played repeatedly on the news from a working mother to her family. The reports had featured her picture—a vacation shot probably; she was tanned and smiling, long blond hair glowing in the bright sunlight. Her voice was tearful but courageous as she said, "I'm stuck on the ninety-fifth floor, and I don't think I'll be able to get out. I love you all." Each time he'd heard the recording, it had ripped his guts out a little more.

The woman's death was more than just a rallying point for Punk, but something more unsettling. He'd spent the short span of his adult life in a profession that ensured that working American mothers didn't die at the hands of terrorists. That's why he'd gone on deployment for all those months. That's why he'd flown over hostile nations in the Middle East.

Punk recalled the trust in Platt's eyes at the terminal and how he'd said, "Kick some ass for me." All of the air shows, coffee table books, movies, and cable TV specials seemed a thin veneer now. Punk felt a strong need to prove his worth.

"We picked the wrong time to be on shore duty," Punk said over the intercom.

"I was just thinking the same thing," Spud replied.

Punk reclined on a chaise lounge in Suzanne's backyard and continued to fight the torment of the intercept that wasn't made. He worked the time/distance problem over and over in his head. He'd heard in the ready room that two F-15s out of Langley Air Force Base had been the first to scramble. As he figured it, with as little as five minutes' more time they could've easily made the intercept. Why did the defense authorities wait? What was the normal tripwire? And if the Eagles had made the intercept, when would the order to fire have been given? At what point would it have been obvious that it was not a simple hijacking but a suicide mission bent on flying into the World Trade Center?

Suzanne emerged from the house after putting Jason to

bed and lay back on the adjacent lounge. She joined Punk staring blankly into dark space.

"Is he down?" Punk asked.

"I think so," Suzanne said with a sigh. "He had a million questions."

"Don't we all?"

Jets rumbled in the southern distance. A few seconds later a pair of anticollision lights crept above the treeline. The two flashing red dots fused as the fighters completed their rendezvous and headed north to the now lonely but well-patrolled skies over New York. Punk reached into a side pocket of his cargo shorts and produced a copy of the flight schedule. In the dim light of the patio he could just make out that, if the schedule was still accurate, Eagle and Scuzz piloted the two planes now passing thousands of feet directly overhead.

The engine noise slowly died away, and Punk was surprised to hear Suzanne softly crying next to him. Although over the last few weeks he'd borne witness to her mood swings, she'd put on a good face throughout this evening. But now with Jason in bed she must've let her emotional guard down. Without a word Punk extended his arms, and she went over to him. Once his arms were around her, her crying intensified. He stroked her hair and soothingly shushed her.

"So many new widows," Suzanne strained to say through the tears. "So much pain."

"Everything's going to be all right," Punk replied reflexively.

Suzanne raised her head off of Punk's collarbone. "Really?" she shot back at him, wiping her eyes with the back of a wrist. "How do you know that? What if everything's not all right?"

"It will be."

"How do you know?" she asked again, more forcefully this time.

Punk attempted an answer by leaning over to buss her cheek. Just before he reached her, Suzanne turned her head to meet him. The kiss began innocently enough, a friendly, comforting gesture, but it rapidly ignited beyond friendship. Her lips barely parted before each mouth was eagerly working against the other. Suzanne's sorrow faded for the moment as she rolled on top of him and threaded her fingers through his hair. His hands worked along the small of her back and then down to the curves of her buttocks. She reached down for him and he began to stiffen.

Punk pulled back. "No," he said. "Not like this."

"Don't stop," she insisted.

"We have to."

"No, we don't." She sat up with her legs straddling him and threw her hair back. "It's been a long time," she said as her hands maniacally worked his belt. "Months of pain, too much pain. I'm tired of it. I want to feel good about something again."

"I want you too," Punk said, gently but firmly warding her hands off of his midsection. "I want you *badly*. But not today. It wouldn't be right. Today can only be remembered for one thing from now on." His cell phone buzzed, and as he grabbed it Suzanne let out a sad laugh and dejectedly slinked back into the house.

"Hello?"

"Punk, it's Spud."

Punk struggled to get his wits about him. "Your timing is impeccable, as always."

"Sorry. Where are you?"

"Out and about. Where are you?"

"At the squadron."

"Still? Did you ever go home?"

"No. I've been on the phone since we got back from our flight this afternoon. I finally talked to Smoke. He's in the hospital with a broken arm. Part of a wall fell on him."

"He's alive, though."

"Yeah. A few of the folks he works with weren't so lucky."

There was silence between them. Spud finally said, "I've got orders."

"Orders? Where?"

"Back to sea. To the *Arrowslingers*. They're in the North Arabian Sea as we speak."

"Our old squadron? When do you leave?"

"Tomorrow morning. There's a charter flight leaving out of Norfolk that's headed for Bahrain."

Punk released a long exhale. "Damn, this is kind of crazy, isn't it?"

"Real crazy, trust me. There are a lot of moving parts in the wake of the attacks. Beamer's move to the Joint Staff has been sped up. That'll send Smooth to the commanding officer spot, and I'll slide into the executive officer job."

Another short silence followed. "So you're off to be a war hero without me, huh?" Punk said.

"Not necessarily," Spud said. "I'm not calling about me: I'm calling about you."

"What about me?"

"The detailer mentioned the *Arrowslingers* needed a pilot or two, including a flight lead, and I took the liberty of telling them I thought I knew one who fit the bill."

"You gave my name to the detailer?" Punk cut his eyes back toward the house. Through the window he could see Suzanne moving about the kitchen.

"No . . . well, *yes,* and you should thank me. A lot of guys are trying to volunteer for this thing. Look, we don't have time to fart around here. Are you up for it?"

"Would I be leaving with you tomorrow?"

"That's affirmative. Flight leaves at noon."

"How long will we be gone?"

"The Boat has already been on cruise for three months. I reckon we'll be home in time for Christmas."

"I need to get my flight gear."

"It's already packed up and staged."

"It is?" Punk chuckled sardonically. "I appreciate you giving me the illusion of a choice here."

"Oh, you still have a choice, technically speaking," Spud offered. "But I was pretty sure you wouldn't be happy watching this thing happen from the sidelines."

Punk got off the lounge and strode a few steps across the backyard. The grass felt cool against his bare feet.

"So you're in?"

"The terminal tomorrow at noon?"

"Tomorrow at noon. And don't worry about packing much more than flight suits. I don't think the Boat will be making any port calls."

As Punk folded his phone he turned toward the house and was startled to find Suzanne a step away from him. She had a glass of wine in each hand and held one of them up to him. "Who was that?" she asked warily.

"Spud," he said as he wrapped his fingers around the stem of the glass.

"Oh." She lowered her eyes to her feet. "What did he want?"

Punk cleared his throat. "I've been ordered back to sea, back to my old squadron."

Suzanne raised her head. "Of course you have." She took the wineglass back from Punk and silently started back inside. Before she entered the house, she poured the contents of both glasses into a bush by the back door.

Punk trailed her, following her upstairs to her bedroom where she curled up on the bed with her back to the door. He stopped in the doorway.

"When are you leaving?" she asked quietly.

"Tomorrow," Punk replied. "I have to be at the terminal at noon."

"How long will you be gone?"

"A couple of months, I guess. Not that long."

"Not that long . . ."

Punk moved onto the bed, spooning against her back with his arms around her. She wept until she fell asleep. He found a blanket and threw it over her. He then switched the bedside lamp off and plopped into a nearby chair and studied the angles of her face, visible by the light from the street that streamed through the venetian blinds. For now she appeared at peace.

A few hours later a stirring from the adjacent bathroom awakened Punk. He looked toward the bed and saw that Suzanne had risen. The bathroom door opened; the light temporarily blinded him. As her silhouette moved across the room, he could just make out that she had nothing on but a towel wrapped around her.

"You see that clock?" she inquired. "What time is it?"

Punk rubbed his eyes and looked over at the nightstand. "Two-thirty," he said.

"So what does that make it?"

"I don't know."

"It's not today anymore. It's tomorrow." The towel fell away.

Her logic was irrefutable. Punk removed his T-shirt and shorts and met her underneath the covers.

*   *   *

The terminal was a busy place. Outside, a procession of trucks with beds stacked high with cruise boxes and fork-lifts bearing net-covered pallets headed toward the three chartered planes parked on the ramp—jets, Punk noted, from airlines he'd never heard of: two from Magnum Air and the other from Associated. Were these the pseudo-companies fronted by the CIA that he'd heard whisper-ings about?

Once inside the building he was surrounded by scores of people hurrying along, most in uniforms or flight suits. Two-man security teams armed with M-16s, a postattack reality, made themselves a conspicuous presence at every turn. Punk moved toward the passenger lounge, past lines of pay phones occupied by teary-eyed sailors bidding adieu to their significant others.

He passed the smoking lounge and snuck a peek at the pathetic beings therein, slaves to the nicotine fix. Just be-fore he looked away he spotted Corky McBride in the far corner. What was he doing at the terminal? Punk almost stopped to find out, but the impulse was suppressed by his desire to find Spud.

The main lounge was jammed with people. Punk focused on the others in flight suits but didn't recognize any of them. He managed to find an empty seat and gathered his hanging bag under his legs. He scanned around him again and wondered if he was in the right place. He checked his watch and figured he'd arrived a bit too early.

The first face he recognized was the last one he expected to see. Muddy shuffled into the lounge area burdened by a large pack across her back and a duffel bag in each hand. She dropped her bags at the head of one of the aisles, took a deep breath, and wiped the sweat from her red face. She noticed Punk just as he raised a second arm into the air above his head, and she lumbered over, scraping her bags across the legs of those seated along the way.

"Did you get the call from DC, too?" Muddy asked as she approached.

"DC?" Punk asked back. "I got a call from Spud. Who called you from DC?"

She put her bags down and attempted to shake the circulation back into her arms. "Some captain at the Office of Legislative Affairs."

Legislative Affairs, the Navy's congressional liaison command? *Of course,* Punk thought, *Senator Meyers meddling again. What could be a better validation than a female war hero?*

The petty officer next to Punk got out of his seat, probably feeling a bit crowded by the officers surrounding him, and excused his way past Muddy. Muddy took her backpack off and sat down. "So are you headed to the *Arrowslingers* too?" she asked like a cocksure fleet veteran.

"Yep," Punk said.

"I must admit I was a little surprised by the call," Muddy said. "I mean, I know we RAG graduates all have to be assigned somewhere, but I didn't think I'd be the one to get the nod to go right on cruise, especially now." She cut her eyes toward Punk. "I swear I didn't have anything to do with these orders."

"I'm sure you didn't," Punk said.

As Muddy tried to figure whether Punk was being sarcastic or not, Flex appeared and plopped his hanging bag on the floor at Punk's feet. "Punk, are you show-bound?" Flex asked.

Muddy mumbled something about one last pit stop before they boarded the airplane and shuffled past Flex. Flex took her seat and faced Punk. "Did you get the call from DC?"

"No, I didn't. The only call I got was from Spud."

"Are you sure Legislative Affairs didn't call you?"

"Why would Legislative Affairs call to give me my orders?"

"Because I gave them your name."

Punk winced in confusion. "You gave them my name?"

"Well, not exactly," Flex said, focusing on his flight boots. "I called Big Top and gave *him* your name. I figured he would do the rest."

"Big Top?"

Flex twisted around and grabbed Punk's biceps. "I told you I wasn't going to miss this war without a fight, didn't I? I wasn't getting anywhere with our asshole detailer, so I called Big Top and planted a seed or two."

"What kind of seeds?"

"I knew he'd be interested in having Muddy on the front lines, and I reminded him that most of her success in the RAG came with me in her backseat . . . and with you on her wing."

"Actually, most of the times she's been on my wing, she's fucked it up."

"Whatever. I'm sure Platt got the senator all fired up about the idea of Muddy in action, and the rest obviously took care of itself. You don't have to thank me."

"I told you, *Spud* gave me the call."

"Okay, so the senator's help was a tiebreaker between you and the hoards of other guys looking to get into this war. Like I said, you don't have to thank me."

A slightly distorted female voice came through the speaker over their heads: "Passengers traveling to Bahrain on Magnum Air Flight 5 should proceed to Gate One. Passengers for Magnum Air Flight 5 to Bahrain proceed to Gate One."

"Where's Spud?" Punk wondered aloud as he threw his hanging bag over his shoulder and fell into the crowd headed for Gate One.

"Are you sure he's supposed to be here?" Flex asked over Punk's shoulder. "Legislative Affairs didn't say anything about him to me."

Punk tried not to snap. "Flex, you're seriously going to have to shut up about Legislative Affairs now, okay?"

A corpulent, silver-haired guy dressed in short sleeves and a tie waved the procession down as they approached Gate One. "Line up right here," he commanded, indicating the desired line with an outstretched arm. "Put your bags on the scale, write their weight on the manifest next to your name, then put them on those carts over there. Once you've done that, you can proceed through the metal detector straight ahead of you and out to the airplane."

One by one the passengers complied with the flight attendant's instructions. Punk stole glances up and down the line of fifty or so fellow travelers, hoping to find Spud among them. Flex was right behind Punk, and Muddy was about ten back. Soon they were outside on the tarmac lined up at the base of the boarding ladder waiting their turn to climb into the 747.

Punk focused on the door from Gate One as he neared the ladder. He reached for his cell phone and cursed Spud's aversion to them. Just before it was his turn to mount the first step, he spotted one of the pilots near the left landing gear. Punk exited the line and jogged over to him.

"Excuse me, sir," Punk said to the pilot bent down between the gigantic wheels and checking the brake lines. "Do you think we could delay starting the jet up for a few minutes? My executive officer isn't here yet, and we definitely don't want to leave without him."

The man stood erect, both taller and older-looking than Punk had gleaned during his approach toward him, and considered the lieutenant. "We don't, huh? Where is he?"

"I don't know," Punk replied. "I'm sure he's on his way."

The pilot looked at Punk's rank insignia embroidered on the shoulder of his flight suit and at his own watch. "We've got a very long flight ahead of us, Lieutenant. We're starting engines in ten minutes, with or without your executive officer."

Punk stepped away and dialed Spud's home number. As he expected and hoped he would, he got his voicemail. He cut the connection and dialed the RAG's duty officer:

"Death Boxer duty office, Lieutenant Thomas."

"Hammer, it's Punk."

"Punk? Aren't you supposed to be on an airplane headed across the pond?"

"I'm about to board. Have you seen Spud?"

"He's not with you?"

"He must've got held up in a traffic jam or something. I'm trying to hold up the flight until he gets here, but I don't know how much patience this crew has." Punk looked back to the double doors from Gate One; still no sign of the lanky, balding, newly assigned XO. "Call me on my cell phone if you hear anything in the next ten minutes or so."

"Will do. Oh, by the way: We've all decided we hate you for getting those orders."

"That's something I'll just have to live with, I guess."

"We're pretty surprised you played the political card," Hammer said. "We figured you'd be the last guy to do that."

"Political card?" Punk returned. "I didn't play any political card."

"Hey, man, desperate times require desperate measures. I guess I can understand that."

"I didn't—"

"I've got another call here. Fly safe, Punk, and don't forget the little people after you're a war hero." There was a click in the earpiece.

Punk folded his phone and shook his head. He saw the line to get on the airplane was down to a few and then shot another glance toward Gate One. Still no Spud. Punk queued up in the line and considered again asking the pilot to delay starting the aircraft, but he figured that would do nothing but further irritate the man.

Punk ascended the stairs and stepped into the jumbo jet. Fifty passengers had little impact on the cavernous interior of the plane, and although he had over two hundred seats to choose from, he sat in the first window seat he came to, on the left side of the airplane just aft of the main cabin door. He tried to look out the window toward Gate One, but the angle at which the jet was parked prevented him from seeing anything but the traffic streaming along the highway adjacent to the air station.

Again he plucked his phone from the clip at his waist and redialed Spud's home number. "Leave a message," Spud's recorded voice concisely instructed after four rings. Punk waited for the beep.

"Spud, it's Punk. I'm sitting on the airplane wondering where you are. We're about to taxi out. I'll leave the phone on as long as I can, so call me if you get this."

The fat flight attendant moved past and closed the cabin door and just as it sealed there was a banging from the outside. Punk perked up as the miffed attendant reopened the door but was disappointed to see Corky, not Spud, slink into the fuselage.

Punk was further dismayed when Corky slid into the seat next to him, reeking of cigarettes and ready to chat up a storm. "Damn, that was close," he said as he loosened his necktie and rolled up his shirtsleeves. "I don't think Mr. Rainno would be happy if I missed this flight because I was trying to sneak in one last smoke before the trip, huh?"

Punk raised his eyebrows in response.

"How long is this flight anyway?" Corky asked. Punk shrugged. "Well, it doesn't matter. I'm prepared." He rolled his left sleeve up nearly to his shoulder and revealed a large, flesh-colored nicotine patch. "And I've got plenty where this one came from."

The ventilation stopped momentarily and the cabin lights flickered as the first engine started up. Punk used the diversion to attempt a graceful exit from Corky's immediate presence. "I'm going to take a quick piss before we get moving," Punk explained before sliding across the civilian's legs and starting down the aisle.

"The nearest head's right there," Corky offered, pointing toward the front of the cabin.

Punk squinted down the extended line of Corky's finger and said, "I heard the ones in the back are nicer."

The lieutenant strode aft, past Muddy and Flex, who'd both established a three-seat footprint. He continued toward the bathroom, taking note of the insignia and patches that adorned the flight suits of the others as he passed. A pair of F-16 pilots, Air Force captains, already had a card game going. Directly behind them a KC-10 driver read a paperback, head bobbing in time to the music pumping through the headphones he wore. Across the aisle, a Tomcat guy slept with his head against the window, pillow over his face and body sprawled out, toes of his flight boots in the aisle. *Tomcat guy?* Punk reached across the man and removed the pillow. *Spud.*

"What's the deal?" Spud muttered as he grimaced against the light and defensively raised his arms.

"Goddammit, asshole," Punk railed. "You scared the shit out of me. Where were you?"

Spud drew his legs in and sat up in the seat. "Where was I? When?"

"I never saw you in the terminal. I thought you were either stuck in a traffic jam or had mixed up the times or something."

Spud checked his watch. "I walked aboard this jet nearly an hour ago."

"I called the duty officer looking for you," Punk said. "I even left a message on your machine at home."

"My machine at home? What did you say?"

"Just that I was wondering where you were and—"

"Jeesus, Punk." Spud reached over and snatched the cell phone from the lieutenant's waist. He punched the keys and held the phone to his head, brow knit as he waited for a response on the other end of the line. "Dear, it's me. Disregard Lieutenant-for-life Reichert's earlier message. Everything's fine. I'm on the airplane and have been for some time. Rick didn't see me and lost his mind for a second. I love you and miss all of you already. Don't worry about anything else, either. Bye-bye for now." Spud feigned crushing the phone before handing it back. He then slouched down again and flipped the pillow back over his face.

Punk took the hint and set up camp a few rows back. He pulled a magazine out of the seatback and split his attention between it and the rapidly changing scenes out the window. The jet rolled down the runway and took off, and soon nothing but the vast ocean dotted by an occasional ship could be seen beneath them.

The dull murmur of conversation between excited travelers around the cabin eventually died away. These were the lonely times; times when each of them realized that there were limits on how long things like conversation could keep the sting of family separation at bay. As Punk joined the others withdrawing into themselves, his mind flitted to Suzanne. For years he'd suppressed these sorts of thoughts— she'd been his best friend's wife, after all—always feeling guilty for considering what sex with her would have been like. But as he conjured up the details from the night before he felt no remorse. Punk was witness to her exorcism, demons cast off with each passionate shudder. He'd seen a new light in her eyes over morning coffee. And her last words in the parking lot when she'd dropped him off had been, "I'll be here when you get back." He'd searched Suzanne's countenance then and, after a final kiss, parted confident that she'd meant what she'd said.

The eastward passage caused night to come quickly to the chartered jet, and it was pitch black through the windows by the time a pilot's voice came over the intercom and announced they were passing over the Azores. Napping travelers awoke and moved to each other in tribal conjoining as the attendants distributed military meals-ready-to-eat, MREs, another bit of evidence that Magnum Air was no normal airline.

Spud, Punk, Muddy, and Flex shared a center row of seats, tearing open the drab olive food containers and spooning the contents into their mouths, cautiously at first.

"What did you get?" Spud asked Punk.

"Spaghetti with meat sauce," Punk said. "I always get spaghetti with meat sauce when I eat these things."

"I'm not even sure what I'm eating," Flex said, holding up the bag to read the side of it. "Beef stew with potatoes . . . *not*."

"I'm not very hungry," Muddy said. "Anybody want mine?"

"Eat," Flex said. "Once you get behind the power curve there's no catching up."

"Spud, how well do you know Smooth?" Punk asked.

"I've never served with him," Spud said. "But I know him."

"And?"

"And?" Spud's eyes went to the overhead. "He's a good pilot and a reasonable guy."

"And?"

"And what?"

"And what are you leaving out?"

"Nothing."

"There's nothing not to like about him?"

"Not that I know about."

Punk shook his head. "Already the XO, huh, Spud?"

"I know you were jaded by Soup Campbell during your first tour, but sometimes good guys win, Punk. Look at Eagle." He patted his chest and smiled wryly. "Hell, look at me."

"Who's Smooth?" Muddy asked.

"Commander Robert Renforth," Spud replied. "Your new commanding officer."

"I know both of you guys are *Arrowslinger* alums," Flex said, leaning forward to see around Muddy. "But I noticed your patches are different. Which one is the official one?"

Punk and Spud each focused on the left breast of the other's flight suit. "What's different about them?" Spud asked.

"They changed the patch right after you left the squadron a couple of years ago," Punk said. "See? They made the spear bigger."

"It's too big now," Spud assessed. "I like the old patch better. It's more elegant."

"When you're talking spears," Punk said, "bigger is always better."

Spud started to counter with something about how he was going to use his executive power to change it back but stopped himself, bemused in the face of the others' laughter. Corky walked back, chuckling although he hadn't heard the exchange. Punk had almost forgotten the civilian was aboard.

"How y'all doing?" Corky said, leaning against the seat-back of a chair in the row ahead of them. "And how are you doing, young lady?" he said to Muddy. She shrugged and tried to ignore him.

Corky took the aisle seat across from the others and leaned over toward Punk and chattered on. Punk nodded occasionally as if he'd been paying attention while his mind wandered. He remembered Corky's reaction to the roll-offs and remained sure that there had been more to the story than two confused coneheads. Punk saw the fireball over the target at Dare County. That day seemed like it had happened years ago now. He conjured up Crud's smile and tried to hear his laugh, and then his mind went back to Suzanne, where it stayed for the balance of the civilian's string of bon mots.

Hours later, Muddy's face came into the circle of light generated by the reading lamp over Punk's head. "Who are we fighting?" she asked.

"What?" he asked back, startled by the broken silence and Muddy's sudden emergence out of the surrounding darkness of the cabin.

"Who are we fighting?" Muddy repeated, parking herself on the armrest of the aisle seat across from where Punk had taken station after their MRE feast. Her voice was steady but barely audible. Sleepers dotted the seats around them.

"The bad guys." Punk said in a plain voice, eyes refocused on the paperback in front of his face.

"Where are they?"

"Afghanistan, last I heard . . . maybe Pakistan."

"Is that where we'll strike?"

"Most likely."

Muddy sighed and sat pensively. "I wonder if I should be here," she said after nearly a minute of silence. "I don't feel like I'm ready."

Punk dropped the book and considered her. She looked tired, vulnerable, and—dare he think it?—*female,* and that wasn't what he wanted to see on his way to certain conflict. And ten hours on the flight with crappy food and little sleep hadn't helped his mood.

"You'd better *get* ready," he snapped. "What did you think flying fighters was all about, anyway? It was just a game; a game that you just had to win, right? Well, you won, Muddy, and now you get the payoff. You get to go to war."

Muddy's mouth twitched as she stared at the bulkhead over his left shoulder. "You're right," she mumbled, and rose to move back from where she came.

Punk suddenly felt like an asshole. She wasn't guilty of being female; she was guilty of being an FNG—a fucking new guy, a nugget. He remembered his own apprehensions a few years back when he'd joined his first fleet squadron—not deployed and certainly not with war looming. He furtively studied her as she sulked back to her seat and wondered if she'd become the warrior they all insisted she be.

A C-2 Greyhound—the COD—was sitting on the ramp several hundred yards away with its propellers turning. The newly arrived passengers stood next to the charter jet and waited for their bags to be unloaded by a ground crew of Bahraini nationals who moved slowly and constantly yelled at each other in their native tongue, an ugly, guttural sound to Punk's ear. Soldiers in desert cammies cradled rifles and watched the process. One of them marched over to Corky, who'd moved away from the action to try to smoke a quick cigarette, and told him that smoking was unauthorized on the flight line. Corky's posture stiffened and he looked as if he might exchange words with the sentry, but instead he took one last long draw and then stamped the butt out on the ground. Behind him, a Humvee with a machine-gun mounted on the back tore across the tarmac.

The heat of midmorning worsened the effects of Punk's jetlag. His body buzzed; he was floating, detached from the surroundings. He deciphered the world through a thin haze. The expressions of the others evinced a similar state, most likely triggered by the realization that they were a long way from home.

A helmeted figure in a flight suit approached, only the lower half of his face visible with his visor down. "Who here is going out to the aircraft carrier?" he asked, speaking louder than he needed to. A few of them raised their hands. "Grab your bags and follow me. We're leaving ASAP."

Of the fifty-some original travelers, only ten followed the crew chief over to the C-2. Punk figured those left behind were either headed to the joint staff in Riyadh or would stay in Bahrain to serve at Fifth Fleet headquarters. He shielded his eyes from the sun and thought about the time spent in these parts during his last deployment. He and his squadronmates had pulled some all-world liberty in Manama, the capital of Bahrain. He'd heard someone in the crowd say the city was now off limits to Americans. There would be no pints in British expatriate bars, no dance-a-thons in the discothèques, no all-night parties with Gulf Air flight attendants in their hotel rooms. American presence wasn't about engagement with the locals any more.

The crew chief was joined by another near the COD, and the two of them lugged a large canvas bag to the feet of the group. "Put on these cranials and life preservers while we stow your gear," the first crew chief shouted over the hum of the turboprops. "Once we give you the signal, enter the aircraft through the aft ramp."

Ten minutes later the C-2 was loaded and the signal was rendered. As he stepped up the ramp, Punk was happy to spot his flight gear bag among the other gear strapped down in the forward part of the bay. The seats in the airplane were facing aft. Whether riding the subway or an amusement park ride, Punk had an aversion to facing opposite the direction the machine was traveling. He didn't suffer from motion sickness; the sensation just bothered him.

The COD lurched as it started to taxi, and one of the crew chiefs stumbled against the right bulkhead near the rear of the fuselage. The man steadied himself and, once he was more surefooted, mated the comm chord dangling from his helmet into a junction box along one of the frames. He swiveled his boom mike against his lips and announced that the first leg of the flight would last about two hours before landing in Fujayrah, in the United Arab Emirates, where they'd take on fuel, supplies, and a few more passengers.

Spud was asleep in the next seat before the COD had its landing gear fully retracted after takeoff, which was of no real consequence to Punk because conversation was almost impossible in the noisy transport. Punk had never enjoyed Spud's gift of narcolepsy and the engines were rattling his head too much to read, so he spent the first leg of the flight in the windowless cabin staring blankly at the crest of the cranial of the person seated in front of him. The haze of jet lag served him well; the flight passed quickly.

The ramp of the C-2 came down as the transport cleared the runway at Fujayrah, and those inside the fuselage grimaced at the bright light and turned away from the blast of desert heat. When the engines finally shut down it seemed very quiet. The passengers sat in their seats, unsure of what to do, until a crew chief ordered them to the terminal.

The U.A.E. felt at least twenty degrees hotter than Bahrain, and strong wind whipped across the scorched earth and whistled in Punk's ears. With an assassin's fluidity, and impervious to the breeze, Corky fired up another cigarette and then sucked on it like a swimmer coming up for air. His eyes darted wildly, looking for the sentry who would stunt his pleasure. Punk surveyed the surroundings as he walked toward the terminal—a low roofed building the same color as the dirt and the sole structure for miles around—and was reminded of Hollywood's vision of other planets. The land was mostly flat with sand dunes dotted with half-bush, half-tree tangles of vegetation forming the only contours.

The travelers were greeted by stale air conditioning and the distinct sound of Ping-Pong being played as they entered the terminal and moved toward the "lounge," a small corner of the open bay furnished with hydraulic cans gathered around barrels filled with industrial fluid. Along an adjacent wall a line quickly formed outside of the sole commode.

The rhythmic meter of the Ping-Pong rally ended with a sharp crack of paddle on ball, and then a voice Punk recognized said, "That's the match!" Punk looked toward the table and couldn't believe his eyes: There, with khaki uniform shirt removed and T-shirt soaked with sweat, was Master Chief Bobby Callaghan.

"Master Chief!" Punk yelled across the room. "Master Chief, what the hell are you doing here?"

Callaghan grew a wide grin. "I might ask you the same question, Lieutenant," he yelled back, pulling a towel out of a bag on the floor near his feet and wiping his face and arms. They met at the center of the room and shook and patted each other on the shoulder.

"You're going to be the maintenance master chief for the *Arrowslingers*?" Punk asked.

"No. Master Chief 'Wild Bill' Jones has that job."

"What squadron, then?"

"None of them. I'm escorting a landing gear assembly out to the Boat. That's how I beat you guys out here. I left the afternoon before you."

"That sounds like a petty officer's job. Since when do master chiefs get ordered to make equipment runs?"

"Ordered?" The master chief smiled. "They don't get *ordered*. I volunteered."

A crew chief walked up, helmet still on and visor down, and said, "Master Chief, we're ready to load that landing gear."

"Be right there," Callaghan returned before turning back toward Punk. "I'll save you a seat in the COD."

"Need some help with the gear?" Punk asked.

The master chief raised his eyebrows. "What's this? Officers doing grunt work?"

"Master Chiefs babysitting replacement parts?" Punk retorted. "It's wartime."

Punk and Callaghan followed the crew chief around the side of the terminal. The landing gear was propped against the building, swathed with bubble wrap generously secured in rings of duct tape. It took six of them to carry it to the COD.

They stood broiling in the sun outside of the C-2. Callaghan craned his big head through the side hatch and monitored the two crew chiefs' efforts to strap the gear down along the deck in the forward portion of the cargo bay. Punk saw something behind the master chief's concerned demeanor. The big man was harried, sure, but he also seemed content, maybe even happy.

After offering loadmaster guidance to the crew chiefs, Callaghan turned to Punk and said, "I might just be able to get this gear to the carrier without breaking it." The master chief chuckled mostly to himself as he snatched a handkerchief out of his back pocket and wiped his face. "Did I tell you Seamus came home?"

Punk's eyes widened. "No," he said. "When?"

"Yesterday . . . or whenever Tuesday was. I think the terrorist attacks got to him. We actually had a decent conversation at the kitchen table right before I left."

"You think he's home for good?"

Callaghan shrugged. "Who the hell knows? I'm sure it doesn't hurt that I'm gone again." Punk tried to read the master chief's expression but got nothing from it.

Over the master chief's shoulder, Punk spotted a line of people headed for the COD, bodies distorted by the waves of heat radiating off the ramp. The procession was led by a figure in a flight suit, one of the transport's pilots, he figured, since the rest of the crew was already at the airplane.

"The Boat just called," the pilot said as he approached, nearly jogging now. "Our overhead time has been moved up an hour and a half. We've got to haul ass." He rushed through the side hatch and a second later the upper part of his body reappeared in the cockpit. Punk watched him don his helmet and then maniacally move his head and arms about as he went through his prestart checklist.

The pilot's panic was infectious, and Punk felt a wave of apprehension wash over him. The Boat had called; the Boat knew that they were there. Punk joined the line to walk up the COD's aft ramp, and in the shape the sweat made on the back of Spud's flight suit Punk had a vision of men in long-sleeved khaki shirts arguing. The Boat, frenetic by tradition if not by nature, would be an even better model of chaos now. And they were already late.

CHAPTER FOURTEEN

The C-2 had been airborne for nearly four hours by the time it started a counterclockwise orbit, and Punk cursed the absence of a window. He figured they'd taken their place in starboard delta, the holding pattern off the right side of the aircraft carrier generally reserved for helicopters and CODs. He checked his watch. The recovery would most likely be scheduled on the hour or the half hour, so they either had a short or moderate wait ahead of them.

The constant turning motion played tricks on the passengers' inner ears and that, combined with heat and fatigue, began to make many who'd otherwise made the journey unscathed airsick. Through his mouse ears Punk heard the muffled sound of retching all around him and the air was soon tinged with the unmistakable smell of vomit, which caused a chain reaction of nausea in still more passengers. Punk stole furtive glances at Muddy across the aisle from him as she methodically removed the contents of her helmet bag and then threw up into it.

A while later the COD leveled its wings and the pitch of the engines increased as the pilot commanded more power. Punk figured it was finally their turn to enter the landing pattern, a theory supported a few seconds later by a hard left hand turn. The wings leveled again, and Punk heard the gear and then the flaps come down. In his mind's eye he pictured where the COD was in the pattern and what the pilot was focused on. He felt the approach turn start, and when the frequency of the power changes increased he knew the pilot was flying the ball. Any second they'd be touching down . . . hopefully.

Punk thought about this leap of faith while strapped helplessly in the cargo bay. His life was in the hands of a prop pilot, a guy who probably finished near the bottom of his class in flight school. The C-2 slammed onto the deck and the engines revved to full power. In a couple of heartbeats the hook grabbed the wire and the airplane stopped. Punk breathed a sigh of relief and thanked the heavens that the minimum standard in flight school was still good enough.

The ramp came down once again, and shrill shriek of jets filled the bay. Flight deckhands scurried across the flight deck between newly recovered aircraft taxiing into the spots where they'd be chained down and groomed for the next launch. The COD stopped and its engines shut down, and the passengers were led to the ATO shack, many on wobbly legs.

Punk stepped down the ramp and onto the nonskid of the fight deck and considered the deck through the scratches in the goggles attached to his cranial. The ship was heeled to port, turning out of the wind in its persistent attempt to maintain its assigned position between launching and landing jets while headed into the wind. The salt air across the deck was replaced by the scent of jet fuel and grease. Punk breathed it in and, as he'd been during the presail conference a few weeks ago, he was hit with the feeling that he'd never left. Real life was simply illusive punctuation between months on the Boat.

Spud emerged from the skipper's stateroom and pushed by Punk, Muddy, and Flex against the passageway's bulkhead without a word. He'd gone a few steps aft when Punk called, "Spud? What's going on?"

Spud turned and ran his eyes across all three before looking at Punk. "You need to start calling me XO," he said sharply. "And a war is what's going on, or at least that's what will be going on very soon, so we've all got a lot to do." Spud pointed toward the skipper's door. "Commander Renforth will see you now."

Caught a bit off guard by Spud's terse tenor, Punk watched him spin on his heel and race aft. *Must've been quite an in-brief,* Punk thought. He rapped on the skipper's door and pushed it open.

"Permission to come aboard, sir?" Punk asked, face wedged into the small opening he'd created.

"Yes," the skipper replied. "Come in. Come in."

Unlike the passageway, the stateroom was pleasantly cool. Commander Smooth Renforth came around the gray metal desk at the far end of the small room and greeted the three officers lined up shoulder-to-shoulder just inside the door. Punk had heard idle ready-room banter about how Smooth was naval aviation's poster boy, and as the man stood before him and shook his hand, the lieutenant understood what they'd meant. The skipper was tall, about Punk's height, with wider shoulders. His flight suit was up to Crud's standards: clean, pressed, and adorned with patches that looked brand-new. He had longish dark hair with some hints of gray around the edges. A single thick eyebrow ran above his dark brown eyes. The smile that accompanied each greeting showed perfect white teeth bookended by deep dimples. He reminded Punk of an older and more rugged version of the cartoon character Speed Racer.

"Welcome to the *Arrowslingers*," the skipper said, gesturing toward the lone couch in the space—a piece of furniture that transformed into the bed by folding the back of it down—and an adjacent chair. "Please have a seat, and let's chat for a second." The skipper returned to the desk chair. Among the group of pictures on the wall behind him was a big picture of the skipper shaking hands with the president, and next to it was a plaque adorned with the presidential seal and a brass plate that read "White House Fellow." Punk had heard that White House fellowships were reserved for the most upwardly mobile officers in the military.

"First, I'd like to thank you for coming out and joining us," the CO said. "The XO tells me your trip was long and tiring, so we'll try to give you a few hours to catch up."

The skipper focused on Muddy seated on the couch next to Flex. Her face was as white as it had been just after she'd pulled her head out of her helmet bag on the COD. "Are you feeling all right?" the commander asked.

She ran a sweaty strand of hair behind her ear, offered a forced smile, and said, "I'm fine, sir."

The skipper shot quick glances at the other two and asked, "Everyone else okay?" Punk, who felt a propeller-induced headache coming on, nodded, as did Flex.

Commander Renforth got out of his chair and sat on the front of the desk, his well-polished flight boots dangling just off the deck. His demeanor was low-key, along the lines of a doctor trying to assuage his patient's fears while at the same time being realistic about the chances for medical success. "We'll need you all up to speed as soon as possible," the commander said, eyes on Muddy a hair longer than the other two. "We've got a lot of work ahead of us and not a lot of time to get it done. Our target is Afghanistan, and that's official as of this morning. When we left on this cruise that wasn't one of the places we'd thought we'd be fighting, so the intelligence center didn't bring any planning charts for that area. But that's fixed now. Bundles of charts of Afghanistan, all sizes and scales, were on the COD with you. The XO will be leading one of the strike teams, and you three are on it. At this point we don't have time to get new crew pairings comfortable, so I'm going to stick the XO in your backseat, Punk; and Muddy, you'll be flying with Flex as your RIO on Punk's wing." The skipper gauged their reactions and then nodded, apparently pleased there were no objections to the news. He checked his watch and moved to shake hands with the new arrivals again. "I've got to scoot to a meeting with the air wing commander. Get some rest."

Punk awoke from a dead sleep, unsure of where he was but pleased that his headache had disappeared. It was cold in the stateroom, and he drew the wool blanket that had gathered around his feet back over the sheet across his body. He laid his head on his understuffed pillow and walked his eyes around the dark space, a two-man stateroom he'd be sharing with Flex for the next number of months.

Months. He'd only been gone twenty-four hours, and that seemed like forever. He was disoriented and craved the comfort of a soft touch. He was overwhelmed with the sensation that he was drowning; he labored to breathe. In his panic Anita's face appeared in his mind, which surprised him, and he wondered if she knew he'd gone to war, and how she'd reacted when given the news. He conjured up an image of Suzanne and tried to stay with her but couldn't. His brain was short-circuiting. He feared that he'd forget what she looked like as the days wore on. He realized he didn't even have a picture of her and resolved to E-mail her and ask for one. He'd hint that he wanted something risqué, maybe something flat-out pornographic. No, that could backfire. They'd consummated the relationship, but he still didn't know her well enough to gauge how she'd react to that sort of request.

Had it really been more than two years? How did he get back here so quickly? How depressing it was to embrace the notion of a photograph as his most intimate companion when hours ago he'd had the real thing. He wanted the real thing now, and the ache of the longing stuck in his throat and chest.

Just as Punk's anxiety threatened to debilitate him further, he was embarrassed by it enough to suppress it. He filled his mind with the horrors of those running from the towers as they fell. He saw their faces caked with ash. That day was what had brought him to this place. "Kick some ass for me," Platt had said. And so he'd try. He'd repaint his war face.

"Punk, are you awake?" Flex asked from the bunk above him.

"Yeah."

"It's 1800. You want to go eat dinner?"

Punk realized he hadn't eaten anything since the MRE on the charter jet. The two aviators put their flight suits back on and walked to Wardroom One, nearly to the bow on the 0–3 level of the Boat. As they waited in the food line, Punk was surprised that he didn't recognize anyone, even the few with *Arrowslinger* patches on their flight suits. He'd never been a big fan of veal patties, so he opted for a hamburger, or "slider" in underway parlance.

After a quick stop at the soda machine, the two surveyed the lines of tables for the appropriate place to sit down. Both knew that by this point in a deployment, squadrons had carved out their turf in the wardroom and wouldn't take kindly to interlopers. Punk spotted Spud, now known as "XO," and the skipper at the far end of the room seated among a group of *Arrowslinger* junior officers, including Einstein, the lone remaining lieutenant from Punk's previous tour.

Einstein, brand-new in the *Arrowslingers* at the time, had had the dubious honor of riding in Commander Soup Campbell's back seat when the then-skipper was bagged after foolishly wandering into an Iraqi SAM trap. Once on the ground after ejecting, Einstein had deftly evaded the Iraqi troops bearing down on him until the SAR helicopter picked him up, with Punk and Spud providing close air support. Soup had fallen into Iraqi hands, where he stayed for five days before being repatriated and spun a hero by the Pentagon. Punk hadn't kept in close touch with Einstein after leaving the squadron but had heard through the grapevine that the young RIO had blossomed into one of the superstars among the *Arrowslinger* lieutenants, which wasn't surprising.

"Welcome back, Punk," Einstein said as Punk approached. He stood and they shook across the table. "There's just no keeping you off the Boat, is there?"

"I guess not," Punk said. "It feels like I never left."

After Flex and Einstein introduced themselves to one another, the newcomers stood in the aisle between tables, hunting for places to sit. Just as they were about to look elsewhere, the first wave of diners, including the CO and XO, rose en masse, leaving a sudden abundance of empty seats. Spud seemed preoccupied at the skipper's heel, and he didn't acknowledge Punk's presence before walking out.

Although he was finished eating, Einstein remained behind, and Punk and Flex each took a seat across from him. Einstein had put on a few pounds and shorn his hair to stubble since Punk had seen him last. "Nice haircut," Punk cracked.

"Mid-deployment malaise," Einstein explained. "I got tired of combing my hair."

Punk chuckled and took his first bite of slider. "So," he said with his mouth full, "how's it going out here?"

"We had a nice little routine working until the attacks,"

Einstein replied. "You know, the standard Gulf cruise: a little no-fly zone action over Iraq, a little liberty in Dubai or Bahrain, repeat. Now that's all history."

"How's morale?" Flex asked.

"Nothing like a war to improve that, I guess; at least for the short term."

"What about the squadron?" Punk asked.

"The squadron?"

"The skipper."

"None better," Einstein said. "Of course, my frame of reference for commanding officers is skewed." His attention was diverted by something across Punk's left shoulder. His eyes widened and he said, "That has got to be the tallest woman I've ever seen in a flight suit."

Punk and Flex turned, both attempting subtlety, and saw Muddy filling a glass with milk. The two of them laughed. "That's Muddy, your new squadronmate," Punk said. "She's not a first, is she? Aren't there other female *Arrowslingers*?"

"Two," Einstein said. "Cat and Peaches, both RIOs. What's Muddy?"

"A pilot," Punk said.

Einstein hummed and said, "A pilot, huh? She must've kicked ass in the RAG to get orders straight out here."

Punk and Flex exchanged smirks. "Oh, yeah, she kicked ass," Flex said. *"Not."*

"Our first female pilot," Einstein mused aloud. "This should be interesting."

"I'm afraid you're right," Punk agreed. "But you don't need to worry about it. Flex is crewed with her."

Muddy walked over, trailed by three civilians and a short black lieutenant in long-sleeved khakis who sported an afro bigger than regulations allowed, although Punk would've been hard pressed to cite the regulation. "I picked up some new friends in the ready room," she said with a bemused wince.

The officer in khakis pushed past her and extended his hand down toward Punk. "Ronnie Wheedle, ship's public affairs officer."

Punk didn't bother standing but halfheartedly offered a hand over his shoulder. "Rick," Punk said wearing a plastic smile as they shook. He cut a glance at the pin above the man's left chest pocket and noticed the PAO sported wings, which made him the first public affairs guy Punk had ever met who wasn't a former ship driver. Punk motioned to Einstein and Flex: "This is Paul and that's Jim."

"Fantastic to meet you," Wheedle said with a wave to each as he slid into the seat next to Punk. "I haven't seen you guys around before. Did you just get out here?"

"Yeah," Punk said.

"Well, on behalf of the ship's company, allow me to welcome you aboard. We have a great relationship with the air wing out here. Together, we're Team Victory."

"Team Victory?"

"Yeah. I made that up, and the captain loved it. We've got patches and everything. I could get you some if you're interested. They're really colorful and only cost ten bucks."

"Yeah," Punk said with the same enthusiasm he gave to telemarketers. "I'll definitely have to think about that."

"Are you guys in Evelyn's squadron?"

"Evelyn?" Punk asked with eyes narrowed. He hadn't heard her called by that name since before her FAM days in the RAG. "Oh, yeah. *Evelyn*. Yeah, we're in Evelyn's squadron."

"These gentlemen are in Evelyn's squadron," Wheedle explained to the civilians. They nodded vigorously, bending forward at the waist like Japanese tourists.

The PAO introduced the civilians, who were members of the press corps aboard the Boat, as they took their seats. Across the table, slicing her veal into small pieces, was a mousy unsmiling female newspaper reporter. Next to her was a wire service correspondent, a pale-skinned Ichabod Crane-type with a narrow face and thin hair that fell across his forehead in unkempt, wet-looking ringlets. And to Wheedle's left was a sweaty fat man with stubble across his beet-red face, who silenced the lieutenant with a wave of a knife-wielding fist midsentence and clarified that he wasn't a best-selling adventure novelist but the researcher for a best-selling adventure novelist, which, he further explained, was harder work than simply writing best-selling adventure novels.

"Do you think you're ready for war?" the female reporter asked Punk over the arrhythmic clatter of silverware against plates. He saw she'd pulled out a small pad of paper

and waited for his answer with pen poised. Punk started to
answer but stopped and looked at the PAO. The PAO
seemed surprised by the recognition but then emboldened
in his role. He returned the go-ahead to Punk: a single,
subtle nod, like a millionaire making a bid at a high-
priced auction.

Punk looked back at the reporter and replied, "Yes,"
omitting the fact he'd only been on the Boat an hour or
so longer than the press corps.

"What makes you think so?" Ichabod asked, pushing his
plate aside and producing his own writing materials.

Punk wiped his face and threw his napkin on the table.
"We're well trained."

The reporter turned her attention to Flex and asked,
"How do you feel about women in combat?"

Flex shrugged and crunched loudly on a piece of ice.

She shifted her eyes back on Punk. "How about you?"

"It's policy," Punk said.

"Do you agree with the policy?"

Punk paused, staring blankly at his plate. "I have no
problem with it as long as standards aren't compromised."

The reporter's thin eyebrows furrowed. "Have standards
been compromised?"

"Of course standards have been compromised," the researcher said, jumping into the conversation with a sardonic
laugh. "Where have you been for the last ten years? We're
lucky the military didn't crash more jets than they did."
Although Punk couldn't completely disagree with the sentiment, it rang vulgar coming from the fat man. It was the
same feeling he got at air shows when cornered by self-
proclaimed military aviation aficionados, guys who'd never
spent a day in uniform but who'd earned their expertise
through movies, professional journals, television documen-
taries, and comic books.

"Were standards compromised for you?" the reporter
asked Muddy.

"It's not about just her," the researcher argued before
Muddy could respond, "and the standard isn't about just
being able to fly the jet. Did you read my boss's last book?"

"You're kidding, right?"

"It sold nearly two and a half million copies."

"So did Bee Gees albums in their heyday."

"Over a year ago, this man predicted everything that's happened."

"He predicted that terrorists would hijack airliners and fly them into the World Trade Center and the Pentagon?"

"Well, not those places, exactly. But in his books, he did predict that terrorists would attack."

"What do they attack?"

"The Eiffel Tower."

"With an airliner?"

"No, with a nuclear bomb."

"Are these terrorists Islamic fundamentalists?"

"No, they're neo-Nazis."

"Uncanny prescience . . ." the reporter deadpanned. "What does that have to do with standards being compromised?"

"One of the characters in the book is a female Air Force pilot who gets shot down and taken prisoner by the terrorists."

"What kind of airplane is she flying when she gets shot down?" Punk asked.

"A stealth bomber," the man replied, jerking a little, as if hit in the forehead by a flying bug. He frowned at the lieutenant. "You haven't read his book either?"

"No," Punk said. "How did the terrorists shoot down a stealth bomber?"

"They exploited stealth technology so it wasn't stealthy anymore," the researcher explained patronizingly. "Those passages were actually some of my best work. Scared the hell out of the Pentagon. But that's not the point. While the female pilot's being held prisoner, she's raped by the terrorist leader." He cut his eyes toward Muddy, who seemed unmoved.

"Oh, I see what you're saying," the reporter said with mock clarity. "Men *never* get raped in prison."

"What happened to the other guy in the airplane?" Punk asked.

"The other guy?" the researcher asked back.

"There are two pilots in a stealth bomber. Where did the other guy go?"

The fat man sat silently with his brow furrowed. An *Arrowslinger* lieutenant Punk hadn't met approached the table and addressed Einstein: "There's an all-aircrew briefing in the ready room in five minutes. The ops officer wanted to make sure the new folks knew about it."

The aviators excused themselves and started out of the wardroom. Punk had gone a few steps when he was pulled aside by Lieutenant Wheedle and escorted to the nearest corner. "The press corps is going to be a fact of life out here," the PAO said, tossing his head back toward the table. "It's best if Team Victory gets along with them."

"Fine," Punk said.

"You'll also find that life around them is easier if you stick to one- and two-word answers; you know, if the press asks you if you agree with females in combat roles you could say yes. How 'bout that?"

Punk started to walk away.

The PAO grabbed his biceps with a spidery hand. "I was a good helicopter pilot," he said. Punk eyed the man's hand on his sleeve until he released his grip. "I didn't get boarded out. I know you were wondering. I saw you look at my wings."

Punk nodded and feigned interest in a loose thread near the waist of his flight suit. "I'd better get going to this meeting," he said, and moved for the exit.

"I wanted to be a public affairs officer," Wheedle continued, now talking to Punk's back, "and I'm damn good at it. And I'll tell you part of this story is already written."

Punk made a half turn. "Which part?"

Wheedle pointed toward the hatch that Punk's squadronmates had just passed through. "The part where that female fighter pilot succeeds."

The intelligence team didn't look or act like the guys who usually gave the squadrons threat assessments before the aviators operated in a new area. These two were the real deal, their aura akin to what Punk had felt from most of the SEALs he'd dealt with over the years: understatedly cool beneath their tanned and sinewy exteriors. One of them had a bushy mustache and the other a full beard. Their eyes were mysterious, revealing no hint of emotion. They wore desert cammies unadorned with names, unit emblems, or even rank insignias.

Without introduction or fanfare, the one with the full beard, presumably the senior man, moved center front of the ready room. "This brief is classified Secret," he said, eyes deliberately working across the gathered seated in their high-backed, faux leather chairs. "But parts of it are really Top Secret." Only a handful of aviators in the room were cleared for Top Secret, but the briefer's expression was read by Punk as a summary clearance upgrade. In any case the statement only enhanced the atmosphere of importance surrounding the presentation. This was war. Rules got bent.

The briefer gestured for the duty officer to turn off the overhead lights and then pointed the remote mouse at a laptop perched on the small table between the CO's and XO's chairs. The darkness was split by light on the pull-down screen at the front of the room, upon which a color map of greater central Asia appeared. The briefer produced a laser pen and began dancing a red dot around the screen. "A quick geography lesson: Afghanistan . . . here. Bordered by Pakistan to the south and east, Iran to the west, and Turkmenistan, Uzbekistan, and Tajikistan to the north. Five major cities: Kandahar to the south, Herat, west, Kabul in the middle, Mazar-e-Sharif in the north, and Khost, northeast. The country is flat in the south and gets more rugged toward the northeast, with the most extreme elevations in the Hindu Kush Mountains. Peaks top out at over twenty two thousand feet MSL in some parts. The mountains are full of thousands of cave complexes. They know them; we don't. Overall, this is challenging topography."

A new slide came on the screen, a photo of what Punk assumed were two locals, each bedecked in a loose-fitting shirt covered with a vest and a black turban on his head. They appeared to be posing by a cave opening. Both were smiling broadly. One of the men held an AK-47 aloft and the other had a Stinger missile slung over his shoulder.

"Afghanistan's sole resource is its location, and any wars fought there involving a foreign power were about using Afghanistan as a bridge to somewhere else. War is not new to the Afghans. They've been fighting wars for centuries, sometimes against a foreign power, sometimes against each other. They're currently fighting a civil war that has been going on since the Soviets left, and they fought the Soviets for ten years before that.

"Civil war is what brought the Taliban to power in 1996. The population was tired of fighting between the rival war-lords and the Taliban offered the best hope for stability, if not peace. Although recognized as the official ruling body of the nation by only two countries, Saudi Arabia and the United Arab Emirates, the Taliban have been courted by several major powers, including the United States. But these efforts waned once the true face of the Taliban appeared. In the course of blowing up centuries-old Buddhist statues, effecting summary justice in the streets, and harboring terrorists, the Taliban have become pariahs. The international community has basically shunned the government for the last several years, but the Taliban haven't really seemed to care too much. This is how they found a friend in Osama Bin Laden and al Qaeda, and why they won't turn him over. The Taliban do whatever they please regardless of outcries or sanctions, and they do it in the name of Islamic law."

The briefer focused on the pull-down screen, where the photo was replaced by a video. The video was slightly out of focus and shot at a low angle with the picture severely jerking from time to time. The scene showed two figures, each covered from head-to-toe in what looked like a blue sheet, being led across a dirt field by several bearded men. The figures were made to kneel on a white line scribed in the dirt, at which point one of the men produced an automatic rifle and fired a single round into the top of each blue bundle. The figures toppled, dark pools spreading across the ground beneath them.

"The Taliban found those two women guilty of the high crime of listening to music," the briefer said. He pointed at the screen. "Now watch what they do to people they *don't* like . . ."

The video switched to a clearly focused presentation of a man lashed spread-eagle to two poles against a brown and ominous sky. In slow motion, the ropes fell slack and the poles snapped outward, each taking an arm and leg with it. The man's torso, now just a flesh sack with a head mounted on it, made only a quarter turn before bouncing on the ground, testimony to how precisely the grizzly device had been engineered.

The map of Afghanistan reappeared, and the bearded

man passed the laser pen to his mustached partner. "Operation Enduring Freedom has already begun," the other briefer said. "Caseworkers are linked up with elements of former rival warlords, known as the Northern Alliance, united only in their dislike for the Taliban. The Northern Alliance will be the main force in this war. Our job is to support them to the degree where they're able to bounce the Taliban out of power and wipe out al Qaeda. History shows that stability beyond that is an ambitious goal, and that's not our mission."

The laser spot came alive again as he spoke. "When the bubble goes up you guys will be hitting fixed targets around Kandahar and Kabul. The Air Force heavies, B-2s, will be working the northern part of the country, taking off from Whiteman Air Force Base in Missouri, hitting their targets, and then landing in Diego Garcia, a small island in the middle of the Indian Ocean about three hundred miles south of where we are right now." Punk did a quick time/distance calculation and figured those flights would last more than thirty hours. And Air Force guys thought landing on the Boat was insane.

"The Taliban don't have much of an integrated air defense," the briefer continued, "so our initial salvo of TLAMs should take care of the fixed-site SAM threat. Mobile AAA and shoulder-fired SAMs are another matter. When planning your attacks, pay close attention to the altitude of the surrounding terrain. The Soviets learned the hard way that these guys know how to use the peaks to get shots off.

"The targeteers at CENTCOM have come up with counter-industrial, counter-military, counter-regime, and counter-economic target lists that should take only a couple of weeks to work through, weather cooperating, of course. After that, we anticipate your role will shift to on-call strikes and close air support. Regardless of the mission, you can plan on long flights, probably longer than any you've ever flown before. It's roughly six hundred miles to Kandahar, and the flights just get longer from there." He signaled for the lights. "The details of this operation will be promulgated in separate correspondence, so don't worry about that right now." He scanned the room, squinting along with the others as their eyes got readjusted to the light. "I know

that was quick and dirty, but we have six other ready rooms
to brief. Any questions?"

The skipper raised his hand. "Where are the tanker
tracks?" he asked.

"We're still working that out," the bearded briefer
replied.

"If we're going six hundred miles minimum," the CO
said, "we're going to need to hit the tanker two, maybe
three times, at least."

"We realize that, sir. As I said, we're working that out."

"Is there an emergency divert field?" the XO asked.

"Yes," the briefer said. "Let me bring the map back up."
The ready room went dark again. "There are actually two
diverts: Pasni, here on the southern coast of Pakistan, the
one that you'll use for flight operations around the carrier,
and Qwadabad, in central Pakistan, the one that you'll go
to if you have a problem during a mission over Afghanistan. Pasni is already secured and we're working on Qwadabad." He signaled for the lights.

"Any other questions?" the bearded man asked as he
checked his watch, suggesting to those gathered that he was
ready to move on. There were a million other questions, but the
junior aviators were too intimidated to ask, and the senior ones
knew they'd get answered along the way right up to the last
minute like always. The man nodded and offered a simple,
"Good luck," before folding up his laptop and exiting with
the other briefer through the front door of the ready room.

The skipper stood and stilled the murmur. "You know,
a lot of comparisons have been made between the terrorist
attacks and Pearl Harbor," he said, raising one knee and
placing his foot on the surface of the low table next to his
chair. "But once you get past the fact we were caught off
guard, this thing we're calling Operation Enduring Freedom and World War Two won't have much in common. I
guarantee you this operation won't provide the closure that
the nation got in 1945. You won't see the Taliban and Bin
Laden averting their eyes and looking remorseful on the
deck of one of our warships. We're all riding an emotional
high, but it won't last. After the flags stop waving, we'll
still be here, seeing this thing through." The CO eyed his
charges and didn't speak further. At that moment, Punk
thought him a very wise man.

CHAPTER FIFTEEN

"Don't call me 'XO' in the airplane," Spud said over the intercom as the Tomcat climbed through seven thousand feet. "Rank goes away once we get between the canopy rails."

"It does, huh?" Punk seethed in return, making no attempt to rein in his ire. Spud had finally given him an opening into an exchange that had, in his mind, been a long time coming. "We've been out here nearly three weeks now. *Three weeks,* Spud. And in that time you've turned into a different guy, and quickly, I might add."

"What the hell are you talking about?"

"You swore you wouldn't change, Spud. For years, flight after flight, you swore you'd never change if you ever got into the position you're in now."

"*Change?* I did become the executive officer of this squadron once we stepped aboard, if that's what you mean."

"I'm talking about more than becoming the XO," Punk said. "I'm talking about the stuff around that."

"I still don't know what you're talking about, Punk, and although I'd love to probe this issue further, I have to find our tanker now." Spud keyed the radio tuned to the carrier's primary control frequency known as Strike. "Strike, Slinger one-one-zero, looking for our tanker."

"One-one-zero, your tanker is Viking seven-oh-six," the Strike controller said. "He should be up this freq."

"Viking seven-oh-six, are you up?" Spud asked.

"Viking's up," the S-3 pilot replied.

"This is Slinger one-one-zero. Say your posit."

"Seven-oh-six is ten miles north of Mother at angles ten, left-hand orbit."

"Slinger copies," Spud said. "We're about five miles away."

"Viking copies."

Punk calmed himself by looking over at Muddy flying at a loose cruise on his right wing. He shifted his thoughts to her performance over the last three weeks, both in and out of the air. They hadn't done anything tactically taxing so far, only benign combat air patrol hops over the North Arabian Sea, so she hadn't been tested yet. Along with continuing her learning process around basic flight operations at sea, she'd been brought up to speed on the use of night vision devices and made comfortable with both day and night tanking from the S-3.

Muddy still wasn't vying for Top Hook honors, though. Her landings had been low average—a No-Grade for every two Fairs—and she'd suffered only two "nights in the barrel," nights where she'd had trouble getting aboard. The first time she went around the pattern four times before snagging a wire, and the second time she stopped on her third attempt. She was on the LSO watch list along with a handful of other pilots in the air wing, but to Punk's knowledge there'd been no talk about a performance board. So far she was being treated like a typical below-average nugget pilot, and that was good news for her.

Muddy appeared comfortable around the ready room, self-assured but appropriately deferential. With her wit and locker room savvy, she was a welcome addition to the female aviator population in the squadron, as it turned out that Cat and Peaches, the female RIOs, were both phlegmatic dullards who'd dutifully fly their hops and then retreat to their stateroom. Muddy fit in much better, and in fact, Punk had heard more than one type-A male pay her the back-handed compliment of "I don't even think of her as female," which was as good as compliments got around a fighter squadron.

The press corps certainly did think of Muddy as female, and while they waited for the war to cook off, they took advantage of their access to the *Arrowslinger* ready room, courtesy of Lieutenant Ronnie Wheedle. But over the course of a feature or two even the press grew tired of the female angle, and while initially Punk had feared he'd be intervening on her behalf, within the first week the press corps stopped coming around at all. The only times he saw them were during meals.

Punk knew that would change once the shooting started, although he had no greater sense than anyone of when that would be. Like everyone else aboard the Boat, he watched the twenty-four-hour news reports and listened to the pundits with a mix of amusement and frustration, the latter growing over the former as the weeks dragged on. Retired flag officers on network retainer droned on in the company of sycophantic anchors and together they answered their own questions, if a polemic could pose as questions. They knew things: complements, times, places, things that the Joint Chiefs hadn't figured out yet, and in spite of the former senior officers' previously sworn duties to the defense of the nation and the well-being of the men and women of the armed forces, they were now compelled to share all that they knew with the American people and the rest of the satellite-facilitated world.

Punk drilled holes in the sky over the Boat. Until today. Just as he feared he might never be assigned a mission of any consequence, that he was being held back because of his pairing with Muddy, his section was slated for an intelligence/surveillance/reconnaissance (ISR) mission over Pakistan with a route of flight along the Afghanistan border. The wing had been flying ISR missions for the last two weeks and their purpose was twofold: First, they were to take photographs of possible ingress routes into Afghanistan for special forces units. Second, they got the Afghan air defense operators used to seeing American planes coming toward them from the sea. One day the jets wouldn't stop at the border, but because the planes had established a routine of coming north, their mere presence wouldn't be the tipper that the war was about to begin.

Spud groomed the Tactical Airborne Reconnaissance Pod System (TARPS), a device strapped to the bottom of the jet that housed two cameras, one film and one digital, while Punk got a tally on the S-3. He signaled Muddy to cross underneath him and joined abeam the left side of the tanker.

As the aviators had briefed, the tanker picked up a northerly heading as soon as Punk was in the basket and receiving gas. While Punk concentrated on staying plugged into the drogue, Spud pressed the digits for the latitude and longitude of Karachi into the dinosaur of a computer integrated into the console along his left thigh. Over one hundred miles away. Good.

By the assertion of the American diplomats, the Pakistanis were great allies, but they'd been nothing but a pain in the air wing's collective ass so far. From the start, they'd demonstrated that they had little interest in making life easy for American military forces. Several times without warning or explanation, they declared the skies over Pakistan closed. The restricted airspace around Karachi grew daily, and depending on how far east the Boat was operating, it was sometimes impossible to avoid without taking a big detour, something aviators weren't too keen on doing during gas-critical missions. CAG, the air wing commander, had complained to the battle group commander, but the admiral had ultimately declared himself powerless to do anything about the situation.

Punk took on the two thousand pounds of JP-5 he was scheduled for and moved to the tanker's right wing. As he continued to fly formation on the Viking, he unstrapped his mask and let it dangle from the left side of his helmet and treated himself to a quick sip of water from a small plastic bottle he kept in the front of his survival vest. A brief look in the mirrors showed that Spud's head was down, and after a glance at the tactical display under the attitude indicator in the center of his instrument panel, he knew that the RIO was busy hammering the rest of the waypoints for their photo mission into the Tomcat's computer.

In the other fighter, Flex worked Muddy through the pretanking checklist, the steps of which had become nearly automatic to her over the last few weeks. She selected "left engine" on the air source panel to keep any gas sprayed from the drogue and down the right engine from circulating through the air conditioning system. Then she cracked the wing sweep angle back to thirty-five degrees so that the airplane would fly with its nose cocked up a bit more and so the horizontal stabs would droop out of the turbulence coming off of the tanker, giving the F-14 a more stable ride. Finally, she extended the refueling probe. It moved into the wind stream with a distinct rumble of disturbed air, and caused just enough drag to allow her to fall behind the tanker.

But even as Muddy fenced with the S-3's basket, she worried about the *next* time she'd have to tank. It would be another first for her: After the TARPS run they were scheduled to in-flight refuel from a heavy tanker, an Air Force KC-135.

Over the last three weeks she'd been deluged with horror stories about the KC-135 or, more specifically, the refueling apparatus attached to the back end of the KC-135. The refueling boom, designed with Air Force jets in mind, was incompatible with Navy jets unless it was fitted with an adaptor that made the male device into a female one. The adaptor was no marvel of modern technology, just ten feet of thick hose attached to a rigid basket. Because there was no take-up reel and the basket was made of solid metal instead of the Kevlar spokes and canvas rim found on other drogues, there was less room for error.

Across the wardroom table there had been tales told of probes ripped off and canopies smashed. Like horror story raconteurs around campfires, they'd related how the KC-135's rig had earned a nickname in carrier aviation circles: the "wrecking ball." They'd watched her reaction, perched to draw perverse pleasure from her anxiety.

She'd attempted to keep her concern in check by reasoning that the veterans were just putting her through the typical nugget rites. Smitty had warned her before she'd left about wild goose chases, that she should be guarded about being scheduled for a flight simulator event because there were no flight simulators on the carrier. She took solace in the odds. How many times a day did jets off the Boat tank from the KC-135? And they all returned with their probes and canopies intact.

Muddy finally plugged the Viking's drogue, and as the indicator light on the bottom of the tanker's refueling store turned green, indicating good gas flow, she wondered when the hurdles would stop coming. There was always the next

thing. You can land a propeller-driven trainer? Now land
this jet. You can land a jet? Now land a jet on an aircraft
carrier. You can land a jet on an aircraft carrier? Now land
a jet on an aircraft carrier at night. You're comfortable
with tanking? How 'bout we take this nice, soft basket and
replace it with a steel one with spikes on it.

Muddy took her gas without incident and then crossed
under and behind Punk and attached herself to his right
wing. With a wave from the COTAC, the S-3 banked left
and started back for the Boat.

As Punk drove the flight north, Spud signaled Flex that
he was switching up the mission check-in frequency. Once
he saw a thumbs-up from the other RIO, he checked in
with the E-2 Hawkeye early warning aircraft, the carrier-
based platform tasked with controlling the flow of traffic to
and from the Boat. "Seabird six-oh-five, Slinger one-one-
zero's proceeding north."

"Roger, one-one-zero," the controller replied, one of
three naval flight officers seated side by side along the
length of the E-2's fuselage. "Stand by for hand-off to Zeus
just before you go feet dry."

"Copy."

Punk kicked Muddy into combat spread formation. She
moved nearly two miles abeam and was thankful for the
little liberty of being able to look around a bit while maintaining station. Staring at nothing but the flight lead's jet
while flying parade formation was both monotonous and
mentally taxing. She also welcomed a color other than the
blue-gray of the ocean as the southern coast of Pakistan
came into view over the fighter's nose: arid-looking as she'd
imagined it would be but a change of scenery in any case.

"Slinger, contact Zeus on Button Five," the E-2 controller said. "Check in using your air tasking order call sign."

"Roger. Slinger switching," Spud said, again signaling
Flex and waiting for a thumbs-up before talking on the new
frequency. "Zeus, Fuji one-one is checking in as fragged."

"Roger, Fuji. Zeus reads you five by five. Picture clear."

Muddy was at once relieved and disappointed to hear
"picture clear." She was the fighter cover for the photo
bird, armed with four air-to-air missiles and five hundred
rounds in the nose cannon. She figured a MiG kill would

relieve most of the stigmas of being a nugget. Intelligence reports had said that the Taliban had a dozen or so working MiG-21s, and the JOs in the ready room had handicapped them as the perfect opponent: crappy pilots willing to die for their cause, zealots with more balls than brains.

At the same time she feared she might still fuck it up. Sometimes reaching for the brass ring and falling off the beast was worse than keeping your ass planted in the saddle. Better that she survive the basics first. She checked her watch. Just over an hour until her appointment with the wrecking ball . . .

The weather was ideal: cloudless blue skies and no turbulence at altitude. Punk looked down the canopy rail as they crossed the coastline and wondered if the surf was any good. He then checked his handheld GPS for the distance to the first turn point: two hundred and fifty miles to go. These were going to be long-ass hops.

"How far is it to Kandahar?" Punk asked over the intercom.

Spud moved his cursor over a waypoint near the top of the tactical display. "Three hundred and fifty miles," he replied.

"How about Mazar-e-Sharif?"

"Is your GPS broken?"

"I've got our mission route in there, and I don't want to mess with it."

"All right, stand by . . ." Spud rifled through several cards tacked to the kneeboard on his right thigh until he found the one labeled "Nav points." "You know, the XO wouldn't do this for a lieutenant, but Spud willingly does this for Punk. You see the difference?"

"I always did," Punk intoned. "I'm glad you finally seem to."

"Mazar-e-Sharif is six hundred and fifty miles from here," Spud said.

"Goddam," Punk exclaimed, "that's about eight hundred miles from the Boat."

"Right."

"Do you think we'll go up there?"

"We might. It depends on how much the Air Force can do flying out of Missouri."

"Eight hundred miles? Those will be quadruple-cycle events, maybe more. We'll be logging nine hours of flight time on those hops."

"Uh-huh."

"We'll have to hit the tanker four or five times."

"Yep."

"Damn, I'll fill four piddle packs at least." Punk thought about his two-hour bladder and then wondered aloud, "What's Muddy going to do?"

Spud chuckled. "That topic came up at an air wing CO/XO meeting last night, as a matter of fact," he said. "The flight surgeons are going to issue 'absorbent undergarments' to the female aviators."

"That's dignified," Punk said.

"The docs are actually afraid that the females won't wear them and will dehydrate themselves instead."

"Maybe they shouldn't be scheduled for the long ones."

Spud guffawed with exasperation. "You've seen the plan, Punk. Once this thing kicks off we're going to need every aviator up and running, and even then crew rest minimums will be violated big time."

The conversation gave Punk the sudden urge to urinate, so he reached along the right console and fumbled through his nav kit until he found the thick plastic bag with a thin, dry sponge in the middle of it. He put the Tomcat on autopilot and went through the always-awkward drill of freeing himself from the grips of zippers, harness webbing, and Nomex. Once sure he was pissing in the bag and not on his hand, he cut a glance toward Muddy and wondered if she was sporting a diaper on this five-hour flight.

The radios were mostly silent as they continued north. Airplanes occasionally checked in or out with the AWACS, but beyond that it was quiet. Their radars were absent any contacts, and their SAM warning receivers were still. All of that was fine with Punk. Walk before running, especially with a nugget on your wing.

Pakistan reminded Punk of the area around Fallon, Nevada, where the Navy's strike warfare center was located. They crossed diagonally over a handful of brown mountain ridgelines that topped out around five thousand feet. As they closed the first point on their TARPS route, the terrain flattened into desert for about sixty miles before trans-

forming into another rise that marked the border with
Afghanistan.

"Ten seconds to first point," Punk said. "Check cameras on."

"Cameras on and running," Spud replied.

They drove north for another ten miles and then ran just
north of east along the border. On his center display Spud
watched the digital camera's images, occasionally freezing
the picture for closer study using the Mark button on the
TARPS control panel, mounted in the right console. Punk
studied the land below, the rises and ravines, and noted
how many places there would be to hide from an air strike,
even an air strike armed with precision-guided bombs. And
Afghanistan's changes in elevation were even more dramatic.

Punk wondered if the locals could see them from the
ground, and what their thoughts would be as they spied
the jets passing overhead. Were the Americans liberators
bringing peace and stability to a war-torn region, or crusad-
ers forcing their ideals on an unwilling population? He'd
seen a report on the news that said that the southern Af-
ghanis and the Pakistanis were from the same religious sect
and that the border between the countries meant nothing
to anyone but westerners. Glints from below the jet made
him think that maybe they were already taking potshots
at him.

Punk checked the range back to the Boat when they
reached the third turn point and saw they were three hundred and forty miles away. He read his fuel gauge: six thousand pounds. He was hit with the lonely fact that for the
first time in years he didn't have enough gas in the jet to
get home. It was time to head for the tanker track.

"I'm feeling kind of vulnerable, Spud," Punk said. "I'm
ready to get some gas."

"Roger that," Spud replied before keying the rear cockpit radio. "Zeus, Fuji is ready for Texaco. Proceeding to
Bradley."

"Roger, Fuji," the AWACS controller, an Air Force captain, replied. "Initial steer for Bradley is one-zero-three for
ninety-four miles."

"Concur. Is our tanker on station?"

"That's affirmative. Exxon two-two is on station."

Muddy fought the feeling that she wasn't ready yet, the

same feeling she'd had when she was a kid approaching the end of the high dive board at the community pool. Flex found the tanker with the radar. "Contact, zero-nine-nine for sixty-five miles," he said over the control frequency. "Left-hand turn passing through west."

"One's clean," Spud replied.

"Contact is steady south now," Flex said. "TCS confirms Exxon. Recommend a heading of one-two-zero for intercept." Muddy glanced down at the television display, saw it filled with KC-135, and was hit with another wave of foreboding.

"Tally the tanker," Punk passed over the radio. "One o'clock, slightly high."

She trained her eyes to his call. "Muddy's tally."

Minutes later the flight was stabilized on the tanker's left wing. "Fuji flight is port observation, nose cold," Spud said.

"Cleared to precontact," the boomer said, lying prone in the rear of the tanker, looking down the boom through his observation window.

Punk threw his probe out and slid the Tomcat behind the big tanker, establishing the fighter several feet short of the drogue. "Fuji's precontact," Spud said.

"Cleared to contact," the boomer replied.

Muddy watched closely from the left wing of the tanker as Punk drove the Tomcat forward and mated the probe with the drogue. Once coupled, he moved forward a few more feet until he'd established a decent bow in the refueling hose and then froze the jet relative to the boom. It looked so easy.

The tanker reached the southern end of its ten-mile racetrack pattern and turned back to the north while Punk continued to take the eight thousand pounds of gas he was allotted. Muddy watched him hang in there and hoped the tanker would stay straight and level for the time she was refueling. She had enough variables to wrestle with already without worrying about bank angle.

Punk finished and moved to the tanker's right wing. "Fuji dash-two is port observation, nose cold," Flex said to the boomer.

"Cleared precontact," the boomer replied.

The roar of disturbed air around the probe as it extended cued Muddy to try to forget childhood fear. She slid the wings back a few degrees and retrimmed the jet and took a deep breath through her oxygen mask, steeling herself for the effort.

"Okay, Muddy," Flex intoned over the intercom, "no big deal. No different than the S-3."

"Roger," she returned in a quick clip.

"Two's precontact," Flex said.

"Cleared to contact."

Muddy tweaked the throttles forward and cautiously closed the basket, trying not to look at it until the last moment, the technique that Punk had recommended in the brief. "Fly formation on the knuckle," he'd said, referring to the joint where the solid metal boom turned to heavy rubber hose, "then make the final small corrections once you're in close." But she couldn't help but look at it—mesmerized, eyes walking up the length of the boom to the boomer's window and back down to the basket flying rock-solid in the air stream, the mouth of it beckoning yet evincing danger, like a Venus flytrap.

The hugeness of the KC-135 was intimidating on its own, but with the refueling rig attached it was like something out of a Jules Verne novel. In Muddy's mind, the day ceased to be bright in its presence; she could have sworn she heard the din of machinery, the industrial clanking of metal on metal.

"Keep the closure coming," Flex coaxed, which caused her to pull power a little more, a reaction that made her curse silently into her mask. She feared that the beast in her subconscious that willed her to fail might be taking over. She fought with it for dominion over her limbs. She wished she hadn't had so much time to think about this, that somehow she could've arrived behind the heavy tanker without any preconceived notions or anxieties. Those bastards and their jokes . . .

Muddy stabilized ten feet away and huffed another deep breath into her mask. She bumped the throttles forward. Voices came at her over the intercom and radio, but she stowed them with the imaginary noise of the machine as she closed the basket. She concentrated on the knuckle while using her peripheral vision to judge when the probe had broken the plane of the basket rim. Once sure she was close, she looked at the probe tip and was elated to see she'd placed it dead smack in the middle of the basket. All she had to do now was ease forward a bit to put a bow in the hose.

But as her focus shifted to the knuckle, the hose suddenly went taut. She stared up at the rig, arms momentarily frozen on the controls, shocked at how quickly the plug had gone to hell. Her mind fired with a million signals in an instant. She momentarily marveled at the sight with a detached curiosity. The hose appeared to be stretching and she wondered how elastic it was.

"Fly off of the knuckle!" Punk called in earnest over the squadron common frequency, which snapped her out of her dreamlike trance and caused her detachment to yield to an overwhelming desire to get away from the tanker *now*. But before Flex could say, "Climb!" the basket ripped off in a spray of gas, taking the tip of the Tomcat's refueling probe with it.

"Back away," Flex cried over the intercom. "Back away!"

"Emergency breakaway," the boomer called over the radio, which caused his pilot to jam all four throttles as far forward as they would go.

"Keep the probe out, Muddy," Punk instructed. "How's your right motor look?"

Muddy studied her gauges for a moment then dejectedly passed, "Fine."

"What's your state?"

"Five thousand pounds," she said.

"Zeus, Fuji flight is going to have to head into the primary divert," Spud said to the AWACS controller.

"Say reason for divert," the controller said.

"Our wingman had a problem tanking and is now unable to take gas airborne."

"Understand both jets are diverting?"

"Affirmative," Spud said.

"Zeus copies. Exxon say your status."

"We're down," the boomer said without any attempt to mask his disgust. "We'll need to return to our home base ASAP."

Punk knew that wouldn't be good news for the AWACS crew or the chain of command above them. He had a vision of generals in Saudi Arabia slamming their fists onto the tops of conference tables in the current operations cell at the Joint Task Force–Southwest Asia. The heavy tanker inventory was already spread thin across the theater; a broken one at this point probably meant that all events over Pakistan would be cancelled until the next tanker was scheduled to be on station. Punk unfolded a copy of the air tasking order and then looked at his watch. The next tanker wasn't supposed to arrive for four hours. Muddy's gaffe would be noticed, to say the least.

"Fuji, the divert field is ready for you," the AWACS controller passed. "Contact tower at this time."

"Switching," Spud said.

Qwadabad, the divert field, was nearly underneath the Bradley tanker track, only twenty-five miles to the southeast. As Spud checked the flight in with the tower controller, Punk thumbed out the speed brake and dumped the nose to lose altitude.

"Ever been to Pakistan?" Flex asked Muddy over the roar of air around the still-extended probe, a noise that taunted her like fans jeering a visiting team's marquis player.

"I don't know what happened," Muddy said in a distant voice.

"If you play tug-of-war with the One-thirty-five, the One-thirty-five wins," Flex said.

"Muddy, I'll let you land first," Punk said. "Don't forget you have carrier-pressure tires. Roll out all the way to the end of the runway."

"Roger."

"Fuji flight, you're cleared to land runway one-two," the tower controller said. "Report short final with the gear."

"Fuji copies," Spud said.

"In the event of missed approach," the controller continued, "we're recommending that you stay north of the field. We've heard gunfire from the south off and on all day long."

"Appreciate the heads-up," Spud said. "We'll stay to the north if we have to go around."

Muddy dropped her gear and flaps and quickly reviewed the landing checks with Flex. After three weeks of landing on the Boat, the runway looked odd to her, and she had to remind herself that once she touched down she'd be pulling the power to idle instead of jamming the throttles to military power like at the Boat. But landing at the field proved to be an easy adjustment to make, and as she rolled out she looked forward to the days after the deployment when she'd have a nice long runway at her disposal once again.

They taxied past rows of revetments filled with MiGs in various states of disrepair. Some looked flyable; most did not. After a few more turns, Muddy spotted several figures in desert cammies waving them down. She followed their hand signals and parked and shut down. Punk did the same next to her.

A hot wind filled the cockpits with the smell of earth as the canopies were opened. A ground crewman opened the steps and ladder folded into the side of each jet, and the aviators made their ways to the ground.

"Welcome to Qwadabad, gentlemen," a young-looking guy with curly brown hair and bright eyes said as he ripped his cranial off. His eyes widened as he caught sight of Muddy. "Oh, sorry. Welcome, *ladies* and gentlemen."

Spud extended his hand. "I'm Commander O'Leary, executive officer of the *Arrowslingers*."

"Chief Ponce," the man said as they shook. "I'm the head of the air wing maintenance detachment here in Pakistan."

"How many folks do you have with you?"

"Four."

"Has that been enough?"

"It's been enough to set our tents up with. You're our first real customer." He squinted his tanned face and looked up at Muddy's extended probe. "I guess somebody just tangled with the tanker."

"Something like that, chief," Spud said. "How quickly can you get us out of here?"

"Fuel truck is on the way. We'll make sure the probe doesn't have any loose pieces hanging from it and have you on your way within the hour. CENTCOM doesn't want you on deck here any longer than you do. These guys are supposedly on our side, but I'll tell you what, there's shit going on all around here." He jabbed a thumb to his left. "We've heard gunfire from that direction all day."

"That's what the tower was telling us," Spud said. "Do you have a phone I can use to call the carrier?"

"Affirmative. Follow me, sir."

"Is there a head around here?" Punk called to the chief headed away from him.

"That way," the man said, pointing under the parked fighters. "Good luck."

Good luck? Punk, Flex, and Muddy walked in the general direction the chief had pointed, and after a dozen steps they understood his meaning. Even from seventy-five yards away the stench from the latrine was overpowering. And there was more in the mix than just human waste; it was an unfamiliar blend of foulness to Punk's nose. He wondered if he smelled the oft-described redolence of death.

Ten steps from the building, Muddy gagged and said she'd wait until later. Punk watched her walk back toward the Tomcats, focusing on her midsection, curious as to whether she was wearing one of those diapers Spud had talked about.

"After you, sir," Flex said with a sweeping bow.

"Thanks . . ." Punk took one last gulp of semiclean air and rushed into the latrine. He passed a line of sinks that had obviously not hosted water for some time and parked himself in front of the commodes, which were nothing more than holes cut into a sheet of plywood. He felt his heart pounding in his chest and throat as he continued to hold his breath. His eyes began to tear up; he seethed "goddamit" at the stream of urine that seemingly had no end. He finally forced himself done after he thought he saw movement across the surface of the ooze below the hole.

Punk gasped for air as he cleared the building. " 'Good luck' is right," he said to Flex, who was standing arms akimbo and grinning. "Your turn."

"I'm done," Flex said, gesturing toward a dark circle near the corner of the building. "This is the Old World, right? From the smell of things I assume you can piss wherever you want. These people obviously care about sanitation . . . *not.*"

Spud was waiting for them once they got back to the Tomcats, the first of which was already being fueled from a truck. "The Boat knows what happened," Spud said.

"Who did you talk to?" Punk asked.

"Smooth."

"How did he take it?" Punk asked.

"In stride, like everything else. He was actually about to launch for an ISR mission of his own, but he got cancelled along with the rest of the air wing headed feet dry after the tanker went down. For once, an over-water hop was a good deal."

Muddy snorted a sorry laugh. "Nothing like impressing the boss right off the bat," she said.

In spite of a heated discussion that Punk feared might come to blows between the English-speaking chief and the Pashto-speaking Pakistani fuel truck driver, both F-14s were gassed up in short order. Spud gathered the four aviators and went through a cursory brief for their four-hundred-mile flight back to the carrier. The ground crew had trouble getting both the electrical power and air start units to work, growing pains associated with their first visitors, but eventually all four of the General Electric F-110s were shrieking at idle power. Once the RIOs had entered the navigational data into the computers, the fighters again weaved their ways past the dilapidated MiGs, Punk leading the way this time. As he passed the temporary tower erected near the runway, he gave a wave to the controllers and several of them enthusiastically waved back.

The Tomcats parked in the hold short and waited for clearance to launch. Punk peered down the approach corridor and was reminded of the scenes at most major civilian airports: He counted five transports in a descending conga line approaching the field. One by one they rolled out and taxied to the other side of the base, and only then did Punk notice the level of activity in that direction. There were a dozen transports parked over there: C-5s, C-17s, and C-130s. Through the waves of heat he could make out the movement of vehicles. War was coming; Punk wondered when.

Two hours later Punk was hawking the flight deck from two thousand feet above the Boat, while at twelve hundred feet and five miles behind the stern, Muddy orbited her jet with the refueling probe still sticking out of her jet like a campy salute. As the last Hornet on the launch hooked up to catapult one, the air boss instructed her to commence her straight-in approach. At that point Punk started heading toward the break, trying to sequence his jet in the wires fifty seconds behind Muddy.

Punk dove down to eight hundred feet and matched the carrier's heading, lining up the jet with the right side of the Boat and shooting glances over his left shoulder, gauging his pattern on Muddy's distance from touchdown.

"Are we sweeping the wings today?" Spud asked sardonically. Damn, Punk thought. There were few things that would get you on the hit board as quickly as coming into the break on a gorgeous day with your wings fully forward. And they were nearly overhead the carrier now. Punk tugged the wing sweep switch with his left thumb and hoped for the fat chance of getting the wings fully aft before anybody on the flight deck noticed otherwise.

Punk's helmet was suddenly slammed against the right side of the canopy as the Tomcat snapped to the left without warning . . . and without his input. With stars in his eyes he instinctively moved the stick to the right and fed in right rudder and commanded the wings forward. "Hold on here, Spud," he gasped.

"What's going on?" Spud asked.

"Uh, stand by." The controls seemed to be working again. Punk glanced down at the DFCS control panel and saw no lights; he depressed the test switch and received a normal readout. The gremlins that had possessed the jet were gone for the time being.

"Spud, we need to depart the pattern for a control check."

"Why?"

"The jet just rolled off without me moving the stick."

"Ah, shit. Understand you have control now?"

"Yes."

As Spud relayed their situation to the air boss, Punk pictured Muddy studying in the Three Wire and Pugsly walking dejectedly onto the transport plane in Key West. Then, in his mind's eye, he saw Corky. Punk added power and climbed back over the ocean, head filled with a wave of faces and statements about how the roll-offs had all been misperceptions and a system was in place to ensure those things never happened, and in the unlikely event they did happen they would be corrected immediately. And this time he wasn't trying to convince the principals to trust a replacement; the problem had happened to him. But would that matter to Corky McBride?

Punk wasn't going to fall into any goddam RDI loopholes. He was flying a fucked-up airplane, a warped gift from the gods of chance, and he wasn't going to let the evidence slip away. Before confronting the tech rep and others, he'd be armed with hard facts: airspeeds, altitudes, wing sweep angles—everything he needed to convince the unbelievers that they had a problem on their hands.

"Spud, are you ready to go to test pilot school?" Punk asked.

"That's what flying with you has always been like," Spud said. "Remember, the air boss only gave us five minutes to get this done. Otherwise, we'll have to divert to Pasni."

"We're not going to have to divert. I just want to see if I can replicate the roll-off. We might be able to solve this thing once and for all. Make sure you have your pencil handy. I need you to jot down whatever instrument readings I call out."

Twenty miles away from the Boat, Punk leveled the jet at five thousand feet. "All right, Spud. Write this down: Five thousand feet, three hundred and fifty knots, wing sweep . . ." Punk tugged the switch aft, focused on the wing sweep tape next to the angle of attack gauge against the left side of the forward canopy bow, and waited for the airplane to roll off. "There's thirty-five degrees . . . forty-five . . . sixty . . . sixty-eight. Wings are all the way aft." The airplane stayed straight and level.

"I didn't feel anything," Spud said. "Did anything happen up there?"

"No," Punk fumed. "I'm dropping down to fifteen hundred feet to try this one more time."

Punk descended the Tomcat to fifteen hundred feet and turned back toward the Boat. "Okay, here we go again," he said to Spud, which caused the RIO to stare intently at his kneeboard and white-knuckle the grip on his pencil. "Fifteen hundred feet, three hundred and fifty knots, wing sweep at twenty degrees . . . thirty-five degrees . . . forty-five . . . fifty-five . . . all the way back. Goddamit. No roll-off at all."

"Are you sure it rolled off the first time?" Spud asked.

"Maybe it was something else; maybe you hit it with your leg or something."

"I'm sure," Punk snapped, "and we should've trusted the coneheads months ago." Punk's voice grew quieter as he thought aloud over the intercom: "It's got to be the roll computer that's causing these roll-offs. It's also got something to do with the wing sweep."

"Boss, Slinger is ready to land now," Spud said over the radio.

"Understand you want a straight-in?" the air boss asked.

"That's affirmative."

"Are you declaring an emergency?"

Spud looked over Punk's left shoulder and the pilot shook his head into one of the three mirrors mounted on the canopy bow. "Negative," Spud said. "No emergency."

"Copy. You've got a ready deck. Come on in."

As they started the approach, Spud keyed the intercom again: "Just write a gripe after we get on deck. Tell Corky. Get the problem fixed."

"Wake up, man; Corky's not on our side here," Punk said as he lowered the gear handle. "Why hasn't he volunteered to have the roll computers checked out before now? And I've met the CEO, too. He's another greasy son of a bitch." The Tomcat slowed to two hundred knots and Punk put the flaps down. "Think about it: There's no way they want to weather the bad press they'd get if word got out that a product they manufacture was responsible for the deaths of two guys and the loss of two Tomcats. Not to mention the company's already in financial trouble. I've read the reports."

"The reports . . ."

"We need to ground all the F-14s until we figure this thing out."

Spud hummed to himself for a few seconds. "On second thought, don't write a gripe. We'll convene a little pow-wow instead."

The skipper's stateroom was a crowded place. Smooth sat awash in fluorescent light from above as he moderated the discussion from the chair behind his desk. Spud sat in the chair in front of the desk and Punk leaned forward on the couch, wedged between Master Chief Callaghan and Corky McBride.

"We've already chased this ghost," Corky said, cutting his eyes toward Punk. "Nothing came of it."

"What about the wing sweep interlocks?" Punk asked.

"Checked them," Corky replied.

"Have you checked the roll computers?"

"We looked at everything."

"How did you check the roll computers?"

"It's engineering stuff. The details would bore you."

"Try me."

The skipper made the "time out" signal and asked Corky, "Are these jets as safe as they can be at this time?"

Punk fought the desire to rephrase the question for the skipper.

"They are, Commander," Corky replied with a sure nod.

"Thank you for your time." The skipper extended an arm toward the back of the closed door, and after a few beats Corky took the hint and showed himself out, making it a point to catch Punk's eye and offer him a gentlemanly nod on the way out.

A few seconds passed, presumably enough time for the civilian to get beyond earshot, before the skipper turned to Callaghan and asked, "What do you think, Master Chief?"

Punk sensed that the master chief wasn't completely relaxed and figured it was because he didn't know Commander Renforth very well. "Well, skipper," Callaghan said, wringing his big, freckled hands, "I know we tore those RAG jets apart pretty good a few months back. Like Corky said, we didn't find anything." He cleared his throat and straightened himself up a bit taller on the couch. "I also trust Lieutenant Reichert. If he tells me there's something wrong with the jet, there's something wrong with the jet. It just might take some time to find it."

"What's your guess on the problem?"

"I don't think the lieutenant's analysis is too far off the mark, but as you know, sir, we don't do computer testing at the squadron level."

The skipper hummed and reached across his desk, picking up several sheets of paper and perfunctorily thumbing through them. "So, Punk, what do you propose we do?"

"We need to ground our jets and tell the chain of command that we've got a problem, skipper," Punk said. "Even at chow tonight, guys were coming up to me saying they might have had the same malfunction; they'd just assumed it was air in the hydraulics or something. Grounding them will force RDI to expedite the fix. They might even be able to make it happen before the war starts."

The skipper returned Punk's expression with his own dour countenance and held up the papers he'd been flipping through. "This is the warning order," he said. "We go to war tonight." Punk cut his eyes to Spud, who simply nodded at the news. This hadn't been the first meeting in the stateroom recently. "I don't doubt your perception, Punk, but we're going," the CO continued, holding up another sheet. "Operation Enduring Freedom starts with one hundred and forty sorties in the next twenty-four hours, and nearly one-third of those are Tomcat flights. The Tomcats are the closest thing we've got to deep precision strike right now, and we can't fight this war without them."

The skipper pushed away from his desk and stood behind the chair, running his hands along the curved lines of the chair back. "I've been flying this airplane since 1987, waiting for this sort of chance. And you want us to ground the force now for something that's happened three times in the last six months?"

"I didn't know about the warning order, sir," Punk said. "All I can say is that my best friend was killed along with a promising replacement pilot during one of those three times, skipper. I'd at least like to know what caused it."

"I'm not saying we throw safety out the window," the CO said, working his eyes across each person in the space. "You know that's not what I'm saying."

"You wrote the gripe on the jet, Punk," Spud said. "The problem's documented. The master chief and the rest of maintenance will continue to check it out."

"We've got the best maintenance effort in the fleet," the skipper said, offering a double thumbs-up to the master chief before refocusing on the lieutenant. "This is a new matrix for you, Punk. It's a new matrix for all of us. We're not enforcing the no-fly zone now; we're going to war. And in a war, warriors have to win with what they've got."

The skipper glanced at the brass ship's clock on the wall above the couch. "I have to head down to CVIC to put the finishing touches on my brief. I'm leading the first wave over Kabul." He took a few steps and leaned against the front of his desk. "I'm not going to force any pilot to fly who doesn't feel like the machine he's taking over the beach is safe." He allowed a heavy silence to hang over them for a few moments, and then said, "You do what you have to do, Punk."

Punk barged through the back door to the ready room and immediately ran into the broad back of the fat researcher. The man didn't readily move, so Punk offered a brusque "excuse me" and threaded his way by him and the rest of the press corps. As he passed, he saw the reporters were crowded around Muddy standing next to Lieutenant Ronnie Wheedle. Punk slowly continued toward the duty desk at the front of the ready room but kept an ear trained on the exchange behind him.

"So she saved the jet?" the female reporter asked.

"That's right," Wheedle replied. "The failure of the tanking apparatus caused damage to Lieutenant (junior grade) Greenwood's probe. Only her quick actions kept chunks of metal from going down the right intake and destroying the engine. At that point, the jet could have been lost. It was impressive airmanship on her part."

Punk couldn't help but glance over his shoulder to see Muddy's reaction. She stood nonplussed, wearing the same bland expression she'd always seemed to favor around PAOs and the media. She looked like she wanted to say something, but didn't.

Wheedle looked at his watch and said, "All right, folks, they're about to start launching cruise missiles from the ships around the carrier. Let's go up to the island and watch the show." Punk found it curious the PAO knew so much about the supposedly secret strike timeline.

Wheedle shepherded the press corps out of the room while Muddy walked over to Punk. "Rewriting history?" Punk asked once she reached him.

"I didn't say a word," Muddy said.

"Exactly," Punk said.

Muddy took a deep breath and ran a hand through her hair. "You know, Punk, I wish you could walk a mile in my shoes before you get all self-righteous. I'm not trying to forward an agenda; I'm just trying to serve my country." She chuckled quietly. "Hell, I'm just trying to keep my

wings. I don't know this Wheedle guy. I do know he out-
ranks me and he's got his own thing going on out here and
I'm not sure I have the power to change that. I guess all I
can do is try to stay un-newsworthy."

Punk hadn't realized how raw the nerve he'd tried to hit
was. "I was just giving you shit," he said. "Fighter pilots
do that to each other."

"Fighter pilots . . ." she mused aloud and then puffed
another sad laugh. "Fighter pilots also tank without wrecking the jet in the process."

"You'll have a chance to redeem yourself very soon,"
Punk said. "I just saw the lineup. We're on for tomorrow
night, a strike supporting a Special Operations force insert
near Kandahar."

"How long is the mission?" Muddy asked.

"Quadruple cycle . . . nearly eight hours."

"How many times do we have to tank?"

"Three, maybe four," Punk said.

Muddy was silent for a time, eyes to the floor, and then
she said, "Maybe I shouldn't—"

"Look at this flight schedule," Punk interrupted in a
sharp voice, pointing at the dry erase board behind the
duty desk. "Every aviator in the squadron has to play to
make it work. Crew rest requirements are already a joke.
If you drop out, somebody's going to go two days without
any sleep at all." He read the apprehension on Muddy's
face and calmed himself. "You'll be fine," he said paternally. "I told you what you did wrong. Just don't do that
again."

"Sounds simple," she muttered.

"Don't dwell on that now. The XO needs us down in
CVIC to help plan this thing. Let's go."

Muddy followed Punk out of the ready room and wondered how she was going to keep from dwelling on her
future behind the heavy tanker.

After four hours of strike planning in the confines of the carrier's intelligence center, or CVIC—*sivvic,* in carrier parlance—
Spud announced they needed a half-hour break and suggested
they hike up to pri-fly to watch some of the Tomahawk Land
Attack Missiles, or TLAMs—*tee-lams,* as they were called—
fly off of the destroyers and cruisers stationed around the

Boat. At the top of the island the four aviators—Spud, Punk, Flex, and Muddy—pressed their noses against the Plexiglas and marveled at the plumes as the cruise missiles left the rails in uneven intervals, each like a smaller version of a night-time space shuttle launch, and started the long journey to Afghanistan. "The small boys are launching forty-nine of those suckers at targets across the country over a two-and-a-half-hour period," Spud said. "And those forty-nine are all going to hit within twenty seconds of each other."

"And they said all America was good for was movies," Flex said.

An S-3 Viking sailed down catapult four and was immediately transformed into a small constellation of lights climbing against the black sky. "Those tanker drivers are going to be flying their asses off," Spud said. "Them and the Brits with their VC-10s."

"What about our Air Force buds?" Punk asked.

"Rumor has it they're down to three tankers in theater and two of them are dedicated to the stealth bombers working the northern targets. The skipper's strike got shifted to a more southerly target just before the brief because they didn't have the in-flight refueling support to get to Kabul."

"That sucks," Flex said.

"Actually, it's not that big of a deal," Spud explained. "Kabul is merely symbolic. Kandahar is where most of the high-level Taliban are."

"Still, it's a hell of a way to have to fight a war," Flex said.

"Semper Gumbi," Punk quipped. "And we're lucky we've got the U.K. on our side."

"We need to get back to CVIC," Spud said while looking at his watch. "That Special Forces guy is probably wondering where those lazy aviators ran off to."

The foursome stepped back down the stairway that twisted through the island and then threaded down the passageway on the 0-3 level until they reached the cipherlocked entrance to CVIC. The enlisted specialist on duty saw the flight-suited officers through the bulletproof glass that framed his post and buzzed them through.

"While you were away I managed to pull down some additional imagery," Army captain Pete Jablonski—the obligatory "Ski" for short—said once the aviators had gathered around one of the large rectangular tables in CVIC's mission planning area. Ski was on loan to the air wing from the Army's Fifth Special Operations Group. He was a big guy—Punk guessed roughly six-foot-three and probably more than two hundred and twenty pounds—with a crew cut and close-set, piercing blue eyes. He'd played linebacker at West Point, graduating the same year that Punk had graduated from Annapolis, and made it a point to remind his fighter pilot peer that Army had beat Navy in the annual football showdown three out of the four years they'd attended their respective military academies. Ski had a competent manner and seemed to know a lot, enough that Punk felt his own point of view myopic by comparison. The captain referred to the mission as the "op," his coworkers as "snake eaters," the targets as "objectives," and the enemy as "gomers."

Ski centered a large photograph on the surface of the table. "Again, this is Garmabak Ghar," he said with a slight southern drawl, running his finger around the picture as he spoke. "This fort is made of sandstone and was built nearly two hundred years ago. A rich history of conflict surrounds it. Right now it's being used as the headquarters for the terrorists' chief of security." Ski held up of photograph of a bearded man who looked pretty much like all the other bad guys who'd been paraded in front of them for the last three-plus weeks. Punk wondered why the aviators were even shown the photos. If the aircrews ever got close enough to recognize them, things had gone horribly wrong for the visiting team.

The captain refocused the aviators back to the table. "As you can see from the chart, the fort is located about one hundred and ten miles north of Kandahar. I'll leave it to you to figure out the specifics of your tanking requirement, but I understand you'll tank twice on the way in and at least once on the way out." Ski scanned the faces of the aviators and each of them nodded and shrugged without objection to his understanding.

"The objective has the secondary benefit of being near an airfield. The gomers aren't stupid. Hopefully they don't know when we're coming, but they know we're eventually coming. So they've positioned a large-caliber antiaircraft gun at each end of the fort." Ski scribed a circle around each gun's location on the photograph. "Now, there is a large concentration of personnel at the fort, so we need the element of surprise in order to overwhelm them. That's why we won't be bombing preemptively or using TLAM. Instead we'll be employing concurrent suppression. That's where you guys come in.

"Two C-130s full of Rangers will be dropping down to low altitude twenty miles out and flying right next to the fort for the insert. As soon as they hit the ground they'll reconstitute and take the objective with a two-axis attack . . . here . . . and here. We need the Tomcats to take out the two AAA sites with precision-guided bombs exactly as the first man leaves the first C-130. Again, the element of surprise is the key here. Without it we might get our asses handed to us. Precise timing is crucial."

A prematurely balding lieutenant from one of the Hornet squadrons rushed into the space looking for an enlisted technician. "The copier's broken!" he said in a panic. "My strike lead will absolutely lose it if I can't get the kneeboard packs completed." After the lieutenant hurried back out, Punk scanned the room full of state-of-the-art intelligence equipment and found it ironic that success came down to whether or not the Xerox machine was working.

Ski tossed the target photo aside and pointed to the chart again. "Tonight is about taking down the gomers' integrated air defense and other strategic targets. Tomorrow night we start taking ground; we start getting our hands dirty. If we can get a foothold, take the fort and the airfield . . ." He tapped on the chart and then swept his hand toward the top of it. ". . . the rest of the country will fall." Again the captain considered the faces of the aviators gathered before him. "Can you do it?"

Maybe not, thought Muddy. The other junior officers instinctively looked to Spud. The XO paused for a moment, staring at the chart, and then he nodded at the captain.

CHAPTER SIXTEEN

The two Tomcats launched into a clear sky at midnight on the second night of the war. Stars were few, but the horizon was discernible. The original plan had called for them to be accompanied by a pair of EA-6B Prowlers, electronic attack airplanes armed with antiradiation missiles, but because the first night had exceeded expectations in shutting down the SAM threat and tanker gas was limited, the fighters were now going alone. That was fine with both Spud and Punk. At night, the fewer machines you had flying around you, the better.

Climbing through three thousand feet, Punk called "Goggle up" over the squadron common frequency. On that transmission the aviators switched their cockpit lighting from red to green and reached into bags velcroed to bulkheads and clipped night-vision goggles to their helmets.

The darkness suddenly had definition. The shapes around the blinking lights in the distant sky were revealed along with the coastline of Pakistan. Punk got a tally on the S-3 tanker before Spud could even think to check in with Strike and found it remarkable that in some ways he could see better with goggles on at night than he could without them in broad daylight.

Technically, pilots weren't supposed to tank while wearing the night-vision devices but Punk did anyway. He'd transitioned to the world of modified night, a place of greens and blacks and limited depth perception, and ruled to himself that he wasn't coming back to the darkness on this flight. He'd found the goggles distracting and downright disorienting the first few times he'd worn them, but now he'd grown accustomed to their quirks and was a believer in their magic.

In the ready room Muddy had heard pilots whisper about tanking with the goggles on, and as she flew formation on the Viking's left wing with the lines of the boxy jet in plain view she was tempted to try, but she elected to play it straight. While Punk was in the basket getting his first ration of airborne gas, she unclipped the goggles from the housing on the front of her helmet and returned to the true night, a blackness that seemed even blacker after time spent peering through the night vision devices.

After Spud cut her loose from CVIC, Muddy had spent the handful of hours she was afforded to rest fitfully tossing in her rack. Her mind conjured up incredible scenarios. She imagined herself pretending to take gas from the heavy tanker, simply sitting behind the drogue without actually plugging it, and then flying off and flaming out and claiming engine failure.

But during the flight brief something had clicked inside of her. She'd suddenly realized a determined calm and optimistically sensed the feeling wasn't fleeting. It hadn't hurt that the air tasking order showed their gas would be coming from a Royal Air Force VC-10 with its gentle hose and soft, forgiving basket.

Her confidence was reinforced as she smoothly slipped the F-14's probe into the S-3's drogue. "All night long," Flex said over the intercom. "That's what I want to see all night long." She allowed herself to smile under her mask.

Because they had a longer way to go until they hit the next tanker, they each took on more gas from the S-3 than they had the previous day on the ISR mission. This time they were almost feet dry over Pakistan once Muddy had finished gassing up. The Viking flashed its lights and turned back for the Boat. Punk watched the jet bank away and wondered if the tanker pilot was envious of the fighters' task, or thankful he was returning to the sanctuary of the skies over American-held waters.

"Zeus, Yankee two-five's up," Spud said over the radio.

"Roger," the AWACS controller replied. Now that the

bubble had gone up, communications between aircraft were short and to the point.

The ATO had assigned New York–themed call signs to all of the missions over Pakistan, which Punk thought was a nice touch. Some of the boys in the ready room had agreed that they'd of late reached the point of symbolic patriotic saturation. They didn't need any more signed flags from civic groups or country music songs about eagles kicking ass; they just needed latitudes and longitudes to drop bombs on.

And now they had plenty of them. Punk had sat in on the skipper's early morning debrief and was pleased to hear the mission had gone well. They'd seen sporadic gunfire from Kandahar proper but that was it. All but one of their bombs had fused on impact. The CO's only bone of contention was that the tanker tracks were too far away from the targets. Even though he'd jumped on the secure phone to complain to the current operations cell at CENTCOM, the tracks stayed where they were, a function of intransigent staffers and the huge bureaucracy the U.S. military had established over more than a decade in theater.

And so Punk drove his flight due north, headed directly for the Gipper refueling track, one hundred miles west of Kandahar and two hundred miles from the fort and runway at Garmabak Ghar. Campfires along the border shone brightly through his goggles, and as they disappeared under the wing line, Punk realized they had crossed into Afghanistan. With that realization came another: People on the ground were shooting at them.

Punk verified their altitude against the elevation of the surrounding terrain, double-checking that they were beyond the range of small-arms fire and light AAA. The goggles showed them every flash of light for hundreds of miles. They seemed to get brighter and come closer to the jets as they traveled farther north. He saw too much and was tempted to take the goggles off and fly around in ignorant bliss but reasoned they were above the reach of their enemy. He decided to just enjoy the show beneath him.

Half an hour later Spud reported, "I've got radar on the VC-10," over the intercom.

Punk sighted through the symbols projected against his

HUD and with the goggles spotted what appeared to be a large airplane coaltitude with them. "I think I'm tally, Spud," he said.

"Roger. It looks like he's steadying up on the westbound leg of his racetrack pattern."

"Copy."

As they got closer to the VC-10 Punk could see the hose was already streamed out behind the tanker. Without any words between the airplanes Punk extended the probe and drove into the basket and was welcomed with a green light on the tanker's flow indicator. At the same time Muddy positioned her jet on the left wing, unclipped her goggles, and readjusted her eyes once again to the extremely black world.

"Going east, mate?" a voice with an English accent asked over the radio, presumably that of one of the pilots.

"That's affirmative," Spud replied, assuming the guy was referring to the target's direction from them. The VC-10 immediately went into a smooth left turn and eventually steadied up eastbound.

"Worry not, Muddy," Flex said as Punk moved to the right wing. "This thing has got a big fluffy basket. Soft as a Nerf ball."

Muddy extended the probe and maneuvered into position, pleasantly surprised by the size of the drogue. It was like a training basket, nearly twice the size of the S-3's, well-lit and as gentle as Flex promised it would be. God save the queen. Suddenly tanking was a pleasure.

With a "Good hunting, lads," from the tanker the fighters detached, topped off and ready for the attack phase of the mission, only one hundred and fifty miles away from the target thanks to the easterly drag from the tanker. Punk peered under the goggles and checked his watch; their timing looked good.

As the crews continued toward the objective in silence, the pilots checked their bomb station status indicators and arming logic while the RIOs groomed the LANTIRN pods. Short for Low Altitude Navigation and InfraRed Targeting at Night, LANTIRN had been adapted for use on the Tomcat several years earlier and had given the aging fighter a new lease on life. With LANTIRN strapped on, the Tomcat went from Cold War air-to-air relic to preeminent precision striker.

Spud double-checked that he'd entered the correct coordinates and then slaved the pod to the target. "There it is, Punk," he said, relief evident in his voice as he studied the distinctive shape of the fort centered on his high-resolution display. He couldn't make out the gun emplacement yet but was happy to be in the ballpark. For all the hours spent planning a strike, doubt still hung heavy until the target was located.

Punk calmed himself. It wasn't showtime yet. The clarity of the LANTIRN view belied the fact that the F-14s were still about one hundred miles away.

Muddy felt her heart start to race and tried to tell herself that for her, the hard part was already over: She'd managed to tank without tearing the jet apart. LANTIRN was mostly Flex's game. He controlled where the pod looked and when the laser fired. All she had to do was switch the master arm on and wait for his cue to depress the bomb button.

Bombs. On the dark flight deck before the launch, with a flashlight in her hand, Muddy had carefully preflighted the two GBU-12s hanging from her jet, paying special attention to the fuse settings, and she'd high-fived the ordies after seeing "New York sends its best" scrawled on the side of one of the bombs and "Eat this, Osama!" on the other. Many times she'd wondered how the moment of truth would hit her, whether she'd feel any remorse toward killing, but now all she felt was a strong desire to get the job done.

As the Tomcats reached fifty miles from the target, the two C-130s checked in with the AWACS: "Zeus, Twin Tower two-two flight is at the initial point, heading for drop zone."

"Roger, Twin Tower," the AWACS controller replied. "Yankee flight is up this freq."

"Copy," the lead C-130 pilot said. "Yankee, on time?"

"Affirmative," Spud said.

Punk dropped the flight down to twenty-four thousand feet as he and Spud went through the final items in the attack checklist. Punk was going to make a comment about how light the resistance from the ground seemed when the blackness just over the nose came alive with streaks of light. These rounds were topping out much higher than the others had. Punk also saw several plumes corkscrew between the bullets—Stinger missiles, the deadly shoulder-fired heat seekers brought to this part of the world by the CIA a decade earlier.

"Western target designated," Spud said over the squadron common frequency, indicating that he had the crosshairs on his assigned aim point.

"Eastern target designated," Flex called in return.

"Twenty seconds to bomb release," Spud said over the intercom. "Check master arm on."

Punk moved the switch to the "on" position and a bolt of dread shot through him. The red "armed" light didn't illuminate. He maniacally flicked the switch up and down a few times, but the light remained out.

"I can't get a hot pickle," Punk said frantically.

"Cycle the switch," Spud advised.

"I did already. It won't come on. Do you have the right stations selected?"

"It's not me. Everything's set up back here."

"Well, it's not me, either." Punk flicked the master arm switch a few more times. "Fuck!"

"We must've taken a stray round or something," Spud said. "We're out of time to troubleshoot. Muddy's going to have to drop on both targets."

Perfect, Punk thought. *Success is in the hands of the choke artist nugget.* He remembered Creepy on the LSO platform saying, "She isn't ready to go to the fleet," and cursed Longo and Senator Meyers and the rest of the politicos who'd brought them to this place. Punk wanted all of them here now; he wanted them to witness what they'd wrought as the Rangers faced a certain pounding at the hands of a poorly opposed enemy.

"Muddy's bomb's away," Flex called, snapping Punk out of his reverie. "Laser's on and firing."

"Twin Tower is thirty seconds from jump point," the C-130 pilot said.

"If Muddy's dropping on both targets, we need the C-130s to delay at least a minute," Punk said to Spud over the intercom.

Spud keyed the AWACS freq: "Twin Tower, this is Yankee lead. Can you delta one?"

"That's a negative, Yankee. First man's out the door as we speak."

At that call the first bomb hit and transformed the eastern site into a huge ball of flame that washed out every pair of night-vision goggles that happened to be looking that way.

"Good hit on the east," Flex said.

"Flex, we can't drop," Punk said on the squadron common freq. "You guys are going to have to hit our target, too."

A surge of adrenaline stiffened Muddy's already tight body another turn. Suddenly it wasn't just Flex's game. She wasn't just going to be able to sit back and wait for him to tell her what to do. They'd briefed this contingency, but she'd never imagined that she'd actually be the one taking up the slack.

The eastern gun was silent now, but as she pushed the throttles to military power and started a hard left turn to get set up for the second drop, she noticed the western emplacement training its stream of fire toward the flight of C-130s. She figured the enemy couldn't see the lumbering transports but were firing at the noise from the turboprops as they passed, a crude sort of targeting that nevertheless could still find its mark.

"Let's get back to the run-in point," Flex said. "We need to get at least six miles away to get back in the drop window."

As Muddy threw the stick against her left thigh an idea hit her. She pushed the throttles into full afterburner, hoping to divert the gunners' attention and give them something other than the C-130s to shoot at. After the first ninety degrees of turn she looked back down at the remaining AAA site and saw her plan was working: The gun had swung around and was now firing in her direction. Punk watched the twin plumes shoot out of her motors and saw how the gunners responded, so he also selected afterburner and mirrored her turn in the opposite direction, which seemed to confuse the enemy even more.

"What's our range from the target now?" Muddy asked.

"Four miles. I'm typing in the coordinates for the other target now. This will take a few seconds . . ."

"Don't worry about that," Muddy said. "I'll cue the pod

from up here." She glanced down at the groundspeed read-out, saw they were doing nearly nine miles a minute, and then looked at the clock. A heartbeat later she started back toward the fort. "I'm centering the western target in the HUD," she told Flex as she dragged the nose of the F-14 through the last portion of the turn to the run-in heading.

"Roger," Flex said, watching the infrared images on the screen, impressed that Muddy knew how to perform the varsity move of a target designation using the heads-up display. Before he went to a more magnified view on the LANTIRN display for the bomb delivery, he noticed the two C-130s toward the bottom of his screen, each trailing a growing daisy chain of parachutes. He could see flashes of small-arms fire streaking toward the fort from where the first of the Rangers landed and from the northeastern wall of the fort back toward the Rangers.

The enemy AAA gunners figured out the ruse just as Muddy pickled the second bomb. "They're coming back on us," one of the C-130 pilots said, voice rife with concern as Flex steadied the crosshairs and willed the bomb to hit. The "time to impact" counter along the right edge of the LANTIRN display went to zero.

A second felt like an hour, and just as Muddy said, "Maybe it's a dud," a huge explosion erupted on their screens and the ground below them. The large-caliber fire from the site ceased.

Muddy and Flex's elation was cut short by a call of "missile in the air" over the radio. She looked down through the goggles and saw a rocket motor blazing toward her. She instinctively pulled the throttles out of afterburner to cool the engines and depressed the flare button on the side of the control stick. Flashes in the mirrors from beneath the jet indicated that the decoys had deployed. The Stinger arced behind the fighter and then fell harmlessly away.

"Twin Tower two-two is clear of the objective," the C-130 pilot reported. "All jumpers away."

"Zeus copies."

"Thanks for the assist, Yankee. Great work."

The radio was silent until Spud came up the squadron common freq and said, "Answer them, Muddy."

"Er . . ." she sputtered on the AWACS freq, surprised

and flattered that Spud had given her the nod. "Our pleasure, Twin Tower."

"Well, Muddy," Flex said with a laugh. "You're officially a war hero now."

Several more Stingers piercing the dark sky around them interrupted the pleasantries.

"Let's keep climbing," Punk commanded. At thirty thousand feet he checked his fuel state. Down to six thousand pounds. "Muddy, say your gas."

She read the gauge and fought another wave of dread. "Five point two," she replied.

Damn. They'd dropped well below their fuel ladder. Punk had Spud check the range to both of the divert fields. "Spud, right now we don't have enough gas to get out of Afghanistan, not to mention to make it to Qwadabad or Pasni," Punk said.

Spud keyed the radio: "Zeus, Yankee flight needs the tanker at Gipper to head for us at best speed. The target area maneuvers drove us very low on fuel."

"Zeus copies," the AWACS controller said, now a female voice. "Exxon two-five, do you copy?"

"Exxon copies," a decidedly American voice replied. "We'll bring it east." The absence of an English accent over the airwaves surprised Muddy, who'd been looking forward to visiting the friendly Brits and their gentle tanker again. And Exxon? What had happened to the nine-eleven theme? Suddenly she feared an unplanned change had been made to the program.

A few minutes later her fears were realized as Flex managed an air-to-air contrast lock with the LANTIRN pod and announced, "The tanker's a KC-135."

Muddy blew an exasperated exhale into her oxygen mask and pulled her goggles off much earlier than required, convincing herself that she needed plenty of time to readjust to the darkness when the real truth was she didn't want to see the wrecking ball any sooner than she had to. She cursed under her breath and slapped her thigh in anger with her throttle hand. How elusive success was; Flex had just called her a war hero, and now she was about to flame out over Afghanistan. Somebody in a big room somewhere was fucking with her. She wanted to jump on the radio and demand an explanation. Who'd let the VC-10 go? And who'd approved the KC-135 in its place?

"You can do this, Muddy," Punk said on squadron common after wrestling with what and how much to say to her. "Remember what I told you: Fly off of the knuckle. If it doesn't look good, back straight out. Don't descend."

"Roger," she replied. She waited for Punk to set the scene, to perhaps add the fact that if she didn't tank successfully, she wasn't going to make it out of Afghanistan, but he said no more for now.

Flex echoed, "Just do it, Muddy," from the back seat, which she figured was probably his way of saying, "If you don't tank successfully, we're not going to make it out of Afghanistan!"

The section of fighters rendezvoused with the heavy tanker and again Punk silently moved right to precontact without stopping at port observation. The eastern sky was beginning to lighten as dawn crept up on them, and as the tanker continued its turn, Muddy watched the silhouette of Punk's jet gracefully slide into the basket. The tanker steadied up on a westerly heading, moving back to the Gipper track. Muddy wondered why the tanker wouldn't just continue the turn and drag them south, back toward the Boat, but then realized that they were just two small jets in a war that was going on around the clock. Others would be waiting at Gipper. The pressure weighed even heavier on her mind. It had been bad enough breaking the tanker before the shooting had started. What chaos would she cause if it happened now? How much planning would go to waste? How many lives might be lost?

Punk knew that Muddy would be apprehensively studying his technique, so he did his level best to fly smoothly and by the numbers. As the Tomcat drew gas from the tanker, Punk maintained a slight curve in the hose and held it as if the rig was permanently shaped that way. Once he'd received his ration, Punk eased straight back at a controlled pace, and the basket detached from the probe with nary a wiggle.

"It's not hard, Muddy," Punk counseled a final time once he was parked on the tanker's right wing. "Fly the knuckle."

Muddy extended the refueling probe and deliberately

moved from the left wing to precontact with a chorus of voices in her head, a multitude of senior officers opining, "It's all about bombs on target." But it wasn't, was it? Bombs on target was the easy part.

She froze the jet in the precontact position and fought to clear her head. As long as she stayed back here she wouldn't do any harm. They'd been airborne for nearly five hours now, and she suppressed the sudden urge to pee. "Anytime, Muddy . . ." Flex said. "They're ready for us, and we could really use the gas."

She nudged the throttles and coaxed the Tomcat forward. Once she sensed they were close enough, she looked over at the probe tip and saw it had contacted the metal drogue off to one side. She tried to finesse it into the center by driving forward a bit more, a move she'd pulled off on the S-3's basket a number of times before, but instead of feeding the probe into the center, the wrecking ball tilted about its universal joint and flung off to the side. She tried to back away before the drogue swung back and hit them and only partially succeeded. The basket missed the probe but struck the nose just forward of it with a loud thud. She couldn't see in the darkness but was sure the collision had left a noticeable dent in the fuselage, another badge of shame she'd be presenting to the maintenance folks back on the flight deck . . . if she'd ever make it back to the flight deck.

"Don't force it, Muddy," Punk said. "That basket's not forgiving. You've got to hit it right in the middle. If you don't, just back away and try again."

"We've got plenty of time to do this safely, Muddy," Flex said, voice growing more disingenuous with each chestnut he threw out. "No hurry."

No hurry except she was tired and hungry and had a full bladder. Then she caught dim green lights out of the corner of her eye and glanced to her left and saw the strip lights of four jets waiting on the left wing for their turn to tank. She suddenly understood how terminally ill patients reach a stage where they simply yield to their diseases, and she wished the jet would just flame out. At that point Flex could eject if he wanted. She was going to ride it in.

Muddy stayed in the precontact position, paralyzed by

her anxiety, until one of the pilots on the left wing cut through the multi source din in her brain with, "C'mon, we've got a target time to meet."

That transmission was like a spur in her side, and without another thought she drove the probe into the basket. "That's it, Muddy," Punk said. "Now fly the knuckle."

Muddy made a few jerky corrections but managed to keep a decent bend in the hose. Flex said, "Good flow," over the intercom, and she fought to settle down. She nursed the trim and stabilized the jet under the knuckle. It hit her that she might not flame out after all. She suddenly felt a bit sheepish for making much ado about nothing and was reminded of the days of her youth when she'd balked at amusement park rides that turned out to be no big deal.

Muddy saw a glow in her right mirror and cut her eyes to it and saw that the sun had just crested above the horizon, which buoyed her spirits another few notches. She wouldn't have to land at night.

"Muddy, I'm pleased to announce we've got enough gas to make it back to the Boat now," Flex said. "That suspense was a lot of fun, though . . . *not*."

She allowed herself to chuckle and smoothly backed out of the basket. The rig made one more harrowing swing as it detached but didn't touch the jet. She moved to the right wing outside of Punk. The stillness that followed the probe retracting into the nose was a symphony of sweetness to her.

"Good work, Muddy," Punk said. "You'll only have to do that fifty more times or so this cruise."

She was in too good a mood now to worry about that. In fact, she felt so relaxed that she treated her diaper to a good soaking.

The goggles were long stowed as the sun was well into a blue sky by the time they crossed the coastline of Pakistan and returned feet wet over the North Arabian Sea. The Boat's wake stretched for miles across the still, glassy water. Punk shamelessly brought the flight into the break with the wings fully forward and both bombs still on his jet and made an OK pass to the three wire. Muddy got a No-Grade.

Punk's legs buckled as he took his first steps on the flight deck and only then did he think to check his watch. They'd been in the jet for over seven hours, a new personal record for him. He did a few deep knee bends and shook his feet and steadied Spud as the RIO reached the base of the ladder. "That hurts," Spud said.

"That might just be one of the shorter missions we fly over here, Spud," Punk said, peeling off his helmet now that the last jet had shut down.

"I hope you're wrong," Spud returned before giving his pilot a wry smile, "and it's 'XO,' if you please."

Punk shook his head and started for the catwalk. Along the way he noticed Corky McBride working on one of the Tomcats parked across catapult one. Next to him was a cartload of black boxes . . . roll computers. Punk told the XO he'd meet him down in maintenance control and walked over to the civilian, anger swelling along the way.

"Let me guess, Corky," Punk said as he approached. "New roll computers?"

Corky turned, obviously a bit surprised by the lieutenant's presence, but he quickly shifted into his usual oily self. "We just got OFP four-point-six." He pointed toward the sky and grinned. "You can start sweeping the wings in the break again."

Punk felt his blood boiling. His fists balled involuntarily. "You knew all along, didn't you?"

Corky raised his hands defensively. "Now, Punk, this is just a routine computer upgrade. We do it all the time, son. You've got no reason to think otherwise."

Punk's anger threatened to turn into all-consuming rage. He knew that punching a tech rep wouldn't go over very well with anyone on the Boat, so he took several deep breaths and calmed himself. The civilian started to turn away to grab another black box off of the cart, but Punk seized him by the shoulder and aimed an index finger at him. "I'm watching you, Corky. Remember that." He gave the man's shoulder a little push as he released his grip and then headed for the catwalk.

"Well, I've got something for you to remember," Corky called to him in a shaky voice after Punk had taken a handful of steps away. "We're all on the same team here. You remember that, okay? One team to win this thing. God bless America!"

Punk stepped down the ladder into the catwalk and felt

the burden of post-mission letdown land on him. He paused to lean on the railing and take in the ocean as it frothed away from the carrier's hull. In the white foam he saw Crud's face, and he wondered if his friend's death was the cost of doing business or if he'd been the victim of supreme injustice. Either way, Punk was going to keep paying attention, to keep giving a shit. And he'd care for Suzanne. That was all he could do. For now there was a mission to debrief and another to get ready for.

Punk finished the maintenance paperwork and entered the front door of the ready room just as the media pool and Lieutenant Ronnie Wheedle burst through the back door and glommed on Muddy like hungry mosquitoes. They shouted questions as they circled around her like, "How did you dodge missiles coming at you?" and "How hard was it to drop two bombs?" and "When did you realize you had to hit both targets?"

Muddy waited for them to settle themselves, and before she spoke, she made it a point to catch Punk's eye. He considered her for a moment, sweaty hair tucked behind her ears and a red line made by her oxygen mask bright across the bridge of her nose and down her cheeks, and then smiled and gave her an approving nod. She'd earned her right to crow. After all, she was a fighter pilot at war.